TO QUOTE A
QUEER

A COMPENDIUM OF WIT, WISDOM, AND DEVASTATING REMARKS

Edited by John Lessard

QUIRK BOOKS
PHILADELPHIA

Library of Congress Cataloging in Publication Number: 2007937403

ISBN 978-1-59474-223-1

Printed in China

Designed by Headcase Design
Cover illlustrations © CSA Images

Distributed in North America by Chronicle Books
680 Second Street
San Francisco, CA 94107

10 9 8 7 6 5 4 3 2 1

Quirk Books
215 Church Street
Philadelphia, PA 19106
www.quirkbooks.com

INTRODUCTION

A stodgy Victorian (Matthew Arnold) once defined culture as "the best which has been thought and said in the world." And as it happens, much of the best that has been thought and said has been thought and said by queers.

Although quote books have been around for a long time, never was there more need than now to collect and celebrate the words of our gay, lesbian, bisexual, and trans communities. Stonewall has given us unprecedented visibility, but that visibility is as recent as the previously unspoken histories of LGBTQ folk is long. Though by no means exhaustive—it would take far more pages to contain our genius—*To Quote a Queer* offers a cross section of voices from many centuries and generations.

I have tried at all times to represent only those voices that are self-proclaimed or very probably lesbian, gay, bisexual, trans, or queer, but I leave it up to you to decide how you want to understand those terms. The LGBTQ community is remarkably diverse, as are the people and ideas you'll find here. We have a lot to say about a lot of things, from politics to partying.

A quote book may not be as stimulating a meeting place as a bathhouse or back alley, but the acquaintances one makes here can be more substantial and longer lasting. I hope that the many incisive and entertaining—not to mention bitchy—insights gathered in *To Quote a Queer* will offer you the same pleasure they have given me in the process of putting them together. Many of these voices may already be old friends to you, but I hope that you will also make a few new exciting acquaintances too.

ACTIVISM

SEE ALSO GAY RIGHTS, POLITICS

I am gay, black, British, smart, dumb, patronizing, stubborn, all these other things—flawed in many ways—and I am now asserting my activism.

—JOHN AMAECHI (1970-)
BRITISH NBA BASKETBALL PLAYER

I think any gay person who's true to himself and out is in some form or another an activist.

—THOMAS BEZUCHA (1964-)
AMERICAN SCREENWRITER AND DIRECTOR

Within seven months I was arrested twice for participating in Peace Masses inside the Pentagon. It seemed the epitome of theatre of the absurd, enacted in real life.

—MALCOLM BOYD (1923-)
AMERICAN MINISTER AND INSPIRATIONAL WRITER

Our proper work now if we love mankind and the world we live in is revolution.

—JOHN CAGE (1912-1992)
AMERICAN COMPOSER

We all have opportunities to change people's minds, and I think a lot of that is cumulative. You have to hear alternative voices a lot sometimes for something to sink in, for there to be a shift.

—ANI DIFRANCO (1970-)
AMERICAN SINGER-SONGWRITER

I think anyone who encourages people to think is an activist.

—MICHAEL THOMAS FORD (1968-)
AMERICAN WRITER

When the youth of America gets together, amazing things happen.
College campuses were once a hotbed of political activity. Students in the '60s
were responsible for great changes, politically and socially. The youth movement
launched and defined what we've become since the '60s.
I would like to see that happen again.

—TOM FORD (1962-)
AMERICAN FASHION DESIGNER

We as a community have a tendency to confuse cultural self-expression with
political activity. Nobody ever had a rally saying, "We're black, and we're here."
. . . Yes, you have to come out, but that can't be all you do.

—BARNEY FRANK (1940-)
AMERICAN CONGRESSMAN

There has been an evolution in activism. The 1990s are different from the late
'70s. Activism is being redefined. But I don't think that a professional organization and activism are mutually exclusive. I think we need them both.

—JOAN GARRY (1958—)
AMERICAN GAY RIGHTS ACTIVIST

Hip consciousness is the realization that authoritarianism of any nature is a
usurpation of human consciousness—open manipulation, brutalization and
arbitrary manhandling of bodies and consciousness.

—ALLEN GINSBERG (1926-1997)
AMERICAN POET

It is always exciting when a gay person of accomplishment comes out. But in our haste to turn these people into role models, we frequently expect them to drop what they're doing and become activists overnight. We forget what made them newsworthy in the first place.

—BRUCE HAYES (1963–)
AMERICAN OLYMPIC GOLD MEDALIST, SWIMMING

———————

There is such a flood of precepts and so few examples—so much preaching, advising, rebuking and reviling, and so little doing.

—HENRY JAMES (1843–1916)
AMERICAN WRITER

———————

Some people still think I'm a traitor. . . . But some people call me and say, "Please don't stop. Keep doing what you're doing."

— JEFF KEY (1966–)
AMERICAN WRITER, DOCUMENTARIST, AND U.S. MARINE

———————

I have not felt all that comfortable as an activist. It's true I have never sat down with NFL executives to talk about the issue. I was sort of hoping people would take that on without me, that I would simply be the spark.

—DAVE KOPAY (1942–)
AMERICAN NFL FOOTBALL PLAYER

———————

I do feel a sense of responsibility to the gay community, but I also have to take care of myself.

—GREG LOUGANIS (1960–)
AMERICAN OLYMPIC GOLD MEDALIST, DIVING

I used to worry that I might be involved with AIDS because I was concerned only about my own health and saving my own skin. . . . But when I tested negative in 1985, I was relieved to find that I was still very concerned.

—JOSEPH LOVETT (1945-)
AMERICAN DIRECTOR

———

It was said inside the organizational walls that I couldn't be pro-life as long as I was a lesbian. . . . And I said, "Just watch me."

— NORMA (AKA "JANE ROE") MCCORVEY (1947-)
AMERICAN ABORTION ACTIVIST

———

If there was anything that characterized the men and women of the "Rubyfruit generation," it was our innocence and our idealism. We really believed that we could make things better, for ourselves and for our brothers and sisters.

—JESSE MONTEAGUDO (1953-)
CUBAN-BORN WRITER AND ACTIVIST

———

I can no longer believe in revolution, but I cannot fail to be on the side of the young who are fighting for it.

—PIER PAOLO PASOLINI (1922-1975)
ITALIAN FILM DIRECTOR

———

They say you have to work within the system, but that's hard to do if you can't get in there to do it.

—LESLIE PEREZ (BORN LESLIE DOUGLAS ASHLEY) (ca. 1940-)
AMERICAN FORMER DEATH ROW INMATE AND TRANS ACTIVIST

———

I think cultivated protest is just as dreamlike as idealism.

—ROBERT RAUSCHENBERG (1925-)
AMERICAN ARTIST

Honestly. If the GLAAD Awards get any more mainstream, they'll be held on the South Lawn of the White House.

—CHRISTOPHER RICE (1978-)
AMERICAN WRITER

It felt like I could celebrate activism, and I could celebrate wanting to be involved. I just felt like we did what we could, you know? We put our yard sign in our yard, and our yard just happened to be a stage.

—MICHAEL STIPE (1960-)
AMERICAN MUSICIAN

I want to get better and better at living life fully and being grounded in the present. . . . All activism starts from a feeling that you have in your personal spaces.

—REBECCA WALKER (1969-)
AMERICAN FEMINIST WRITER

ACTIVISM FOR THE ENVIRONMENT

It's scary to hang off the side of a building with a giant banner, or slide information about clear-cut logging under investors' doors at a fancy hotel while being followed by security guards and police. But what antiabortionists, homophobic bigots, and CEOs are doing to people and this planet is so much scarier.

—BRIANNA CAYO COTTER (1981-)
AMERICAN ENVIRONMENTALIST

Everyone knows that global warming is a huge and important issue but one that challenges our right to consume ourselves stupid. It's easy even for gays to dismiss challenging voices by calling the issue not a queer one.

—PIP STARR (1968-)
AUSTRALIAN DOCUMENTARIST AND ENVIRONMENTALIST

I was vegetarian for 17 years, because of factory farming. It wasn't political, more a gut reaction. I knew I could no more eat a battery chicken egg than jump off Big Ben. Then I discovered organic farming and started eating meat again. You've got to do something with the boys, after all.

—JEANETTE WINTERSON (1959-)
BRITISH WRITER

ACTORS AND ACTING

SEE ALSO ART AND ARTISTS, ENTERTAINMENT, HOLLYWOOD, MOVIES

Actors deal in illusion . . . every public persona is a bit of a show.

—RICHARD CHAMBERLAIN (1934-)
AMERICAN ACTOR

———————

You ask my advice about acting? Speak clearly, don't bump into the furniture, and if you must have motivation, think of your pay packet on Friday.

—NOËL COWARD (1899-1973)
BRITISH ACTOR AND PLAYWRIGHT

———————

An actress has to be more than an ordinary woman, and an actor somehow has to be less of a man.

—GEORGE CUKOR (1899-1983)
AMERICAN FILM DIRECTOR

———————

For working actors, every time you do a film, you have to pass a physical in order to qualify for bond insurance. Before the advent of protease inhibitors, people with HIV and AIDS couldn't get bond insurance. And that's why you haven't seen people step forward about this issue.

—MICHAEL JETER (1952-2003)
AMERICAN ACTOR

I'm a sober, gay actor who is trying very hard to not have my self-worth be dictated by whether I'm working or not. For years and years, I was my job.

—LESLIE JORDAN (1955-)
AMERICAN EMMY AWARD-WINNING ACTOR

Why should actors, whose job it is to understand and interpret human nature and who professionally parade their individuality, lie and lie hidden in the closet?

—SIR IAN MCKELLEN, CBE (1939-)
BRITISH ACTOR

I prefer the kind of screen personality that goes backward to the 50s, when actors were quiet and kept their dignity. . . . They never made faces because good-looking people keep their own council, they keep secrets. They're not looking to draw attention to themselves like little people.

—PAUL MORRISSEY (1938-)
AMERICAN DIRECTOR

I am surrounded with scores of straight producers making sure I am as gay this week as I was last week.

—GRAHAM NORTON (1963-)
IRISH COMEDIAN AND ACTOR

Most children have theatre in them. Those who carry it over into adolescence and, more or less, maturity, commit the ultimate indecency of becoming professional actors.

—PATRICK WHITE (1912-1990)
AUSTRALIAN WRITER AND NOBEL LAUREATE

ROLES

If all I ever do is play gay roles for the rest of my life, that ain't such a bad thing.
A lot of actors out there don't even get to work.

—WILSON CRUZ (1973-)
PUERTO RICAN–AMERICAN ACTOR

———————

People said, "Gee, now you're going to be typecast as a dyke." Well, so?
What's the problem? If I only did lesbian roles for my entire career, I'd be thrilled.

—PATRICE DONNELLY (ca. 1960-)
AMERICAN ACTOR

———————

[On getting into character] It's a combination of two parts cynicism
and one part Red Bull. Shake well. Drink with a chaser.

—NEIL PATRICK HARRIS (1973-)
AMERICAN ACTOR

———————

The Academy generally frowns on out gays playing gays—it's not really acting,
after all. Trophies have been reserved for "courageous" straights playing gay.
Alas, whenever another *X-Men* movie rolls around, no one says,
"Wow, Sir Ian was so brave to play straight! What a stretch!"

—MICHAEL MUSTO (1954-)
AMERICAN WRITER AND COLUMNIST

———————

I've always had that argument with my work in the theater, too, about, "can
straight actors play gay roles?" Is it politically and morally better to have gay
actors playing those roles? It's an endless kind of debate. I always go with casting
whoever is the most talented.

—PAUL RUDNICK (1957-)
AMERICAN SCREENWRITER AND PLAYWRIGHT

Acting has been fun, especially the roles out of drag, because I can't really fall back on just the way I look. In drag, the character comes from the outside in, and out of drag, it's totally inside out.

—RUPAUL (1960-)
AMERICAN DRAG PERFORMER AND MUSICIAN

I am an openly gay man playing an openly gay character on a network television show in the family hour . . . and I think it's no mistake that it's a black family.

—JASON STUART (1959-)
AMERICAN ACTOR AND COMEDIAN

Alexis Arquette will play so many gay roles that people will start thinking he's straight.

—BRUCE VILANCH (1948-)
AMERICAN COMEDY WRITER

AGE AND AGING

I'm a little less angry. As you get older you get less angry.

—DOROTHY ALLISON (1942-)
AMERICAN WRITER

We shall become middle aged, tied with more and more ties, busier and busier, fussier and fussier; we shall become old, disinterested, peevishly or placidly old men . . . we shall swollenly, stupidly, and uninterestedly die!

—RUPERT BROOKE (1887-1915)
BRITISH POET

There've been other people in other generations who swore not to get old,
who found Life as good as we do, and vowed to keep it so, to stay young
and clean-eyed. Where are they now? Dead.

—RUPERT BROOKE (1887–1915)
BRITISH POET

I am old, and death has robbed me of the thoughts of youth,
and just let anyone who doesn't know what old age is wait until it comes,
for he cannot know beforehand.

—MICHELANGELO BUONARROTI (1475–1564)
ITALIAN PAINTER, SCULPTOR, POET, AND ENGINEER

I almost rejoice when one I love dies young, for I could never bear
to see them old or altered.

—LORD BYRON (1788–1824)
BRITISH POET

Maybe the older you grow and the less easy it is to put thought into action,
maybe that's why it gets all locked up in your head and becomes
a burden. Whenever I read in the paper about an old man disgracing himself,
I know it's because of this burden.

—TRUMAN CAPOTE (1924–1984)
AMERICAN WRITER

I am past my fifties. This means that death does not have very far to go to meet
me. The play is almost over. Not much dialogue remains.

—JEAN COCTEAU (1889–1963)
FRENCH WRITER AND FILMMAKER

A young woman can always teach her elders how to grow old.
Later on, she stops to consider the matter, and finds she has forgotten
the lesson she once taught herself.

—SIDONIE-GABRIELLE COLETTE (1873-1954)
FRENCH WRITER

I feel a dreadful sense of loss but I must be prepared and armed for the future.
I shall be fifty in December, and as one gets older people begin to die
and when each one goes a little light goes out.

—NOËL COWARD (1899-1973)
BRITISH ACTOR AND PLAYWRIGHT

The older you get, the more you become your true, essential self.
You whittle away the parts of yourself that mean less to you.

—TOM FORD (1962-)
AMERICAN FASHION DESIGNER

Barring mysticism and the possibility of love explaining the universe—what are we
to do where we are now? Like all our contemporaries I am vexed by decreasing
powers and by named disease or diseaselets, and have to summon such defenses
as I can. The two best seem to be the old ones: courage and unpossessiveness.

—E. M. FORSTER (1879-1970)
BRITISH WRITER

I'm too old now to get married again. Too old to raise children—I think.
And why get married if you don't want children?

—ROCK HUDSON (1925-1985)
AMERICAN ACTOR

I got a lot of notoriety for doing *Will and Grace*, but I was sort of an aging show pony. They'd trot me out on stage, I'd do my thing, then they'd trot me back off.

—LESLIE JORDAN (1955-)
AMERICAN EMMY AWARD-WINNING ACTOR

I used to walk with a brisk stride; now I walk with tiny old-man steps, and I don't like it. My worst dread is Alzheimer's. Every so often I have what they colloquially call a "senior moment," and I think, "Oh, my God, has it started?"

—FRANK KAMENY (1925-)
AMERICAN GAY RIGHTS ACTIVIST

If the accretions of vested interest were to grow without mitigation for many generations, half the population would be no better than slaves to the other half.

—JOHN MAYNARD KEYNES (1883-1946)
BRITISH ECONOMIST

What else can one do but grow old gracefully?

—JAMES MERRILL (1926-1995)
AMERICAN PULITZER PRIZE-WINNING POET

As you get older you start to realize that it really doesn't matter what other people think.

—JONATHAN MURRAY (1955-)
AMERICAN TV PRODUCER

I figured that dykeness would protect me from the ravages of midlife crises . . . . We're saved by the grand lesbian tradition of "the older woman."

—B. RUBY RICH (1948-)
AMERICAN SCHOLAR AND FILM CRITIC

Since I broke my hip, I think I lost a couple of inches. Don't break your hip:
I lost an inch and a half off my height and an inch and a half off my cock.

—HAROLD ROBBINS (1916-1997)
AMERICAN WRITER

———

And as I get older . . . I find I get more and more disagreeably solitary,
in fact I foresee the day when I shall have gone so far into myself that there
will no longer be anything to be seen of me at all.

—VITA SACKVILLE-WEST (1892-1962)
BRITISH POET, NOVELIST, AND GARDENER

———

The fact is that five years ago I was, as near as possible,
a different person to what I am tonight. I, as I am now, didn't exist at all.
Will the same thing happen in the next five years? I hope so.

—SIEGFRIED SASSOON (1886-1967)
BRITISH POET AND WRITER

———

I think the older you get, the fussier you get about "less is more."

—STEPHEN SONDHEIM (1930-)
AMERICAN MUSICAL THEATER COMPOSER AND PLAYWRIGHT

———

Though my terrible state of health gives me warning now, it talks,
I'm afraid, to a deaf man.

—PAUL VERLAINE (1844-1896)
FRENCH POET

———

I'm only eighty, for god's sake. I'm in the springtime of my senescence.

—GORE VIDAL (1925-)
AMERICAN WRITER AND POLITICAL ACTIVIST

Kiehl's makes you look younger and Absolut makes you look older.

—LYNN WARREN (1977-)
AMERICAN REALITY TV STAR

I wonder if a lot of misery and loneliness among the elderly isn't due to what they call retirement?

—ETHEL WATERS (1896-1977)
AFRICAN-AMERICAN ACTOR AND MUSICIAN

It's one thing to be twenty and touring the world, but doing it in your forties, you wake up with aches and pains. We've all got tendinitis and carpal tunnel in our arms from playing guitar.

—JANE WIEDLIN (1958-)
AMERICAN MUSICIAN

ALCOHOL

SEE ALSO DRUGS, ENTERTAINMENT, FOOD AND DRINK, VICE

Charming though the Japanese are, their national tipple, saké, is a very poor brew. I drank it all the time I was there, but it was an undeniable pleasure to meet gin once more when I had left their pretty shores.

—J. R. ACKERLEY (1896-1967)
BRITISH WRITER AND EDITOR

I wasn't a very happy drunk. I felt the responsibility of telling everybody how they should be living their lives. I found anybody's hopeless weakness, and I would just zero in on it and publicly humiliate people. I was awful with alcohol.

—EDWARD ALBEE (1928-)
AMERICAN TONY AWARD- AND PULITZER PRIZE-WINNING PLAYWRIGHT

I like the way that alcohol can change me, I'm interested in change in practically everything, and alcohol is a good way of doing it. . . . Sometimes I think the idea of fun is being absolutely drunk with a bottle of poppers.

—LEIGH BOWERY (1961-1994)
BRITISH PERFORMANCE ARTIST

———————

I am very low-spirited on many accounts, and wine, which, however, I do not quaff as formerly, has lost its power over me.

—LORD BYRON (1788-1824)
BRITISH POET

———————

The only trouble about not drinking is that other people who are drinking are liable to look a little silly.

—NOËL COWARD (1899-1973)
BRITISH ACTOR AND PLAYWRIGHT

———————

I am grateful only for wine. I have neither women nor song.

—HART CRANE (1899-1932)
AMERICAN POET

———————

Everything that one thinks while in a state of intoxication appears to one to have the touch of genius: and afterwards one is ashamed of it. . . . Only beings composed of nothingness and mediocrity are capable of elevating themselves a little with alcohol.

—SALVADOR DALÍ (1904-1989)
SPANISH ARTIST

———————

I am deeply suspicious of men who carry martinis to the lunch or dinner table.

—MARLENE DIETRICH (1901-1992)
GERMAN-BORN ACTOR

Alcohol's the most dangerous drug for artists, because it ends up
really making you stupid.

—RAINER WERNER FASSBINDER (1945-1982)
GERMAN DIRECTOR

———————

Martinis should never be shaken. . . . They should always be stirred
so that the molecules lie sensuously on top of each other.

—W. SOMERSET MAUGHAM (1874-1965)
BRITISH WRITER AND PLAYWRIGHT

———————

O Moscow! Scarcely has one set foot in it before one must needs begin
to drink! . . . I cannot tell you how strange and repugnant to me is this
Moscow atmosphere of swilling.

—PETER ILYICH TCHAIKOVSKY (1840-1893)
RUSSIAN COMPOSER

———————

I'd get a new car on Friday and by Monday I had nothing left;
I'd get drunk and go sing on the streets and be late for the show.
I used to drink tequila. I drank everything I ever owned.

—CHAVELA VARGAS (1919-)
COSTA RICAN MUSICIAN

———————

Let's talk of the one vice which, among all my others, is perhaps unpardonable.
My passion and mania for drinking.

—PAUL VERLAINE (1844-1896)
FRENCH POET

What I've learned is that people will get me home no matter how much I drink and pick me up no matter how little I said or offered the night before.

—EDMUND WHITE (1940-)
AMERICAN WRITER AND CRITIC

AMBITION

The way to riches, to greatness, lies before me. I can, I will, cut myself a path through the world or perish in the attempt.

—LORD BYRON (1788-1824)
BRITISH POET

———————

At the age of six I wanted to be a crook. At seven I wanted to be Napoleon. And my ambition has been growing steadily ever since.

—SALVADOR DALÍ (1904-1989)
SPANISH ARTIST

———————

Our goal should be to achieve joy.

—ANA CASTILLO (1953-)
CHICANA POET, NOVELIST, AND ESSAYIST

———————

I simply wasn't ambitious, nor have I ever been. Perhaps that's what allowed me to survive all those years in Hollywood.

—MARLENE DIETRICH (1901-1992)
GERMAN-BORN ACTOR, SINGER, AND ENTERTAINER

———————

A gangster has the same bourgeois desires as the ordinary citizen.

—RAINER WERNER FASSBINDER (1945-1982)
GERMAN DIRECTOR

I can't join in any "build-a-new-world" stuff. Once in a lifetime one can swallow that, but not twice.

—E. M. FORSTER (1879-1970)
BRITISH WRITER

It is not wise to look too far ahead; our powers of prediction are slight, our command over results infinitesimal.

—JOHN MAYNARD KEYNES (1883-1946)
BRITISH ECONOMIST

The people in the right are not those who fasten their eyes on the little jaws of the ticket window and shout, "Now! Now!" but those who think of tomorrow and who sense that new life will soon be hovering over the world.

—FEDERICO GARCIA LORCA (1898-1936)
SPANISH POET AND PLAYWRIGHT

Possibility is neither forever nor instant. It is not easy to sustain belief in its efficacy.

—AUDRE LORDE (1934-1992)
AFRICAN-AMERICAN WRITER, POET, AND ACTIVIST

Nothing is worse in life than a missed opportunity or an unfulfilled dream.

—ROB ROSEN (1966-)
AMERICAN WRITER

Don't be afraid of missing opportunities. Behind every failure is an opportunity somebody wishes they had missed.

—LILY TOMLIN (1939-)
AMERICAN ACTOR AND COMEDIAN

Focus on the positive—it's harder to see than the negative things in life.

—LYNN WARREN (1977–)
AMERICAN REALITY TV STAR

AMERICA

SEE ALSO CITIES, EUROPE, TRAVEL

Oh beware of America when you get there! You cannot be too much
on your guard! The world is ruled from there, in the American imagination,
and everything the world contains. And they stop at nothing.

—J. R. ACKERLEY (1896–1967)
BRITISH WRITER AND EDITOR

There's one state worse [than South Carolina]. That's Mississippi. I used to think,
"Thank God for Mississippi. They are more uneducated than here."

—DOROTHY ALLISON (1942–)
AMERICAN WRITER

I tend to be like a sponge. . . . I absorb stuff from all around, like TV, O. J.
Simpson, the Menendez brothers. I live in America and in this society,
and that's what's reflected in my movies.

—GREGG ARAKI (1959–)
JAPANESE-AMERICAN DIRECTOR

I grew up in, you know, the principal American vacuum, you know,
television mostly.

—JEAN-MICHEL BASQUIAT (1960–1988)
AMERICAN ARTIST

Today, we still live in two Americas—one in which homosexuality
is taken for granted as a part of everyday life and one in which gays
are still demonized and abused.

—BRUCE BAWER (1956-)
AMERICAN CRITIC AND WRITER

We need urgently to put behind us an ideology that quixotically rejects and
ridicules everything the average American believes in.

—BRUCE BAWER (1956-)
AMERICAN CRITIC AND WRITER

I don't realize what a drag the U.S. can be until I hit a free country
and get relief in every direction.

—WILLIAM BURROUGHS (1914-1997)
AMERICAN WRITER

Whenever an American requests to see me (which is not unfrequently), I comply:
firstly, because I respect a people who acquired their freedom by firmness without
excess; and secondly, because these transatlantic visits, "few and far between,"
make me feel as if talking with Posterity from the other side of the Styx.

—LORD BYRON (1788-1824)
BRITISH POET

To us and all those who hate us—that the U.S.A. may become just another
part of the world, no more, no less.

—JOHN CAGE (1934-1992)
AMERICAN COMPOSER

It's partly our Puritan roots . . . sex in America is thought to be basically evil,
I think. You know, even heterosexual sex is very questionable.

—RICHARD CHAMBERLAIN (1934–)
AMERICAN ACTOR

I am most grateful to America; it stimulates me and changes my direction.
I do not intend another year to go by without going again.

—NOËL COWARD (1899–1973)
BRITISH ACTOR AND PLAYWRIGHT

I've been in trouble before for saying that Americans are too perfect in their
approach to dressing, but Americans are descended from Puritans,
and sometimes that comes through in their style.

—TOM FORD (1962–)
AMERICAN FASHION DESIGNER

The U.S. used to be perceived as the moral leader of the world,
and we have absolutely lost that. I think we appear as the most
morally corrupt country on the planet. It is sad.

—TOM FORD (1962–)
AMERICAN FASHION DESIGNER

There isn't a single district in America with a gay majority.

—BARNEY FRANK (1940–)
AMERICAN CONGRESSMAN

I think that to be American is an excellent preparation for culture.
We can deal freely with forms of civilization not our own, can pick and choose
and assimilate and, in short, claim our property wherever we find it.

—HENRY JAMES (1843–1916)
AMERICAN WRITER

There's an atmosphere of fear in America right now that is deadly.
Everyone is too career-conscious . . . there was a moment about a year ago
when you couldn't say a word about anything in this country for fear of your
career being shot down by people saying you are un-American.

—SIR ELTON JOHN, CBE (1947–)
BRITISH GRAMMY- AND ACADEMY AWARD-WINNING MUSICIAN

———

It is a matter of values—of what we in America think is important. We spend
money on military hardware, liquor, hairdressers, automobiles. We could—if we
were so inclined—spend money on making America beautiful.

—PHILIP JOHNSON (1906–2005)
AMERICAN ARCHITECT

———

To me, the essence of the American small town has always been the drugstore,
with its high-school kids and their cokes. It is where happens
that which is going to happen.

—PHILIP JOHNSON (1906–2005)
AMERICAN ARCHITECT

———

We act like teenagers in this country. "I want it now. It doesn't matter what it costs."
We are still a relatively young nation. But the credit card bills ultimately come.

— JEFF KEY (1966–)
AMERICAN WRITER, DOCUMENTARIST, AND FORMER U.S. MARINE

———

I'm homesick, not for America, but for Negroes. That's the trouble.

—NELLA LARSEN (1891–1964)
AFRICAN-AMERICAN WRITER

Israel is many things. . . . It can be very liberal and openminded—and parts
can be the opposite of that. It's something you can say about America too.

—IVRI LIDER (1974-)
ISRAELI MUSICIAN

———————

Increasingly I get a feeling that American standards are sort of an unspoken
norm, and that whether one resists them, or whether one adopts them,
they are there to be reckoned with. This is rather disappointing.

—AUDRE LORDE (1934-1992)
AFRICAN-AMERICAN WRITER, POET, AND ACTIVIST

———————

Increasingly I get a feeling that American standarl would think of America as one
vast City of Night stretching gaudily from Times Square to Hollywood Boulevard—
jukebox-winking, rock 'n' roll moaning:
America at night fusing its dark cities into the unmistakable shape of loneliness.

—JOHN RECHY (1934-)
AMERICAN WRITER

———————

In America the Indian is relegated to the obligatory first chapter—
the "Once Great Nation" chapter—after which the Indian is cleared away
as easily as brush, using a very sharp rhetorical tool called an "alas."

—RICHARD RODRIGUEZ (1944-)
MEXICAN-AMERICAN WRITER

———————

The border is real enough; it is guarded by men with guns. But Mexicans
incline to view the border without reverence, referring to the American side
as *el otro cachete*, the other buttock.

—RICHARD RODRIGUEZ (1944-)
MEXICAN-AMERICAN WRITER

That's one of the reasons why I enjoy America, because in Britain we live a somewhat secluded life. We don't let everything hang out like the Americans do. But I rather like that; it's all grist to the mill.

—JOHN SCHLESINGER, CBE (1926-2003)
BRITISH DIRECTOR

People ask if I miss it, but they don't understand that American culture is so ubiquitous that there's nothing to miss.

—DAVID SEDARIS (1956-)
AMERICAN WRITER

America is my country, but Paris is my hometown.

—GERTRUDE STEIN (1874-1946)
AMERICAN EXPATRIATE WRITER

Something happens in America which is like the change when water reaches freezing point or boiling point, and I suddenly see Americans in a warm and sympathetic light, which makes their furnishing of their houses, their conformism by which one might so easily judge them, irrelevant.

—STEPHEN SPENDER (1909-1995)
BRITISH POET AND WRITER

I felt that inside I was always American. I've always been very straightforward, honest, pushy, and gregarious, and the general honesty of this culture is a boon.

—ANDREW SULLIVAN (1963-)
BRITISH-BORN POLITICAL COMMENTATOR AND BLOGGER

The United States, the country, has no doubt damned its soul because of how it has treated others, and if it is true that we reap what we sow, as a country we have only to recognize the poison inside us as the poison we forced others to drink.

—ALICE WALKER (1944–)
AFRICAN-AMERICAN FEMINIST AND PULITZER PRIZE-WINNING WRITER

In my opinion it is by a fervent, accepted development of Comradeship, the beautiful and sane affection of man for man, latent in all the young fellows, North and South, East and West—it is by this, I say . . . that the United States of the future . . . are to be most effectually welded together.

—WALT WHITMAN (1819–1892)
AMERICAN POET

ANIMALS

I'm a sucker for any animal show that comes on. I don't care whether they're snakes or elephants. I love animals, and I watch them all.

—EDWARD ALBEE (1928–)
AMERICAN TONY AWARD- AND PULITZER PRIZE-WINNING PLAYWRIGHT

I have taken my own vet out to lunch and pumped him, and you will be pleased to hear that he is in the fullest agreement with all my guesses about the anal glands.

—J. R. ACKERLEY (1896–1967)
BRITISH WRITER AND EDITOR

A hotel room is always improved by the presence of an animal.

—SIDONIE-GABRIELLE COLETTE (1873–1954)
FRENCH WRITER

Yesterday we had to see the three little newborn bulldogs that her bitch Bellotte has just produced. She was delirious. I'm sure she would feel less passion for her own child.

—SIDONIE-GABRIELLE COLETTE (1873-1954)
FRENCH WRITER

I've lost too many friends to AIDS. So I do believe in animals losing their lives to eradicate cancer and AIDS from our lives; I believe in that.

—MELISSA ETHERIDGE (1961-)
AMERICAN GRAMMY AWARD-WINNING MUSICIAN AND BREAST CANCER ACTIVIST

From one end of the animal scale to the other we have been obliged to acknowledge, in all animal mating, the glaring supremacy of male beauty.

—ANDRÉ GIDE (1869-1951)
FRENCH WRITER

ABUSE

To get the confidence of any animal and then let it down seems to me almost the worst crime anyone can commit. Human relationships matter less—people understand people, suffer though they may; animals understand nothing, only loss.

—J. R. ACKERLEY (1896-1967)
BRITISH WRITER AND EDITOR

DOGS

People talk to you a lot more when you have a dog. I was walking him one night and this homeless guy jumped out and said, "That dog gonna wind up in a pot of rice!" And he probably wouldn't have said that if I was by myself.

—MARGARET CHO (1968-)
KOREAN-AMERICAN COMEDIAN

You get a Griffon if you take a Pug and cross it with a Jack Russell terrier—
a bit unusual looking. Some people think they look like monkeys. They're very—
well, just think primates. They're wonderful pets though.

—JOSH WESTON
AMERICAN PORN STAR

APPEARANCES

SEE ALSO BEAUTY, FASHION, STYLE

[On *Desperate Housewives*] I love the idea of a beautiful neighborhood that represents
the very best of American values, but also as a fun backdrop to some darker, deli-
ciously sneaky things going on in people's lives. The truth is I see both in the suburbs.
I think that is one of the secrets of our success. Unlike other writers who are incredibly
cynical about suburban life, I think my love of this world comes through in the project.

—MARC CHERRY (1962-)
AMERICAN TV WRITER AND PRODUCER

My hair is obviously radical—it's red!

—PATRICIA FIELD (1943-)
AMERICAN COSTUME DESIGNER

I was a fat naked fag. I'm still a big naked fag, most of the time.

—RICHARD HATCH (1961-)
AMERICAN REALITY TV STAR

Lookin' cute is feelin' cute!

—CARSON KRESSLEY (1969-)
AMERICAN FASHION EXPERT AND REALITY TV STAR

[On the diet on which he lost 90 pounds] Yes, but you know, it depends how superficial you are and what you are ready to accept to achieve something, you see.

—KARL LAGERFELD (1938-)
GERMAN FASHION DESIGNER

I am sure the time will come when I say, "I like the way I used to look better." But until then I'm okay.

—ROBERT MAPPLETHORPE (1946-1989)
AMERICAN PHOTOGRAPHER

I suspect that Gertrude Stein opted for tweeds and dowdiness because she didn't have a lot of choices when she went shopping.

—INGRID SISCHY (1952-)
AMERICAN WRITER AND EDITOR

The Kiehl's PR person let me go to the store and pick out one of everything. I would love to do that again. It was like a religious experience for me, it was so beautiful.

—LYNN WARREN (1977-)
AMERICAN REALITY TV STAR

It's not all facial hair. If you miss when you're shaving you have to draw it on . . . a little Maybelline thrown in. White people can't grow moustaches like this.

—JOHN WATERS (1946-)
AMERICAN DIRECTOR

Like anyone's going to look good that early in the morning with no makeup on, let alone beautiful babes in their forties.

—JANE WIEDLIN (1958-)
AMERICAN MUSICIAN

ART AND ARTISTS

SEE ALSO ACTORS AND ACTING, BEAUTY, CREATION AND CREATIVITY, DANCING, FASHION, IMAGINATION, LITERATURE, MUSIC, PHOTOGRAPHY, STYLE, TALENT, THEATER, WRITING

I'm interested in how people create themselves. All artists do it. I told a lot of visual artists that I was doing this play and they said, "That fascinates me—how we do that, how we become our art."

—EDWARD ALBEE (1928–)
AMERICAN TONY AWARD- AND PULITZER PRIZE-WINNING PLAYWRIGHT

As an artist my job isn't to preach, but to lay open the truth about certain situations, gently.

—JANE ANDERSON (1954–)
AMERICAN ACTOR AND DIRECTOR

We are all of us tempted to read more books, look at more pictures, listen to more music, than we can possibly absorb; and the result of such gluttony is not a cultured mind but a consuming one.

—W. H. AUDEN (1907–1973)
ANGLO-AMERICAN POET AND CRITIC

There must always be two kinds of art: escape-art, for man needs escape as he needs food and deep sleep, and parable-art, that art which shall teach man to unlearn hatred and learn love.

—W. H. AUDEN (1907–1973)
ANGLO-AMERICAN POET AND CRITIC

Ideas always acquire appearance veils, the attitudes people acquire of their time and earlier time. Really good artists tear down those veils.

—FRANCIS BACON (1909–1992)
BRITISH ARTIST

How awful that the artist has become nothing but the after-dinner mint of society.

—SAMUEL BARBER (1910-1981)
AMERICAN COMPOSER

Oh, expressionism—well, art should be expressive. Or something or other.

—JEAN-MICHEL BASQUIAT (1960-1988)
AMERICAN ARTIST

Art can be absolutely anything. . . . Art, I suppose, is anything the artist says it is . . . and anybody can say they're an artist.

—LEIGH BOWERY (1961-1994)
BRITISH PERFORMANCE ARTIST

I want to be able to continually surprise myself as an artist. I think if that element is not there, then things dissipate and you get into a sort of regularity of concept that becomes vegetating, if you're not careful.

—DAVID BOWIE (1947-)
BRITISH MUSICIAN

It may be that in Art I can forget Life, and in dreams of God escape from my own dreams.

—RUPERT BROOKE (1887-1915)
BRITISH POET

I am a poor man of little worth, who keeps laboring in the art God gave me, to prolong my life as far as I can.

—MICHELANGELO BUONARROTI (1475-1564)
ITALIAN PAINTER, SCULPTOR, POET, AND ENGINEER

We used to have the artist up on a pedestal.
Now he's no more extraordinary than we are.

—JOHN CAGE (1934-1992)
AMERICAN COMPOSER

———————

Art is a recompense for the difficulties of simply living.

—TRUMAN CAPOTE (1924-1984)
AMERICAN WRITER

———————

Picasso taught me to run faster than beauty. . . . He who runs less fast than
beauty will accomplish only something mediocre. As for him who runs faster
than beauty, his work will seem ugly, but he forces beauty to join it and then,
once joined, it will become beautiful for good.

—JEAN COCTEAU (1889-1963)
FRENCH WRITER AND FILMMAKER

———————

The Muses are ladies accustomed to attentions. If you fail them,
they will be avenged.

—JEAN COCTEAU (1889-1963)
FRENCH WRITER AND FILMMAKER

———————

Much of the art we see in the world's museums reflects the heterosexual male's
desires. . . . But if the artist has a different gender or orientation, the gaze shifts,
offering other possibilities based on different standards. It changes the
balance of power.

—STEVE COMPTON
AMERICAN ARTIST AND CURATOR

In Western culture, artists have historically been used as agents of propaganda. We've either proselytized a religion or depicted the glory of a king or queen. . . . Art reflects the ideology of the time.

—STEVE COMPTON
AMERICAN ARTIST AND CURATOR

The modern artist has got to harden himself, and the walls of an ivory tower are too delicate and brittle a coat of mail for substitute.

—HART CRANE (1899-1932)
AMERICAN POET

I cannot figure out what Dadaism is beyond an insane jumble of the four winds, the six senses, and plumb pudding.

—HART CRANE (1899-1932)
AMERICAN POET

With me no one could ever tell where humor ended and my congenital fanaticism began, so that people soon got used to letting me do whatever I wanted, without discussion: "That's just Dalí!" they would say, shrugging their shoulders.

—SALVADOR DALÍ (1904-1989)
SPANISH ARTIST

The dress-designer is not a painter . . . his creation is more likely to be akin to poetic expression. A certain nostalgia is necessary.

—CHRISTIAN DIOR (1905-1957)
FRENCH FASHION DESIGNER

Quilts are definitely where it's at in this big land of ours right now.

—ALLAN GURGANUS (1947-)
AMERICAN WRITER

An artist might be attracted to hedonism, but of course an artist is not a hedonist.
He's a worker, always.

—DAVID HOCKNEY (1937-)
BRITISH ARTIST

You shouldn't talk about art. You should do it.

—PHILIP JOHNSON (1906-2005)
AMERICAN ARCHITECT

One of the reasons that we need art and value art is that it
allows you a confrontation with something that's almost too frightening
or too upsetting or too wonderful to encounter in waking life.
It gives you a safe environment in which you can encounter it.

—TONY KUSHNER (1956-)
AMERICAN PLAYWRIGHT

I don't think of myself as a photographer. I think of myself as
an artist who uses photography.

—ANNIE LEIBOWITZ (1949-)
AMERICAN PHOTOGRAPHER

An exhibition doesn't begin when you enter a gallery. . . .
It begins the minute you get an invitation in the mail.

—ROBERT MAPPLETHORPE (1946-1989)
AMERICAN PHOTOGRAPHER

To my mind the most interesting thing in art is the personality of the artist;
and if that is singular, I am willing to excuse a thousand faults.

—W. SOMERSET MAUGHAM (1874-1965)
BRITISH WRITER AND PLAYWRIGHT

Popular art, in a society without ritual, can only be that which entertains, is consumed, and is replaced at once by the next thing. Its admirers include, to a man, us aesthetes. That the admiration isn't mutual needn't bother anyone.

—JAMES MERRILL (1926-1995)
AMERICAN PULITZER PRIZE-WINNING POET

_____

You listen to Handel operas, right? And there are a thousand of them, right? And they all sound alike and they're all ravishing, right? You think to yourself, "Oh, it all sounds alike." But when Handel was writing them, he was having a baby every time. And he thought, "Oh, my God, am I really going to depart from my normal style and write this?" And then it sounds like everything else—but he doesn't know that. You know what I mean? If I look back on my work, maybe it's the same thing, the same thing, the same thing. But I think I'm always having a revelation.

—ISAAC MIZRAHI (1961-)
AMERICAN FASHION DESIGNER

_____

I think that when the funding is down, everybody looks at the first thing they can cut, and they see everything as " extras." . . . Art is not an extra.

—CYNTHIA NIXON (1966-)
AMERICAN TONY AND EMMY AWARD-WINNING ACTOR

_____

Without craft, I think art is nonsense—it's a sort of masturbation. Whereas, with craft, it's a form of teaching.

—STEPHEN SONDHEIM (1930-)
AMERICAN MUSICAL THEATER COMPOSER AND PLAYWRIGHT

_____

What I discovered about Japanese art, what I finally cottoned on to, is they're the ultimate culture in "less is more." They are the minimalist culture.

—STEPHEN SONDHEIM (1930-)
AMERICAN MUSICAL THEATER COMPOSER AND PLAYWRIGHT

The Catholic Church makes a very sharp distinction between a hysteric and a saint. The same thing holds true in the art world.

—GERTRUDE STEIN (1874-1946)
AMERICAN EXPATRIATE WRITER

———————

To reveal art and conceal the artist is art's aim.

—OSCAR WILDE (1854-1900)
IRISH PLAYWRIGHT AND WRITER

———————

We can forgive a man for making a useful thing as long as he does not admire it. The only excuse for making a useless thing is that one admires it intensely. All art is quite useless.

—OSCAR WILDE (1854-1900)
IRISH PLAYWRIGHT AND WRITER

———————

The whole purpose of art is to show us other realities—and I don't mean other realisms—I mean other worlds.

—JEANETTE WINTERSON (1959-)
BRITISH WRITER

———————

You make the choice whether you want to be a political artist or an entertainer, or somebody who's very aware.

—PATRICK WOLF (1983-)
BRITISH MUSICIAN

It is a constant idea of mine . . . that the whole world is a work of art; that we are parts of the work of art. *Hamlet* or a Beethoven quartet is the truth about this vast mass that we call the world. But there is no Shakespeare, there is no Beethoven; certainly and emphatically there is no God; we are the words; we are the music; we are the thing itself.

—VIRGINIA WOOLF (1882–1941)
BRITISH WRITER

ARCHITECTURE

The real object in architecture must be to make you excited.

—PHILIP JOHNSON (1906–2005)
AMERICAN ARCHITECT

There is nothing more poetic and terrible than the skyscrapers' battle with the heavens that cover them.

—FEDERICO GARCIA LORCA (1898–1936)
SPANISH POET AND PLAYWRIGHT

PAINTING

I would like my pictures to look as if a human being had passed between them, like a snail, leaving a trail of the human presence and memory trace of past events, as the snail leaves its slime.

—FRANCIS BACON (1909–1992)
BRITISH ARTIST

It's also always hopeless talking about painting—one never does anything but talk around it.

—FRANCIS BACON (1909–1992)
BRITISH ARTIST

I had some money, I made the best paintings ever. I was completely reclusive,
worked a lot, took a lot of drugs. I was awful to people.

—JEAN-MICHEL BASQUIAT (1960-1988)
AMERICAN ARTIST

I used to feel that sculpture was the lantern of painting, and that there was
the difference between them that there is between the sun and moon.
Now . . . I have changed my opinion, and say that . . .
painting and sculpture are one identical thing.

—MICHELANGELO BUONARROTI (1475-1564)
ITALIAN PAINTER, SCULPTOR, POET, AND ENGINEER

Boldness in the painter is almost always confused with boldness of the brush.

—JEAN COCTEAU (1889-1963)
FRENCH WRITER AND FILMMAKER

Painting has to extract the figure from the figurative.

—GILLES DELEUZE (1925-1995)
FRENCH PHILOSOPHER AND CRITIC

It is a mistake to think that the painter works on a white surface. . . .
The painter has many things in his head, or around him, or in his studio.
Now everything he has in his head or around him is already in the canvas.

—GILLES DELEUZE (1925-1995)
FRENCH PHILOSOPHER AND CRITIC

People get something from living with a painting. I love living with paintings.

—KEITH HARING (1958-1990)
AMERICAN ARTIST AND ACTIVIST

Nobody had painted L.A. to me—I didn't know of any. Paris, London had been painted by marvelous artists actually. L.A. had not. . . . So, it was unknown visually, and I was attracted to that.

—DAVID HOCKNEY (1937-)
BRITISH ARTIST

––––––––––

[Willem] De Kooning used to say: "I'm a house painter, and you're a sign painter."

—JASPER JOHNS (1930-)
AMERICAN ARTIST

––––––––––

I think a painting has such a limited life anyway. Very quickly a painting is turned into a facsimile of itself when one becomes so familiar with it that one recognizes it without looking at it.

—ROBERT RAUSCHENBERG (1925-)
AMERICAN ARTIST

AUDIENCES

SEE ALSO ACTORS AND ACTING, COMMUNICATION,
ENTERTAINMENT, HOLLYWOOD, THE PUBLIC

When people pay to see you live, they already connect with you on a much deeper level than people who just buy your records. It's a very intimate, one-on-one experience with two thousand people.

—SANDRA BERNHARD (1955-)
AMERICAN ACTOR, COMEDIAN, AND MUSICIAN

I think it's good for my immune system to encounter the general public close up, even if some of you do live in rented accommodation and clearly choose not to invest in expensive skincare products.

—JULIAN CLARY (1959-)
BRITISH COMEDIAN

Now they're actually bringing extra bras to my shows; they are not just wearing them. I guess soon they'll be selling bra launchers for the people in the back rows.

—MELISSA ETHERIDGE (1961-)
AMERICAN GRAMMY AWARD-WINNING MUSICIAN AND BREAST CANCER ACTIVIST

Whenever I speak before a large group I always think I must have taken the wrong door.

—FEDERICO GARCIA LORCA (1898-1936)
SPANISH POET AND PLAYWRIGHT

It's madness to think of an audience. It's madness also not to think of one.

—JAMES MERRILL (1926-1995)
AMERICAN PULITZER PRIZE-WINNING POET

I've stopped autographing female breasts. . . . This one girl lifted up her top and said, "Will you sign my chest?" I said . . . "If your boyfriend has a really cute ass, I'll autograph his butt."

—CHUCK PANOZZO (1948-)
AMERICAN MUSICIAN

There's a phrase in the Catholic Church they use for the nuns: custody of the eyes. . . For a long time eye contact was an issue for me. "How can I entertain these people when I'm afraid to look at them?"

—CHUCK PANOZZO (1948-)
AMERICAN MUSICIAN

BEAUTY

SEE ALSO APPEARANCES, ART AND ARTISTS, FASHION, IMAGINATION, STYLE, TALENT

So long as I live, the love of Beauty will be my guide.

—NATALIE BARNEY (1876-1972)
AMERICAN WRITER

Beauty (unlike ugliness) cannot really be explained: in each part
of the body it stands out, repeats itself, but it does not describe itself.
Like a god (and as empty), it can only say: I am what I am.

—ROLAND BARTHES (1915-1980)
FRENCH CRITIC AND THEORIST

Beauty at its inception is always invisible. A fairy godmother protects it,
either saying, "You will appear ugly," or enveloping it in a cloud.

—JEAN COCTEAU (1889-1963)
FRENCH WRITER AND FILMMAKER

Beauty has most often appeared to me in moments of penitence
and even, sometimes, distraction and worry.

—HART CRANE (1899-1932)
AMERICAN POET

Americans are obsessed with physical beauty.
In England beautiful women are under suspicion.

—QUENTIN CRISP (1908-1999)
BRITISH WRITER AND PERSONALITY

In the movies beauty is not a woman but a man's idea of a woman.
What made Marlene Dietrich great was what Mr. Von Sternberg thought of her.
What made Garbo great was what Mr. Stiller thought of her.

—QUENTIN CRISP (1908-1999)
BRITISH WRITER AND PERSONALITY

We agree we want modern beauty—not yesterday's beauty,
which ranges us with schoolmasters and clergymen, but a quality so up to date
that no one has had time to note it down.

—E. M. FORSTER (1879-1970)
BRITISH WRITER

Darwin was no more of a uranist than many other explorers who,
traveling among naked tribes, have marveled at the beauty of young men.

—ANDRÉ GIDE (1869-1951)
FRENCH WRITER

I brought myself to despise, if not to abhor, the beauty of women,
looking on it as the greatest snare to which mankind are subjected, and though
young men and maidens, and even old women (my mother among the rest),
taxed me with being an unnatural wretch, I gloried in my acquisition;
and, to this day, am thankful for having escaped the most dangerous of all snares.

—JAMES HOGG (1770-1835)
SCOTTISH NOVELIST AND POET

For what does one do with beauty—that oddest, most irrational of careers? There
were boys in that room—bank tellers, shoe salesmen, clerks—who had been given
faces and forms so extraordinary that they constituted a vocation of their own.

—ANDREW HOLLERAN (1944-)
AMERICAN WRITER

I see nothing wrong with describing someone as beautiful—straight or gay—
if they are. Even more to the point, after reading of themselves as powerless
freaks and criminals, gays need to read of other gays as dynamic,
bright, successful, powerful, handsome, and able.

—FELICE PICANO (1944-)
AMERICAN WRITER

Look at me—I'm a big old black man under all of this makeup,
and if I can look beautiful, so can you.

—RUPAUL (1960-)
AMERICAN DRAG PERFORMER AND MUSICIAN

The aesthete sustains standards that make it possible to be pleased
with the largest number of things; annexing new, unconventional,
even illicit sources of pleasure.

—SUSAN SONTAG (1933-2004)
AMERICAN WRITER AND CRITIC

I believe that recognizing beauty wherever and whenever it occurs
is not just about the desire for sex.

—GIANNI VERSACE (1946-1997)
ITALIAN FASHION DESIGNER

Beautiful people are sometimes more prone to keep you waiting than plain people
are, because there's a big time differential between beautiful and plain.

—ANDY WARHOL (1928-1987)
AMERICAN ARTIST

The most beautiful thing in Tokyo is McDonald's.
The most beautiful thing in Stockholm is McDonald's.
The most beautiful thing in Florence is McDonald's.
Peking and Moscow don't have anything beautiful yet.

—ANDY WARHOL (1928-1987)
AMERICAN ARTIST

I have noticed that those who are observant of beauty only in women,
and are moved little or not at all by the beauty of men,
seldom have an impartial, vital, inborn instinct for beauty in art.

—JOHANN JOACHIM WINCKELMANN (1717-1768)
GERMAN ART HISTORIAN AND ARCHEOLOGIST

BUSINESS

If a Haitian wants to produce cars or TVs in Haiti, he has to make the items in
Haiti, export them to the U.S., import them to Haiti. That's the only way the
Haitian government can make the luxury taxes they so desperately need.

—KATHY ACKER (1947-1997)
AMERICAN WRITER

Nowadays it's capitalism that brings forth terrorism, to boost itself and strengthen
its hegemony.

—RAINER WERNER FASSBINDER (1945-1982)
GERMAN FILM DIRECTOR

The hereditary principle in the transmission of wealth and the control of business
is the reason why the leadership of the Capitalist cause is weak and stupid.
It is too much dominated by third-generation men.

—JOHN MAYNARD KEYNES (1883-1946)
BRITISH ECONOMIST

Gays are the epitome of capitalism.

—STEVEN SHIFFLETT (1953-1992)
AMERICAN POLITICAL ACTIVIST

―――――――

There are many Paris picture dealers who like adventure in their business;
there are no publishers in America who like adventure in theirs.

—GERTRUDE STEIN (1874-1946)
AMERICAN EXPATRIATE WRITER

―――――――

I do personally wrestle with the idea of the capitalistic model.
It can never really be equitable. I wrestled with it as I became wealthy.

—LISA THOMAS (1957-)
AMERICAN ENTREPRENEUR

―――――――

It is very vulgar to talk about one's business. Only people like stockbrokers
do that, and then merely at dinner parties.

—OSCAR WILDE (1854-1900)
IRISH PLAYWRIGHT AND WRITER

―――――――

What is true of a bankrupt is true of everyone else in life.
For every single thing that is done someone has to pay.

—OSCAR WILDE (1854-1900)
IRISH PLAYWRIGHT AND WRITER

CAREERS

SEE ALSO WORK

It is neither nice nor gay to earn money with what one loves,
but we live almost entirely that way.

—SIDONIE-GABRIELLE COLETTE (1873-1954)
FRENCH WRITER

————————

Career is such a small part of what we are right now. . . .
I went from selling less than a million copies 'til I came out, then I sold
six million—[being gay] actually amplified my career.

—MELISSA ETHERIDGE (1961-)
AMERICAN GRAMMY AWARD-WINNING MUSICIAN AND BREAST CANCER ACTIVIST

————————

You tell yourself, I can have this really great public life, and that will
make up for an empty private life. That's bullshit.

—BARNEY FRANK (1940-)
AMERICAN CONGRESSMAN

————————

A satisfying career cannot be a substitute for the emotional and
physical needs you have as a human being.

—BARNEY FRANK (1940-)
AMERICAN CONGRESSMAN

————————

I think one of the things they hate [in the U.K.] is that once you've had
your go, whatever it may be, they want you to piss off, and they can't
bear it if you come back—they can't bear it.

—BOY GEORGE (1961-)
BRITISH MUSICIAN

I did the professional and then the personal. Ideally, it goes the other way around—get your house in order and then deal with the world.

—GERRY STUDDS (1937-2006)
AMERICAN CONGRESSMAN

CELEBRITIES

SEE ALSO FAME, GAY ICONS, HOLLYWOOD, ROYALTY, SUCCESS

CLAY AIKEN

I don't even care if Clay Aiken is gay or not. It's none of my business.

—SIR ELTON JOHN, CBE (1947-)
BRITISH GRAMMY- AND ACADEMY AWARD-WINNING MUSICIAN

————

And I've found during my exploration that a "Claymate" is to an "Anderfan" as John Hinckley Jr. is to a Gawker Stalker.

—JOSH KILMER-PURCELL (1969-)
AMERICAN WRITER AND DRAG PERFORMER

CHER

I might choose my mom to be vice president. I think she would do a good job. She would be a very good politician, 'cause she's so honest.

—CHASTITY BONO (1979-)
AMERICAN GAY RIGHTS ACTIVIST AND DAUGHTER OF CHER AND SONNY BONO

MONTGOMERY CLIFT

I wanted to start my own club, a fan club. The I-Love-Montgomery-Clift-Because-He-Understands-Me-Like-No-Other club. Membership: one. Club member requirements: An intense yearning to worship a dead matinee star because he provides comfort, because he provides hope. Club dues: Be willing to give up your soul. Club Activities: Watch Monty movies no matter what hour his movies come on.

—NOËL ALUMIT (1970-)
PHILLIPINO-BORN WRITER AND PLAYWRIGHT

ANDERSON COOPER

If you were trying to promote yourself as Anderson Cooper, are you gay first and foremost, or are you Anderson Cooper? If he does agree to talk about it, well then you can't talk about anything else, and no one wants to talk about anything else.

—RUPERT EVERETT (1959-)
BRITISH ACTOR

MARLENE DIETRICH

Marlene Dietrich was the original performance artist . . . without Marlene, you couldn't have had David Bowie or Madonna.

—SEAN MATHIAS (1956-)
BRITISH DIRECTOR

CELINE DION

I hate Celine Dion's fashion sense. I don't like her music either, and I think she often looks terrible. . . . it's really the whole package because her choreography is so stank.

—LADY BUNNY (1962-)
AMERICAN DRAG PERFORMER AND DJ

GRETA GARBO

Someday there'll have to be a new world. A new kind of woman. In that future time the woman will be beautiful and be the hottest number whose eyes breathe fire, who works hard, who's honest and blunt, who demands total honesty.
Greta Garbo in *Queen Christina*.

—KATHY ACKER (1947–1997)
AMERICAN WRITER

————

To know Greta [Garbo]—one must know the North. She may live the rest of her life in a Southern climate, but she will always be Nordic with all its sober and introvert characteristics. To know her one must know—really know—wind, rain, and dark brooding skies. She is of the elements.

—MERCEDES DE ACOSTA (1893–1968)
CUBAN-AMERICAN WRITER AND SOCIALITE

JUDY GARLAND

Well Judy was, uh, Judy was a mess, basically. Judy was unbelievably talented. She was like, she was this little fragile bird that, that could just tear up the stage and be so exciting.

—BOB MACKIE (1940–)
AMERICAN FASHION DESIGNER

PARIS HILTON

Yeah, I called her [Paris Hilton] a whore! When I see a whore I see a whore. We were performing, and I see these two bitches sitting there talking like nothing was going on. So the spotlight hits them and I say, "This is what I call a coupla whores."

—JOEY ARIAS (ca. 1955–)
AMERICAN PERFORMANCE AND DRAG ARTIST

ROCK HUDSON

I think he mainly was attracted to blond men that were straight-acting.
Rock himself couldn't act like a queen if you asked him to. I mean, I once said:
"Can you camp?" You know, just to see how far—he couldn't do it. I mean,
he looked really awkward trying to. . . .What you saw on the screen
really was the way he was in real life. He really was very masculine.

—MARC CHRISTIAN (ca. 1953-)
AMERICAN CELEBRITY BOYFRIEND

COURTNEY LOVE

My guru now is Courtney Love.

—SANDRA BERNHARD (1955-)
AMERICAN ACTOR, COMEDIAN, AND MUSICIAN

MARILYN MONROE

There's been an awful lot of crap written about Marilyn Monroe,
and there may be an exact psychiatric term for what was wrong with her,
I don't know—but truth to tell, I think she was quite mad.
The mother was mad, and poor Marilyn was mad.

—GEORGE CUKOR (1899-1983)
AMERICAN FILM DIRECTOR

I planned to go like a '50s movie star, like a brunette Marilyn Monroe,
but I wound up looking more like Queen Elizabeth.

—LILY TOMLIN (1939-)
AMERICAN ACTOR AND COMEDIAN

JACKIE O.

I've drawn from some of the most feminine women, people like Jackie Kennedy—
like, I am totally devastated that she's gone. She had it all. . . .
But, I mean, if I can cover the gamut from Courtney Love to Jackie Bouvier
Kennedy Onassis, I think that says it all.

—SANDRA BERNHARD (1955-)
AMERICAN ACTOR, COMEDIAN, AND MUSICIAN

KEANU REEVES

I'd really love Keanu Reeves to play me, but I know he doesn't do TV.

—GREG LOUGANIS (1960-)
AMERICAN OLYMPIC GOLD MEDALIST, DIVING

Do we need Keanu Reeves to be one of us because it's so awful to be us
that having him in our club will somehow make us feel better about ourselves?
Or is this an elaborate way of making him more attainable . . .
like you or I might have a shot?

—BRUCE VILANCH (1948-)
AMERICAN COMEDY WRITER

ANNA NICOLE SMITH

Anna Nicole Smith was the goddess of all things that are sweet and enveloping.

—MARGARET CHO (1968-)
KOREAN-AMERICAN COMEDIAN

BRITNEY SPEARS

I do like Britney Spears. I think she's cute. I think she's fun. And I like her records.
You know, I'm not a pop snob whatsoever. I think she makes great pop records.

—SIR ELTON JOHN, CBE (1947–)
BRITISH GRAMMY- AND ACADEMY AWARD-WINNING MUSICIAN

ELIZABETH TAYLOR

Liz Taylor when she's on time seems "early." It's like you get a new talent all
of a sudden by being so bad at something for so long, and then
suddenly one day being not quite so bad.

—ANDY WARHOL (1928–1987)
AMERICAN ARTIST

Ohhhh, Elizabeth Taylor, ohhhh. She's so glamorous.

—ANDY WARHOL (1928–1987)
AMERICAN ARTIST

CENSORSHIP

SEE ALSO JOURNALISM, LANGUAGE, MEDIA, THE PUBLIC

I didn't foresee, when I opened my bookshop in 1919, that it was going to profit
by the suppressions across the sea. I think it was partly to these suppressions, and
the atmosphere they created, that I owed many of my customers—all those pil-
grims of the twenties who crossed the ocean and settled in Paris.

—SYLVIA BEACH (1887–1962)
AMERICAN-BORN EXPATRIATE BOOKSELLER

Sex passes the censor, squeezes through between bureaus, because there's always a space between, in popular songs and grade-B movies, as giving away the basic American rottenness.

—WILLIAM BURROUGHS (1914-1997)
AMERICAN WRITER

O God that I should have to live within these American restrictions forever, where one cannot whisper a word, not at least exchange a few words!

—HART CRANE (1899-1932)
AMERICAN POET

[Charlie Chaplin's *The Kid*] was a year late in arriving in Cleveland, I understand, on account of objections from the state board of censors! What they could possibly have objected to, I cannot imagine, It must have been some superstition aroused against good acting!

—HART CRANE (1899-1932)
AMERICAN POET

But there was also another purpose behind the "obscenity" rhetoric: The charge of being too "graphic" or "grossly offensive" offered the perfect pretext for silencing a disfranchised minority's attempt to end its subjugation and challenge the cultural terms of the majority's social control.

—MARLON RIGGS (1957-1994)
AFRICAN-AMERICAN FILMMAKER

CHANCE

I have a notion that Gamblers are as happy as most people
being always excited. . . . Every turn of the card, and cast of the dice,
keeps the Gamester alive.

—LORD BYRON (1788-1824)
BRITISH POET

———————

Things would happen that seemed like chance, but they always meant more,
so I came to believe there was no such thing as chance. If you accept that there
are no coincidences, you use whatever comes along.

—KEITH HARING (1958-1990)
AMERICAN ARTIST AND ACTIVIST

———————

I think it's taught me what I wrote years ago without really knowing
what I was saying—that before the parade passes you by you have to
take a second chance. And there are second chances.

—JERRY HERMAN (1931-)
AMERICAN COMPOSER AND LYRICIST

———————

God is the impulse of things to persist in their Being . . . and it is only Satan,
the Prince of this World, who is responsible for events.
Hence we are shocked by the "accidental."

—RICHARD HOWARD (1929-)
AMERICAN POET, CRITIC, AND TRANSLATOR

———————

Probability is concerned not with objective relations between propositions
but (in some sense) with degrees of belief.

—JOHN MAYNARD KEYNES (1883-1946)
BRITISH ECONOMIST

[On gambling in Atlantic City] Throwing away your life's earnings tends to prompt much praying, not to mention other on-your-knees activities.

—MICHAEL MUSTO (1954-)
AMERICAN WRITER AND COLUMNIST

Even though chance deals with the unexpected and the unplanned, it still has to be organized before it can exist.

—ROBERT RAUSCHENBERG (1925-)
AMERICAN ARTIST

How far can anything in our mental and moral evolution be considered accidental? Nothing, I believe. And yet some of the most decisive turning points in life seem to depend on casual circumstance.

—JOHN ADDINGTON SYMONDS (1840-1893)
ENGLISH POET AND CRITIC

CHANGE

SEE ALSO AGE AND AGING, DEATH, HISTORY, LIFE, THE PAST, THE PRESENT, ROUTINE

Change of life by definition refers to the future; one life is finishing therefore another life must be beginning.

—JUNE ARNOLD (1926-1982)
AMERICAN WRITER

When one begins to search for the crucial, the definitive moment, the moment which changed all others, one finds oneself pressing, in great pain, through a maze of false signals and abruptly locking doors.

—JAMES BALDWIN (1924-1987)
AFRICAN-AMERICAN WRITER

You hope that you change altogether through time. People don't ever stand still, they're in movement from birth to death, the whole psyche is changing all the time. No one ever knows what their psyche ever is.

—FRANCIS BACON (1909-1992)
BRITISH ARTIST

The average personality reshapes frequently, every few years even our bodies undergo a complete overhaul—desirable or not, it is a natural thing that we should change.

—TRUMAN CAPOTE (1924-1984)
AMERICAN WRITER

Things move so rapidly nowadays, that you're old-fashioned almost without knowing it.

—GEORGE CUKOR (1899-1983)
AMERICAN FILM DIRECTOR

For anyone to change, you have to break down.

—DAVID DEL TREDICI (1937-)
AMERICAN COMPOSER

No doubt every thing in human beings is changing all the time. But it's so difficult to remember the change is going on, especially when one establishes what are called "permanent" relationships in daily life.

—E. M. FORSTER (1879-1970)
BRITISH VVWRITER

Desire for acceptance is the antithesis to the desire for change. I fight every day not to return to that desire to be accepted into the familiar order of things.

—JEWELLE GOMEZ (1948-)
AFRICAN-AMERICAN WRITER, POET, AND ACTIVIST

There is only one absolute today and that is change. Old values are swept away by new with dizzying but thrilling speed. Long live Change!

—PHILIP JOHNSON (1906-2005)
AMERICAN ARCHITECT

I am concerned with a thing's not being what it was, with its becoming something other than what it is, with any moment in which one identifies a thing precisely and with the slipping away of that moment.

—JASPER JOHNS (1930-)
AMERICAN ARTIST

Change requires as its catalysts and fuel both good faith and decent intention, as well as deep need.

—TONY KUSHNER (1956-)
AMERICAN PLAYWRIGHT

One must break it all up; the dogmas must clean themselves up and the patterns take on new excitement.

—FEDERICO GARCIA LORCA (1898-1936)
SPANISH POET AND PLAYWRIGHT

The quality of light by which we scrutinize our lives has direct bearing upon the product which we live, and upon the changes which we hope to bring about through those lives.

—AUDRE LORDE (1934-1992)
AFRICAN-AMERICAN WRITER, POET, AND ACTIVIST

The forms in writing . . . do change, but they change as slowly as the forms in Darwin, whereas the pendulum of individual tone from one generation to the next keeps moving briskly.

—JAMES MERRILL (1926-1995)
AMERICAN PULITZER PRIZE–WINNING POET

It is not change I fear or detest—it is that change moves in ways that are strangely ambiguous to me.

— FELICE PICANO (1944-)
AMERICAN WRITER

Yes, the world has changed a lot for teen queens since the 1980s (ahem), but I know from the letters and e-mails I get that it's still pretty tough out there.

—JAMES ST. JAMES (1966-)
AMERICAN WRITER

I'm a chameleon; I know how to change. Also, I don't live for yesterday, I live basically for today and tomorrow.

—JUNIOR VASQUEZ (1946-)
AMERICAN DJ AND RECORD PRODUCER

China is a country which has a long history of gay culture. Because of that, changes are coming much faster in this country.

—DIDIER-ZHENG (1980-)
CHINESE TALK SHOW HOST

CHILDHOOD

SEE ALSO AGE AND AGING, CHILDREN, YOUTH

I am very tired of being grown-up. Have you ever been treated as an adult for eight weeks in succession? It is a dreary experience.

—RUPERT BROOKE (1887-1915)
BRITISH POET

———————

I realized I could get away with murder when I was six.

—TRUMAN CAPOTE (1924-1984)
AMERICAN WRITER

———————

Puberty's disadvantages can hardly be exaggerated.

—ALLAN GURGANUS (1947-)
AMERICAN WRITER

———————

When I was a child, my mother used to say I was sensitive.
My stepfather preferred the word sissy.

—E. LYNN HARRIS (1955-)
AFRICAN-AMERICAN WRITER

———————

I wish I'd had more people to look at [as a kid]—and I'm not talking about
any sort of role models—just more people to look at, more stories,
more honesty, less hate.

—T. R. KNIGHT (1973-)
AMERICAN ACTOR

———————

If you want to get analytical about it, I'm still living out my childhood.

—NATHAN LANE (1956-)
AMERICAN TONY AWARD-WINNING ACTOR AND COMEDIAN

When you're gay, you become a sort of spy at a very early age—
a spy for both sides, almost. A gay teenager can walk into a room and pretty
much figure out what's on everybody's mind, because you see things that other
people don't see. I think that's why a lot of artists are gay.

—ARMISTEAD MAUPIN (1944-)
AMERICAN WRITER

[My grandmother's] ears were going. That's what everyone said, "Oh, your
nana's ears are going, you know," and when I was very young, I would think,
Going where? A child's world is so literal. So many things don't make sense.

—ROSIE O'DONNELL (1962-)
AMERICAN ACTOR, COMEDIAN AND TALK SHOW HOST

When I was little, I liked Walt Disney. Then, as I got big, I got more perverse.

—FRANCOIS OZON (1967-)
FRENCH DIRECTOR AND WRITER

We'd get so fucking high on sugar and salt,
making passionate love to our candy.

—HORACIO N. ROQUE RAMIREZ (ca. 1970-)
EL SALVADORAN WRITER

The upside to being raised by what were essentially a pair of house cats
was that we never had any enforced bedtime.

—DAVID SEDARIS (1956-)
AMERICAN WRITER

The spoon is the utensil of childhood, the friendliest utensil.
The spoon is childlike. Yum-yum.

—SUSAN SONTAG (1933-2004)
AMERICAN WRITER AND CRITIC

CHILDREN

SEE ALSO AGE AND AGING, CHILDHOOD, YOUTH

Kids can think, kids deal with issues, you know kids lose parents, kids have fights at school, kids have to deal with the whole dynamics of society. . . . They deal with it every day. We have to treat them like individuals and people.

—JOHN BARROWMAN (1967-)
SCOTTISH ACTOR AND TV PRESENTER

I abominate the sight of them [children] so much that I have always had the greatest respect for the character of Herod.

—LORD BYRON (1788-1824)
BRITISH POET

Admittedly, someone like me "ought" not to bring children into the world. But that "ought" deserves its quotation marks. All living things not only will their existence because they are alive but have willed it or they would not be alive.

—THOMAS MANN (1875-1955)
GERMAN WRITER

[Before having a child] what else would I spend my money on? Leather pants and party drugs? Past, oh, age 33, a man looks ridiculous wearing leather pants, to say nothing of huge black pupils.

—DAN SAVAGE (1964-)
AMERICAN SEX COLUMNIST AND WRITER

Gay people shouldn't feel they have to have children to be considered a normal part of society. You can contribute in all sorts of ways beyond procreation.

—DANIEL TAMMET (1979-)
BRITISH AUTISTIC SAVANT

The impertinence of boys!

—PETER ILYICH TCHAIKOVSKY (1840-1893)
RUSSIAN COMPOSER

I was on [*The Tonight Show*] in 1973, and [Johnny] Carson said to me, "You're not married, are you?" And I said, "No." And he said, "Don't you want to have any children?" . . . There was kind of a tense moment there, so I said to Carson, "Who has custody of yours?'"

—LILY TOMLIN (1939-)
AMERICAN ACTOR AND COMEDIAN

CITIES AND STATES

SEE ALSO AMERICA, EUROPE, TRAVEL

The city where you live is surrounded by a labyrinth where the unaccredited are lost who do not announce themselves.

—MONIQUE WITTIG (1935-2003)
FRENCH FEMINIST AND WRITER

ATLANTA

For an African-American person, living in San Diego was just not happening. When I got to Atlanta, I realized, Oh, my God! There really are black people in the world!

—RUPAUL (1960-)
AMERICAN DRAG PERFORMER AND MUSICIAN

ATLANTIC CITY

A.C. is all that and a bag of poker chips.

—MICHAEL MUSTO (1954-)
AMERICAN WRITER AND COLUMNIST

BEIJING

There's something really alluring about single white men wandering around
Beijing on their own.

—JUSTIN CHIN (1968-)
ASIAN-AMERICAN WRITER AND PERFORMANCE ARTIST

BEIRUT

When I told people that I lived in Beirut, they often questioned my sanity.
To them Beirut was still that terrifying city of the 1980s of hostages, car bombs,
and massacres . . . [but] this is where the Middle East came to reinvent itself,
where it came to experiment—the San Francisco of the Middle East.

—WARREN SINGH-BARTLETT (ca. 1970-)
JOURNALIST LIVING IN BEIRUT

CALIFORNIA

Oh brother. California. Everyone there is somewhere else.

—KATHY ACKER (1947-1997)
AMERICAN WRITER

I realized then the amount of hatred that there is in California. They hate the Jews, they hate the Poles, they even hate the Pope! They hate everybody! They're all terrified, they all live in cages.

—DIRK BOGARDE (1921-1999)
BRITISH ACTOR AND WRITER

———————

I love California. I adore it. I owe a majority of my success to the state of California. I do have some issues with California . . . California is all about extremes—extreme beauty, extreme ugliness.

—RUFUS WAINWRIGHT (1973-)
CANADIAN MUSICIAN

CLEVELAND

Lately I have grown terribly isolated, and very egoist. One has to, in Cleveland.

—HART CRANE (1899-1932)
AMERICAN POET

KEY WEST

Key West is better than fiction, and spends most of its time writing itself. It's a lazy novelist's paradise.

—TIM ASHLEY (ca. 1970-)
BRITISH WRITER

LOS ANGELES

L.A. is going to seem to you like everyone is moving in slow motion. L.A. is culturally napping sometimes. It's like one long siesta.

—STANLEY BENNETT CLAY (1950–)
AFRICAN-AMERICAN PLAYWRIGHT AND PRODUCER

———————

L.A. is my American city. . . . I think of L.A. as my American urban experience, London as my European urban experience, and Santa Fe as my country escape.

—TOM FORD (1962–)
AMERICAN FASHION DESIGNER

———————

I live in L.A., which isn't exactly the most vibrant literary scene on the planet. I have screenwriter friends. I don't have any friends who write or have published novels. If I lived in New York, that would be different.

—CHRISTOPHER RICE (1978–)
AMERICAN WRITER

———————

The city without a center was everywhere the city. L.A. bestowed metropolitan stature on the suburban.

—RICHARD RODRIGUEZ (1944–)
MEXICAN-AMERICAN WRITER

———————

You're beautiful if L.A. says you're beautiful, goddammit.

—RICHARD RODRIGUEZ (1944–)
MEXICAN-AMERICAN WRITER

L O N D O N

London seemed like really the only place in the world, and I had to go there.

—LEIGH BOWERY (1961-1994)
BRITISH PERFORMANCE ARTIST

When I first went back to have a look at the World Trade Center area, that was the one thing that struck me about it, is I thought, Oh, my God, it looks like London's East End when I was a kid. That's what it looked like when I was about seven. Then it brought it all back, what London was like in that particular time. And it was grey and it was a pretty poor place in those days.

—DAVID BOWIE (1947-)
BRITISH MUSICIAN

You can call it swinging London, but it just sort of expresses something that is there, a splendid liberalism. . . . You can do all sorts of things in London, and long may it remain so.

—JOE ORTON (1933-1967)
BRITISH PLAYWRIGHT

M I A M I

[On Miami, Southbeach] Everybody who isn't gay is Eurotrash, and everybody who isn't Eurotrash is Latin and a print model, and everybody who isn't Latin and a print model is an old Jew wandering around wondering why all these people are making all this noise all of a sudden. Oy.

—BRUCE VILANCH (1948-)
AMERICAN COMEDY WRITER

MOSCOW

For me, as a writer, Moscow is certainly different. It's the first city I've ever lived
in where I could make my living entirely from writing.

—LANGSTON HUGHES (1902-1967)
AFRICAN-AMERICAN POET

Home. . . . Absolutely insurmountable repulsion toward Moscow
and everything that's here.

—PETER ILYICH TCHAIKOVSKY (1840-1893)
RUSSIAN COMPOSER

NEW YORK

The East Village was crumbling and crazy. That's where all the misfits that
couldn't work it out anywhere else gathered. I started meeting up
with all the weirdoes, the real weirdoes.

—JOEY ARIAS (ca. 1955-)
AMERICAN PERFORMANCE AND DRAG ARTIST

I do miss New York, and I wish I could live there, but you gotta come and suck
off the nipple, the great nipple of Hollywood, that's what everyone does.

—ALEXIS ARQUETTE (1969-)
AMERICAN ACTOR AND DRAG PERFORMER

[On Central Park] A bunch of trees surrounded by noise.

—SAMUEL BARBER (1910-1981)
AMERICAN COMPOSER

I really can't make it in the U.S. anymore. Only in N.Y., which is something
special and not pure U.S.; and where I have all my junkie connections.

—WILLIAM BURROUGHS (1914-1997)
AMERICAN WRITER

I am certainly not unique in my memories of New York. Anyone who lived there
from 1900 until late into the twenties can remember the same things I can.
But it seems a shame that the young now know it merely as a
great commercial city—infinitely impersonal.

—MERCEDES DE ACOSTA (1893-1968)
CUBAN-AMERICAN WRITER AND SOCIALITE

My New York [in the '70s] held no families. My New York was a late-night city,
its streets occupied by prostitutes, taxicabs, roaming homosexuals, its parks
trysting places, its ruined neighborhoods mere stage sets on which isolated figures
appeared to fulfill my romantic dreams. That these figures all came from families
enclosed by the walls of the numberless houses that stretched in all directions
around Manhattan was not a fact I dwelled on.

—ANDREW HOLLERAN (1944-)
AMERICAN WRITER

If New York was a city full of fountains that were never turned on,
it was also a town full of churches that were empty.

—ANDREW HOLLERAN (1944-)
AMERICAN WRITER

New York is appalling, fantastically charmless, and elaborately dire.

—HENRY JAMES (1843-1916)
AMERICAN WRITER

Ah, filthy New York . . .

—FEDERICO GARCIA LORCA (1898-1936)
SPANISH POET AND PLAYWRIGHT

———————

The two elements the traveler [in New York] first captures in the big city are
extra-human architecture and furious rhythm. Geometry and anguish.

—FEDERICO GARCIA LORCA (1898-1936)
SPANISH POET AND PLAYWRIGHT

———————

Even though I grew up as a Sephardic Jew in Brooklyn where we ate Syrian food
and went to temple and all that, it was still America. And most of my life I was
occupied with American television and American food. And my ethnicity was my
choice. It still is. That's what's so great about New York. You have selective privacy,
you have selective ethnicity. Everything is your own choice.

—ISAAC MIZRAHI (1961-)
AMERICAN FASHION DESIGNER

———————

[Someone once said] parking lots are the most valuable real estate in
New York City because there's absolutely no overhead. And I thought
this is so absurd, all these officious looking buildings and actually,
the best business would be not to have a building at all.

—ROBERT RAUSCHENBERG (1925-)
AMERICAN ARTIST

———————

The California Look is great, but when you get back to New York
you're so glad to be back because they're stranger looking here
but they're more beautiful even—the New York Look.

—ANDY WARHOL (1928-1987)
AMERICAN ARTIST

NEW YORK VS. LOS ANGELES

That's the big difference between Los Angeles and New York.
in Hollywood they put you in a box and never allow you to stretch.
In the New York theater world, they want to see what you can do.

—LEA DELARIA (1958-)
AMERICAN COMEDIAN AND ACTOR

Whereas New York is claustrophobic, LA is big, wide—one story.

—DAVID HOCKNEY (1937-)
BRITISH ARTIST

NEW YORK VS. PARIS

They were, New York and Paris, exactly as I'd imagined them to be—full of
discoveries, inspirations, the sense of possibility.

—SUSAN SONTAG (1933-2004)
AMERICAN WRITER AND CRITIC

PARIS

I found my poetry being more "influenced" but the sight of clear water flowing in the
street gutters, where it is (or was) diverted or damned by burlap sandbags moved
about by workmen than it was by the French poetry I was learning to read at the time.

—JOHN ASHBERY (1927-)
AMERICAN POET

Paris gave everyone permission to get a character.

—DJUNA BARNES (1892-1982)
AMERICAN WRITER

We have learned well or less well, how to live with the décor of custom,
habit, and hope. Remove that suddenly and you have Paris.

—DJUNA BARNES (1892–1982)
AMERICAN WRITER

———————

Paris: Home which keeps its promise.

—MARLENE DIETRICH (1901–1992)
GERMAN-BORN ACTOR

———————

When a man has seen Paris somewhat attentively, he has seen (I suppose)
the biggest achievement of civilization in a certain direction and he will always
carry with him a certain little reflet of its splendor.

—HENRY JAMES (1843–1916)
AMERICAN WRITER

———————

Paris is a big city, in the sense that London and New York are big cities and that
Rome is a village, Los Angeles a collection of villages and Zürich a backwater.

—EDMUND WHITE (1940-)
AMERICAN WRITER AND CRITIC

———————

The French have such an attractive civilization, dedicated to calm
pleasures and general tolerance, and their taste in every domain is so sharp,
so sure, that the foreigner (especially someone from chaotic,
confused America) is quickly seduced into believing that if he can only
become a Parisian he will at last master the art of living.

—EDMUND WHITE (1940-)
AMERICAN WRITER AND CRITIC

PARIS VS. BERLIN

The early American traveler commuted between Paris and Berlin, for drug-taking was the fashion, and while the streetwalkers and the seamstresses sold "snow" in Paris to eke out their scant earnings, it could be got "over the bar" in Berlin.

—DJUNA BARNES (1892-1982)
AMERICAN WRITER

———

Wasn't Berlin's famous "decadence" largely a commercial "line" which the Berliners had instinctively developed in their competition with Paris? Paris had long since cornered the straight-girl market, so what was left for Berlin to offer its visitors but a masquerade of perversions?

—CHRISTOPHER ISHERWOOD (1904-1986)
BRITISH-BORN WRITER

PROVINCETOWN

My years in Provincetown—which fills up every summer with gays and lesbians from all over the world—have taught me that gay people come in as many sorts of varieties as everyone else, and therefore it's impossible to essentialize them; I wouldn't want to claim that gay people are by nature this or that, or like this or that.

—MARK DOTY (1953-)
AMERICAN POET

RALEIGH

When we moved to Raleigh, it felt like a definite place, but now it's become just like anywhere else in the country, you know, here's your Long John Silver's, here's your Kmart, it could be anywhere.

—DAVID SEDARIS (1956-)
AMERICAN WRITER

ROME

Rome is expensive and cold, and seemingly offers nothing for a
man of my caliber. I am going to have something to say to Gore Vidal,
and all these characters talking about how great Italy is and anything goes,
and they like a renaissance of culture. What a crock of shit!

—WILLIAM BURROUGHS (1914-1997)
AMERICAN WRITER

––––––––

No one looks handsome in Rome—besides the Romans.

—HENRY JAMES (1843-1916)
AMERICAN WRITER

––––––––

Rome doesn't disappoint me. It is myself that fails. Why am I so dreary and unre-
ceptive, incapable of imaginative enthusiasm and romantic youthfulness?

—SIEGFRIED SASSOON (1886-1967)
BRITISH POET AND WRITER

––––––––

Rome and Roman life are too characteristic, too exciting and full of variety,
to permit of my sticking to my writing table.

—PETER ILYICH TCHAIKOVSKY (1840-1893)
RUSSIAN COMPOSER

SAN FRANCISCO

The queers here in Mecca [San Francisco] get very righteous, and they don't like
their secrets, like shaved testicles, shared with the straights.

—SCOTT CAPURRO (1962-)
BRITISH COMEDIAN AND WRITER

Atlantis, to Pompeii, to the Pillar of Salt, we add the Golden Gate Bridge, not golden at all, but rust red. San Francisco toys with the tragic conclusion.

—RICHARD RODRIGUEZ (1944-)

MEXICAN-AMERICAN WRITER

TOKYO

What is the good of having a lover in Tokyo, unless one can stay on forever.

—J. R. ACKERLEY (1896-1967)

BRITISH WRITER AND EDITOR

VENICE

To enter Venice at night is fit and proper. But it is disheartening to wake the next morning . . . to cosmopolitan hotels and Americans and all the other evils that our civilized age gives.

—RUPERT BROOKE (1887-1915)

BRITISH POET

CLASS

SEE ALSO OPPRESSION, MONEY

[Genealogy is] not a big thing among white trash, no. Rednecks don't want to be found. It ain't a family in which we have many things we can boast about.

—DOROTHY ALLISON (1942-)

AMERICAN WRITER

I tolerate anchovies on my Caesar salad. But people shouldn't be tolerated. Accepted, embraced, all of these things, but tolerated suggests a power differential between two types of people. It suggests that one is one class of citizen, and the other is another class, a lower class.

—JOHN AMAECHI (1970-)
BRITISH NBA BASKETBALL PLAYER

I haven't met that many refined people. Most people are generally crude.

—JEAN-MICHEL BASQUIAT (1960-1988)
AMERICAN ARTIST

I knew then that noble people can only live their lives in two ways—either religiously or poetically—and both these ways, in a measure, are the same.

—MERCEDES DE ACOSTA (1893-1968)
CUBAN-AMERICAN WRITER AND SOCIALITE

No writer who knows the working classes seems to find in them the good temper and charm which I find in them during my superficial contacts. It's all poverty, exasperation, disease, and attempts to free oneself: and this, untransfigured by poetry, makes difficult reading.

—E. M. FORSTER (1879-1970)
BRITISH WRITER

I think it is important for people to know that an open, working-class lesbian poet who surfaced in 1970 with the word "dyke" in the title of her first book is now considered literary canon.

—JUDY GRAHN (1940-)
FEMINIST POET AND GAY RIGHTS ACTIVIST

I do think you can be working class and have your sexuality accepted by your family.

—JONATHAN HARVEY (1968-)
BRITISH PLAYWRIGHT

———

He was suffering from an inhibition, then not unusual among upper-class homosexuals; he couldn't relax sexually with a member of his own class or nation. He needed a working-class foreigner.

—CHRISTOPHER ISHERWOOD (1904-1986)
BRITISH-BORN WRITER

———

While the peasant world has completely disappeared in the major industrialized countries like France and England (you can't talk about the peasantry in the classic sense of their word there), in Italy it still survives. . . . My mother used to have to go to bed by candlelight.

—PIER PAOLO PASOLINI (1922-1975)
ITALIAN FILM DIRECTOR

———

Well, when I was in school I would see all these people in class who . . . you know, they wanted to be raised by wolves. They had a suburban experience, but in their minds that was something to be ashamed of. Nobody would own up to it.

—DAVID SEDARIS (1956-)
AMERICAN WRITER

———

What essential difference indeed is there between making books or boots, driving in a donkey-cart or a barouche, embracing a duchess or a dairymaid, dining off ortolans or porridge?

—JOHN ADDINGTON SYMONDS (1840-1893)
ENGLISH POET AND CRITIC

If you're poor or working class, and don't have the privilege of coming
from within the academy, DIY isn't just some cute craftsy idea,
it's the only way you will survive as an artist.

—MICHELLE TEA (1971–)
AMERICAN WRITER

COMING OUT

SEE ALSO GAY COMMUNITY, GAY RIGHTS, HOMOSEXUALITY, IDENTITY, LESBIANS,
SELF-AWARENESS

There was no k.d. lang. There was no Melissa Etheridge. There was no Janis Ian.
No one was out then. . . .Being outed was the most destructive, terrifying thing
anyone could imagine. I panicked. We all panicked.

—CHASTITY BONO (1979–)
AMERICAN GAY RIGHTS ACTIVIST AND DAUGHTER OF CHER AND SONNY BONO

I discover that I have been all-too easy all along in letting out announcements
of my sexual predilections. not that anything unpleasant has happened or
is imminent. But it does put me into obligatory relations to a certain extent with
"those who are in the know," and this irks me to think of sometimes.
After all when you're dead it doesn't matter, and this statement proves
my immunity from any "shame" about it.

—HART CRANE (1899–1932)
AMERICAN POET

What happened to me is exactly the opposite of what closeted people fear:
They think they'll lose everything if they come out. This did not happen to me
at all. In fact, everything came back tenfold.

—MELISSA ETHERIDGE (1961–)
AMERICAN GRAMMY AWARD-WINNING MUSICIAN AND BREAST CANCER ACTIVIST

Everybody has had this situation where you come out to an individual and you're told, "Hey, that's fine, I don't care, I love you; but don't tell mother, don't tell Grandma, don't tell your uncle." That reinforces the view that you're not supposed to not be prejudiced.

—BARNEY FRANK (1940-)
AMERICAN CONGRESSMAN

When I first came out—at nineteen—I was still illegal. There was this irony that living as an adult, I could vote, drive, and drink, but I could not fuck.

—JOHN GREYSON (1960-)
CANADIAN FILM DIRECTOR

The word outing is not part of my vocabulary. I don't out anybody. I report on the private lives of public figures.

—PEREZ HILTON (1978-)
CUBAN-AMERICAN CELEBRITY BLOGGER

It's one thing to tell your parents you're gay . . . and quite another to write a book about bathhouses and have them be supportive. I'm lucky.

—WAYNE HOFFMAN (1982-)
AMERICAN WRITER

When you work in obscurity and suddenly you have the spotlight thrust upon you, the gay press announces you're coming out. I've always been out, but nobody ever asked before.

—CHERRY JONES (1956-)
AMERICAN TONY AWARD-WINNING ACTOR

We had a huge argument, all of us at dinner last night, about Tom Cruise . . .
It's like what Tallulah Bankhead said about Tab Hunter when asked if he was gay.
"I don't know dahling. He hasn't sucked my cock."

—LESLIE JORDAN (1955-)
AMERICAN EMMY AWARD-WINNING ACTOR

———————

When I was outed, I felt I was then out. It was like, "That's done."
But I guess the gay community never felt that way, that's for sure. . . . I felt very
violated. It's like rape. . . . To be outed means you weren't ready.

—BILLIE JEAN KING (1943-)
AMERICAN TENNIS CHAMPION

———————

How selfish it would be to only think of myself and my life as an actor when you
are weighing it [coming out] against severe homophobia.

—T. R. KNIGHT (1973-)
AMERICAN ACTOR

———————

Actually my wife told me I was gay. I would not approach the subject at all.
I was taught you didn't talk about things, you put them in God's hands.

—STEVE KMETKO (1953-)
AMERICAN TV HOST

———————

[In honor of his former boyfriend, Lance Bass] It's to be outed by someone in the
public media . . . they're calling it a "lancing." It's to "be lanced."

—REICHEN LEHMKUHL (1973-)
AMERICAN REALITY TV STAR AND CELEBRITY

Scrawling "I'm gay" in lipstick on your parents' bedroom mirror may demonstrate a personal signature of the highest style, but is not particularly sensitive to their feelings. Upon hearing me utter those words almost twenty years ago, my own mother did what and self-respecting middle-class mom would do: went directly into a seizure. Unfortunately, she was behind the wheel of our family station wagon. As I was coming out of the closet, our car was hurtling over an embankment. The moment was terrifying—but exactly right.

—LANCE LOUD (1951-2001)
AMERICAN COLUMNIST AND REALITY TV STAR

I was sleeping with my male friends in high school without ever thinking that I might be gay. It was only after a couple of years that I thought to myself, Gee, I haven't slept with a woman. I wonder if that means I'm gay.

—GREGORY MAGUIRE (1954-)
AMERICAN WRITER

It's more possible now that kids will have friends who are gay . . . but you know from the get-go that even if your family loves you, you just know that something is deeply strange.

—JAMES MCCOURT (1941-)
AMERICAN WRITER

Whenever a subject tells me, "I won't discuss who I'm dating" or "I resent labels," I generally know not so much that they're passionate about privacy but that they're gay, gay, gay.

—MICHAEL MUSTO (1954-)
AMERICAN WRITER AND COLUMNIST

I was able to do it [come out] with some grace. What I was wanting to do at the time was shout at them, "Hey, your son is a fucking faggot!" I was feeling very violent about telling them.

—ROBERT O'HARA (1970-)
AMERICAN PLAYWRIGHT AND DIRECTOR

———

[On Lance Bass's coming out] He said some things in the *People* article that got me pissed. That he doesn't want to be the poster boy or marching down side-walks for gays. That's ignorant. First off, just because you are out doesn't make you the poster boy for gay community. But secondly, you are on the cover of *People* magazine for being gay. That's why you are there. Don't forget that.

—JAI RODRIGUEZ (1979-)
AMERICAN ACTOR AND REALITY TV STAR

———

[After coming out] it feels like a huge weight has been lifted off my shoulders. . . . I feel very empowered.

—DAN PINTAURO (1976-)
AMERICAN ACTOR

———

I know in college there was a period where it was cool to be gay. There was a point where people were coming out and it was like, "Oh, cool, he's gay."

—DAVID PICHLER (1968-)
AMERICAN OLYMPIC DIVER

———

What began with the outing wars back in the early 1990s—when I and other gay journalists began reporting on closeted public figures in a small, feisty New York weekly called *OutWeek*, causing an uproar while challenging the rest of the media to normalize the discussion of homosexuality—is finally coming to fruition in the age of 100 million blogs.

—MICHELANGELO SIGNORILE (1960-)
AMERICAN JOURNALIST, WRITER, AND GAY ACTIVIST

A lot of gay men need to be away from where they grew up in order to come out.

—ANDREW SULLIVAN (1963–)
BRITISH-BORN POLITICAL COMMENTATOR AND BLOGGER

But no matter what anybody says, the list I see over and over again of [show business] people who could be outed is not terribly long.

—LILY TOMLIN (1939–)
AMERICAN ACTOR AND COMEDIAN

COMING OUT AND THE CLOSET

The closet corrupts you and will ruin your life.

—WILSON CRUZ (1973–)
PUERTO RICAN-AMERICAN ACTOR

Like many young gay men, divided from my self, from the authentic character of my desire, I felt I had to hide for years! And the result of that for me, once I began to break through the dissembling, was a thirst for the genuine.

—MARK DOTY (1953–)
AMERICAN POET

No human being can get through the day and give honest answers to questions without telling people what his sexual orientation is: "What did you do last weekend?" "What are you doing tonight?" "Where do you live down in Washington?"

—BARNEY FRANK (1940–)
AMERICAN CONGRESSMAN

It probably wouldn't be a good idea to date a closeted celebrity.

—T. R. KNIGHT (1973–)
AMERICAN ACTOR

When I came out of the closet, I nailed the door shut, and I'm not going back in it
for anybody, including some politician who says he'll help me out as soon as
I get him into power—if I'll just stay out of the way until he gets elected . . .
When I was a kid in the South, I saw black people who behaved the same way.
We called them Uncle Toms. And that's what's going on.

—ARMISTEAD MAUPIN (1944–)
AMERICAN WRITER

———

If a bullet should enter my brain, let that bullet destroy every closet door.

—HARVEY MILK (1930–1978)
AMERICAN POLITICIAN AND GAY RIGHTS ACTIVIST

———

A glass closet—that complex but popular contraption that allows
public figures to avoid the career repercussions of any personal disclosure
while living their lives with a certain degree of integrity.

—MICHAEL MUSTO (1954–)
AMERICAN WRITER AND COLUMNIST

———

At the time, I figured that once people knew you could come out of the closet,
everybody would come out. . . . This belief reflected nothing but my naïveté.

—RANDY SHILTS (1951–1994)
AMERICAN JOURNALIST, AIDS ACTIVIST, AND WRITER

COMMUNICATION

SEE ALSO AUDIENCES, DECEIT, FEELINGS, FORGIVENESS, FRIENDS AND FRIENDSHIP,
HONESTY, HUMOR, JOURNALISM, MEDIA, SECRETS, UNDERSTANDING, WRITING

When you interview people . . . you seduce them.

—JANE ANDERSON (1954–)
AMERICAN ACTOR AND DIRECTOR

We have no further use for the functional, the beautiful, or for whether or not something is true. We have only time for conversation.

—JOHN CAGE (1934-1992)
AMERICAN COMPOSER

Who knows how to write? Trying to be understood is like fighting with ink.

—JEAN COCTEAU (1889-1963)
FRENCH WRITER AND FILMMAKER

At present, I am sociable, attentive to conversation, very nice, and futile.

—SIDONIE-GABRIELLE COLETTE (1873-1954)
FRENCH WRITER

I have a horror of speaking about something I know nothing about.

—SIDONIE-GABRIELLE COLETTE (1873-1954)
FRENCH WRITER

I'll tell you what I don't believe in: improvisation. I think it's a lot of crap, because I can always tell when people are improvising.

—GEORGE CUKOR (1899-1983)
AMERICAN FILM DIRECTOR

Whenever someone asks a question in two parts, always answer the first part and never the second.

—HARRY HAY (1912-2002)
BRITISH-BORN GAY RIGHTS ACTIVIST

Properly to see things you need to talk about them.

—HENRY JAMES (1843-1916)
AMERICAN WRITER

Too much conversation, too much disturbance, all to too little purpose.

—JOHN MAYNARD KEYNES (1883-1946)
BRITISH ECONOMIST

———

I prefer to be wrong than to compromise.

—KARL LAGERFELD (1938-)
GERMAN FASHION DESIGNER

———

Conversation is an art . . . something entirely unrelated to sense or reality or logic.

—ROBERT MCALMON (1896-1956)
AMERICAN WRITER AND PUBLISHER

———

I was filled, like an empty jar, by the words of other people streaming
in through my ears, though I'm so stupid that I've even forgotten
where and from whom I heard them.

— PLATO (427-347 BC)
GREEK PHILOSOPHER

———

I think people can figure out if you're a bullshit artist or if you mean it.

—ANDREW SULLIVAN (1963-)
BRITISH-BORN POLITICAL COMMENTATOR AND BLOGGER

———

[I] would like so much to give myself over to contemplation without interference, but
here and now I am afraid they will force conversation! It spoils all the pleasure.

—PETER ILYICH TCHAIKOVSKY (1840-1893)
RUSSIAN COMPOSER

———

Communicate as you confront. The key to our future lies in communication.

—URVASHI VAID (1958-)
AMERICAN GAY RIGHTS ACTIVIST

Rumor has a hundred mouths.

—PAUL VERLAINE (1844-1896)
FRENCH POET

My facial expressions are sort of huge and over the top, and I think that does come from having to sign. When you use sign language to communicate it's mostly from the shoulders up—and mostly in your face.

—JIM VERRAROS (1983-)
AMERICAN IDOL FINALIST

Ultimately the bond of all companionship, whether in marriage or in friendship, is conversation.

—OSCAR WILDE (1854-1900)
IRISH PLAYWRIGHT AND WRITER

COURAGE

SEE ALSO ACTIVISM, COWARDICE, SUCCESS, VANITY

Nay, it were better to meet some dangers half way, though they come nothing near, than to keep too long a watch upon their approaches; for if a man watch too long, it is odds he will fall asleep.

—SIR FRANCIS BACON (1561-1626)
BRITISH PHILOSOPHER AND STATESMAN

The English do not always take their pleasures sadly,
at least not when they are surrounded by death and destruction.

—NOËL COWARD (1899-1973)
BRITISH ACTOR AND PLAYWRIGHT

I had to dare a little bit. Who am I kidding—I had to dare a lot.
Don't wear one ring, wear five or six. People ask how I can play with
all those rings, and I reply, "Very well, thank you."

—LIBERACE (1919-1987)
AMERICAN ENTERTAINER AND MUSICIAN

All over the world there are wonderful stories to be written if only
you've got the balls to write them.

—W. SOMERSET MAUGHAM (1874-1965)
BRITISH WRITER AND PLAYWRIGHT

If someone is chasing you, stop running. And then they'll stop chasing you.

—CYNTHIA NIXON (1966-)
AMERICAN TONY AND EMMY AWARD-WINNING ACTOR

I was a scared kid, but you'd never have known it. I'm a scared adult.
I don't think it shows.

—ROSIE O'DONNELL (1962-)
AMERICAN ACTOR, COMEDIAN, AND TALK SHOW HOST

Nothing like bravado to overcome stark terror.

—B. RUBY RICH (1948-)
AMERICAN SCHOLAR AND FILM CRITIC

For being American, for being anything, for just being myself, someone might want
to destroy me. That concept is so terrifying that it constantly bears exploration.

—BRYAN SINGER (1965-)
AMERICAN FILM DIRECTOR

I've had to fight to be myself and to be respected. I'm proud to carry this stigma and call myself a lesbian. I don't boast about it or broadcast it, but I don't deny it.

—CHAVELA VARGAS (1919-)
COSTA RICAN MUSICIAN

———————

For all the people in the world who are afraid to be themselves, there also have to be people who say, "Fuck it—if you don't like me as I am, I don't care."

—JANE WIEDLIN (1958-)
AMERICAN MUSICIAN

CREATION AND CREATIVITY

SEE ALSO ART AND ARTISTS, TALENT, WRITING

I don't know how to describe my work because it's not always the same thing. It's like asking Miles, well, how does your horn sound?

—JEAN-MICHEL BASQUIAT (1960-1988)
AMERICAN ARTIST

———————

I enjoy creating in a form that is considered lightweight because so many "heavy" ideas can be slipped in.

—JEWELLE GOMEZ (1948-)
AFRICAN-AMERICAN WRITER, POET, AND ACTIVIST

———————

Part of growing is trying to teach yourself to be empty enough that the thing can come through you completely so it's nor affected by your preconceived ideas of what a work of art should be or what an artist should do.

—KEITH HARING (1958-1990)
AMERICAN ARTIST AND ACTIVIST

These places of possibility within ourselves are dark because they are ancient and hidden; they have survived and grown strong through that darkness. Within these deep places, each one of us holds an incredible reserve of creativity and power.

—AUDRE LORDE (1934-1992)
AFRICAN-AMERICAN WRITER, POET, AND ACTIVIST

———————

Scenes of childhood [are] . . . after all, the purest well from which the creative artist draws.

—PATRICK WHITE (1912-1990)
AUSTRALIAN WRITER AND NOBEL LAUREATE

CRIME

There is not one of us who, given an eternal incognito, a thumbprint nowhere set against our souls, would not commit rape, murder, and all abominations.

—DJUNA BARNES (1892-1982)
AMERICAN WRITER

———————

Murderers almost always laugh when they're discussing their crimes. I've met few killers who didn't start laughing when I finally managed to force them to discuss the murder—which isn't easy.

—TRUMAN CAPOTE (1924-1984)
AMERICAN WRITER

———————

Now, I'm no bleeding heart about murderers. . . . I know them, and I'm realistic about them. But as capital punishment functions today, it is so erratic in its application and so creakingly accomplished that it really does constitute "cruel and unusual" punishment as proscribed by the Constitution.

—TRUMAN CAPOTE (1924-1984)
AMERICAN WRITER

Spare a thought for London cabbies. My driver told me he doesn't work after 7 p.m. because it's too dangerous. "I've been attacked twice by machetes and knives. The police don't do anything because they all look the same." Well, quite. I wouldn't know one machete from another, although they've always been very nice to me.

—JULIAN CLARY (1959-)
BRITISH COMEDIAN

There is a close relationship between flowers and convicts. The fragility and delicacy of the former are of the same nature as the brutal insensitivity of the latter.

—JEAN GENET (1910-1986)
FRENCH WRITER, CRIMINAL, AND POLITICAL ACTIVIST

I killed Freda because I loved her, and she refused to marry me. I asked her three times to marry me, and at last she consented . . . I sent her an engagement ring and she wore it for a time. When she returned it I resolved to kill her. I would rather she were dead than separated from me living.

—ALICE MITCHELL (1873-1898)
AMERICAN TEENAGED MURDERER

I still think everybody looks better under arrest.

—JOHN WATERS (1946-)
AMERICAN DIRECTOR

CRITICS AND CRITICISM

SEE ALSO JUDGMENT, SOCIETY

[If] you are ready enough to pull my knitting to pieces, but provide none of your own, the only sock is a sock in the jaw!

—J. R. ACKERLEY (1896-1967)
BRITISH WRITER AND EDITOR

I am getting sick of other people's silly unimaginative minds trailing all over my work.

—NOËL COWARD (1899-1973)
BRITISH ACTOR AND PLAYWRIGHT

———————

If a choice is in order . . . I'd rather have people hiss than yawn.

—JAMES DEAN (1931-1955)
AMERICAN ACTOR

———————

It's frightening how much power critics and curators have. People like that may have enough power to completely write you out of history.

—KEITH HARING (1958-1990)
AMERICAN ARTIST AND ACTIVIST

———————

The stories they were printing were upsetting—but I was rich enough and fortunate enough to be wealthy enough to fight them.

—SIR ELTON JOHN, CBE (1947-)
BRITISH GRAMMY- AND ACADEMY AWARD-WINNING MUSICIAN

———————

Demands and struggle, with a depth of stern love, temper an artist's soul. Facile praise makes it effeminate and destroys it.

—FEDERICO GARCIA LORCA (1898-1936)
SPANISH POET AND PLAYWRIGHT

———————

I just want to be written about as a normal artist.

—ROBERT MAPPLETHORPE (1946-1989)
AMERICAN PHOTOGRAPHER

Critics work hard, but they do not really work for the sake of art.
They only write about it.

—VASLAV NIJINSKY (1890-1950)
RUSSIAN DANCER

———————

In spite of all one hears to the contrary, critics are human beings, and human
beings make snap judgments.

—JOE ORTON (1933-1967)
BRITISH PLAYWRIGHT

———————

When you're an artist you make a bargain—whatever you do is going to be
reviewed by people. Some of them are going to be good, some of them are
going to be bad, some of them are going to be in between.

—MARTIN SHERMAN (1938-)
AMERICAN PLAYWRIGHT AND SCREENWRITER

———————

An author never judges his own works with justice.

—PETER ILYICH TCHAIKOVSKY (1840-1893)
RUSSIAN COMPOSER

———————

You can survive being trashed . . . you move to a different place inside.
And there's growth once you're there.

—ALICE WALKER (1944-)
AFRICAN-AMERICAN FEMINIST AND PULITZER PRIZE-WINNING WRITER

DANCING

SEE ALSO ART AND ARTISTS, ENTERTAINMENT, MUSIC

I have found myself suddenly seized with a need to stop speaking, and to express myself with gestures, body movement, dance rhythms instead.

—SIDONIE-GABRIELLE COLETTE (1873-1954)
FRENCH WRITER

I am more interested in the facts of moving rather than in my feelings about them.

—MERCE CUNNINGHAM (1919-)
AMERICAN CHOREOGRAPHER AND DANCER

No art lends itself so aptly as dance to metaphors borrowed from the spiritual life.

—SUSAN SONTAG (1933-2004)
AMERICAN WRITER AND CRITIC

Nobody would dance if they could see the actual reality. It's a very short career.

—STANTON WELCH (1969-)
AUSTRALIAN DANCER AND CHOREOGRAPHER

I have delighted in dancing with boys since that long ago
summer of 1945 in Mexico City when I learned to follow and was,
for that reason, the belle of the balls.

—TENNESSEE WILLIAMS (1911-1983)
AMERICAN PLAYWRIGHT

DISCO

Call me old-fashioned, but I'm a disco queen.

—LADY BUNNY (1962-)
AMERICAN DRAG PERFORMER AND DJ

———————

The funny thing about Studio 54 is that the bartenders were so much at the center of everything; they were at the core of desire. And they became sort of famous.

—MARK CHRISTOPHER (1963-)
AMERICAN FILM DIRECTOR

———————

That winter I . . . began asking everyone I knew, "What will we be doing after disco?" For I was certain that form of diversion was kaput. The disco beat, which devotees of rock and jazz detest, suddenly seemed idiotic even to me, a certified disco maven.

—ANDREW HOLLERAN (1944-)
AMERICAN WRITER

———————

DEATH

SEE ALSO AGE AND AGING, GRIEF, THE HOLOCAUST, LIFE, TRAGEDY AND SUFFERING

In each generation's flesh is the knowledge of a million generation's death.

—DJUNA BARNES (1892-1982)
AMERICAN WRITER

———————

Do not put too much value on the words of the dying—they also lie.

—DJUNA BARNES (1892-1982)
AMERICAN WRITER

The slow death of my lover Joan from cancer . . . taught me that life is far too short and precious to be lived in fear or as a lie.

—CHASTITY BONO (1979-)
AMERICAN GAY RIGHTS ACTIVIST AND DAUGHTER OF CHER AND SONNY BONO

I am thinking out a really humorous method of dying. One might do it quite wittily. It is an opportunity not to be lost.

—RUPERT BROOKE (1887-1915)
BRITISH POET

There is one consolation in death—where he sets his seal, the impression can neither be melted nor broken, but endureth for ever.

—LORD BYRON (1788-1824)
BRITISH POET

Nothing which relates to death disgusts me except the pomp which goes with it. Funerals are not pleasing to my memory.

—JEAN COCTEAU (1889-1963)
FRENCH WRITER AND FILMMAKER

I used to laugh at one of the mortuary ads that boasted about the quality of its earth. "Warm, dry soil—no seepage!"

—GEORGE CUKOR (1899-1983)
AMERICAN FILM DIRECTOR

Death is the face of God.

—COUNTEE CULLEN (1903-1946)
AFRICAN-AMERICAN POET

I found in Death a constant lover:
Here in his arms I lie.

—COUNTEE CULLEN (1903-1946)
AFRICAN-AMERICAN POET

I have always felt the greatest moral uneasiness before the anonymity
of names in cemeteries, engraved as far as the eye can see in a
symmetrical vista to be found only in cemeteries.

—SALVADOR DALÍ (1904-1989)
SPANISH ARTIST

I did not know then as I do now that there is no excuse for suicide . . .
the cause of every suicide is essentially and solely ignorance,
no matter what the motive appears to be.

—MERCEDES DE ACOSTA (1893-1968)
CUBAN-AMERICAN WRITER AND SOCIALITE

There were these caskets. I got into one of them and lay down. . . .
I always wanted to see how I'd look in a casket.

—JAMES DEAN (1931-1955)
AMERICAN ACTOR

Part of the reason that I'm not having trouble facing the reality of death is that it's
not a limitation, in a way. It could have happened any time, and it is going to
happen sometime. If you live your life according to that, death is irrelevant.

—KEITH HARING (1958-1990)
AMERICAN ARTIST AND ACTIVIST

A man who dies at forty is at every moment of his life, we say,
a man who has died at forty.

—RICHARD HOWARD (1929-)
AMERICAN POET, CRITIC, AND TRANSLATOR

I've recently started looking for a cemetery, which is sort of like looking for a
good apartment in New York City. People are afraid to talk about death.

—ANNIE LEIBOWITZ (1949-)
AMERICAN PHOTOGRAPHER

You know, I'm seventy-two. At my time of life one finds all one's friends and
acquaintances dying like flies around one. . . . But perhaps it's just as well . . .
for, you see, it does remove further risks of libel actions.

—W. SOMERSET MAUGHAM (1874-1965)
BRITISH WRITER AND PLAYWRIGHT

I don't feel there is any ending written to the story of my life until it ends.

—PAUL MONETTE (1945-1995)
AMERICAN WRITER AND AIDS ACTIVIST

What will happen to the world when you leave it? Nothing, in any case,
will remain of what is now visible.

—ARTHUR RIMBAUD (1854-1891)
FRENCH POET

Suicides are inexplicable to me. No amount of scandal would make me want to
spoil my noble cranium with a revolver.

—SIEGFRIED SASSOON (1886-1967)
BRITISH POET AND WRITER

I've always called death my third tit. . . . I was just around death so much
that I was weaned on it.

—KEVIN SESSUMS (1956-)
AMERICAN JOURNALIST AND CELEBRITY INTERVIEWER

————————

Through me shall the words be said to make death exhilarating.

—WALT WHITMAN (1819-1892)
AMERICAN POET

————————

[On the death of her mother] The tragedy of her death was not that it made one,
now and then and very intensely, unhappy. It was that it made her unreal.

—VIRGINIA WOOLF (1882-1941)
BRITISH WRITER

D E C E I T

SEE ALSO DOUBLE LIVES, SECRETS

I was raised in the Baptist church so I have trouble of being proud of being a liar.
But God knows, I'm a good one. God does know.

—DOROTHY ALLISON (1942-)
AMERICAN WRITER

————————

People who are having a love-sex relationship are continuously lying to each other
because the very nature of the relationship demands that they do, because you
have to make a love object of this person, which means that you editorialize about
them. . . . You cut out what you don't want to see, you add this if it isn't there.

—TRUMAN CAPOTE (1924-1984)
AMERICAN WRITER

No artist can deceive God.

—VASLAV NIJINSKY (1890-1950)
RUSSIAN DANCER

If you're phony, you're going to see phoniness in other people.

—ETHEL WATERS (1896-1977)
AFRICAN-AMERICAN ACTOR AND MUSICIAN

DESIRE

SEE ALSO BEAUTY, FANTASIES, INTIMACY, LOVE, ROMANCE, SEX

Watch desire carefully. Desire burns up all the old dead language morality.

—KATHY ACKER (1947-1997)
AMERICAN WRITER

But my gratitude is enduring—if only for that once, at least, something beautiful approached me and, as though it were the most natural thing in the world, enclosed me in his arm and pulled me to him without my slightest bid.

—HART CRANE (1899-1932)
AMERICAN POET

Lad, never dam you body's itch
When loveliness is seen.

—COUNTEE CULLEN (1903-1946)
AFRICAN-AMERICAN POET

The fact that I want so much is what makes me completely awkward.

—ANDRÉ GIDE (1869-1951)
FRENCH WRITER

I think so much of attraction is about the things that we don't believe we are.

—ROBERT GANT (1968-)
AMERICAN ACTOR

DETERMINATION
SEE ALSO AMBITION, COURAGE

I love Midwest personalities, and I love the Midwest mentality that says
if your crops are destroyed by the locusts, you don't sit on your porch and cry,
you hop on your tractor and start plowing all over again.

—JANE ANDERSON (1954-)
AMERICAN ACTOR AND DIRECTOR

———

They said, "It's a race, and you finish a race, win or lose!" That didn't make sense
to me. I like to think that quitting that race was the last honest thing I ever did!

—RICHARD CHAMBERLAIN (1934-)
AMERICAN ACTOR

———

Our age tries hard enough to kill us, but I begin to feel a pleasure in sheer stub-
bornness, and will possibly turn in time into some sort of a beautiful crank.

—HART CRANE (1899-1932)
AMERICAN POET

———

Marathon running is an extreme . . . like living with AIDS. You hit the wall, and
then you get a handle on why it's worth hanging on.

—STEVE KOVACEV (1952-)
AMERICAN HIV-POSITIVE MARATHON RUNNER

I have doggedly refused to become a mess.

—JOHN RECHY (1934-)
AMERICAN WRITER

———————

When faced with life's crises, there are two possible responses:
despair or determination. Despair often seems more logical. But determination
is far more productive and usually far better for the soul.

—GERRY STUDDS (1937-2006)
AMERICAN CONGRESSMAN

DIFFERENCE

SEE ALSO GENDER BENDING, IDENTITY, INDIVIDUALISM, SELF-AWARENESS

When did I realize I was on another planet? . . . Any immigrant child is defined
by that experience—you're different, and it compounds differences that you find
as your identity becomes more apparent or more conscious to you.

—ANTONY HEGARTY (1971-)
BRITISH MUSICAN

———————

Savoring non-relatedness. Put the emphasis on savoring.

—SUSAN SONTAG (1933-2004)
AMERICAN WRITER AND CRITIC

———————

Two-headed people, like blacks, lesbians, Indians, "witches," have been
suppressed, and, in their case, suppressed out of existence.

—ALICE WALKER (1944-)
AFRICAN-AMERICAN FEMINIST AND PULITZER PRIZE-WINNING WRITER

DOUBLE LIVES

SEE ALSO COMING OUT, DECEIT, SECRETS

As fathers they punish what they cherish as lovers.

—MARIE-CLAIRE BLAIS (1939–)
CANADIAN WRITER AND PLAYWRIGHT

Over a long period of time, living as if you were someone else is no fun.

—RICHARD CHAMBERLAIN (1934–)
AMERICAN ACTOR

I think he [Leigh Bowery] was an intelligent, fairly shy person, until he dressed up. And then he became something of a monster.

—JULIAN CLARY (1959–)
BRITISH COMEDIAN

I'm not really into the whole "birdcage" thing.

—STEWART LEWIS (ca. 1970–)
AMERICAN MUSICIAN AND WRITER

Jane Roe has had to sit in a lot of rooms with a lot of women's organizations and listen to what people think about her who don't know beans about her. But Jane is pretty passive and she's going to let things slide. Norma McCorvey, on the other hand, is nothing but a rompin', stompin' bitch. . . . Put the two together, and you get trouble with a big red T. So Jane's sleeping and Norma carries on.

—NORMA (AKA "JANE ROE") MCCORVEY (1947–)
AMERICAN ABORTION ACTIVIST

I began going to Greece . . .very much in the spirit of one who embarks upon a double life. . . . I felt for the first time that I was doing exactly as I pleased. How we delude ourselves! As if there were ever more than one life.

–JAMES MERRILL (1926-1995)
AMERICAN PULITZER PRIZE WINNING POET

I've never had any time for the closet and double lives.

–JEANETTE WINTERSON (1959-)
BRITISH WRITER

[On having sex with Thornton Wilder] Thornton always went about having sex as though it were something going on behind his back and he didn't know anything about it.

–SAMUEL STEWARD (1909-1993)
AMERICAN WRITER, SCHOLAR, AND TATTOO ARTIST

I hope you have not been leading a double life, pretending to be wicked and being really good all the time. That would be hypocrisy.

–OSCAR WILDE (1854-1900)
IRISH PLAYWRIGHT AND WRITER

DRAG

SEE ALSO ENTERTAINMENT, GAY COMMUNITY, HOMOSEXUALITY, SEXUALITY, STYLE

People don't even know the meaning of the word "transvestite." I don't live in drag. Now, Candy Darling was a transvestite, and a very beautiful one. But I don't sit around in negligees and I don't wear little Adolfo suits to lunch. Of course, if I had a couple of Bob Mackie outfits, things might be different . . .

–DIVINE (1945-1988)
AMERICAN ACTOR AND SINGER

I think [drag]'s been an art for centuries. From Japan's kabuki theater to boys playing all the female roles of Shakespeare's plays to Michael Jackson, the larger than life quality of drag has made it an entertainment staple for centuries.

—LADY BUNNY (1962-)
AMERICAN DRAG PERFORMER AND DJ

When a queen is rigged up in all her flashy finery it can be quite regal— hence the term "queen." I think it's hilarious to temper this grandness with lunacy or else the drag risks being a snooze.

—LADY BUNNY (1962-)
AMERICAN DRAG PERFORMER AND DJ

Drag is about icons, archetypes—a fabrication of femininity.

—JOHN GRAYSON (1960-)
CANADIAN DIRECTOR

The Barbara Bush look is, sadly, the drag I look best in.

—NATHAN LANE (1956-)
AMERICAN TONY AWARD-WINNING ACTOR AND COMEDIAN

I am hoping to play a dame in a pantomime soon.

—SIR IAN MCKELLEN, CBE (1939-)
BRITISH ACTOR

I knew that Divine had to have a name, and I gave her that one while I was thinking up the credits for *Roman Candles*. . . . I went to Catholic school, and they were always saying this was divine and that was divine, and if you look it up in the dictionary it has a good definition.

—JOHN WATERS (1946-)
AMERICAN DIRECTOR

DRUGS

SEE ALSO ALCOHOL, CRIME, VICE

I'm pretty puritanical. I never buy pot, though I take it if someone offers it to me.

—KATHY ACKER (1947-1997)
AMERICAN WRITER

———————

I didn't feel "normal" for months after being sober, maybe even years . . . And it was a gradual thing, not a sudden jolt. I began to notice small things: emotions, physical feeling, smell, returning to me over time. But it took almost two years.

—MICHAEL ALIG (1966-)
AMERICAN FOUNDING MEMBER OF THE CLUB KIDS AND CONVICTED MURDERER

———————

I knew a doctor who asked a few of us to take LSD. It was his theory that the state LSD induces is a chemically exact replica of schizophrenia. Well, I took it twice and was interested in the images and fantasies, but I quite disagree with his theory. Because all the time you're under LSD, some part of your mind is saying, "My isn't this interesting." You know that what you're seeing is not reality, which the true schizophrenic does not.

—TRUMAN CAPOTE (1924-1984)
AMERICAN WRITER

———————

Pot is an insidious drug because it can steal your life away from you, without you even being aware of it. I had a love affair with pot for ten years. Pot was my most devoted partner.

—MARGARET CHO (1968-)
KOREAN-AMERICAN COMEDIAN

I affirm that opium, if the technique were not so complicated, would prepare many souls for elevation. The difficulty consists in knowing when it ceases to be charitable.

—JEAN COCTEAU (1889-1963)
FRENCH WRITER AND FILMMAKER

———

Did I tell you of that thrilling experience this last winter in the dentist's chair when, under the influence of aether and amnesia, my mind spiraled to a kind of seventh heaven of consciousness and egotistic dance among the seven spheres—and something like an objective voice kept saying to me, "You have the higher consciousness."

—HART CRANE (1899-1932)
AMERICAN POET

———

If we've learned anything at all in twenty-plus years of this [AIDS] crisis, it's that dread and humiliation of "forbidden love" equate with excessive use of drugs and alcohol.

—KYAN DOUGLAS (1970-)
AMERICAN REALITY TV STAR

———

I've always used various addictions to anesthetize myself— drag, drugs, fame, sex, religion, food—and there's been a lot of things in my life that I've wanted to run away from. Therapy opens up a window. You can try to close it, but the realization remains.

—BOY GEORGE (1961-)
BRITISH MUSICIAN

———

All the antidrug things on television at the time only made me want to do them more. They showed all these things to scare you: a gas burner turning into a beautiful flower. I thought, That's great! You mean I can see like that?

—KEITH HARING (1958-1990)
AMERICAN ARTIST AND ACTIVIST

I was more ashamed that I couldn't work the washing machine than the fact that I was taking drugs.

—SIR ELTON JOHN, CBE (1947-)
BRITISH GRAMMY- AND ACADEMY AWARD-WINNING MUSICIAN

––––––––

When I was loaded I had no trouble being gay. So I stayed loaded for 30 years!

—LESLIE JORDAN (1955-)
AMERICAN EMMY AWARD-WINNING ACTOR

––––––––

There's a lot more wrong with the world than teenage sex and drug taking.

—JOE ORTON (1933-1967)
BRITISH PLAYWRIGHT

––––––––

I've know fear and terrible solitude. Tranquilizers and drugs, those phony friends. The prison of depression and hospitals. I've emerged from all this dazzled but sober.

—YVES SAINT LAURENT (1936-)
FRENCH FASHION DESIGNER

––––––––

[On drugs in Manhattan] There is this kind of Babylonian village that exists in this city. I am happy it does exist, but it is not where you want to end up.

—RUFUS WAINWRIGHT (1973-)
CANADIAN MUSICIAN

EDUCATION

Earlier she [my grandmother] had taught me my letters, and at first I could not get past the letter G, which for some time I felt was far enough to go. My alphabet made a satisfying short song, and I didn't want to spoil it.

—ELIZABETH BISHOP (1911-1979)
AMERICAN POET

Knowledge is so disillusioning.

—RUPERT BROOKE (1887-1915)
BRITISH POET

The lecturer is often a pedant who does not try to get close to his listeners and who speaks on what is old hat to him, without spending energy and without force of love, until the audience is seized with such hatred it wants to see him trip on leaving the podium or sneeze so furiously that his spectacles go crashing into the water glass.

—FEDERICO GARCIA LORCA (1898-1936)
SPANISH POET AND PLAYWRIGHT

Although there exists on all campuses a distinct cleavage between the younger and older members of the faculties, almost everywhere the younger teachers, knowing well the existing evils, are as yet too afraid of their jobs to speak out.

—LANGSTON HUGHES (1902-1967)
AFRICAN-AMERICAN POET

I have always loved education, even though it is such a sadomasochistic affair— or maybe this is why I like it so much.

—FRANCISCO IBAÑEZ-CARRASCO (1963-)
CHILEAN-CANADIAN WRITER

Education is atmosphere, nothing more.

—THOMAS MANN (1875-1955)
GERMAN WRITER

We [Bobby Lopez and I] decided to write a musical about this aspect of
American society—the whole generation of people our age who graduate
from college thinking they're pretty special and then find, to their shock,
the rude reality that they're only about as special as everyone else.

—JEFF MARX (1970-)
AMERICAN COMPOSER AND LYRICIST

I got a very big arty education, so I have a big artistic overview of
it all, but I also believe that ivory tower art is not a reasonable response
to a world that is disintegrating like ours is.

—PAUL MONETTE (1945-1995)
AMERICAN WRITER AND AIDS ACTIVIST

We can't just have an attitude as parents and educators of "Eat your spinach."
You can't just say, "Eat your spinach" for 7 hours a day. Just do math and that's
it. We can't just educate the brain in one narrow way.

—CYNTHIA NIXON (1966-)
AMERICAN TONY- AND EMMY AWARD-WINNING ACTOR

I should, therefore, be no advocate for any plan of introducing English
literature into the course of university studies. . . . Intelligent Englishmen
resort naturally for a liberal pleasure to their own literature. Why transform
into a difficult exercise what is natural virtue in them?

—WALTER PATER (1839-1894)
BRITISH CRITIC AND WRITER

I think what you study is not as important as knowing you're capable of graduating.

—DAN SAVAGE (1964-)
AMERICAN SEX COLUMNIST AND WRITER

———————

I couldn't write a simple declarative sentence because when you're an English major, they don't teach you how to write; they teach you how to read.

—RANDY SHILTS (1951-1994)
AMERICAN JOURNALIST, AIDS ACTIVIST, AND WRITER

———————

The real danger of high school is that the social hierarchies take the power away from the parents. They become the dominant authority over the student. . . . That kid's like, "You can't help me between the hours of 8 and 3. So why should I even trust you?"

—CHRISTOPHER RICE (1978-)
AMERICAN WRITER

———————

High school is a private hell for everyone in their own way. It's only certain individuals who manage to navigate the social hierarchy of it successfully, especially in America.

—CHRISTOPHER RICE (1978-)
AMERICAN WRITER

———————

Education is an admirable thing, but it is well to remember from time to time that nothing that is worth knowing can be taught.

—OSCAR WILDE (1854-1900)
IRISH PLAYWRIGHT AND WRITER

HOMOSEXUALITY

You are taught that you are wrong, that you are bad . . . and you wrap yourself
in a little straitjacket, and you put yourself in your little room. . . "Don't do it!
Don't look at someone, don't touch them, don't kiss them, don't do anything!"

—T. R. KNIGHT (1973-)
AMERICAN ACTOR

———

Every boy of good looks [at school] had a female name,
and was recognized either as a public prostitute or as some bigger fellow's
"bitch." Here and there one could not avoid seeing acts of onanism,
mutual masturbation, the sports of naked boys in bed together.

—JOHN ADDINGTON SYMONDS (1840-1893)
ENGLISH POET AND CRITIC

———

I didn't attend lesbian classes. No one taught me to be this way.
I was born this way, from the moment I opened my eyes in this world.

—CHAVELA VARGAS (1919-)
COSTA RICAN MUSICIAN

ENEMIES

SEE ALSO RELATIONSHIPS

A number of people seem to have taken a violent, irrational dislike to me.
Especially people who run bars.

—WILLIAM BURROUGHS (1914-1997)
AMERICAN WRITER

O I have killed them already so many times and in so many ways in my mind that now I don't know which death is most bitter for them to die.

—COUNTEE CULLEN (1903-1946)
AFRICAN-AMERICAN POET

We have to learn how to stop being afraid of people who are different than us, who are supposedly our enemies.

—EYTAN FOX (1964-)
ISRAELI DIRECTOR

ENTERTAINMENT

SEE ALSO ACTORS AND ACTING, AUDIENCES, HOLLYWOOD, MOVIES, TELEVISION

You can call me a lousy entertainer, but you can't call me a killer.

—MICHAEL BARRYMORE (1952-)
BRITISH COMEDIAN AND ACTOR

I hate clowns. . . . They're evil and mean. . . . Never trust anyone whose face you can't really see.

—JUSTIN CHIN (1967-)
ASIAN-AMERICAN WRITER AND PERFORMANCE ARTIST

As long as our enjoyment is—or is said to be—instinctive, it is not enjoyment, it is terrorism.

—RICHARD HOWARD (1929-)
AMERICAN POET, CRITIC, AND TRANSLATOR

Everything comes in cycles in show business. There are times when at first they fall in love with you, then they get sick of you and then . . . then they love you again.

—NATHAN LANE (1956-)
AMERICAN TONY AWARD-WINNING ACTOR AND COMEDIAN

BROADWAY

It's easy to pick on musicals . . . Like the Western, they are few and far between. Each bad one is supposed to kill off the genre. Until *Unforgiven* wins the Oscar.

—NEIL MERON (1955-)
AMERICAN FILM PRODUCER

———————

Writing a book for a musical is not "playwriting lite." It's hard to write a play, and it's hard to write a musical.

—TERRENCE MCNALLY (1939-)
AMERICAN PLAYWRIGHT

———————

I don't even go to see the [musical theater] shows; it's so boring to me. But it's really hard to write a song, and nobody writes songs anymore in the musical theater—they write extended pieces.

—STEPHEN SONDHEIM (1930-)
AMERICAN MUSICAL THEATER COMPOSER AND PLAYWRIGHT

———————

I righteously and wrongly confronted Chita Rivera when I misunderstood something she'd said about the male dancers in her Broadway show *Bajour*. Chita has a bit of a New York accent, and I misheard her say the word "personally" as "purse nellie."

—LILY TOMLIN (1939-)
AMERICAN ACTOR AND COMEDIAN

The fact that I was the first director of color to direct a major
white play in the history of Broadway is ridiculous.

—GEORGE C. WOLFE (1954-)
AFRICAN-AMERICAN PLAYWRIGHT AND DIRECTOR

DISNEYLAND

Khrushchev was here, and Twentieth-Century Fox put on a lunch for him
at the studio. Khrushchev's patience was tried on all occasions . . . finally he got
quite angry and said, "You won't let me go to Disneyland, I'll send the hydrogen
bomb over," and frankly I wondered why he didn't.

—GEORGE CUKOR (1899-1983)
AMERICAN FILM DIRECTOR

[On visiting Disneyland in Paris] Incidentally, disgruntled employees at
Walt Disney Studios in Burbank, California, call their headquarters Mouschwitz
or Duckau. I remembered that just as we were approaching the iron gates,
having just disembarked from a train. But enough of all that—
we're in the happiest place on earth!

—ALAN CUMMING (1965-)
BRITISH ACTOR

The prize for selling 146 subscriptions to the *Catholic Herald* was a red bicycle
and a trip to Disneyland. . . . I wasn't all that thrilled about Disneyland.

—RICHARD RODRIGUEZ (1944-)
MEXICAN-AMERICAN WRITER

EUROPE

SEE ALSO AMERICA, CITIES AND STATES, TRAVEL

I'm a bestseller in France—me and Jerry Lewis. Let's let it go.

—DOROTHY ALLISON (1942-)
AMERICAN WRITER

———————

The French carved out an existence that so exactly executed
the needs of man's soul and body that this has produced the saying that
man has two countries, his own and France.

—DJUNA BARNES (1892-1982)
AMERICAN WRITER

———————

Possibly homosexual behavior is so deeply ingrained in the German race
as to appear, to certain Germans, quite natural.

ANDRÉ GIDE (1869-1951)
FRENCH WRITER

———————

All Germans are an excessively clean people and they shine their very hide
so it glistens.

—MARSDEN HARTLEY (1877-1943)
AMERICAN ARTIST

———————

If Europe does not wholly solve the problem of existence, it at least
helps the flight of time—or beguiles its duration.

—HENRY JAMES (1843-1916)
AMERICAN WRITER

Spain is the only country where death is the national spectacle.

—FEDERICO GARCIA LORCA (1898-1936)
SPANISH POET AND PLAYWRIGHT

Russia is a very anti-Semitic and homophobic society.

—MICHAEL LUCAS (1972-)
RUSSIAN-BORN PORN PRODUCER

If I must describe what Europe means to me as an American, I would start with liberation. Liberation from what passes in America for a culture.

—SUSAN SONTAG (1933-2004)
AMERICAN WRITER AND CRITIC

EXISTENCE

SEE ALSO IDENTITY, INDIVIDUALISM, LIFE

"You are you," something said. "How strange you are, inside looking out . . . you are you and you are going to be you forever." It was like coasting downhill, this thought, only much worse, and it quickly smashed into a tree.
Why was I a human being?

—ELIZABETH BISHOP (1911-1979)
AMERICAN POET

What did we do to be born? Did we, after consideration, choose life here rather than on another planet or in another solar system, feeling there were better opportunities on Earth? That we would get farther?

—JOHN CAGE (1934-1992)
AMERICAN COMPOSER

It is the duty of each to perform his own function as faithfully as he can;
his privilege to obtain his pleasure where he finds it; his dignity
to suffer pain as cheerfully as he is able.

—JOHN ADDINGTON SYMONDS (1840-1893)
ENGLISH POET AND CRITIC

A great part of every day is not lived consciously. One walks, eats,
sees things, deals with what has to be done. . . . When it is a bad day
the proportion of non-being is much larger.

—VIRGINIA WOOLF (1882-1941)
BRITISH WRITER

EXPERIENCE

SEE ALSO AGE AND AGING, LIFE

To play Trivial Pursuit with a life like mine could be said to be a form
of homeopathy.

—ALAN BENNETT (1934-)
BRITISH WRITER AND ACTOR

One learns nothing by experience but caution, if you want to learn that.
I don't, because that way you defeat yourself, removing pleasure with the pain
so the whole maneuver is pointless.

—WILLIAM BURROUGHS (1914-1997)
AMERICAN WRITER

I am a pear that has survived a hailstorm: When it does not rot, it becomes better
and sweeter than the others, in spite of its little scars.

—SIDONIE-GABRIELLE COLETTE (1873-1954)
FRENCH WRITER

Desolation, Desolation, I owe so much to Desolation, thank you forever for guiding me to the place where I learned all.

—JACK KEROUAC (1922-1969)
AMERICAN WRITER

None of the experiences I've had in my life have been for nothing. Even if I felt bad, I learned something, and they served me somehow.

—IVRI LIDER (1974-)
ISRAELI MUSICIAN

I cannot stand old people. It is not that I hate them or fear them; they just make me uneasy. I cannot talk to them. . . . Above all, I mean those old people who think that just by being old they are in on all of life's secret's. What they call "experience" and talk so much about I just cannot conceive of.

—FEDERICO GARCIA LORCA (1898-1936)
SPANISH POET AND PLAYWRIGHT

There is no such thing as the gay experience. To expect as much reduces our humanity.

—MARIA MAGGENTI (1962-)
SCREENWRITER AND DIRECTOR

Is it not possible—I often wonder—that things we have felt with great intensity have an existence independent of our minds; are in fact still in existence?

—VIRGINIA WOOLF (1882-1941)
BRITISH WRITER

FAILURE

SEE ALSO DETERMINATION, THE PAST, SUCCESS

Here is someone who is nobody in particular, there even an obvious failure,
yet they do not seem to mind. How is that possible? What is their secret?

—W. H. AUDEN (1907-1973)
ANGLO-AMERICAN POET AND CRITIC

———————

As always the things that fail are the ones that you have a lot of affection for.

—ALAN BENNETT (1934-)
BRITISH WRITER AND ACTOR

———————

No occasion is ever adequate to the impulse that wants to make it an occasion—
all poetry is in this sense the acknowledgment of failure.

—RICHARD HOWARD (1929-)
AMERICAN POET, CRITIC, AND TRANSLATOR

———————

Surely evil was a real thing, and . . . not to have been, by instinctive election,
on the right side, was to have failed in life.

—WALTER PATER (1839-1894)
BRITISH CRITIC AND WRITER

———————

Once your teeth get crummy then it's really over. You know what I mean?
You can't even pass as a good, middle-class kid. Your teeth start going,
then you have nothing to prove that you ever grew up in a house with a
dishwasher, and if you tell people you did they don't believe you.

—DAVID SEDARIS (1956-)
AMERICAN WRITER

I had a flash of my whole life's achievement, and it seemed to me to be a succession of botched beginnings, of tasks inadequately done, few real achievements. A dozen jewels perhaps in a refuse dump of failures.

—STEPHEN SPENDER (1909-1995)
BRITISH POET AND WRITER

I prefer to tell stories of defeat. I have a soft spot for lonely souls and destinies beat by reality.

—LUCHINO VISCONTI (1906-1976)
ITALIAN ARISTOCRAT AND DIRECTOR

FAME

SEE ALSO AUDIENCES, CELEBRITIES, GAY ICONS

Warhol was a huge influence. But he was almost too famous. I never thought what I was starting would ever become a scene in itself. I was just hoping to be accepted by the existing scene. The thought of replacing that scene never even crossed my mind.

—MICHAEL ALIG (1966-)
AMERICAN FOUNDING MEMBER OF THE CLUB KIDS AND CONVICTED MURDERER

We live in such a cult of personality. I go to meetings, and I am constantly pitched actors as characters. They'll go, "Oh, we have this great idea. Winona Ryder is Goldie Hawn and Danny DeVito's daughter." I mean, I actually went to a meeting where somebody said that.

—ALAN BALL (1957-)
AMERICAN SCREENWRITER

If somebody's uncomfortable about the irony of celebrity, that says a lot about where they're at.

—SANDRA BERNHARD (1955-)
AMERICAN ACTOR, COMEDIAN, AND MUSICIAN

When one has a good reputation, one shouldn't tempt fortune; it is better to be silent than to fall from a height.

—MICHELANGELO BUONARROTI (1475-1564)
ITALIAN PAINTER, SCULPTOR, POET, AND ENGINEER

As far as fame goes, I have had my share.

—LORD BYRON (1788-1824)
BRITISH POET

Fame is only good for one thing—they will cash your check in a small town.

—TRUMAN CAPOTE (1924-1984)
AMERICAN WRITER

It is better to live contented than to be famous.

—COUNTEE CULLEN (1903-1946)
AFRICAN-AMERICAN POET

Nowadays it seems if you don't put a record out every year, you pretty much have disappeared off the face of the planet.

—MELISSA FERRICK (1970-)
AMERICAN SINGER-SONGWRITER

I just hope I can live long enough to see the fame.

—ROBERT MAPPLETHORPE (1946-1989)
AMERICAN PHOTOGRAPHER

I've been seriously offended by the lack of decent jokes on the subject [of my arrest], and believe me, if there were any more out there, I would have heard them.

—GEORGE MICHAEL (1963-)
BRITISH MUSICIAN

We just had a tour of the Philippines. We [*Queer Eye for the Straight Guy*] are huge there. Like Michael Jackson in 1983.

—JAI RODRIGUEZ (1979-)
AMERICAN ACTOR AND REALITY TV STAR

When you become a public figure, you become at the same time a product, and people actually look at your "expiration date," you know? They look at your age and say, "Hmm. How fresh is this one?"

—RUPAUL (1960-)
AMERICAN DRAG PERFORMER AND MUSICIAN

I think to be famous, you have to be known by more than ten percent of the population.

—MATTHEW RUSH (1972-)
AMERICAN PORN STAR

It used to be said of me, "Oh, she needs to be a star" . . . Well, once I did. But although I still need to exercise my creativity, it's no longer a case of needing to be loved, hoping to be adored, being desperate to hear that applause. If I never heard it again, I think I'd still be fine.

—DUSTY SPRINGFIELD (1939-1999)
BRITISH MUSICIAN

Fame! What contradictory sentiments that word awakes in me!
On the one hand I desire and strive for it; on the other I detest it.

—PETER ILYICH TCHAIKOVSKY (1840-1893)
RUSSIAN COMPOSER

———

Being famous isn't all that important. If I weren't famous, I wouldn't
have been shot for being Andy Warhol.

—ANDY WARHOL (1928-1987)
AMERICAN ARTIST

———

Between the famous and the infamous there is but one step, if so much as one.

—OSCAR WILDE (1854-1900)
IRISH PLAYWRIGHT AND WRITER

DIVAS

It's gotten very important for me now to work with people who are not
Divas or egomaniacs, and boy, I've worked with a few believe me.
I just don't have time for all that. The people that I'm involved with now
are well balanced and know who they are.

—DAVID BOWIE (1947-)
BRITISH MUSICIAN

———

Stars are NO maintenance. Divas are nothing BUT.

—TERRENCE MCNALLY (1939-)
AMERICAN PLAYWRIGHT

I think the word *diva* has lost its true meaning in today's society. A true diva is someone who delivers the goods at the highest level possible on a consistent basis, whose success is based on hard work and a deep, true talent.

—RICK SKYE (ca. 1975–)
AMERICAN DRAG PERFORMER

———

As every gay person knows, you can't fuck with a diva.

—RUFUS WAINWRIGHT (1973–)
CANADIAN MUSICIAN

FAMILY

SEE ALSO CHILDREN, COMING OUT, FATHERS AND FATHERHOOD, GAY COMMUNITY, INDIVIDUALISM, MARRIAGE, MOTHERS AND MOTHERHOOD, SOCIETY

You know, we're [the Arquette family] not quirky, we're not zany. They're quirky, they're zany. We're normal. We're the most normal people you'll ever meet. We're way more normal than most of Hollywood. We have our shit together. Hollywood's fucked-up. We're not in therapy. We deal with our problems in our family, we confront each other, we don't live in denial.

—ALEXIS ARQUETTE (1969–)
AMERICAN ACTOR AND DRAG PERFORMER

———

I would not want to be Christopher Ciccone [Madonna's brother], if you know what I'm saying. Because you have no identity of your own, you're merely "the brother of." And inherently you're competitive, even if you don't want to be.

—ALEXIS ARQUETTE (1969–)
AMERICAN ACTOR AND DRAG PERFORMER

My feelings for Jerry [Falwell] are mixed. . . . He said a lot of hateful and hurtful things, but blood is thicker than water. You can't pick your relatives.

—BRETT BEASLEY (ca. 1962-)
COUSIN OF AMERICAN TELEVANGELIST JERRY FALWELL

—————

Mismanagement is the hereditary epidemic of our brood.

—LORD BYRON (1788-1824)
BRITISH POET

—————

Without much accuracy, with strangely little love at all, your family will decide for you exactly who you are, and they'll keep nudging, coaxing, poking you until you've changed into that very simple shape.

—ALLAN GURGANUS (1947-)
AMERICAN WRITER

—————

Finding families for kids who need them is beyond fulfilling, it is addictive. I like to help. I need to help. I help a lot, sometimes too much.

—ROSIE O'DONNELL (1962-)
AMERICAN ACTOR, COMEDIAN, AND TALK SHOW HOST

—————

The fact that my kids have got two Mums doesn't even bother them. It's not like they're fine with it, they don't even think about whether they are fine with it.

—SANDI TOKSVIG (1958-)
DANISH COMEDIAN, WRITER, AND RADIO PERSONALITY

—————

I love hearing my relations abused. It is the only thing that makes me put up with them at all. Relations are simply a tedious pack of people who haven't got the remotest knowledge of how to live, nor the smallest instinct about when to die.

—OSCAR WILDE (1854-1900)
IRISH PLAYWRIGHT AND WRITER

FANTASIES

SEE ALSO IMAGINATION, MAGIC, SEX

I was inspired by the Old Guard. Andy Warhol, Michael Musto, Rudolf, Diane Brill, Sister Dimension, John Sex—these people seemed magical to me. Like some sort of crazy character actors who were always in character, living life the way I'd always wanted to, like it was some kind of game.

—MICHAEL ALIG (1966-)
AMERICAN FOUNDING MEMBER OF THE CLUB KIDS AND CONVICTED MURDERER

———

Some people want to be shocked. And they are disappointed when the world does not come up to their own dirty fantasies of it.

—PERRY BRASS (1947-)
AMERICAN WRITER

———

I am not personally into role playing. Fake firefighters and policemen don't quite do it for me. I like gay guys as they really are, whether they are fashion designers, hair dressers, students, or trading stocks.

—MICHAEL LUCAS (1972-)
RUSSIAN-BORN PORN PRODUCER

———

If I had all the money in the world, I would have a center for modeling where young girls could come—not that I would grope them, but I would watch them putting on make-up and trying on clothes.

—CAMILLE PAGLIA (1947-)
AMERICAN SCHOLAR AND CRITIC

———

Hollywood Boulevard is the imitation of a Dream.

—JOHN RECHY (1934-)
AMERICAN WRITER

The world has changed, little gay person. Now we don't just fantasize over pictures of Greek gods, we get to be them.

—BRUCE VILANCH (1948-)
AMERICAN COMEDY WRITER

The more oppressed you are and the more hopeless it seems, the more you take off into fantasyland. The more the government gives you things, the more boring you become.

—RUFUS WAINWRIGHT (1973-)
CANADIAN MUSICIAN

FASHION

SEE ALSO APPEARANCES, BEAUTY

Fashion seeks equivalences, validities—not verities.

—ROLAND BARTHES (1915-1980)
FRENCH CRITIC AND THEORIST

They thought I was going to hate the dress . . . but I loooved it. Everyone likes to play dress-up once in a while.

—LEA DELARIA (1958-)
AMERICAN COMEDIAN AND ACTOR

Don't follow it [fashion] into every dark alley. Always remember that you are not a model or a mannequin for which the fashion is created.

—MARLENE DIETRICH (1901-1992)
GERMAN-BORN ACTOR

If those multicolored horrors make you feel carefree and gay, wear them.
If they don't have that effect on you, wear them only if your mother has given
them to you at Christmas, birthdays or Father's Day.

—MARLENE DIETRICH (1901-1992)
GERMAN-BORN ACTOR

Today's fashion is above all a question of general line: from the shoes
to the hat, the silhouette is whole.

—CHRISTIAN DIOR (1905-1957)
FRENCH FASHION DESIGNER

In this world of ours, that seeks to give away its secrets one by one,
that feeds on false confidences and fabricated revelations, it [fashion] is the
very incarnation of mystery, and the best proof of the spell it casts is that,
now more than ever, it is the topic on everyone's lips.

—CHRISTIAN DIOR (1905-1957)
FRENCH FASHION DESIGNER

For me, having a good fashion day is when I'm wearing clean socks.

—JOE DIPIETRO (1945-)
AMERICAN PLAYWRIGHT

I don't consider myself a woman or a man professionally. Half the creative industry is gay, so if anything, I would almost say it's a plus. I mean, I'm not a politicians. I don't work for the government. At the end of the day, I'm a hairdresser.

—PATRICIA FIELD (1943-)
AMERICAN COSTUME DESIGNER

Fashion is a very gay place to be. . . . I honestly think it's harder for a straight
kid trying to work in it. You know, when you're standing there with your shirt off
and some gay photographer says, "Oh, you're gorgeous, gorgeous,"
a straight guy might have trouble with that.

—RYAN FINDLAY (1972-)
SOUTH AFRICAN MODEL

Real fashion change comes from real changes in real life.
Everything else is just decoration.

—TOM FORD (1962-)
AMERICAN FASHION DESIGNER

Fashion is, after all, a form of escapism, and in fact people are buying more
special things than ever, right now. They deny and deny themselves, and wait
and wait, and then they get sick of it and spend to make themselves feel better.

—TOM FORD (1962-)
AMERICAN FASHION DESIGNER

We are living in an era of instant gratification, and [*Project Runway*] is built on
that premise. The fact is that fashion is an art form. . . . When they just use
personalities, they miss a lot of the hard work that goes into our industry.

—TIM GUNN (1953-)
AMERICAN FASHION EXPERT AND REALITY TV STAR

A man in a brown suit is not as exciting to watch as a woman in a gown.

—JERRY HERMAN (1931-)
AMERICAN COMPOSER AND LYRICIST

If you've ever seen guys in a sheer shirt—you know, we don't need to see the nipples. We'll leave that to Janet Jackson. Thanks for the mammaries, Janet.

—CARSON KRESSLEY (1969-)
AMERICAN FASHION EXPERT AND REALITY TV STAR

For a long time now I have believed that fashion was not only supposed to make women beautiful, but to reassure them, to give them confidence, to allow them to come to terms with themselves.

—YVES SAINT LAURENT (1936-)
FRENCH FASHION DESIGNER

Mixing lesbianism and fashion makes for a kind of mysticism.

—KELLY LINVILLE (1970-)
AMERICAN PHOTOGRAPHER

I like sex, nighttime in the city, Latin music, and women in high heels.

—EDUARDO LUCERO (1969-)
MEXICAN-BORN FASHION DESIGNER

I had to be honest. Edith Head was not a great designer.
She was a great promoter of Edith Head and that's it, she spent more time doing that than she did anything else.

—BOB MACKIE (1940-)
AMERICAN FASHION DESIGNER

My [fashion] shows are about sex, drugs, and rock and roll. I want audiences quaking with nerves. I want heart attacks. I want ambulances.

—ALEXANDER MCQUEEN (1969-)
BRITISH FASHION DESIGNER

In fashion there aren't big revolutions; there are small changes that have an enormous influence.

—INGRID SISCHY (1952-)
AMERICAN WRITER AND EDITOR

Fashion can be a form of both bondage and liberation.

—INGRID SISCHY (1952-)
AMERICAN WRITER AND EDITOR

At sixteen I clipped articles from *Vogue* when Diana Vreeland was editor. There's a famous picture of Mrs. Vreeland in her office measuring the millimeter of a pearl—wearing white gloves. That picture was on my wall. Some people had pictures of rock stars; I had pictures of Diana Vreeland.

—ANDRE LEON TALLEY (1949-)
AMERICAN FASHION EDITOR, *VOGUE*

Spandex is a privilege, not a right, and should be considered only if a quarter can bounce eagerly off your bum.

—DANIEL VOSOVIC (1981-)
AMERICAN FASHION DESIGNER AND REALITY TV STAR

If I am occasionally a little overdressed, I make up for it by being always immensely overeducated.

—OSCAR WILDE (1854-1900)
IRISH PLAYWRIGHT AND WRITER

I never saw anybody take so long to dress, and with such little result.

—OSCAR WILDE (1854-1900)
IRISH PLAYWRIGHT AND WRITER

No one had ever dared blend a simulated pearl with real diamonds, or fake sapphires with real ones as Chanel had done. . . . She was the centre of almost everything artistic in French life this century.

—FRANCO ZEFFIRELLI (1923–)
ITALIAN FILM DIRECTOR

COUTURE

A couturier must be: an architect for design, a sculptor for shape, a painter for color, a musician for harmony and a philosopher for temperance.

—CRISTOBAL BALENCIAGA (1895–1972)
SPANISH FASHION DESIGNER

———

Unfortunately the true couture client is a dying breed. . . . Nowadays it is new money rather than old; it is no longer the same clients. This is something that saddens me, because my clients were once a great source of inspiration.

—TOM FORD (1962–)
AMERICAN FASHION DESIGNER

DESIGN

A beautiful dress is one which follows the body, and only the body.

—CRISTOBAL BALENCIAGA (1895–1972)
SPANISH FASHION DESIGNER

———

I wanted my dresses to be constructed, molded upon the curves of the feminine body whose sweep they would stylize.

—CHRISTIAN DIOR (1905–1957)
FRENCH FASHION DESIGNER

We were emerging from a period of war, of uniforms, of women-soldiers built like boxers. I drew women-flowers, soft shoulders, flowering busts, fine waists like liana, and wide skirts like corolla. But it is well known that such fragile appearances are obtained only at the price of a rigorous construction.

—CHRISTIAN DIOR (1905-1957)
FRENCH FASHION DESIGNER

As a fashion designer, I was always aware that I was not an artist, because I was creating something that was made to be sold, marketed, used, and ultimately discarded.

—TOM FORD (1962-)
AMERICAN FASHION DESIGNER

It's the poor look. It's the '90s. You don't want to look rich.

—CALVIN KLEIN (1942-)
AMERICAN FASHION DESIGNER

They're the devil's playground, the pleated khakis.

—CARSON KRESSLEY (1969-)
AMERICAN FASHION EXPERT AND REALITY TV STAR

I drew that, that fancy all diamond dress that she wore to sing "Happy Birthday" to Kennedy.

—BOB MACKIE (1940-)
AMERICAN FASHION DESIGNER

There are a lot of gay women hairdressers and a lot of gay women makeup artists, and there are certainly a lot of gay women models. But . . . there are very, very few gay women designers, which gets back to what I was saying before: how much fashion has failed women.

—INGRID SISCHY (1952-)
AMERICAN WRITER AND EDITOR

Grunge? That was lesbian feminist clothing and fashion in the 1970s.

—URVASHI VAID (1958-)
AMERICAN GAY RIGHTS ACTIVIST

People judge me avant-garde, people judge me rock and roll, and I am smiling. I am the most classically influenced of the Italian designers, which no one seemed to realize until the last year.

—GIANNI VERSACE (1946-1997)
ITALIAN FASHION DESIGNER

FADS

Take a fad and make it your own. And if it works for you, and you own it, stick with it even after its time has passed.

—CARSON KRESSLEY (1969-)
AMERICAN FASHION EXPERT AND REALITY TV STAR

Whenever I'm interested in something, I know the timing's off, because I'm always interested in the right thing at the wrong time. I should just be getting interested after I'm not interested any more.

—ANDY WARHOL (1928-1987)
AMERICAN ARTIST

FRENCH

Things are changing with globalization. You never used to see a Frenchman
wearing tennis shoes at night, and now you see it all the time.

—TOM FORD (1962-)
AMERICAN FASHION DESIGNER

You know, there's still this puritanical thing in the back of a lot of Americans'
minds. You're not even supposed to admit that you like fashion, let alone are
willing to play with it and indulge in it. For the French, especially those in Paris,
it's a birthright. You're talking about the only city in the world where a cab driver
says, "Oh, I heard the Saint Laurent show today was terrific."

—MICHAEL KORS (1959-)
AMERICAN FASHION DESIGNER

SUPERMODELS

I've had dalliances with other women. I appreciate anyone who follows the
nature of the spirit of their soul. I applaud gay men, and I applaud gay women.

—JANICE DICKINSON (1955-)
AMERICAN SUPERMODEL, AGENT, AND REALITY TV STAR

Linda Evangelista is not a bitch!

—DOUGLAS KEEVE (1956-)
AMERICAN FILM DIRECTOR

FATHERS AND FATHERHOOD

SEE ALSO CHILDREN, GAY MARRIAGE, MARRIAGE, MOTHERS AND MOTHERHOOD,
ROLE MODELS

My father was very cool about my coming out. He said, "Son, if it makes you feel
any better, I've sucked a cock before.

—ALEXIS ARQUETTE (1969–)
AMERICAN ACTOR AND DRAG PERFORMER

––––––––

Whosoever sees his father threatened or struck is obligated to interpose
his own life.

—MICHELANGELO BUONARROTI (1475–1564)
ITALIAN PAINTER, SCULPTOR, POET, AND ENGINEER

––––––––

I was on a [business] trip to New York city when I turned on MTV's *My Super Sweet
16*. I called Rebecca that night to check in, and I left a message saying, "Oh, my
God! I'm going to be seventy-six years old at my daughter's sweet sixteen!

—BEVAN DUFTY (1955–)
AMERICAN POLITICIAN ON THE SAN FRANCISCO BOARD OF SUPERVISORS

––––––––

I always thought I hated my father, but in fact I didn't hate him; I was in conflict
with him, in a state of permanent, even violent, tension with him. . . . I realized
that basically a great deal of my erotic and emotional life depends not on hatred
for my father but on love for him.

—PIER PAOLO PASOLINI (1922–1975)
ITALIAN FILM DIRECTOR

––––––––

No, I'm a baseball fan because my eight-year-old son, D. J., somehow succeeded
where my father failed: He made a man of me.

—DAN SAVAGE (1964–)
AMERICAN SEX COLUMNIST AND WRITER

At one point my mother withdrew with my sister, leaving my father to acquaint me, I began to sense, with the facts of life. . . . My heart was beating horribly, but at least it wasn't up to me to speak; the onus was on my unfortunate father. At last he accepted his duty. He warned me against the seats of public lavatories.

—PATRICK WHITE (1912-1990)
AUSTRALIAN WRITER AND NOBEL LAUREATE

FEELINGS

SEE ALSO COMMUNICATION, DECEIT, GRIEF, HAPPINESS, PESSIMISM, UNDERSTANDING

A dreadful bitterness is beginning to grow in me, and I count on it for comfort— yes, a dreadful bitterness against the sort of wretch who can neither take care of nor defend a woman.

—SIDONIE-GABRIELLE COLETTE (1873-1954)
FRENCH WRITER

The high is exactly the contrary of the low: and there you have a fine definition of dizziness!

—SALVADOR DALÍ (1904-1989)
SPANISH ARTIST

People use the white handkerchief to say goodbye and the warm hand to say hello. . . . Between the handkerchief that sends him away and the hand that receives him lies the sailor's true greeting, both arrival and departure, both happiness and sadness.

—FEDERICO GARCIA LORCA (1898-1936)
SPANISH POET AND PLAYWRIGHT

Within living structures defined by profit, by linear power, by institutional dehumanization, our feelings were not meant to survive. . . . Feelings were expected to kneel to men. But women have survived.

—AUDRE LORDE (1934-1992)
AFRICAN-AMERICAN WRITER, POET, AND ACTIVIST

———

Is the need to save people good or bad, compulsion or compassion? Maybe compassion is compulsion, creativity is insanity. If this is so, then is craziness a good thing, the source of our humanity?

—ROSIE O'DONNELL (1962-)
AMERICAN ACTOR, COMEDIAN, AND TALK SHOW HOST

———

As an end within itself, when it became impotent pity, was compassion merely another subterfuge to grasp at, to resort to in guilt when we questioned ourselves?

—JOHN RECHY (1934-)
AMERICAN WRITER

———

It is absolutely essential to be patient and to remember that nothing one feels is the last word; all feeling passes over me and as far as the life of the motions goes there is only one rule: to wait.

—STEPHEN SPENDER (1909-1995)
BRITISH POET AND WRITER

———

I can't be too maudlin.

—JILL SOBULE (1961-)
AMERICAN SINGER-SONGWRITER

———

A way of feeling is a way of seeing.

—SUSAN SONTAG (1933-2004)
AMERICAN WRITER AND CRITIC

I guess jealous is the worst feeling you can have. . . .
Nothing warps and eats on you like jealousy.

—ETHEL WATERS (1896–1977)
AFRICAN-AMERICAN ACTOR AND MUSICIAN

———————

The sentimentalist is always a cynic at heart. Indeed sentimentality
is merely the bank holiday of cynicism.

—OSCAR WILDE (1854–1900)
IRISH PLAYWRIGHT AND WRITER

———————

A sentimentalist is simply one who desires to have the luxury of an
emotion without paying for it.

—OSCAR WILDE (1854–1900)
IRISH PLAYWRIGHT AND WRITER

FEMINISM

SEE ALSO ACTIVISM, GAY RIGHTS, LESBIANS, WOMEN

When people ask me if I am a feminist filmmaker, I reply I am a woman
and I also make films.

—CHANTAL AKERMAN (1950–)
BELGIAN DIRECTOR

———————

For feminist theory, the development of a language that fully or adequately
represents women has seemed necessary to foster the political visibility of women.
This has seemed obviously important considering the pervasive cultural condition
in which women's lives were either misrepresented or not represented at all.

—JUDITH BUTLER (1956–)
AMERICAN CRITIC AND PHILOSOPHER

According to our social pyramid, all men who feel displaced racially, culturally, and/or because of economic hardships will turn on those whom they feel they can order and humiliate, usually women, children, and animals—just as they have been ordered and humiliated by those privileged few who are in power. However, this definition does not explain why there are privileged men who behave this way toward women.

—ANA CASTILLO (1953-)
CHICANA POET, NOVELIST, AND ESSAYIST

Feminism—not just for babes anymore.

—ANI DIFRANCO (1970-)
AMERICAN SINGER-SONGWRITER

It is shamefully easy for us to enjoy our own fantasies of biological omnipotence while despising men for enjoying the reality of theirs.

—ANDREA DWORKIN (1946-)
AMERICAN FEMINIST, CRITIC, AND ANTI-PORN ACTIVIST

On the pedestal, immobile like waxen statues, or in the gutter, failed icons mired in shit, we are exalted or degraded because our biological traits are what they are. Citing genes, genitals, DNA, pattern-releasing smells, biograms, hormones, or whatever is in vogue, male supremacists make their case which is, in essence, that we are biologically too good, too bad, or too different to do anything other than reproduce and serve men sexually and domestically.

—ANDREA DWORKIN (1946-)
AMERICAN FEMINIST, CRITIC, AND ANTI-PORN ACTIVIST

The oppression of women knows know ethnic nor racial boundaries, true, but that does not mean it is identical within those difference.

—AUDRE LORDE (1934-1992)
AFRICAN-AMERICAN WRITER, POET, AND ACTIVIST

Despite the fact that all the fashion magazines write about "the modern woman" or "the working woman," what's amazing is how little fashion reflects those concepts, how so much of fashion is still the same old form of bondage.

—INGRID SISCHY (1952-)
AMERICAN WRITER AND EDITOR

When I started in comedy if you were a woman and you wanted to say something other than, "The Doctor will see you now!" and try and get a laugh, you had to write your own material!

—SANDI TOKSVIG (1958-)
DANISH COMEDIAN, WRITER, AND RADIO PERSONALITY

Consider how much different the women's movement would look if there had been as high a premium placed on raising perfectly healthy daughters . . . as there was on educational and professional advancement.

—REBECCA WALKER (1969-)
AMERICAN FEMINIST WRITER

FOOD AND DRINK

SEE ALSO ALCOHOL

A meal without mushrooms is like a day without rain.

—JOHN CAGE (1934-1992)
AMERICAN COMPOSER

I have made a bet with myself to eat four hundred nuts between lunch and dinner. Oh! That's not a record, of course, but when one must gather as well as shell the nuts . . .

—SIDONIE-GABRIELLE COLETTE (1873-1954)
FRENCH WRITER

How wonderful to crunch a bird's tiny skull! How can one eat brains any other way!

—SALVADOR DALÍ (1904-1989)
SPANISH ARTIST

———————

The British have an umbilical cord which has never been cut and through which
tea flows constantly.

—MARLENE DIETRICH (1901-1992)
GERMAN-BORN ACTOR

———————

That oxymoron: the butter knife.

—SUSAN SONTAG (1933-2004)
AMERICAN WRITER AND CRITIC

———————

When I am in trouble, eating is the only thing that consoles me.
Indeed, when I am in really great trouble, as anyone knows me intimately
will tell you, I refuse everything except food and drink.

—OSCAR WILDE (1854-1900)
IRISH PLAYWRIGHT AND WRITER

FORGIVENESS

SEE ALSO COMMUNICATION

A little mercy is nice now and again.

—EDWARD ALBEE (1928-)
AMERICAN TONY AWARD- AND PULITZER PRIZE-WINNING PLAYWRIGHT

———————

Forgiveness to me is realizing there was nothing to forgive.

—RICHARD CHAMBERLAIN (1934-)
AMERICAN ACTOR

FREEDOM

SEE ALSO AMERICA, INDIVIDUALISM, OPPRESSION, SOLITUDE

I am an anachronism. A free man.

—JEAN COCTEAU (1889-1963)
FRENCH WRITER AND FILMMAKER

Money, believe it or not, isn't money to me. It's freedom.

—TOM FORD (1962-)
AMERICAN FASHION DESIGNER

In short, the greater my guilt in your eyes . . . the greater will be my freedom.
The more perfect my solitude and uniqueness.

—JEAN GENET (1910-1986)
FRENCH WRITER, CRIMINAL, AND POLITICAL ACTIVIST

"A state may be voluntary without being free," said Leibniz, among others,
and it's rather banal, but here is what is not banal: working to make all one's
states voluntary, whether one is under compulsion or not.
(That is not acceptation—on the contrary—it is the choice after the test,
the counting of one's chickens after they're hatched).

— ANDRÉ GIDE (1869-1951)
FRENCH WRITER

Trees were free when they were uprooted by the wind; ships were free when they
were torn from their moorings; men were free when they were cast out of their
homes—free to starve, free to perish of cold and hunger.

—RADCLYFFE HALL (1880-1943)
BRITISH POET AND WRITER

If you are free, you are not predictable and you are not controllable. To my mind, that is the keenly positive, politicizing significance of bisexual affirmation . . .

—JUNE JORDAN (1936-2002)
AFRICAN-AMERICAN ACTIVIST

The white fathers told us: I think, therefore I am. The Black mother within each of us—the poet—whispers in our dreams: I feel, therefore I can be free.

—AUDRE LORDE (1934-1992)
AFRICAN-AMERICAN WRITER, POET, AND ACTIVIST

I would go back to darkness and to peace,
But the great western world holds me in fee,
And I may never hope for full release.

—CLAUDE MCKAY (1889-1948)
JAMAICAN WRITER

Some people think the home is restrictive; when you go out into the street or to a big bar or club, this is what freedom looks like. For me it's the reverse. When you go into a public space there are codes about what you can eat, what you can drink, what you can say; you're restricting yourself the moment you enter the public sphere. At home those codes don't exist.

—DANIEL TAMMET (1979-)
BRITISH AUTISTIC SAVANT

I am an energetic champion of religious freedom.

—PETER ILYICH TCHAIKOVSKY (1840-1893)
RUSSIAN COMPOSER

Don't imagine, please, that this life of flying free and unencumbered across Persia is in any sense a romantic life; it isn't; the notion that one escapes from materialism is a mistaken notion; on the contrary, one's preoccupation from morning to night is: Have we cooked the eggs long enough? Have we enough Bromo left?

—VITA SACKVILLE-WEST (1892-1962)
BRITISH POET, NOVELIST, AND GARDENER

Liberty relies on itself, invites no one, promises nothing, sits in calmness and light, is positive and composed, and knows no discouragement.

—WALT WHITMAN (1819-1892)
AMERICAN POET

FRIENDS AND FRIENDSHIP

SEE ALSO COMMUNICATION, GAY COMMUNITY, MARRIAGE, RELATIONSHIPS, SOCIETY, UNDERSTANDING

For who will not betray a friend or, for that matter, himself, for a whisky and soda, caviar and a warm fire?

—DJUNA BARNES (1892-1982)
AMERICAN WRITER

Actually, I think friendship and love are exactly the same thing.

—TRUMAN CAPOTE (1924-1984)
AMERICAN WRITER

Losing money is less important than losing a friend.

—SIDONIE-GABRIELLE COLETTE (1873-1954)
FRENCH WRITER

At school, friendship is a passion. It entrances the being; it tears the soul. All loves of after life can never bring its rapture, or its wretchedness; no bliss so absorbing, no pangs of jealousy or despair so crushing and so keen! What tenderness and what devotion; what illimitable confidence; what infinite revelations of inmost thoughts; what ecstatic present and romantic future; what bitter estrangements and what melting reconciliations; what scenes of wild recrimination, agitating explanations, passionate correspondence; what inane sensitiveness, and what frantic sensibility; what earthquakes of the heart, and whirlwinds of the soul, are confined that simple phrase—a schoolboy's friendship.

—BENJAMIN DISRAELI (1804-1881)
BRITISH PRIME MINISTER AND LITERARY FIGURE

What rose out of Shakespeare's soul was universal; he was angry because his buddy went off with a Dark Lady on another motorcycle.

—ALLEN GINSBERG (1926-1997)
AMERICAN POET

The fact is that now no one wants to be my friend because I have lost my reputation, something that I cannot remedy. I will have to be friends with those who like me just the way I am.

—FRIDA KAHLO (1907-1954)
MEXICAN ARTIST AND INTELLECTUAL

When on New Year's Eve . . . I hear people singing that song in which they ask themselves the question "Should old acquaintance be forgot?" I can only tell you that my own answer is in the affirmative.

—W. SOMERSET MAUGHAM (1874-1965)
BRITISH WRITER AND PLAYWRIGHT

If you were to choose the best of those who are in love with you, you'd have a pretty small group to pick from; but you'll have a large group if you don't care whether he loves you or not and just pick the one who suits you best; and in that larger pool you'll have a much better hope of finding someone who deserves your friendship.

— PLATO (427-347 BC)
GREEK PHILOSOPHER

I do my best to observe my own law: no sex with friends if you want to keep the friend . . . a friend in the bed is either an enemy in the making or, simply, heartbreak.

—GORE VIDAL (1925-)
WRITER AND POLITICAL ACTIVIST

Of all the people that have worked together with me, who've known each other for years, I don't think any of them have fucked any of the other ones. I can't think of any combination that ever has. That's probably why we're all still friends.

—JOHN WATERS (1946-)
AMERICAN DIRECTOR

But merely of two simple men I saw to-day on the pier in the midst of the crowd, parting the parting of friends. The one to remain hung on the other's neck and passionately kiss'd him—while the one to depart tightly prest the one to remain in his arms.

—WALT WHITMAN (1819-1892)
AMERICAN POET

Time doesn't take away from true friendship, nor does separation.

—TENNESSEE WILLIAMS (1911-1983)
AMERICAN PLAYWRIGHT

GARDENING

SEE ALSO NATURE

Gardens, gardens upon gardens. . . . I don't really like this country [Naples], but its gardens, draped in vines and roses and heavy with oranges are delicious. And I have yet to see them in summer!

—SIDONIE-GABRIELLE COLETTE (1873-1954)
FRENCH WRITER

———

We have reached the era of simplification in gardening; and, so far as one can ever feel sure about any question of taste, always a dangerous venture, I feel almost sure that we are now traveling along the right lines.

—VITA SACKVILLE-WEST (1892-1962)
BRITISH POET, NOVELIST, AND GARDENER

———

Garden history is an enthralling branch of art history, opening on to the history of outdoor spectacles (the masque, fireworks, pageants), of architecture, of urban planning—and of literary history as well.

—SUSAN SONTAG (1933-2004)
AMERICAN WRITER AND CRITIC

———

[In the garden at the White House] man's beauty blended with God's overwhelming beauty. . . . The atmosphere was somehow exquisitely pastoral, as though the city had fallen back, so that only the gentle quiet of a country garden was there.

—ETHEL WATERS (1896-1977)
AFRICAN-AMERICAN ACTOR AND MUSICIAN

GAY COMMUNITY

SEE ALSO COMING OUT, DOUBLE LIVES, GAY MARRIAGE, GAY PRIDE, GAY RIGHTS,
GAYS VS. LESBIANS, GAYS VS. STRAIGHTS, GENDER BENDING,
HOLLYWOOD, HOMOSEXUALITY, INDIVIDUALISM, LESBIANS, OUTSIDERS,
QUEERNESS, SOCIETY, UNDERSTANDING

I was not treated very well by most of the gay activists I came in
contact with. Most of them were also antiwar activists and felt I had
no business being in the military to begin with.

—COPY BERG (1951–)
AMERICAN NAVAL OFFICER AND GAY RIGHTS ACTIVIST

———————

I hated the gay community. . . . This gay bar called the Cubbyhole had its bathroom wallpapered with my tabloids. They were selling T-shirts of me at Gay Pride.

—CHASTITY BONO (1979–)
AMERICAN GAY RIGHTS ACTIVIST AND DAUGHTER OF CHER AND SONNY BONO

———————

I find that gay men have their own fundamentalism, that is, the ones who are not
locked into the closet and religious fundamentalism.

—PERRY BRASS (1947–)
AMERICAN WRITER

———————

After you've gone to the city, explored gay identity, immersed yourself
in its culture, lived your gay ghetto fantasies, and then move to a small town
you have to discover who you are in that context. You're not who you
were before you moved to the city.

—ANDREW HOLLERAN (1944–)
AMERICAN WRITER

Having to get undressed in the locker room during P. E. How could people do that? That was too much, exposing myself like that in front of so many strange guys, comparing foreign parts so early on. . . . Early bathhouse etiquette and secrecy, learned at age twelve and refined in my twenties.

—HORACIO N. ROQUE RAMIREZ (ca. 1970-)
EL SALVADORAN WRITER

———————

[In college] I was suddenly surrounded by other gay kids. Up until then I'd felt like the screamingest queen around.

—MATTHEW RETTENMUND (1964-)
AMERICAN WRITER

———————

For most men, the gay world is—warts and all—a paradise of freedom when compared with the heterosexual wasteland we came from. But it's nonetheless a world with a lot of pressure and a lot problems, and you'd think gay men would spend more time debating it and analyzing it and trying to make it better.

—GABRIEL ROTELLO (1953-)
AMERICAN WRITER AND FILMMAKER

———————

The new way of being gay was to be open, not to hide, of being powerful and was asserting your power. When gangs came in to beat us up, we organized our own street patrols. We weren't going to be the sissies anymore.

—RANDY SHILTS (1951-1994)
AMERICAN JOURNALIST, AIDS ACTIVIST, AND WRITER

———————

I realized that, as a producer of these events [circuit parties], I was helping to recruit young gay men into a lifestyle that features drug abuse and promiscuity. I no longer wanted to be responsible for furthering that kind of dangerous activity in my lifetime.

—STEVE TROY (1950-)
AMERICAN PARTY PROMOTER

I [literally] lived in a bathhouse with my first boyfriend in the early seventies.
I was there. I was in the bathhouse, seeing Bette Midler starting out,
during the free, gay sex of the seventies. I know firsthand where that led.

—JUNIOR VASQUEZ (1946–)
AMERICAN DJ AND RECORD PRODUCER

Homosexual is not a noun. It's an adjective describing an activity. . . . I was
supposed to come out on a white horse in the name of gaydom. Well, I didn't,
obviously. And why should I? I don't feel I'm part of a community; do you?

—GORE VIDAL (1925–)
AMERICAN WRITER AND POLITICAL ACTIVIST

There has been a spate of gay plays and films lately that touch on bonding,
but the bonding doesn't seem to be about being gay. It's generally about
experiencing loss. For pure gay bonding all we have is Gay Pride Month.
And we're not terribly kind to one another after that.

—BRUCE VILANCH (1948–)
AMERICAN COMEDY WRITER

GAY ICONS

SEE ALSO CELEBRITIES

I'd like to be the gay Mary Tyler Moore.

—AMANDA BEARSE (1958–)
AMERICAN ACTOR

Really all the great gay icons have talent in common—Barbra, Judy, Liza.
I don't think we'd wait all night in line for tickets to see Britney Spears!

—STEVEN BRINBERG (ca. 1967–)
AMERICAN BARBARA STREISAND IMPRESSIONIST

It was only last year that I discovered that *The Wizard of Oz* is the special province of gay men. . . . What with the association of Judy with Stonewall and the fact that the Scarecrow, the Tin Man, and the Cowardly Lion are all such unregenerately single gentlemen.

—GREGORY MAGUIRE (1954-)
AMERICAN WRITER

———————

Recently I've . . . been called an icon and a legend; I've also been called a sleazy star fucker. Now, who are you going to believe?

— FELICE PICANO (1944-)
AMERICAN WRITER

———————

It's difficult to feel like a legend when you wake up disgruntled and have to go fix breakfast and then wash dishes.

—JOHN RECHY (1934-)
AMERICAN WRITER

———————

[On Tammy Fay Bakker] She's basically the Christian Judy Garland.

—RUPAUL (1960-)
AMERICAN DRAG PERFORMER AND MUSICIAN

———————

If you don't find Liza with a *Z* inspiring then there's something wrong with you.

—PAUL SPICER (ca. 1981-)
BRITISH ACTOR AND MUSICIAN

GAY MARRIAGE

SEE ALSO MARRIAGE, RELATIONSHIPS, SEX

To keep the debate over gay marriage as rational and free of emotionalism
as possible, we must . . . strive to pierce the aura of marriage,
helping people to see it afresh, to think about it objectively, and to acknowledge
the widespread social reality of committed gay unions.

—BRUCE BAWER (1956–)
AMERICAN CRITIC AND WRITER

———————

I want to be legally recognized as married. I want all the benefits that a legal
marriage has. I get crazy when so many heterosexuals take it for granted yet it's
still something that Julie and I cannot have.

—MELISSA ETHERIDGE (1961–)
AMERICAN GRAMMY AWARD-WINNING MUSICIAN AND BREAST CANCER ACTIVIST

———————

At the moment gay marriage—i.e., real marriage and not that compromised crap
you folks settled for—is legal in Canada despite the fact that our hillbilly prime
minister wants to reopen the entire debate.

—BRAD FRASER (1959–)
CANADIAN PLAYWRIGHT AND SCREENWRITER

———————

To me it seems to have been a closer union than that of most marriages.
We know there have been other such between two men, and also between two
women. And why should there not be. Love is spiritual.

—MARY GREW (1813–1896)
AMERICAN PIONEER LESBIAN

I should have spotted something amiss when I saw the bride and groom standing knee-deep in white frosting . . . a bride and a groom on the wedding cake of two women? Maybe they didn't want to splurge on two sets of figurines.

—JANIS IAN (1951-)
AMERICAN GRAMMY AWARD WINNING MUSICIAN

We've gotten increasing numbers of civil union enactments . . . that means we'll be in the back of the bus, but at least we'll be on the bus.

—FRANK KAMENY (1925-)
AMERICAN GAY RIGHTS ACTIVIST

If two human beings want to exchange vows and declare before each other, their families, their friends, the world, and their God that they want to become a sacred union, I don't see why our government has any business stopping them because of their genitalia.

—JEFF MARX (1970-)
AMERICAN COMPOSER AND LYRICIST

There are also a lot of gay and lesbian couples like my partner and me who are ambivalent—still, I call him my boyfriend. My son is always correcting me— "No, he's your husband!" He's more comfortable with the idea now than we are.

—DAN SAVAGE (1964-)
AMERICAN SEX COLUMNIST AND WRITER

Whereas marriage between two people of the opposite sex who are physically attached to one another fails if there is no such bond of understanding, marriage between two people of the same sex may be immensely binding.

—STEPHEN SPENDER (1909-1995)
BRITISH POET AND WRITER

When I take to the House floor to fight for AIDS funding, employment nondiscrimination, or domestic-partner benefits, my anger is fueled by the denial of respect and equality to our community—and to my partner and our relationship.

—GERRY STUDDS (1937-2006)
AMERICAN CONGRESSMAN

Following legalization of same-sex marriage and a couple of other things, I think we should have a party and close down the gay rights movement for good.

—ANDREW SULLIVAN (1963-)
BRITISH-BORN POLITICAL COMMENTATOR AND BLOGGER

GAY PRIDE

SEE ALSO COMING OUT, GAY COMMUNITY, GAY RIGHTS, GAYS VS. LESBIANS, GAYS VS. STRAIGHTS, HOMOSEXUALITY, LESBIANS

More than anything else, Gay Pride Month symbolizes for me the ineffectuality of our movement in comparison with the religious right.

—BRUCE BAWER (1956-)
AMERICAN CRITIC AND WRITER

I don't think you can really be proud of being gay because it isn't something you've done. You can only be proud of not being ashamed.

—QUENTIN CRISP (1908-1999)
BRITISH WRITER AND PERSONALITY

It's 1990, it's hip to be gay, and I'm a big dyke!

—LEA DELARIA (1958-)
AMERICAN COMEDIAN AND ACTOR

How can gays get respect with parades where their meat is hanging out all over the place? . . . That doesn't mean gay to me, it means freak. I'm not one of those.

—MARLA GLEN (1960-)
AMERICAN MUSICIAN

In July 1968 I coined the slogan "Gay is good," which is the one thing, if nothing else, that I want to be remembered for. Our movement doesn't always handle its rhetoric well. It's not that gay is not bad, it's that gay is good. It's not that homosexuality is not sinful and immoral, it's that homosexuality is affirmatively virtuous and moral.

—FRANK KAMENY (1925-)
AMERICAN GAY RIGHTS ACTIVIST

I'm proud of some of my decisions this year. There are some I haven't been proud of, but I'm proud of the ones pertaining to being gay. . . . I'm not happy with what I ate this morning.

—T. R. KNIGHT (1973-)
AMERICAN ACTOR

GAY RIGHTS

SEE ALSO ACTIVISM, GAY MARRIAGE, POLITICS

The invention of the homosexual may have been the precondition of sexual liberation.

—LEO BERSANI (1931-)
AMERICAN LITERARY THEORIST AND PROFESSOR OF FRENCH

Ultimately, if you fight for women's rights, lesbian rights are there. . . . After all, homophobia is based on sexism. The fear and hatred of gay men is based on a straight man's fear of being like a woman. And the hatred of lesbians is the man's fear of women not needing men.

—TAMMY BRUCE (1962–)
AMERICAN FEMINIST ACTIVIST AND TALK SHOW HOST

I'm in the process of rejecting the word gay and especially the concept of "gay rights." The fight is for equality and dignity for all people regardless of what they might like to do in bed.

—BRAD FRASER (1959–)
CANADIAN PLAYWRIGHT AND SCREENWRITER

Let every one of us regard man-to-man romantic relations in whatever personal, aesthetic light desired; their decontrol is a pressing humanitarian and libertarian need of our time. Decontrol will not promote the inversion of a normal person any more than punishment has succeeded in making an inverted person normal.

—KURT HILLER (1885–1972)
JUDEO-GERMAN WRITER AND PACIFIST

Part of me looks at the gay movement now and worries that we're losing our individuality. On the other hand, a good friend of mine just got very badly queer-bashed, so I understand the need for politics.

—BOY GEORGE (1961–)
BRITISH MUSICIAN

[On being gay in the 1920s] In those years we weren't even in the *Encyclopedia Britannica.*

—HARRY HAY (1912–2002)
BRITISH-BORN GAY RIGHTS ACTIVIST

One's view as to what is pathological and what is not, as to whether a sexual abnormality is merely a variation or a sign of degeneracy is important both from the therapeutic standpoint and from that of the criminal law.

—MAGNUS HIRSCHFELD (1868-1935)
GERMAN SEXOLOGIST AND PIONEER GAY RIGHTS ACTIVIST

When I read that drag queens led the Stonewall riots, it made perfect sense— what did they have to lose except losers like me?

—JANIS IAN (1951-)
AMERICAN GRAMMY AWARD-WINNING MUSICIAN

Now you have a lot of people doing a lot of work for gay rights. People come forward and they're there and they speak. Instead of a having a spokesperson, you have a sizable number of spokespeople.

—FRANK KAMENY (1925-)
AMERICAN GAY RIGHTS ACTIVIST

The raw energy of Black determination released in the '60s powered changes in Black awareness and self-concepts and expectations. This energy is still being felt in movements for change among women, other peoples of Color, gays, and the handicapped—among all the disenfranchised peoples of history.

—AUDRE LORDE (1934-1992)
AFRICAN-AMERICAN WRITER, POET, AND ACTIVIST

A few hours in jail were insignificant. This was the fight for liberation.

—MORTY MANFORD (1950-1992)
AMERICAN LAWYER AND ACTIVIST

My life began in the summer of 1969. Before that I didn't exist.

—ROBERT MAPPLETHORPE (1946-1989)
AMERICAN PHOTOGRAPHER

I was so busy enjoying and promoting my career that I had no time or inclination to be aware of the gay liberation movement fighting on my behalf.

—SIR IAN MCKELLEN, CBE (1939-)
BRITISH ACTOR

———————

Conservatives want a homogenous image and are afraid to embrace the transgender community because they think that's going to screw up our ability to gain civil rights.

—ANN NORTHROP (1948-)
AMERICAN WRITER, PRODUCER, AND ACTIVIST

———————

The great cause of gay rights is not served by tolerating mediocrity, pretension, and deceit . . . If gays do not stand for truth, they stand for nothing.

—CAMILLE PAGLIA (1947-)
AMERICAN SCHOLAR AND CRITIC

———————

The Stonewall event was a major one, but it was one of many manifestations of gay resistance throughout the decades.

—JOHN RECHY (1934-)
AMERICAN WRITER

———————

Various movements even in their fragmentation somehow nevertheless yearn towards a wider unity—Women's Lib, Gay Lib, etc—[but] it is forgotten that the 1930s, among other things, was a sexual revolution.

—STEPHEN SPENDER (1909-1995)
BRITISH POET AND WRITER

The gay community has had too many glamourists and not enough sane arguers.
We've forgotten that our best case is a reasonable one,
not an emotional one.

—ANDREW SULLIVAN (1963-)
BRITISH-BORN AMERICAN POLITICAL COMMENTATOR AND BLOGGER

———————

The goal of the gay and lesbian movement is . . . about morality.
And it encompasses much more than legal reform or media visibility.

—URVASHI VAID (1958-)
AMERICAN GAY RIGHTS ACTIVIST

———————

Even bright pink queens and lesbians boys who say they're just here for the fun
have really thought about issues when you start asking them.

—JEANETTE WINTERSON (1959-)
BRITISH WRITER

GAYS VS. LESBIANS

SEE ALSO GAY COMMUNITY, GAYS VS. STRAIGHTS, HOMOSEXUALITY, LESBIANS

Gay men and lesbians have nearly disappeared into their sophisticated awareness of how they have been constructed as gay men and lesbians.

—LEO BERSANI (1931-)
AMERICAN LITERARY THEORIST AND PROFESSOR OF FRENCH

———————

Gay men and lesbians—a forced marriage if ever there was one.

—TORIE OSBORN (ca. 1950-)
AMERICAN GAY RIGHTS ACTIVIST AND COALITION BUILDER

I love the name Lesbians—so noble. I've suggested we gay men call ourselves Trojans, something appropriately grand.

—JOHN RECHY (1934-)
AMERICAN WRITER

For gay male designers, fashion is really an expression of one's gayness. Whereas for gay women, fashion hasn't been the same kind of issue.

—INGRID SISCHY (1952-)
AMERICAN WRITER AND EDITOR

The public discourse on what it means to be queer in America is conducted largely by gay male writers and thinkers.

—URVASHI VAID (1958-)
AMERICAN GAY RIGHTS ACTIVIST

GAYS VS. STRAIGHTS

SEE ALSO GAY COMMUNITY, GAYS VS. LESBIANS, HOMOSEXUALITY, SOCIETY

I'm very interested in building bridges between gay people and straight people, allowing for sexual interchange of experience and, above all, acceptance and understanding.

—PAUL BARTEL (1938-2000)
AMERICAN FILM DIRECTOR

When a boy and girl decide they are going to have sex, they roughly know what to expect. But before two men have sex, they practically have to hold a board meeting in order to figure out the agenda . . .

—QUENTIN CRISP (1908-1999)
BRITISH WRITER AND PERSONALITY

In the last few years straight men have become a little more polished,
and it's hard sometimes to tell who is gay and who is straight.

—WILSON CRUZ (1973-)
PUERTO RICAN-AMERICAN ACTOR

———————

Call me a big, warm-hearted lug, but I think straight people
deserve a show of their own, too.

—JOE DIPIETRO (1963-)
AMERICAN PLAYWRIGHT

———————

I find it inherently beautiful when a straight guy and a gay guy learn
from each other.

—KYAN DOUGLAS (1970-)
AMERICAN REALITY TV STAR

———————

Stop asking permission from the straight world to be who we are.
It has nothing to do with them.

—BOY GEORGE (1961-)
BRITISH MUSICIAN

———————

No one wants to really admit that there is an ambiguous territory there.
That straight people do explore. That gay people explore with straight people.
That there is a meeting place.

—CHARLES HERMAN-WURMFELD (1966-)
AMERICAN FILM DIRECTOR

———————

Even if change were simple, easy, quick, convenient, and possible,
which it is not, why would we want to swap what is first-class,
superior homosexuality for second-class, inferior heterosexuality?

—FRANK KAMENY (1925-)
AMERICAN GAY RIGHTS ACTIVIST

We also put on the first gay dance at the University of Oregon, a gay-straight sock hop. . . . We allowed straight people—you know, we were very liberal.

—RANDY SHILTS (1951-1994)
AMERICAN JOURNALIST, AIDS ACTIVIST, AND WRITER

———————

I love straight people, I do. I have two to clean my house. You're nice people.

—JASON STUART (1959-)
AMERICAN ACTOR AND COMEDIAN

———————

I've had sex with straight men—quite a bit actually.
A lot of them are curious about it.

—RUFUS WAINWRIGHT (1973-)
CANADIAN MUSICIAN

———————

I like mixing it up. I always cast straight people to play gay people and gay people to play straight people. I like it confusing, just like I like it in real life!

—JOHN WATERS (1946-)
AMERICAN DIRECTOR

———————

I have always seen gay life as an alternative to straight life. If gay life meant just reproducing straight life, I'd rather become a monk.

—EDMUND WHITE (1940-)
AMERICAN WRITER AND CRITIC

———————

What is straight? A line can be straight, or a street, but the human heart, oh, no, it's curved like a road through mountains!

—TENNESSEE WILLIAMS (1911-1983)
AMERICAN PLAYWRIGHT

GENDER BENDING

SEE ALSO DOUBLE LIVES, GAY COMMUNITY, GAY PRIDE, GAY RIGHTS,
GAYS VS. LESBIANS, GAYS VS. STRAIGHTS, HOMOSEXUALITY, SEXUALITY

I think when people see a drag queen with a big wig and an over-the-top look, they associate it with partying and tend to scream "Work!" or "You go, girl!" It's the serious "I'm-passing-as-a-woman" looks that tend to be less popular, when the queens aren't passing and there's no hint of fun or glamour. Then straights tend to want to yell stuff like "Hello, sir!" to let the queens know that they aren't fooling anybody.

—LADY BUNNY (1962–)
AMERICAN DRAG PERFORMER AND DJ

From early youth I had absorbed our culture's fear of any gender confusion, giving my utterly harmless sexual orientation the undeserved semblance of villainy. I had to admit to myself that I was as homophobic as the public I sought to please.

—RICHARD CHAMBERLAIN (1934–)
AMERICAN ACTOR

I don't believe in the binary gender system in any way. . . . What I am trying to do is join my feminine and masculine qualities, and I feel this is the best I can ask for in a world that is so bent keeping gender so rigid.

—MORTY DIAMOND (ca. 1976–)
AMERICAN FTM WRITER AND PORN PRODUCER

At the best of times gender is difficult to determine.

—MARLENE DIETRICH (1901–1992)
GERMAN-BORN ACTOR

And Jove oft-times bent to lascivious sport,
And coming where Endimion did resort,
Hath courted him, inflamed with desire,
Thinking some Nymph was cloth'd in boyes attire.

—MICHAEL DRAYTON (1563-1631)
BRITISH POET

In her boots and with a sword by her side, she told the company there present
that she thought many of them were of opinion that she was a man, but if any of
them would come to her lodging they should find that she is a woman.

—ON MARY "MAD MOLL" FRITH (1584-1659)
FROM THE JANUARY 27,1611 CORRECTION BOOK FOR THE CONSTITATORY OF LONDON
BRITISH PIONEER FEMINIST AND TRANSVESTITE

In every living being born of the union of two sexes, the characteristics of one sex
are to be identified to varying degrees alongside those of the other.

—MAGNUS HIRSCHFELD (1868-1935)
GERMAN SEXOLOGIST AND PIONEER GAY RIGHTS ACTIVIST

Talk about a confusing state of affairs: The woman I lusted after was a man?
What did that make me? A lesbian who wanted men? A heterosexual?

—JANIS IAN (1951-)
AMERICAN GRAMMY AWARD-WINNING MUSICIAN

I certainly think becoming a man involves becoming a woman as well.

—PAUL MONETTE (1945-1995)
AMERICAN WRITER AND AIDS ACTIVIST

In the first place there were three sexes, not, as with us, two, male and female; the third partook of the nature of both the others and has vanished, though its name survives. The hermaphrodite was a distinct sex in form as well as in name, with the characteristics of both male and female, but now the name alone remains, and that solely as a term of abuse. . . . The reason for the existence of three sexes and for their being of such a nature is that originally the male sprange from the sun and the female from the earth, while the sex which was both male and female came from the moon, which partakes of both sun and earth.

— PLATO (427-347 BC)
GREEK PHILOSOPHER

―――――――――

The sister was not a mister. Was this a surprise? It was.

—GERTRUDE STEIN (1874-1946)
AMERICAN EXPATRIATE WRITER

―――――――――

The stinging fact [is] that in orthodox society today, if the dresses were changed, the men might easily pass for women and the women for men.

—WALT WHITMAN (1819-1892)
AMERICAN POET

GENIUS

SEE ALSO INTELLIGENCE AND INTELLECTUALS

I'm an alcoholic. I'm a drug addict. I'm a homosexual. I'm a genius.

—TRUMAN CAPOTE (1924-1984)
AMERICAN WRITER

The poverty from which I have suffered could be diagnosed as "Soho" poverty. It comes from having the airs and graces of a genius and no talent.

—QUENTIN CRISP (1908-1999)
BRITISH WRITER AND PERSONALITY

————

If the homosexuality of geniuses does not prove that homosexuality is a higher order, it certainly does prove that homosexuality is not exclusively an affliction of gutter snipes, maniacs, and thugs.

—HENRY GERBER (1892-1972)
GERMAN-BORN GAY RIGHTS ACTIVIST

————

Sometimes people ask me if I am a genius. I always say it's not for me to say. You can't go up to a lunatic and say "Are you mad?"

—DANIEL TAMMET (1979-)
BRITISH AUTISTIC SAVANT

————

No, I'm not interested in developing a powerful brain. All I'm after is just a mediocre brain, something like the President of the American Telephone and Telegraph Company.

—ALAN TURING, O.B.E. (1912-1954)
BRITISH MATHEMATICIAN AND CRYPTOGRAPHER

————

When people have spoken to me of "genius," I have felt an inside pocket to make sure my wallet's still there.

—TENNESSEE WILLIAMS (1911-1983)
AMERICAN PLAYWRIGHT

GRIEF

SEE ALSO FEELINGS, HAPPINESS, PSYCHOLOGY, THERAPY, SUFFERING

Mourning your first love is as important as meeting your first love.
It's the whole cycle.

—JANE ANDERSON (1954-)
AMERICAN ACTOR AND DIRECTOR

———

Grief is like a boomerang. You throw it away and it comes back and hits you.

—RITA MAE BROWN (1944-)
AMERICAN WRITER

———

It's so curious: One can resist tears and "behave" very well in the hardest hours
of grief. But then someone makes you a friendly sign behind a window . . . or a
letter slips from a drawer—and everything collapses.

—SIDONIE-GABRIELLE COLETTE (1873-1954)
FRENCH WRITER

———

When we are five, we don't want to hear a story about the sorrows of the
five-year-old that lives next door; we want to hear about witches and treasures
and dragons. When we get older, we do of course begin to want to know
about the sorrows and joys of people like us, and people unlike us,
but I don't think we lose that other appetite.

—MICHAEL CUNNINGHAM (1952-)
AMERICAN PULITZER PRIZE-WINNING WRITER

———

Grief is not a pathology. It is the body's natural response to devastation.
Anyone who can formulate a stiff upper lip is, to me, already dead.

—CRAIG LUCAS (1951-)
AMERICAN PLAYWRIGHT AND DIRECTOR

HAPPINESS

SEE ALSO FEELINGS, GRIEF, PSYCHOLOGY, THERAPY

Just a little more effort, perhaps merely the discovery of the right terms in which to describe it, and surely absolute pleasure must immediately descend upon the astonished armies of this world and abolish forever all their hate and suffering.

—W. H. AUDEN (1907-1973)
ANGLO-AMERICAN POET AND CRITIC

———

And now I have to confess the unpardonable and the scandalous, in an age which scorns happiness. I am a happy man. . . . I love love. I hate hate.

—JEAN COCTEAU (1889-1963)
FRENCH WRITER AND FILMMAKER

———

There never was a happy man. One man sees brighter days than another, but never yet was there one happy man.

—COUNTEE CULLEN (1903-1946)
AFRICAN-AMERICAN POET

———

I do not think that we have a "right" to happiness. If happiness happens, say thanks.

—MARLENE DIETRICH (1901-1992)
GERMAN-BORN ACTOR

———

There is no happiness in this horrible world but the happiness we have had— the very present is ever in the jaws of fate.

—HENRY JAMES (1843-1916)
AMERICAN WRITER

I'm happy as long as I can keep making movies and get laid every now and then.

—TOMMY O'HAVER (1967–)
AMERICAN SCREENWRITER AND FILM DIRECTOR

―――――――

What is the use of a violent kind of delightfulness if there is no pleasure in not getting tired of it.

—GERTRUDE STEIN (1874–1946)
AMERICAN EXPATRIATE WRITER

―――――――

Nobody thinks it's funny if those girls that win beauty contests stand there with their crowns askew, lookin' kind of silly—cryin'! Why? What's the difference? They're happy and they cry because they're happy. Can't God's people cry because they're happy too?

—ETHEL WATERS (1896–1977)
AFRICAN-AMERICAN ACTRESS AND MUSICIAN

HATRED

SEE ALSO FEELINGS, OPPRESSION, REPRESSION, SUFFERING

We belong to a minority despised not only by the powerful but also, often with greater vehemence and even more self-righteously, by the most luckless racial and economic victims in every part of the world.

—LEO BERSANI (1931–)
AMERICAN LITERARY THEORIST AND PROFESSOR OF FRENCH

―――――――

I had thought for so long that it was somehow noble to hate myself. As if fate would take kindly to me, and say, "You adorable little scamp! Somebody will love you, because you just can't seem to!"

—MARGARET CHO (1968–)
KOREAN-AMERICAN COMEDIAN

To grow up metabolizing hatred like daily bread means that eventually every human interaction becomes tainted with the negative passion and intensity of its by-products—anger and cruelty.

—AUDRE LORDE (1934-1992)
AFRICAN-AMERICAN WRITER, POET, AND ACTIVIST

―――――

I am a giant "Fuck you" to bigotry. Buddha, Krishna, Jesus, and now RuPaul.

—RUPAUL (1960-)
AMERICAN DRAG PERFORMER AND MUSICIAN

―――――

When you die you'll lie dead; No memory of you,
No desire will survive . . .
Once gone, you'll flutter among the obscure.

—SAPPHO (ca. 630-ca. 570 BC)
GREEK POET

―――――

I do now realize that arrows, if they are tipped with venom, have a tendency to reach their target.

—STEPHEN SPENDER (1909-1995)
BRITISH POET AND WRITER

HOMOPHOBIA

A lot of people are not homophobic, but they think they're supposed to be. They think that if they don't express prejudice, people will think there's something the matter with them.

—BARNEY FRANK (1940-)
AMERICAN CONGRESSMAN

I don't want to get into a word comparison—this word versus that word. . . .
All those words are soaked in blood. Whatever word it is, if it's the last word
that someone screams at you before you're killed—whether it's about your
sexuality or your religion or your race—that's hate.

—T. R. KNIGHT (1973-)
AMERICAN ACTOR

HISTORY

SEE ALSO THE HOLOCAUST, THE PAST, THE PRESENT

When the historical process breaks down and armies organize. . . .
When necessity is associated with horror and freedom with boredom,
then it looks good to the bar business.

—W. H. AUDEN (1907-1973)
ANGLO-AMERICAN POET AND CRITIC

At both ends of history, there is something ahistorical.

—LEO BERSANI (1931-)
AMERICAN LITERARY THEORIST AND PROFESSOR OF FRENCH

History in the making can be most exhausting.

—NOËL COWARD (1899-1973)
BRITISH ACTOR AND PLAYWRIGHT

In considering male intellectual and scientific argumentation in conjunction with
male history, one is forced to conclude that men as a class are moral cretins.

—ANDREA DWORKIN (1946-2005)
AMERICAN FEMINIST CRITIC AND ANTI-PORN ACTIVIST

Establishing discontinuities is not an easy task even for history in general.
And it is certainly even less so for the history of thought.

—MICHEL FOUCAULT (1926-1984)
FRENCH PHILOSOPHER AND CULTURAL HISTORIAN

I regard the march of history very much as a man placed astride of a locomotive
without knowledge or help, would regard the progress of that vehicle.

—HENRY JAMES (1843-1916)
AMERICAN WRITER

[In the 1920s] history was not considered a proper study.
And today, how different! We find ourselves now all wrapped up in reminiscence.
We cannot today not know history.

—PHILIP JOHNSON (1906-2005)
AMERICAN ARCHITECT

Great historical crimes reproduce themselves. One injustice breeds new generations of injustice. Suffering rolls on down through the years . . .

—TONY KUSHNER (1956-)
AMERICAN PLAYWRIGHT

The ironic philosopher reflects with a smile that Sir Walter Raleigh is more safely
enshrined in the memory of mankind because he set his cloak for the Virgin Queen
to walk on than because he carried the English name to undiscovered countries.

—W. SOMERSET MAUGHAM (1874-1965)
BRITISH WRITER AND PLAYWRIGHT

Historical figures . . . [are] like figures in a novel read by millions of people at once. What's terrifying is that they're human as well, and therefore no more reliable than you or I.

—JAMES MERRILL (1926-1995)
AMERICAN PULITZER PRIZE-WINNING POET

The effect of time is that it washes thing clean, like the walls of a house in the rain.

—PIER PAOLO PASOLINI (1922-1975)
ITALIAN FILM DIRECTOR

Clergymen, and people who use phrases without wisdom, sometimes talk of suffering as a mystery. It is really a revelation. One discerns things that one never discerned before. One approaches the whole of history from a different standpoint.

—OSCAR WILDE (1854-1900)
IRISH PLAYWRIGHT AND WRITER

HOLLYWOOD

SEE ALSO AUDIENCES, BUSINESS, CELEBRITIES, ENTERTAINMENT, FAME, MOVIES

People only know what they know and they only believe what they see. They're very limited, most people in this town. It's amazing how uncreative so many people in the film business are. They're people who should be CPAs.

—ALEXIS ARQUETTE (1969-)
AMERICAN ACTOR AND DRAG PERFORMER

There's nothing worse than working for some director who thinks they've done you some sort of a favor. They feel that for all actors.

—ALEXIS ARQUETTE (1969-)
AMERICAN ACTOR AND DRAG PERFORMER

I go to commercial Hollywood films and often think how glad I am that I didn't pursue a career in that kind of filmmaking.

—PAUL BARTEL (1938-2000)
AMERICAN ACTOR, WRITER AND FILM DIRECTOR

———————

Working in Hollywood, and not being traditionally beautiful or tall or skinny or blonde or even a guy, I felt invisible a lot of the time. . . . I felt sexless, useless, ugly, and fat, and had no idea how I was going to get past my physical self and show the producers that I actually had a lot of talent.

—MARGARET CHO (1968-)
KOREAN-AMERICAN COMEDIAN

———————

But do you really want to sell your soul so you could play Jerry Lewis in a TV movie? If that's what you want to do, then great! I don't think Jerry Lewis is worth the trouble.

—CRAIG CHESTER (1965-)
AMERICAN ACTOR AND COMEDIAN

———————

I love old movies, and old movies were really about a studio system. It's fascinating because times have not changed. Studios are studios.

—MARK CHRISTOPHER (1963-)
AMERICAN FILM DIRECTOR

———————

[In Hollywood] all the inhabitants are "movie people" of some sort or the media. A strange language is spoken. I think it's called wheelie-dealie. It sounds like English, but it might as well be Greek.

—LOLA COLA (ca. 1963-)
AMERICAN TRANS DOCUMENTARY STAR

I thought I'd write a novel that was so obviously meant to be a movie that
Hollywood would discover me.

—WARREN DUNFORD (1963-)
CANADIAN WRITER

[In Hollywood] there are all these buttons pushed to make us react.
We laugh, we cry. But I think if we can be surprised into an unexpected response,
it's going to resonate in a new way, and we'll discover something.

—JOHN GRAYSON (1960-)
CANADIAN DIRECTOR

I'm not Hollywood beautiful, so my sexuality doesn't matter. . . . Hollywood gets
excited only about someone who's beautiful and just shy of thirty—because then
they'll have a good twelve years of millions of dollars to make off this person.

—CHERRY JONES (1956-)
AMERICAN TONY AWARD-WINNING ACTOR

And while some actors are still advised to disguise their sexuality in public,
it's not that long since Jews in Hollywood felt obliged to change their names
and left-wingers had to lie about their politics.

—SIR IAN MCKELLEN, CBE (1939-)
BRITISH ACTOR

As they say in Hollywood, nobody ever wanted to read one more script
on their deathbed.

—PAUL MONETTE (1945-1995)
AMERICAN WRITER AND AIDS ACTIVIST

The thing about awards is, when you don't get one, you feel terrible, and when you do get one, you realize how little it actually had to do with you.

—DAVID HYDE PIERCE (1959-)
AMERICAN ACTOR

———

Hollywood Boulevard is the heart of the heartless Hollywood legend. Like special moths attracted to the special glitter of the nihilistic movie capital, the untalented or undiscovered are spewed into the streets by the make-it legend.

—JOHN RECHY (1934-)
AMERICAN WRITER

———

You can be the greatest novelist on Earth, but when you walk into a meeting with Hollywood producers, you are just the writer . . . and the writer in film is the lowest.

—CHRISTOPHER RICE (1978-)
AMERICAN WRITER

———

Hollywood is where gay screenwriters churn out offensive teenage sex comedies and do it well because there isn't anything they don't know about pretending to be straight.

—VITO RUSSO (1946-1990)
AMERICAN ACTIVIST, HISTORIAN, AND WRITER

———

I guess unless you play the game, like attaching a star and saying, "We have Jim Carrey to play Issan Dorsey," nobody really listens to you. . . . I just think it's really fake. I mean, you can get the star afterwards.

—GUS VAN SANT (1952-)
AMERICAN FILM DIRECTOR

All of a sudden I was a Hollywood film-maker, and . . . I'm thinking, well, I can get these people, they want to be in my movie. That's weird, because I was used to begging the guy who's my waiter in the restaurant to be in my movie.

—GUS VAN SANT (1952-)
AMERICAN FILM DIRECTOR

The undermining of standards of seriousness is almost complete, with the ascendancy of a culture whose most intelligible, persuasive values are drawn from the entertainment industry.

—SUSAN SONTAG (1933-2004)
AMERICAN WRITER AND CRITIC

I always assume in Hollywood that most women are bisexual.

—JACKIE WARNER (1968-)
AMERICAN REALITY TV STAR AND CELEBRITY TRAINER

THE HOLOCAUST

SEE ALSO HATRED, HISTORY, OPPRESSION, RELIGION

But what matters to the bourgeoisie besides making money and seeing value appreciate? Nothing. So the bourgeoisie needs the Jews so as not to have to despise its own attitudes . . . the ultimate result of such unconscious self-hatred was the mass extermination of the Jews in the Third Reich.

—RAINER WERNER FASSBINDER (1945-1982)
GERMAN DIRECTOR

I think that what happened is that we grew up with the Holocaust within us. It turned us into harsh, emotionally incapable people who have become blind to what they are doing to other people. A lot of times, Holocaust abuse justifies terrible things done to the Palestinians.

—EYTAN FOX (1964-)
ISRAELI FILM DIRECTOR

I spent the best part of my youth in prison. . . . When I met this soldier, I had no idea of homosexuality. I only knew that we were very happy together. Who would punish a 17-year old boy for love?

—TEOFIL KOSINSKI (1925-)
HOLOCAUST SURVIVOR AND GAY RIGHTS ACTIVIST

I was very obsessed with the Holocaust as a child and man's inhumanity to man. And, ultimately, it came from my fear of intolerance.

—BRYAN SINGER (1965-)
AMERICAN FILM DIRECTOR

HOMOSEXUALITY

SEE ALSO GAY COMMUNITY, GAY ICONS, GAY MARRIAGE, GAY PRIDE, GAY RIGHTS, GAYS VS. LESBIANS, GAYS VS. STRAIGHTS, GENDER BENDING, QUEERNESS, S&M

We love our token gay things.

—ALEX ALI (ca. 1983-)
AMERICAN REALITY TV STAR

I liked the Dandies. . . . The truth is, that, though I gave up the business early, I had a tinge of Dandyism in my minority. . . . I had gamed and drank, and taken my degrees in most dissipations.

—LORD BYRON (1788-1824)
BRITISH POET

Homosexuals don't have parents? I always knew we were different, but I hadn't realized that we were self-generating.

—SIMON CALLOW, CBE (1949-)
BRITISH ACTOR

This is what I know of homosexuality. . . . That it is a sin if done wrong. That it is a better sin if done right.

—JUSTIN CHIN (1967-)
ASIAN-AMERICAN WRITER AND PERFORMANCE ARTIST

It has always been easy for me to write about homosexuality and the normalcy of it.

—STANLEY BENNETT CLAY (1950-)
AFRICAN-AMERICAN PLAYWRIGHT AND PRODUCER

Homosexuals recognize each other. . . . The mask dissolves, and I would venture to discover my kind between the lines of the most innocent book.

—JEAN COCTEAU (1889-1963)
FRENCH WRITER AND FILMMAKER

The ladies of earlier years were far smarter. No pants, drinking, swearing and competing with the boys; they just stayed put and, as a general rule, got their own way and held their gentlemen much longer. It really isn't surprising that homosexuality is becoming as normal as blueberry pie.

—NOËL COWARD (1899-1973)
BRITISH ACTOR AND PLAYWRIGHT

Can we hope to be regarded as anything other than biologically unfortunate if we claim we are homosexual because we were born that way? Just by virtue of seeking an explanation for homosexuality, aren't we falling into the trap of believing that "something went wrong" to make us as we are?

—LILLIAN FADERMAN (1940-)
AMERICAN SCHOLAR AND WRITER

Our very lives as homosexuals are disruptive of oppressive social orders, and when we become parents, we model creative alternatives to those orders.

—LILLIAN FADERMAN (1940-)
AMERICAN SCHOLAR AND WRITER

But to be a homosexual was one thing; to be an expatriate was quite another, although perhaps in an unsavory way they were linked after all.

—ROBERT FERRO (1941-1988)
AMERICAN WRITER AND GAY RIGHTS ACTIVIST

I doubt that anything completely gay, or straight for that matter, could be a utopia.

—BRAD FRASER (1959-)
CANADIAN PLAYWRIGHT AND SCREENWRITER

Gay men were at the time prone to actually referring to themselves as "friends of Dorothy." Basically, gay male self-hatred of the masculine animus comes from straight people's stereotype that gay men are not real men, are girly, effeminate, and maybe even, a third sex.

—JACK FRITSCHER (ca. 1950-)
AMERICAN EDITOR AND WRITER

Homosexuality seems more or less frequent according to whether it appears more or less openly.

— ANDRÉ GIDE (1869-1951)
FRENCH WRITER

The Middle East has a long history of tolerance of homosexuality—it was European colonizers who introduced anti-gay laws to the region, and it is those laws that tyrants enforce for political gain.

—DAVE HALL (ca. 1970-)
ARAB-AMERICAN MUSICIAN

Understanding homosexuality presupposes a psychological reorientation, a self-liberation from the tutelage of the legislator who ignorantly subsumes homosexuality and depravity under the same concept.

—MAGNUS HIRSCHFELD (1868-1935)
GERMAN SEXOLOGIST AND PIONEER GAY RIGHTS ACTIVIST

I didn't have a choice being gay—I mean I literally fell out of my mother's womb and landed in her high heels!

—LESLIE JORDAN (1955-)
AMERICAN EMMY AWARD-WINNING ACTOR

My mother cautioned me that being gay and having a career was going to be hard. But it's been much better for my career. It's definitely a community where people help each other.

—TYSON LIEBERMAN (1982-)
AMERICAN SCREENWRITER

In retrospect, the most unnerving aspect of being openly gay was that it turned out to be as disappointingly normal as being straight.

—LANCE LOUD (1951-2001)
AMERICAN REALITY TV STAR AND COLUMNIST

———————

Someone give me the gay rulebook, because they didn't pass it out to me in the sixth grade.

—TYSON MEADE (1962-)
AMERICAN MUSICIAN

———————

Homosexuality was a very useful neutral way to refer to same-sex love, "scientifically" defusing such highly charged words as "bugger," "sodomite" or "degenerate."

—RICTOR NORTON (1945-)
AMERICAN SCHOLAR, CRITIC, AND HISTORIAN

———————

Homosexuals have bade a covenant against nature. Homosexual survival lay in artifice, in plumage, in lampshades, sonnets, musical comedy, couture, syntax, religious ceremony, opera, lacquer, irony.

—RICHARD RODRIGUEZ (1944-)
MEXICAN-AMERICAN WRITER

———————

I mean, people say that I'm gay, gay, gay, gay, gay, gay, gay, gay. I'm not anything. . . . People are people.

—DUSTY SPRINGFIELD (1939-1999)
BRITISH MUSICIAN

———————

I am unable to dissociate in certain cases my friendly feeling for a man from the plastic admiration of his beauty.

—JOHN ADDINGTON SYMONDS (1840-1893)
ENGLISH POET AND CRITIC

I never, ever felt growing up that the [homosexual] feelings that I had
were unusual or anything that I should be self-conscious about.
That may be one of the blessings of my autism.

–DANIEL TAMMET (1979-)
BRITISH AUTISTIC SAVANT

———————

I don't think we'll ever truly understand what makes someone gay or not gay.
It's a flavor of being human. But certainly it's fixed prenatally. I think autism is the
same way. I didn't get it from anything I was exposed to as a child.

–DANIEL TAMMET (1979-)
BRITISH AUTISTIC SAVANT

———————

To be gay and out of shape is almost as much of a stigma as just being gay
used to be. The shoulders stoop with the burden.

–BRUCE VILANCH (1948-)
AMERICAN COMEDY WRITER

———————

I have very high standards. I'm not gonna like someone just because they're gay.

–RUFUS WAINWRIGHT (1973-)
CANADIAN MUSICIAN

———————

For me being gay means being one who usually gets the rotten side
of the stick but who can handle it a little better, someone who sees life
through a slightly different tint.

–RUFUS WAINWRIGHT (1973-)
CANADIAN MUSICIAN

I thought about women, but never sexually. It was in a highly
romantic context. . . . But then the women would turn into chicks with dicks,
and I started noticing the men around me.

—RUFUS WAINWRIGHT (1973–)
CANADIAN MUSICIAN

This empty dish, gallantry . . . this tepid wash, this diluted deferential love,
as in songs, fictions, and so forth, is enough to make a man vomit;
as to manly friendship, everywhere observed in the States,
there is not the first breath of it to be observed in print.

—WALT WHITMAN (1819-1892)
AMERICAN POET

I am more and more willing to agree with certain authorities that
homosexuality is negative—that it is, even when apparently aggressive,
a submission to solicitations. These solicitations are not necessarily those
coming from the outside; they come from within also, from an exorbitant
need for tenderness, i.e., to be valued by another.

—THORNTON WILDER (1897-1975)
AMERICAN PLAYWRIGHT

BEARS

The Bear is a counter-image to the dominant mainstream gay image right now.
I like to look at what's not being focused on, what's not the center of American
images. I like it when any group that's at the margins starts to organize and to
become, in terms of erotic images, its own fetish.

—ERIC ROFES (1954-2006)
AMERICAN WRITER AND ACTIVIST

I noticed that in the late '80s, when AIDS was hitting the gay community hardest and people were wasting because they were ill, big men were seen as healthy, or at least healthier. People started paying more attention in those days to bears . . .

—RICK TROMBLY (1957-)
AMERICAN POLITICIAN AND FORMER STATE LEGISLATOR

HONESTY

SEE ALSO COMMUNICATION, DECEIT, INTIMACY, TRUTH

Only animals who are below civilization and the angels who ho are beyond it can be sincere.

—W. H. AUDEN (1907-1973)
ANGLO-AMERICAN POET AND CRITIC

———

Gay used to stand for pretense and patterned choreography, playing prescribed roles and wearing masks. "Make it gay" was the watchword. It meant "put on the ritz," "keep the act going," "don't let down your guard," "keep on smiling"— especially to conceal one's sadness. But there has been a change. Gay now means new honesty.

—MALCOLM BOYD (1923-)
AMERICAN MINISTER AND INSPIRATIONAL WRITER

———

People keep on saying now, "At least we're more honest." But what does that really mean? I don't think that's enough. Honesty can look just as silly as anything else ten years later.

—GEORGE CUKOR (1899-1983)
AMERICAN FILM DIRECTOR

THE HUMAN BODY

SEE ALSO ILLNESS

A fake nose is fine as long as it never, ever, for one second looks like a fake nose.

—MICHAEL CUNNINGHAM (1952-)
AMERICAN PULITZER PRIZE WINNING WRITER

Without a doubt, the greatest thing about sex is vaginas. Looking at one is like looking to the face of God. Whenever I do, I speak in tongues.

—LEA DELARIA (1958-)
AMERICAN COMEDIAN AND ACTOR

Hips are absolutely key to every shape I do, because whatever you do at the top or bottom, you want to keep it slim and narrow on the hips. One thing is for certain: No one, man or woman, wants big hips.

—TOM FORD (1962-)
AMERICAN FASHION DESIGNER

We're all born nude, and we all put clothes on and take them off. Whoopee.

—RICHARD HATCH (1961-)
AMERICAN REALITY TV STAR

Being scared of nudity is retarded.

—JANE WIEDLIN (1958-)
AMERICAN MUSICIAN

To recite one's own body, to recite the body of the other, is to recite the words of which the books is made up. The fascination for writing the never previously written and the fascination for the unattained body proceed from the same desire.

—MONIQUE WITTIG (1935-2003)
FRENCH FEMINIST AND WRITER

PENISES

I had a very definite idea of how a young man, should present himself, and one key element was that the man has . . . a dick.

—PETER BERLIN (1934-)
GERMAN MODEL AND GAY SEX ICON

The question was posed to them [three girls], what is the strongest thing of all? One girl said "Iron" and gave as her proof that men dig and cut everything with it and use it as a tool for all sorts of purposes. This seemed like a good answer, but the second girl followed her and said that the smith is much stronger, because this man in working iron could bend it, soften it, and do what he wanted with it. The third girl said that the penis is the strongest thing of all, because with this they can screw the smith and make him groan.

—DIPHILUS (342-291 BC)
GREEK PLAYWRIGHT AND POET

We think with our penises too much, and our penises are very, very stupid.

—JOE DI PIETRO (1963-)
AMERICAN PLAYWRIGHT

A small penis—the leprosy of homosexuals . . .

—ANDREW HOLLERAN (1944-)
AMERICAN WRITER

PLASTIC SURGERY

I would never do that [plastic surgery]. I will never undergo surgery for something like that; I feel it's a weakness of character, if you don't accept becoming older.

—RICHARD CHAMBERLAIN (1934-)
AMERICAN ACTOR

———

[The reality TV show that] of course obsesses me is *The Swan*, along with *Extreme Makeover*. Any program where people actually mutilate themselves for our pleasure (laughs) is okay by me.

—PAUL RUDNICK (1957-)
AMERICAN SCREENWRITER AND PLAYWRIGHT

———

I think a person's imperfections make them sexy, so I wouldn't change anything about my appearance with cosmetic surgery.

—MATTHEW RUSH (1972-)
AMERICAN PORN STAR

HUMANITY

SEE ALSO THE PUBLIC, SOCIETY, STEREOTYPES

Human beings are, necessarily, actors who cannot become something before they have first pretended to be it; and they can be divided, not into the hypocritical and the sincere, but into the sane who know they are acting and the mad who do not.

—W. H. AUDEN (1907-1973)
ANGLO-AMERICAN POET AND CRITIC

———

There's a long list of leeches on this planet.

—JEAN-MICHEL BASQUIAT (1960-1988)
AMERICAN ARTIST

If there is one thing I feel sure of it is this: that human life has direction.

—WILLIAM BURROUGHS (1914-1997)
AMERICAN WRITER

———————

To most people a man loses his humanity the minute they learn
he's a murderer. . . . But I find it relatively easy to establish rapport
with murderers. . . . I find that they are ordinary men with extraordinary
problems, set apart only by their ability to kill.

—TRUMAN CAPOTE (1924-1984)
AMERICAN WRITER

———————

There seems to be a vision possible to man, as from some more universal standpoint, free from the obscurity and localism which especially connect themselves
with the passing clouds of desire, fear, and all ordinary thought and emotion.

—EDWARD CARPENTER (1844-1929)
BRITISH SOCIALIST POET AND GAY ACTIVIST

———————

Humanity has been replaced with melodrama.

—GEORGE CUKOR (1899-1983)
AMERICAN FILM DIRECTOR

———————

But everything you need to know about human life, about human experience,
can also be found in two elderly women having tea in a corner of a
little shabby tearoom some place, very much the way the recipe for the whole
organism is contained in every strand of DNA.

—MICHAEL CUNNINGHAM (1952-)
AMERICAN PULITZER PRIZE-WINNING WRITER

As the archaeology of our thought easily shows, man is an invention of recent date. And one perhaps nearing its end.

—MICHEL FOUCAULT (1926-1984)
FRENCH PHILOSOPHER AND CULTURAL HISTORIAN

———

Within each one of us there is some piece of humanness that knows we are not being served by the machine which orchestrates crisis after crisis and is grinding all our futures into dust.

—AUDRE LORDE (1934-1992)
AFRICAN-AMERICAN WRITER, POET, AND ACTIVIST

———

The nature of men and women—their essential nature—is so vile and despicable that if you were to portray a person as he really is, no one would believe you.

—W. SOMERSET MAUGHAM (1874-1965)
BRITISH WRITER AND PLAYWRIGHT

———

I move simply, but the movements of a monkey are complicated. A monkey is stupid. . . . I know that organically a man resembles a monkey, but spiritually he does not.

—VASLAV NIJINSKY (1890-1950)
RUSSIAN DANCER

———

What is the tragedy? It's that there are no longer any human beings; there are only some strange machines that bump up against each other.

—PIER PAOLO PASOLINI (1922-1975)
ITALIAN FILM DIRECTOR

———

Really what odd things grown-up, civilized human beings are, with their dancing and their fancydress . . . and their sports, and their blind man's bluff.

—VITA SACKVILLE-WEST (1892-1962)
BRITISH POET, NOVELIST, AND GARDENER

I hate mankind in the mass, and I should be delighted to retire into some wilderness with very few inhabitants.

—PETER ILYICH TCHAIKOVSKY (1840-1893)
RUSSIAN COMPOSER

HUMOR

SEE ALSO COMMUNICATION, UNDERSTANDING

A sense of humor, you know, is one of the least infectious things in the world.

—J. R. ACKERLEY (1896-1967)
BRITISH WRITER AND EDITOR

———————

No, nothing should be taken completely seriously ever! Especially not drag! . . . There is something innately ridiculous about drag.

—LADY BUNNY (1962-)
AMERICAN DRAG PERFORMER AND DJ

———————

If you really look at anything, there's always a comic note. A painful note, too. One brings the other to life.

—GEORGE CUKOR (1899-1983)
AMERICAN FILM DIRECTOR

———————

Roses are red, violets are blue
I can't write poems, but I've been told I've many other good qualities.

—GRAHAM NORTON (1963-)
IRISH COMEDIAN AND ACTOR

If a person isn't generally considered beautiful, they can still be a success if they have a few jokes in their pockets. And a lot of pockets.

—ANDY WARHOL (1928-1987)
AMERICAN ARTIST

If you can get them to laugh, that's the first step in getting them to change their opinions.

—JOHN WATERS (1946-)
AMERICAN DIRECTOR

Anything having to do with erotic life is humorous.

—GEORGE WHITMORE (1946-1989)
AMERICAN WRITER AND PLAYWRIGHT

The way I established myself, since I wasn't a great athlete, was by being funny.

—GEORGE C. WOLFE (1954-)
AFRICAN-AMERICAN PLAYWRIGHT AND DIRECTOR

IDENTITY

SEE ALSO EXISTENCE, INDIVIDUALISM, LIFE, SELF-AWARENESS, SELF-DECEPTION,

SELF-EXPRESSION, SEXUALITY

As we say in America, I wanted to find myself. This is an interesting phrase,
not current as far as I know in the language of any other people,
which certainly does not mean what it says but betrays a nagging suspicion
that something has been misplaced.

—JAMES BALDWIN (1924-1987)
AFRICAN-AMERICAN WRITER

Be natural, in order that everything may truly come from within you.

—CRISTOBAL BALENCIAGA (1895-1972)
SPANISH FASHION DESIGNER

Who speaks is not who writes, and who writes is not who is.

—ROLAND BARTHES (1915-1980)
FRENCH CRITIC AND THEORIST

There are some people whom we envy not because they are rich or
handsome or successful, although they may be any or all of these, but because
everything they are and do seems to be all of a piece.

—ELIZABETH BISHOP (1911-1979)
AMERICAN POET

Talking about oneself seems more arduous because one can't take
refuge in the role of detached witness faithfully transcribing what an
impartial observer might have remembered.

—MARIE-CLAIRE BLAIS (1939-)
CANADIAN WRITER AND PLAYWRIGHT

I attempt to be "all things to all men"; rather "cultured" among the cultured,
faintly athletic among athletes, a little blasphemous among blasphemers,
slightly insincere to myself.

—RUPERT BROOKE (1887-1915)
BRITISH POET

The deconstruction of identity is not the deconstruction of politics; rather,
it establishes as political the very terms through which identity is articulated.

—JUDITH BUTLER (1956-)
AMERICAN CRITIC AND PHILOSOPHER

"I" is myself—as well as I could find words to express myself:
But what that Self is, and what its limits may be; and therefore what the self
of any other person is and what its limits may be—I cannot tell.

—EDWARD CARPENTER (1844-1929)
BRITISH SOCIALIST POET AND GAY ACTIVIST

[One has] a sense that one is those objects and things and persons that
one perceives (and even that one is the whole universe)—a sense in which
sight and touch and hearing are all fused in identity.

—EDWARD CARPENTER (1844-1929)
BRITISH SOCIALIST POET AND GAY ACTIVIST

Who I am is not a noun, but a narrative.

—JAN CLAUSEN (ca. 1967-)
AMERICAN WRITER

God made me left-handed, God made me black, God made me gay, God made
me an artist. Now these are four things, throughout history, that people have hated.

—STANLEY BENNETT CLAY (1950-)
AFRICAN-AMERICAN PLAYWRIGHT AND PRODUCER

I'm finally emerging from my "vulgarity crisis."

—SIDONIE-GABRIELLE COLETTE (1873-1954)
FRENCH WRITER

———————

Accuracy is alien to my nature.

—QUENTIN CRISP (1908-1999)
BRITISH WRITER AND PERSONALITY

———————

Most of us have more than one choice, and I chose to be what I am, rather than remain a farm boy back in Indiana. Despite endless odds and issues along the way, I've never regretted it.

—JAMES DEAN (1931-1955)
AMERICAN ACTOR

———————

One day I'd be Marie Antoinette, the next day I'd be a nun; that was a good look.

—BOY GEORGE (1961-)
BRITISH MUSICIAN

———————

Indeed personality is itself a mask, through which the idiosyncratic sound is made, sounding through . . . personas.

—RICHARD HOWARD (1929-)
AMERICAN POET, CRITIC, AND TRANSLATOR

———————

I never thought of myself as a Russian even when I lived in Russia.
As all Jews did, I had a paragraph in my passport which read "Jewish."
People called it "5th paragraph."

—MICHAEL LUCAS (1972-)
RUSSIAN-BORN PORN PRODUCER

I don't really feel like a Rosie. Rosie is Nancy Walker selling paper towels. "Bounty, the quicker picker-upper!" Rosie is the maid on *The Jetsons*. Rosie is an elderly aunt who forces you to eat decade-old hard candies that live in the bottom of her crusty purse. No, Rosie never fit me. I feel like a Ro.

—ROSIE O'DONNELL (1962–)
AMERICAN ACTOR, COMEDIAN, AND TALK SHOW HOST

———————

It is wrong to say: I think. One ought to say: People think me.

—ARTHUR RIMBAUD (1854–1891)
FRENCH POET

———————

I am, beyond all doubt, less silly than I was six months ago. But the improvement may be only temporary.

—SIEGFRIED SASSOON (1886–1967)
BRITISH POET AND WRITER

———————

Everybody is admiring my sacrifice. But there is no sacrifice at all. I am complacent, am a glutton. . . . Do nothing and spend money on nonsense, when others are in need of necessities. Am I not a real egoist?

—PETER ILYICH TCHAIKOVSKY (1840–1893)
RUSSIAN COMPOSER

———————

It's too hard to look in the mirror. Nothing's there.

—ANDY WARHOL (1928–1987)
AMERICAN ARTIST

———————

When a straight guy goes on line as a girl, he's just discovering what we've done for years. Identity is what you make it.

—JEANETTE WINTERSON (1959–)
BRITISH WRITER

Do I contradict myself?
Very well, then I contradict myself
(I am large, I contain multitudes).

—WALT WHITMAN (1819-1892)
AMERICAN POET

Lacking flamboyance, cursed with reserve, I chose fiction, or more likely,
it was chosen for me, as the means of introducing to a disbelieving audience
the cast of contradictory characters of which I am composed.

—PATRICK WHITE (1912-1990)
AUSTRALIAN WRITER AND NOBEL LAUREATE

ILLNESS

SEE ALSO THE HUMAN BODY

Just a line to let you know that I am wounded and a prisoner in Germany. . . .
The wound is not bad, but inconvenient, being in the bottom!

—J. R. ACKERLEY (1896-1967)
BRITISH WRITER AND EDITOR

For my part I am kilt . . . by what a Methodist would call a congregation,
a bookseller compilation, and a quack a complication of disorders.

—LORD BYRON (1788-1824)
BRITISH POET

When one of us dies of cancer, loses her mind, or commits suicide, we must
not blame her for her inability to survive an ongoing political mechanism bent
on the destruction of that human being. Sanity remains defined simply by
the ability to cope with insane conditions.

—ANA CASTILLO (1953-)
CHICANA POET, NOVELIST, AND ESSAYIST

[Vitamins] used to come in the food. They don't come in the food anymore.
You have to take them. Pills, capsules, drops.

—MARLENE DIETRICH (1901–1992)
GERMAN-BORN ACTOR

———

Poor hysteria! Don't speak ill of it; it's the most amusing of illnesses.

— ANDRÉ GIDE (1869–1951)
FRENCH WRITER

———

Why do we get sick? Who is to blame for this? It would be so much easier if there
really were a patient zero, a guilty victim, one closeted gay traitor to blame, or the
African monkeys, a CIA conspiracy against homosexuals, Latinos, and blacks.

—FRANCISCO IBAÑEZ-CARRASCO (1963–)
CHILEAN-CANADIAN WRITER

———

My mother told me she had hepatitis. I looked it up in the school dictionary.
Hepatitis was a disease transmitted through dirty needles.
I vowed never to use the sewing machine.

—ROSIE O'DONNELL (1962–)
AMERICAN ACTOR, COMEDIAN, AND TALK SHOW HOST

AIDS

I'd love to have polite relations with drug companies . . . but I don't have time
to put up with the bullshit, because it's going to cost lives.

—JEFF GETTY (1957–2006)
AMERICAN AIDS ACTIVIST

The more I learned about environmental illness . . . the more I was struck
by its many parallels to AIDS. The difference is that environmental illness
has a known origin—chemicals. It is a disease that is embedded in the
very fabric of our material existence.

—TODD HAYNES (1961-)
AMERICAN FILM DIRECTOR

———————

For years I got tested for HIV every six months or so. In November of 1995
I tested negative. The next May I tested positive. And the oddest thing for me—
my immediate reaction to hearing the news that I was HIV-positive—was relief.

—MICHAEL JETER (1952-2003)
AMERICAN ACTOR

———————

And I have no doubt that AIDS was allowed to happen because of Nancy
Reagan's sex life and Ed Koch's sex life and the perception that Ron Reagan Jr.
was gay. All their sexual secrets and hypocrisy.

—LARRY KRAMER (1935-)
AMERICAN WRITER, PLAYWRIGHT, AND ACTIVIST

———————

Back in the '80s, the president had to speak about AIDS and had to speak
about using condoms, because at that time there was no information at all.
So yes he was responsible for many deaths.

—MICHAEL LUCAS (1972-)
RUSSIAN-BORN PORN PRODUCER

———————

People are very bored with AIDS. A lot of that has to do with the fact that most
people working at the networks haven't been affected by it personally.

—JOEY LOVETT (1945-)
AMERICAN DIRECTOR

After all, if homosexuality is the greatest taboo in Hispanic culture,
AIDS is the unspeakable.

—JAIME MANRIQUE (1949-)
COLUMBIAN-AMERICAN WRITER

You know, faggots are dying.

—ROBERT MAPPLETHORPE (1946-1989)
AMERICAN PHOTOGRAPHER

I was buying a suit recently and thought to myself, What the hell are you buying
a suit for, you'll probably be dead in six months? And then I thought,
Well, so you'll be a well-dressed corpse. I bought the suit.

—A. DAMIEN MARTIN (1934-1991)
AMERICAN GAY RIGHTS ACTIVIST

Some friends feel it's their duty to cheer me up. Sometimes I wish they
wouldn't do that. Sometimes in their attempt to avoid talking about AIDS,
it becomes like a turd in the center of the table.

—PAUL MONETTE (1945-1995)
AMERICAN WRITER AND AIDS ACTIVIST

Fortunately I am not the first person to tell you that you will never die. You simply
lose your body. You will be the same except you won't have to worry about rent
or mortgages or fashionable clothes. You will be released from sexual obsessions.
You will not have drug addictions. You will not need alcohol. You will not have to
worry about cellulite or cigarettes or cancer or AIDS or venereal disease.
You will be free.

—COOKIE MUELLER (1949-1989)
AMERICAN ACTOR AND WRITER

We appear to be dying from the very pleasure we wanted to educate the world about.

—GABRIEL ROTELLO (1953-)
AMERICAN WRITER AND FILMMAKER

AIDS was and still is associated with two hated minorities: the faggots and the Africans. This administration would love it if they all died. And so you're up against ignorance and stupidity and malevolence, which is how I would describe our current government.

—GORE VIDAL (1925-)
AMERICAN WRITER AND POLITICAL ACTIVIST

It's one thing to think, We all went through this [AIDS] together and survived it, and here's my story of what I went through. It's going to be another thing to have nobody want to read those stories.

—EDMUND WHITE (1940-)
AMERICAN WRITER AND CRITIC

I think there will be people over 30 now who have survived and who will feel themselves becoming more and more marginalized by younger people who aren't as aware of the whole [AIDS] battle.

—EDMUND WHITE (1940-)
AMERICAN WRITER AND CRITIC

CANCER

Millions and millions of dollars have been raised [for breast cancer], but why are we still sick? . . . Considerable resources are spent each year to encourage women to make changes in their personal lives that might reduce the risk of breast cancer, but many factors that contribute to the disease lie far beyond a woman's personal control.

—BARBARA BRENNER (1952-)
AMERICAN BREAST CANCER ACTIVIST

Generally, you get up in the morning, you fix your makeup, you do your hair. . . .
But when you have cancer it gets to the point where you have nothing to do:
You have no eyelashes, no eyebrows, no hair—and I'm a person
with a ton of hair. It's almost like being reborn.

—GINNY DIXON (1961-)
PULITZER PRIZE-WINNING PHOTOGRAPHER

It was very hard. It was the hardest thing I've ever done in my life. Chemotherapy
tests your sanity. Yet there is an amazing clarity to it that I'm grateful for.

—MELISSA ETHERIDGE (1961-)
AMERICAN GRAMMY AWARD-WINNING MUSICIAN AND BREAST CANCER ACTIVIST

I always wanted to know why tumors were constantly compared to fruits,
generally of the citrus variety.

—DAVID B. FEINBERG (1956-1994)
AMERICAN WRITER AND ACTIVIST

I was the only 21-year-old I knew who had breast cancer.

—TANIA KATAN (1971-)
AMERICAN PLAYWRIGHT

HOSPITALS

Hospitals are places that you have to stay in for a long time, even if you are a
visitor. Time doesn't seem to pass in the same way in hospitals as it does in other
places. Time seems to almost not exist in the same way as it does in other places.

—PEDRO ALMODOVAR (1951-)
SPANISH FILM DIRECTOR

The only people who know anything about medical science are the nurses, and they never tell; they'd get slapped if they did. But the great doctor, he's a divine idiot.

—DJUNA BARNES (1892–1982)
AMERICAN WRITER

MENTAL ILLNESS

I don't know that I shan't end with insanity, for I find a want of method in arranging my thoughts that perplexes me strangely; but this looks more like silliness than madness.

—LORD BYRON (1788–1824)
BRITISH POET

———

I always thought of myself as a kind of two-headed calf. . . . I've never been psychoanalyzed; I've never even consulted a psychiatrist. I now consider myself a mentally healthy person. I work out all my problems in my work.

—TRUMAN CAPOTE (1924–1984)
AMERICAN WRITER

———

I like insane people, I know how to talk to them. . . . I never contradict them, therefore madmen like me.

—VASLAV NIJINSKY (1890–1950)
RUSSIAN DANCER

———

On a good day I think I'm a relatively sane person with a few frayed wires. On a bad day I think, Just lock me up.

—ROSIE O'DONNELL (1962–)
AMERICAN ACTOR, COMEDIAN, AND TALK SHOW HOST

IMAGINATION

SEE ALSO ART AND ARTISTS, CREATION AND CREATIVITY, THOUGHT

The imagination is the only thing worth a damn.

—HART CRANE (1899-1932)
AMERICAN POET

———————

I just think it's one of the dilemmas of the human condition. We are capable of imagining more than we can possibly produce.

—MICHAEL CUNNINGHAM (1952-)
AMERICAN PULITZER PRIZE-WINNING WRITER

———————

There are no tendencies worth anything but to see the actual or the imaginative, which is just as visible, and to paint it.

—HENRY JAMES (1843-1916)
AMERICAN WRITER

———————

Imagination is a Divine gift, as was the Bacchic vine; but each can intoxicate the heedless, and so enslave where it should serve.

—WALTER PATER (1839-1894)
BRITISH CRITIC AND WRITER

———————

I'm just not that fascinating a person to have had all those lives that I've written about.

—MICHAEL STIPE (1960-)
AMERICAN MUSICIAN

But in the case of an artist, weakness is nothing less than a crime, when it is a weakness that paralyses the imagination.

—OSCAR WILDE (1854-1900)
IRISH PLAYWRIGHT AND WRITER

INDIVIDUALISM

SEE ALSO EXISTENCE, IDENTITY, LIFE, SELF-AWARENESS, SELF-DECEPTION,

SELF-EXPRESSION, SEXUALITY

As individuals we do not act; we exhibit behavior characteristic of the biological species and social group or groups to which we belong . . . [But] as persons, who can, now and again, truthfully say I, we are called into being.

—W. H. AUDEN (1907-1973)
ANGLO-AMERICAN POET AND CRITIC

Sentiment, poetry, romance, religion are but mists of our own fancies, too weak for the great nature-forces of individuality and sexual emotion. They only obscure the issue.

—RUPERT BROOKE (1887-1915)
BRITISH POET

Every now and then you run into the assumption that if one person is committed others will commit themselves, following suit, as it were. This is implicit in the current activities involving civil disobedience, to say nothing of education, apprenticeship, and the whole rigmarole. Do we then measure our success by how much we reduce the human race to sheeplikeness?

—JOHN CAGE (1934-1992)
AMERICAN COMPOSER

Are we really separate individuals, or is individuality an illusion, or again is it only a part of the ego or soul that is individual, and not the whole?

—EDWARD CARPENTER (1844-1929)
BRITISH SOCIALIST POET AND GAY ACTIVIST

I seem destined to a truculent eccentricity, whether I wish it or no.

—SALVADOR DALÍ (1904-1989)
SPANISH ARTIST

Individualism leads to hierarchy, which leads to aggression; so I think just the masculine sensibility is not enough to guide us to peace.

—ANI DIFRANCO (1970-)
AMERICAN SINGER-SONGWRITER

You cultivate your strangeness, and then in order not to be ashamed of it you congratulate yourself on not feeling like all the rest.

—ANDRÉ GIDE (1869-1951)
FRENCH WRITER

For the sake of an act, by which only individual pleasure is produced and not a fly in the cosmos is harmed, the state martyrs productive citizens; it shatters flourishing existences.

—KURT HILLER (1885-1972)
JEWISH WRITER AND PACIFIST

We pay high prices for the maintenance of the myth of the Individual.

—TONY KUSHNER (1956-)
AMERICAN PLAYWRIGHT

INTELLIGENCE AND INTELLECTUALS

SEE ALSO GENIUS

The term "intellectual," without qualification of some sort, is in disrepute.

—WILLIAM BURROUGHS (1914-1997)
AMERICAN WRITER

————

I excuse ignorance but I abhor innocence.

—FRANCISCO IBAÑEZ-CARRASCO (1963-)
CHILEAN-CANADIAN WRITER

————

Nothing is my last word about anything—I am interminably super-subtle and analytic. . . . It will take a much cleverer person than myself to discover my last impression . . . of anything.

—HENRY JAMES (1843-1916)
AMERICAN WRITER

————

Purely intellectual thoughts have a soothing effect after embittered brooding on the cheap humbuggery of politics.

—THOMAS MANN (1875-1955)
GERMAN WRITER

————

I know all about ivory towers. An ivory tower is a place into which a man will retire to think of the world in general and himself in particular.

—W. SOMERSET MAUGHAM (1874-1965)
BRITISH WRITER AND PLAYWRIGHT

Intelligence prevents people from developing.

—VASLAV NIJINSKY (1890-1950)
RUSSIAN DANCER

————————

There's simple-minded, and there's simple, and there's a big difference. . . .
"Simple" is really hard to do.

—STEPHEN SONDHEIM (1930-)
AMERICAN MUSICAL THEATER COMPOSER AND PLAYWRIGHT

————————

A man who sets up at the age of twenty-one to be a man of letters exposes
himself to other risks, moreover. He may easily drift into sloth and
dilettantism and self-indulgence.

—JOHN ADDINGTON SYMONDS (1840-1893)
ENGLISH POET AND CRITIC

INTIMACY

SEE ALSO FANTASIES, FRIENDS AND FRIENDSHIP, RELATIONSHIPS, ROMANCE, SEX

I find affectionate contact almost as satisfactory without sex. . . .
I certainly feel a definite need for non-sexual intimacy.
I don't mean necessarily non-sexual, you understand.

—WILLIAM BURROUGHS (1914-1997)
AMERICAN WRITER

————————

The most, the best, we can do, we believe (wanting to give
evidence of love), is to get out of the way, leave space around whomever
or whatever it is. But there is no space!

—JOHN CAGE (1934-1992)
AMERICAN COMPOSER

We all have our own personal scales of intimacy. Perhaps mine was skewed?
It ranged from such relatively impersonal contact like shaking someone's hands,
greeting them on the street, having violent and profound sex with them,
exchanging first names, sharing recreational drugs with them. . . .
Sleeping with someone was rather low on my scale of familiarity.

—DAVID B. FEINBERG (1956-1994)
AMERICAN WRITER AND ACTIVIST

The whole process of intimacy is very difficult, especially when you have two
individuals who want to fulfill themselves. In the old-fashioned kind of relationship,
each one had a role and things were clearer and more absolute.

—IVRI LIDER (1974-)
ISRAELI MUSICIAN

The society of another fellow-creature is only pleasant when a long-standing intimacy, or common interests, make it possible to dispense with all effort. Unless this
is the case, society is a burden which I was never intended by nature to endure.

—PETER ILYICH TCHAIKOVSKY (1840-1893)
RUSSIAN COMPOSER

Sex is synonymous not with physical release but with a frightening intimacy.
Cumming is the final sign of accepting that intimacy.

—GEORGE WHITMORE (1946-1989)
AMERICAN WRITER AND PLAYWRIGHT

Pain . . . is no doubt the first stage of intimacy.

—VIRGINIA WOOLF (1882-1941)
BRITISH WRITER

JOURNALISM

SEE ALSO ART AND ARTISTS, CRITICS AND CRITICISM, MEDIA, WRITING

Cocktail-party chatter and journalism in the pejorative sense are two aspects of the same disease, what the Bible calls idle words.

—W. H. AUDEN (1907-1973)
ANGLO-AMERICAN POET AND CRITIC

There is no liberal movement that blackballs journalists in the sense that there is a self-identified, hardwired conservative movement that can function as a kind of neo-Stalinist thought police that rivals anything I knew at Berkeley.

—DAVID BROCK (1962-)
CONSERVATIVE JOURNALIST

This press persecution of me is bound to amount to very little; they invariably go off at half-cock and destroy their own efforts by their own inaccuracy.

—NOËL COWARD (1899-1973)
BRITISH ACTOR AND PLAYWRIGHT

A peculiarly atrocious and vulgar form of modern torture—the assault of the newspaper—[is one] which all civilized and decent people are equally interested in resisting the blackguardism of.

—HENRY JAMES (1843-1916)
AMERICAN WRITER

Nothing makes sense to me. I have stopped reading the *New York Times*: It's all gossip, fashion, and obscene cruelty I have no power to change.

—CRAIG LUCAS (1951-)
AMERICAN PLAYWRIGHT AND DIRECTOR

Oh! Journalism is unreadable, and literature is not read.

—OSCAR WILDE (1854-1900)
IRISH PLAYWRIGHT AND WRITER

JUDGMENT

SEE ALSO CRITICS AND CRITICISM

Why cannot someone who is looking at something do his own work of looking?

—JOHN CAGE (1934-1992)
AMERICAN COMPOSER

To spot when it's faked and when it's good your senses must be constantly alert. You've got to have complete faith in your own reactions, for better or for worse, so that you can make snap judgments, then and there.

—GEORGE CUKOR (1899-1983)
AMERICAN FILM DIRECTOR

It's really dangerous to judge an image—to say this is a good image, this is a bad image. There are so many ways of reading an image.

—JEFFREY FRIEDMAN (ca. 1960-)
AMERICAN FILM DIRECTOR

Sometimes when you're being quick to judge, you don't notice the delicacy or softness or transient gracefulness of what is around you. In the overexcited mental turmoil of constantly having to judge every thought and perception, you might miss some of the luminousness of the phenomenal world or even not notice some of your own thoughts or feelings.

—ALLEN GINSBERG (1926-1997)
AMERICAN POET

But if you do not even understand what words say,
how can you expect to pass judgement
on what words conceal?

—H. D., BORN HILDA DOOLITTLE (1886–1961)
AMERICAN ESSAYIST, NOVELIST, AND POET

————————

The biggest thing I've achieved in my life is learning that it doesn't matter
if other people approve of me. . . . And I found that out by reading
the words of other gay writers.

—ZACK LINMARK (1968–)
FILIPINO WRITER

————————

Every judgment of relative value is a mere statement of facts and can therefore be
put in such a form that it loses all the appearance of a judgment of value.

—LUDWIG WITTGENSTEIN (1889–1951)
AUSTRIAN PHILOSOPHER

LANGUAGE

SEE ALSO COMMUNICATION, JOURNALISM, LITERATURE, MEDIA, POETRY
UNDERSTANDING, THOUGHT, WRITING

Language is more important than meaning.

—KATHY ACKER (1947-1997)
AMERICAN WRITER

———————

There is no more beautiful word in the language than withered.

—JUNE ARNOLD (1926-1982)
AMERICAN WRITER

———————

Why is language necessary when art so to speak already has it in it?

—JOHN CAGE (1934-1992)
AMERICAN COMPOSER

———————

One of the joys of the English language is that you can play around with the
meaning of words. I don't think it works so well in Spanish.

—JULIAN CLARY (1959-)
BRITISH COMEDIAN

———————

In addition to the meaning words have, they possess a magical power, a charm,
a form of hypnosis, a fluid which functions outside of meaning.

—JEAN COCTEAU (1889-1963)
FRENCH WRITER AND FILMMAKER

———————

I think using four-letter words is not very witty.

—GEORGE CUKOR (1899-1983)
AMERICAN FILM DIRECTOR

I refuse to be a prisoner of verbal automatism.

—JEAN GENET (1910-1986)
FRENCH WRITER, CRIMINAL, AND POLITICAL ACTIVIST

I'm experiencing it now in these FCC regulations, okay? We're experiencing it now, the octopus of the state intruding on our language consciousness.

—ALLEN GINSBERG (1926-1997)
AMERICAN POET

Translation is a very different involvement with a language than merely reading, speaking, even living your life in it.

—MARILYN HACKER (1942-)
FEMINIST POET, CRITIC, AND ACTIVIST

Translation is an effort—though a most flattering one!—to tear the hapless flesh, and in fact to get rid of so much of it that the living thing bleeds and faints away!

—HENRY JAMES (1843-1916)
AMERICAN WRITER

Metaphor links two antagonistic worlds by an equestrian leap of imagination.

—FEDERICO GARCIA LORCA (1898-1936)
SPANISH POET AND PLAYWRIGHT

One doesn't particularly notice that the language is being preserved or purified, no matter how busily the poets function. I know one thing: worrying about it helps not at all.

—JAMES MERRILL (1926-1995)
AMERICAN PULITZER PRIZE-WINNING POET

If you open a book of poetry, you can see the style immediately,
the rhymes and all that: you see the language as an instrument.

—PIER PAOLO PASOLINI (1922-1975)
ITALIAN FILM DIRECTOR

Metaphor alone gives a semblance of eternity to style.

—MARCEL PROUST (1871-1922)
FRENCH WRITER

If there is one thing in this world that astonishes me more than another,
it is the rapidity with which some people talk in French.

—CHARLES WARREN STODDARD (1843-1909)
AMERICAN TRAVEL WRITER

I have also been punished and slapped and chastised because of the
clipped way I speak. To some people, it's clear diction.
To my old neighborhood folks, it was impudence.

—ETHEL WATERS (1896-1977)
AFRICAN-AMERICAN ACTOR AND MUSICIAN

Words and chess pieces are analogous; knowing how to use a word is
like knowing how to move a chess piece. . . . What is the difference between
playing the game and aimlessly moving the pieces?

—LUDWIG WITTGENSTEIN (1889-1951)
AUSTRIAN PHILOSOPHER

LESBIANS

SEE ALSO FEMISIM, GAY COMMUNITY, GAY ICONS, GAY MARRIAGE, GAY PRIDE, GAY
RIGHTS, GAYS VS. LESBIANS, GAYS VS. STRAIGHTS, GENDER BENDING,
HOMOSEXUALITY, QUEERNESS, S&M, WOMEN

Gay women, out or not, have been brilliant comedians because their
point of view is twisted.

—JANE ANDERSON (1954-)
AMERICAN ACTOR AND DIRECTOR

———————

Well, there is a lot of "dyke drama," I have to say, having lived my share.
There is that.

—AMANDA BEARSE (1958-)
AMERICAN ACTOR

———————

Susie Bright is like a *Good Housekeeping* seal of approval . . .
for really good lesbian sex.

—SUSIE BRIGHT (1958-)
AMERICAN FEMINIST AND SEX EDUCATOR

———————

I found myself telling my friends beforehand that I was off to Yale to be a lesbian,
which of course didn't mean that I wasn't one before, but that somehow then,
as I spoke in that context, I was one in some more thorough and totalizing way,
at least for the time being.

—JUDITH BUTLER (1956-)
AMERICAN CRITIC AND PHILOSOPHER

———————

Of course I like dykes themselves. They don't scare me a bit. But stories about
dykes bore the bejesus out of me. I just can't put myself in their shoes.

—TRUMAN CAPOTE (1924-1984)
AMERICAN WRITER

Leaving a woman for a man . . . is still the lesbian equivalent of a mortal sin.

—JAN CLAUSEN (ca. 1947–)
AMERICAN WRITER

––––––––––

Some lesbians curse the power of sexual imagery without ever examining what that power means to lesbians.

—JEWELLE GOMEZ (1948–)
AFRICAN-AMERICAN WRITER, POET, AND ACTIVIST

––––––––––

As Mr. Lesbian says: "Is that a gun in your pocket, or do you always carry zucchini home that way?"

—JANIS IAN (1951–)
AMERICAN GRAMMY AWARD-WINNING MUSICIAN

––––––––––

All my life I've loved women, and that's it. I've never been any other way.

—LINDA PERRY (1965–)
AMERICAN MUSICIAN

––––––––––

I do not care for the best man that ever walked, and never will. Ida is the only one I ever loved and I will continue to love her until I die, and if we are not allowed to go together I will kill myself and her, too.

—DELIA PERKINS (ca. 1880–ca. 1900)
AMERICAN ARRESTED AS A TEENAGER IN 1893 FOR RUNNING AWAY WITH IDA PRESTON

––––––––––

I don't use a vibrator. . . . I use a Harley-Davidson.

—KAREN RIPLEY (ca. 1960–)
AMERICAN COMEDIAN

The women's bar was kind of weird and taboo, and no one went. That was a whole separate world.

—JILL SOBULE (1961-)
AMERICAN SINGER-SONGWRITER

It's time for lesbian feminists to be more vocal about our existence.
Our future is intimately tied to that of gay men, bisexuals, and transgendered people, but most importantly it is tied to our struggle as women.

—URVASHI VAID (1958-)
AMERICAN GAY RIGHTS ACTIVIST

The 1970s revival in pop culture contains a curious omission: any mention of lesbian-feminist culture, even though it invented so much of what is quintessentially '70s.

—URVASHI VAID (1958-)
AMERICAN GAY RIGHTS ACTIVIST

I've never been to bed with a man. Never. That's how pure I am;
I have nothing to be ashamed of.

—CHAVELA VARGAS (1919-)
COSTA-RICAN MUSICIAN

I'm like, "We're two attractive lesbians, we make out, we fight, we bite—
what more do you want?"

—JACKIE WARNER (1968-)
AMERICAN REALITY TV STAR AND CELEBRITY TRAINER

I also have a soft spot for novels in which the lesbians are completely horrible to each other, or end up dead.

—SARAH WATERS (1966-)
BRITISH WRITER

Le Corps Lesbian has lesbianism as its theme, that is a theme which cannot even be described as taboo, for it has no real existence in the history of literature. Male homosexual literature has a past, it has a present. The lesbians, for their part, are silent—just as all women are as women at all levels.

—MONIQUE WITTIG (1935-2003)
FRENCH FEMINIST AND WRITER

BUTCH LESBIANS

I happen to be a butch lesbian, but I know butch heterosexuals too.

—CRIN CLAXTON (ca. 1970-)
BRITISH WRITER OF EROTICA

———

Those goddamned lesbians are going crazy, cutting off their hair. . . . I don't want to take nothing to bed that looks like me, walks like me, or talks like me.

—MARLA GLEN (1960-)
AMERICAN MUSICIAN

———

We manly gals may get grief on the street for looking like high-school boys, but—praise Jesus—at least we don't look like Howard Stern when we get in front of a camera.

—RACHEL MADDOW (1973-)
AMERICAN RADIO TALK SHOW HOST

LIFE

SEE ALSO DEATH, DOUBLE LIVES, EXISTENCE, EXPERIENCE

The very fact of being born is a very ferocious thing, just existence itself as one goes between birth and death.

—FRANCIS BACON (1909-1992)
BRITISH ARTIST

Life would be very boring if it didn't have sordid elements.

—DIRK BOGARDE (1921-1999)
BRITISH ACTOR AND WRITER

———

Life is a burden. There are too many questions I can't find an answer to.

—RUPERT BROOKE (1887-1915)
BRITISH POET

———

I don't think it's possible to go through life, unless you're a complete idiot,
without being continuously hurt one way or another.

—TRUMAN CAPOTE (1924-1984)
AMERICAN WRITER

———

Birth is a crime
All men commit.

—COUNTEE CULLEN (1903-1946)
AFRICAN-AMERICAN POET

———

You can't talk about the meaning of life without using phony words.
Imprecise ones. But there aren't any others.

—RAINER WERNER FASSBINDER (1945-1982)
GERMAN DIRECTOR

———

Life is not all nonsense and cruelty—the inversion of Victorian complacency—
but has hard spots of sense and love bobbing about in it here and there.

—E. M. FORSTER (1879-1970)
BRITISH WRITER

When the highs and lows are so far apart, it's hard to stay in the middle and think of yourself as a good person.

—ALLAN GURGANUS (1947-)
AMERICAN WRITER

There's nothing glamorous about it when people still refer to being gay as a lifestyle and not a life.

—E. LYNN HARRIS (1955-)
AFRICAN-AMERICAN WRITER

No one should be born who can't meet life somehow decently.

—MARSDEN HARTLEY (1877-1943)
AMERICAN ARTIST

It gets to the point where you say either I keep going or I go under. At that point life becomes very simple . . . if you reduce life to that, to "I have no money, I have no prospects, I have two guitars," life becomes very simple.

—JANIS IAN (1951-)
AMERICAN GRAMMY AWARD-WINNING MUSICIAN

As artists and workers, we owe most to those who bring to us most of human life.

—HENRY JAMES (1843-1916)
AMERICAN WRITER

When you think you can deal with life by holding rigid views, then life will laugh right back at you. Rigidity creates difficulty and a couple whose relationship derives from such a stance won't last.

—IVRI LIDER (1974-)
ISRAELI MUSICIAN

We are powerful because we have survived, and that is what it is all about—
survival and growth.

—AUDRE LORDE (1934-1992)
AFRICAN-AMERICAN WRITER, POET, AND ACTIVIST

If I have to change my lifestyle, I don't want to live.

—ROBERT MAPPLETHORPE (1946-1989)
AMERICAN PHOTOGRAPHER

Life's been rather like a party that was very nice to start with but has become
rather noisy as time went on. And I'm not at all sorry to go home. . . .
But I wish I could believe that I shall go home.

—W. SOMERSET MAUGHAM (1874-1965)
BRITISH WRITER AND PLAYWRIGHT

Why be alive if you can't like the battle of measuring your contempt or
indifference or interest against that of others?

—ROBERT MCALMON (1896-1956)
AMERICAN WRITER AND PUBLISHER

I contemplate young mountaineers hung with ropes and ice-axes,
and think that they alone have understood how to live life . . .

—VITA SACKVILLE-WEST (1892-1962)
BRITISH POET, NOVELIST, AND GARDENER

I might pass to-day over with "nothing much happened."
Nothing much! Life is woven of nothing muches.

—SIEGFRIED SASSOON (1886-1967)
BRITISH POET AND WRITER

I think life itself is an epiphany.

—AIDEN SHAW (1966-)
BRITISH PORN STAR

———————

The idea of this remorse is: Life passes, is coming to an end while
I have reached no conclusions; I banish vital problems, or run away
from them when they arise. Is that how I live?

—PETER ILYICH TCHAIKOVSKY (1840-1893)
RUSSIAN COMPOSER

———————

In my youth I found it hard to reconcile life and art; if I did,
I think I suspected I was committing an insincerity.

—PATRICK WHITE (1912-1990)
AUSTRALIAN WRITER AND NOBEL LAUREATE

———————

In life there is really no small or great thing.
All things are of equal value and equal size.

—OSCAR WILDE (1854-1900)
IRISH PLAYWRIGHT AND WRITER

MEANING OF LIFE

You can't talk about the meaning of life without using phony words.
Imprecise ones. But there aren't any others.

—RAINER WERNER FASSBINDER (1945-1982)
GERMAN DIRECTOR

If you're writing a story, you can sort of ramble on and go in a lot of directions at once, but when you are getting to the end of the story, you have to start pointing all the things toward one thing. That's the point that I'm at now, not knowing where it stops but knowing how important it is to do it now.

−KEITH HARING (1958-1990)
AMERICAN ARTIST AND ACTIVIST

The desire to say something about the ultimate meaning of life, the absolute good, the absolute valuable, can be no science. What it says does not add to our knowledge in any sense. But it is a document of a tendency in the human mind which I personally cannot help respecting deeply and I would not for my life ridicule it.

−LUDWIG WITTGENSTEIN (1889-1951)
AUSTRIAN PHILOSOPHER

LIMITATIONS

Man can have everything, but he can keep nothing.

−DJUNA BARNES (1892-1982)
AMERICAN WRITER

Be adventurous, but, of course, with some sense of reality.
You shouldn't say, "There's nothing I can't do," because you know damn well there are things you can't.

−GEORGE CUKOR (1899-1983)
AMERICAN FILM DIRECTOR

Our limitations are a curse and a blessing.

−MICHAEL STIPE (1960-)
AMERICAN MUSICIAN

LITERATURE

SEE ALSO ART AND ARTISTS, LANGUAGE, POETRY, WRITING

Look at the Oprah list. I think she created a brand-name literature that is actually substantial and educated an audience that would not have reached for those books. A lot of her audience would have reached for romances and mysteries. And that's wonderful and that's pop culture too.

—DOROTHY ALLISON (1942-)
AMERICAN WRITER

———————

Literature is like phosphorus.

—ROLAND BARTHES (1915-1980)
FRENCH CRITIC AND THEORIST

———————

Those who fail to reread are obliged to read the same story everywhere.

—ROLAND BARTHES (1915-1980)
FRENCH CRITIC AND THEORIST

———————

I sometimes have the sense that I live my life as a writer with my nose pressed against the wide, shiny plate glass window of the "mainstream" culture. The world seems full of straight, large-circulation, slick periodicals which wouldn't think of reviewing my book and bookstores which will never order it.

—JAN CLAUSEN (ca. 1947-)
AMERICAN WRITER

———————

We are all sick and can read only those books which treat our disease. This explains the success of love stories.

—JEAN COCTEAU (1889-1963)
FRENCH WRITER AND FILMMAKER

Am reading more of Oscar Wilde. What a tiresome, affected sod.

—NOËL COWARD (1899-1973)
BRITISH ACTOR AND PLAYWRIGHT

———

[On starting a literary magazine] I pray you invest your hard-earned money in neckties, theatre tickets, or something else good for the belly or the soul, —but don't throw it away in paper and inefficient typography.

—HART CRANE (1899-1932)
AMERICAN POET

———

I'm always suspicious of people who can't think of a book they like.

—DAVID SEDARIS (1956-)
AMERICAN WRITER

———

Hemingway, remarks are not literature.

—GERTRUDE STEIN (1874-1946)
AMERICAN EXPATRIATE WRITER

———

Growing up in Nevada, which was a very quiet environment, I think, well, I think we grew up entertaining ourselves with books. I've always been a voracious reader. And, of course, in Nevada there's not a lot to do so I at an early age I started picking out books and entertaining myself that way.

—JOSH WESTON (ca. 1980-)
AMERICAN PORN STAR

GAY LIT

It seems just about as pointless to separate the gay books in a bookstore as it does to separate the books written by women from the books written by men.

—MICHAEL CUNNINGHAM (1952-)
AMERICAN PULITZER PRIZE-WINNING WRITER

It seems that any gay book worth anything at all must be accompanied by its author going out and meeting the press and the people. I hope this won't be necessary in the future, but as gay literature is still a hotly disputed subject—the *New York Times*, for example, doesn't believe it exists—such promotion is probably a good thing.

— FELICE PICANO (1944-)
AMERICAN WRITER

———————

People have been writing non-gay stories for three thousand years, and we've got a lot of catching up to do.

— FELICE PICANO (1944-)
AMERICAN WRITER

———————

[On gay fiction] What on earth is that? Does that mean the book only hangs out with other books?

—GORE VIDAL (1925-)
AMERICAN WRITER AND POLITICAL ACTIVIST

———————

Anthologies [of lesbian writing] are a gratifying escape from the advertising-induced conclusion that all lesbians are as bland as k.d. lang's last album.

—JOHN WEIR (ca. 1966-)
AMERICAN SCHOLAR AND WRITER

———————

Every year, the straight press drags some timeworn fag writer out of storage and gets him to stand for everyone in America who has ever had a homosexual feeling. Usually it's Ed White's job.

—JOHN WEIR (ca. 1966-)
AMERICAN SCHOLAR AND WRITER

LOVE

SEE ALSO FAMILY, FRIENDS AND FRIENDSHIPS, GAY MARRIAGE, MARRIAGE,
RELATIONSHIPS, ROMANCE, SEX

I think that "generosity" has always existed, although I do not label it as such.
It's really my life. It is not even part of my life. It is my life itself. . . .
It is probably the closest thing to being in love.

—PEDRO ALMODOVAR (1951-)
SPANISH FILM DIRECTOR

———————

The trouble is, we all think that Christ said "Love thy neighbor.". . .
But in fact he said, "Love thy neighbor as thyself," which is completely different.
If you can't love yourself, you end up saying "beat me."

—MICHAEL ARDITTI (ca. 1960-)
BRITISH WRITER

———————

I began to rue th' unhappy sight
Of that faire Boy that had my hart intangled;
Cursing the Time, the Place, the sense, the sin;
I came, I saw, I viewd, I slipped in.

—RICHARD BARNFIELD (1574-1627)
BRITISH POET

———————

Love becomes the deposit of the heart, analogous in all degrees
to the "findings" in a tomb.

—DJUNA BARNES (1892-1982)
AMERICAN WRITER

At the same time, as you look at your own spiritual health, you don't want to be a bastard. I've been very selfish. . . . To love someone [is] giving and not expecting anything in return.

—ANDY BELL (1964-)
BRITISH MUSICIAN

You are alive for one purpose. To love. Don't let anything—anyone— any idea—get in the way of that insight. Learn about love by not being afraid of being alive. Learn about love by taking risks with it. Look at the person ahead of you in line at the grocery store and imagine what a person who loves them sees. And never forget to look at your lovers the same way.

—TOM BIANCHI (1945-)
AMERICAN PHOTOGRAPHER

He who loves does not sleep.

—MICHELANGELO BUONARROTI (1475-1564)
ITALIAN PAINTER, SCULPTOR, POET, AND ENGINEER

Love—romantic attachments for things marketable for a dollar!

—LORD BYRON (1788-1824)
BRITISH POET

Love should be allowed. I'm all for it. Now that I've got a pretty good idea what it is.

—TRUMAN CAPOTE (1924-1984)
AMERICAN WRITER

Of course it is the return of devotion [that] astounds me so, and the real certainty that, at least for the time, it is perfectly honest.

—HART CRANE (1899-1932)
AMERICAN POET

So many ways love has none may appear
The bitter best, and none the sweetest worst.

—COUNTEE CULLEN (1903-1946)
AFRICAN-AMERICAN POET

———

And if I please you so, my lover,
Remember praise is comely.

—COUNTEE CULLEN (1903-1946)
AFRICAN-AMERICAN POET

———

Love is Lucy van Pelt, Charlie Brown, and that goddamned football. Every
autumn, Lucy convinces Charlie Brown that she won't pull it away at the last
minute. . . . He kicks the air and falls flat on his back. Charlie Brown is in traction
for months; he is psychologically paralyzed for life. Yet he persists in learning
nothing from the experience, repeating it the following fall.

—DAVID B. FEINBERG (1956-1994)
AMERICAN WRITER AND ACTIVIST

———

Since this is a hard and sad truth for the telling; those whom nature has sacrificed
to her ends—her mysterious ends that often lie hidden—are sometimes endowed
with a vast will to loving, with an endless capacity for suffering also, which must
go hand in hand with their love.

—RADCLYFFE HALL (1880-1943)
BRITISH NOVELIST AND POET

———

The more deeply we study the physiology of love the better we are able to judge
what things should be regarded as advantageous and what are disadvantageous,
what are harmful and what are not.

—MAGNUS HIRSCHFELD (1868-1935)
GERMAN SEXOLOGIST AND PIONEER GAY RIGHTS ACTIVIST

It was a democracy such as the world—with its rewards and penalties, its competition, its snobbery—never permits, but which flourished in this little room on the twelfth floor of a factory building on West Thirty-Third Street, because its central principle was the most anarchic of all: erotic love.

—ANDREW HOLLERAN (1944-)
AMERICAN WRITER

I don't have a lover, but I have many loves.

—DAVE KOPAY (1942-)
AMERICAN NFL FOOTBALL PLAYER

I believe in love. I believe in altruism, though I'm unable to practice it myself.

—W. SOMERSET MAUGHAM (1874-1965)
BRITISH WRITER AND PLAYWRIGHT

[I wrote poetry] as if I were writing for someone who could only love me a great deal. I understand now why I have been the object of so much suspicion and hatred.

—PIER PAOLO PASOLINI (1922-1975)
ITALIAN FILM DIRECTOR

A lover keeps his eye on the balance sheet—where his interests have suffered from love, and where he has done well; and when he adds up all the trouble he has taken, he thinks he's long since given the boy he loved a fair return.

— PLATO (427-347 BC)
GREEK PHILOSOPHER

It is better to give your favors to someone who does not love you than to someone who does.

— PLATO (427-347 BC)
GREEK PHILOSOPHER

You should feel sorry for lovers, not admire them.

— PLATO (427-347 BC)
GREEK PHILOSOPHER

Isn't it possible that wanting to be wanted . . . or "loved" . . . could be as much an aspect of what you call "love" as actually loving back?

—JOHN RECHY (1934-)
AMERICAN WRITER

"Love" has ceased to be an adventure into Elysium; it never travels further than Chelsea.

—SIEGFRIED SASSOON (1886-1967)
BRITISH POET AND WRITER

Masturbation, homosexuality, following people in the streets, breaking up relationships because one has failed in one's own, all these compensatory activities form a circle of Hell in which people can never rest from proving that their failures are the same as love.

—STEPHEN SPENDER (1909-1995)
BRITISH POET AND WRITER

Valentine's Day—what the world needs now is love sweet love; more love and pleasure, sex; a more pleasure-filled, happy, sexy world.

—ANNIE SPRINKLE (1954-)
AMERICAN PERFORMANCE ARTIST AND SEX EDUCATOR

Love is giving yourself away. And you can only do that once. Otherwise you're giving away fragments of yourself.

—DANIEL TAMMET (1979-)
BRITISH AUTISTIC SAVANT

I have loved much in my life. Far too much? Oh no, decidedly not! For love you see . . . [is] practically the sole motive of every action worthy of the name. Don't speak to me of other things: ambition, lucre, glory! At most you might perhaps mention Art. And yet, and yet, Art, all by itself?

−PAUL VERLAINE (1844-1896)

FRENCH POET

I sometimes had the experience of loving someone as though we shared each other's dreams.

−STEPHEN SPENDER (1909-1995)

BRITISH POET AND WRITER

Love of some kind is the only possible explanation of the extraordinary amount of suffering that there is in the world.

−OSCAR WILDE (1854-1900)

IRISH PLAYWRIGHT AND WRITER

MAGIC

What's marvelous is that the moon still rises even though we've changed our minds about whether or not we'll ever get there.

—JOHN CAGE (1934-1992)
AMERICAN COMPOSER

———————

For magic beliefs are immensely strong, I think, if only their essential fragility is respected. It's a paradox.

—TONY KUSHNER (1956-)
AMERICAN PLAYWRIGHT

———————

The blind are happiest in the realm of the mystical, where light can be infinite, a landscape without real objects, open to the great cross-winds of wisdom.

—FEDERICO GARCIA LORCA (1898-1936)
SPANISH POET AND PLAYWRIGHT

———————

The magician, yes, performs the essential act. He heals what he has divided. A double-edged action, like his sword. It's what one comes to feel that life keeps doing.

—JAMES MERRILL (1926-1995)
AMERICAN PULITZER PRIZE-WINNING POET

———————

Don't you think there comes a time when everyone, not just a poet, wants to get beyond the self? To reach, if you like, the "god" within you? The [Ouija] board, in however clumsy or absurd a way, allows for precisely that.

—JAMES MERRILL (1926-1995)
AMERICAN PULITZER PRIZE-WINNING POET

I know stuff. Stuff I shouldn't. It scares some people. . . These ethereal moments
where I am given information from some unknown place inside me.
Whatever it is tells me, and then I know. Very Shirley MacLaine.

—ROSIE O'DONNELL (1962-)
AMERICAN ACTOR, COMEDIAN, AND TALK SHOW HOST

———

We live in a culture which does not believe in miracles, and so they
have an unpleasant effect on us.

—PIER PAOLO PASOLINI (1922-1975)
ITALIAN FILM DIRECTOR

———

If you just look at the word *Ta-dah* with no exclamation mark, no full-stop, it's very
abstract. There's magic behind that word, illusion behind that word—you think of
performance, showmanship. But Tah-dah is also about expectations.

—JAKE SHEARS (1978-)
AMERICAN MUSICIAN

MARRIAGE

SEE ALSO FAMILY, FRIENDS AND FRIENDSHIPS, GAY MARRIAGE, MARRIAGE,
RELATIONSHIPS, ROMANCE, SEX

Why were the men one liked not the sort who proposed marriage and the men
who proposed marriage not the sort one liked?

—W. H. AUDEN (1907-1973)
ANGLO-AMERICAN POET AND CRITIC

———

I am not a housewife—men never can be housewives.

—JAMES BALDWIN (1924-1987)
AFRICAN-AMERICAN WRITER

Between husband and wife there should always be at least ten years' difference.

—MICHELANGELO BUONARROTI (1475-1564)
ITALIAN PAINTER, SCULPTOR, POET, AND ENGINEER

I have no humor to marry, I love to lie o' both sides o' th' bed myself, and again o' th' other side; a wife you know ought to be obedient, but I fear me I am too headstrong to obey, therefore I'll ne'er go about it. . . . I have the had now of myself, and am man enough for a woman; marriage is but a chopping and changing, where a maiden loses one head and has a worse i' the' place.

—MARY "MAD MOLL" FRITH (1584-1659)
BRITISH PIONEER FEMINIST AND TRANSVESTITE

The best argument I've heard so far why gay people should be able to get legally married: We should have the full right to suffer like anyone else.

—WIM HELDENS (1954-)
DUTCH PAINTER

Marriage is not a cure-all.

—MAGNUS HIRSCHFELD (1868-1935)
GERMAN SEXOLOGIST AND PIONEER GAY RIGHTS ACTIVIST

I'm uncomfortable generally with public displays of affection, and is there a more public display of affection than a wedding? It's sort of the floor show, the big Broadway extravaganza of affection.

—DAN SAVAGE (1964-)
AMERICAN SEX COLUMNIST AND WRITER

I'm in a relationship with a woman now, and we're committed to a seven-year performance piece to explore love as art. . . . We just had our first wedding, the first of seven we're going to have.

—ANNIE SPRINKLE (1954-)
AMERICAN PERFORMANCE ARTIST AND SEX EDUCATOR

Marriage can be retained for men and women and a separate but equal institution be available to same-sex couples. We are different. Let's not only ask other people to respect our difference but also respect it ourselves.

—DANIEL TAMMET (1979-)
BRITISH AUTISTIC SAVANT

[I am] too indolent to found a family, too indolent to take upon myself the responsibility of wife and children. In short, marriage is to me inconceivable.

—PETER ILYICH TCHAIKOVSKY (1840-1893)
RUSSIAN COMPOSER

I have decided to get married. It is unavoidable. . . . I seek marriage or some sort of public involvement with a woman so as to shut the mouths of assorted contemptible creatures whose opinions mean nothing to me, but who are in a position to cause distress to those near to me.

—PETER ILYICH TCHAIKOVSKY (1840-1893)
RUSSIAN COMPOSER

Oh, the first quarrel in a young household, what an occasion!
A memorable date, often.

—PAUL VERLAINE (1844-1896)
FRENCH POET

MASCULINITY

SEE ALSO APPEARANCES, BEAUTY, GENDER BENDING, HOMOSEXUALITY, IDENTITY,
ROLE MODELS, SISSIES, WOMEN

For the better part of the century they [men's magazines] have been
telling men how to make a drink, how to give a cocktail party,
how to behave so they won't get thrown out of a restaurant. It makes you wonder.
. . . How did we become such wolves?

—TED ALLEN (1965-)
FOOD AND WINE CONNOISSEUR AND REALITY TV STAR

———————

All men are troubled by masculinity.

—DAVID DANDRIDGE (ca. 1970-)
BRITISH PLAYWRIGHT AND WRITER

———————

Figuring out what "Being a Man" means for us is a very important part of who—
and what—we are. In Israel, it always meant—and a lot of that is still true—there
was only one kind of man you could be, there were no alternatives, no options.

—EYTAN FOX (1964-)
ISRAELI FILM DIRECTOR

———————

The mass audience is and may always be much more receptive to lesbian
eroticism than to its gay male equivalent, probably because of
deep-seated anxiety about masculinity—which really does exist and is not,
as silly academics claim, merely a social construction.

—CAMILLE PAGLIA (1947-)
AMERICAN SCHOLAR AND CRITIC

The men who run big-time bodybuilding love to pretend that it is only for straight people. an openly gay champion complicates their efforts to overcome the old 1950s myths that said all bodybuilders were queer.

–BOB PARIS (1959-)
AMERICAN ACTIVIST AND MR. UNIVERSE INTERNATIONAL IN 1983

———————

I've defined my own masculinity, one that's not based on his [my father's] or anyone else's. Now I approve of myself, and I don't need that approval from someone else. Now I'm ready to take the mask off.

–RUPAUL (1960-)
AMERICAN DRAG PERFORMER AND MUSICIAN

MATERIALISM

Antique shops have changed minds as to periods to love, and books, [and] what songs to worship.

–DJUNA BARNES (1892-1982)
AMERICAN WRITER

———————

We are getting rid of ownership, substituting use.

–JOHN CAGE (1934-1992)
AMERICAN COMPOSER

———————

Like all vagabonds, I am obsessed with the mania of owning a house.

–JEAN COCTEAU (1889-1963)
FRENCH WRITER AND FILMMAKER

What can one be sure of if not what one holds in one's arms at the time one is holding it? And we have so few chances to be proprietary . . .

—SIDONIE-GABRIELLE COLETTE (1873-1954)
FRENCH WRITER

I always liked spending my money, even when I was a kid, when I had a paper round—or paper route, as they call it over here. I used to get my money at the end of the week, buy my mum something, or buy a record, and that was it. . . . I'm a lavish kind of guy, and that's the way I am.

—SIR ELTON JOHN, CBE (1947-)
BRITISH GRAMMY AND ACADEMY AWARD-WINNING MUSICIAN

Oh yes, we like at least at church on Sundays to think of commercial values as Mammon, with a capital M, as an evil, but then on Monday through Friday quite the opposite.

—PHILIP JOHNSON (1906-2005)
AMERICAN ARCHITECT

We are all more blind to what we have than to what we have not.

—AUDRE LORDE (1934-1992)
AFRICAN-AMERICAN WRITER, POET, AND ACTIVIST

I begin to feel the necessity for getting superficial enjoyments from superficially pleasurable things. Being nicely dressed and spending money freely are the sort of things that lubricate the machinery of everyday existence.

—SIEGFRIED SASSOON (1886-1967)
BRITISH POET AND WRITER

MEDIA

SEE ALSO CRITICS AND CRITICISM, JOURNALISM, LANGUAGE, WRITING

[The] corruption of language has been enormously encouraged by mass education and the mass media. . . . Today, I would guess that nine-tenths of the population do no know what thirty percent of the words they use actually mean.

—W. H. AUDEN (1907-1973)
ANGLO-AMERICAN POET AND CRITIC

The connections between the media [exist] now in a way there wasn't before. The sale of a book to a movie house can completely change its "hopes." It's all one huge self-serving system and I don't like that at all. . . . It's very good for the people who do the movies, but I don't think it's good for the people who love books.

—CLIVE BARKER (1952-)
BRITISH WRITER AND DIRECTOR

There's something about the media crawling up your ass. It's hard enough to really express yourself in a completely emotional, raw way, but then also to have to explain it to the press and reinterpret it to make them understand where you are really coming from . . .

—SANDRA BERNHARD (1955-)
AMERICAN ACTOR, COMEDIAN, AND MUSICIAN

A book tour is, I believe, as physically and emotionally demanding as Wimbledon or the U.S. Open. F. Scott Fitzgerald never rose at dawn for an author's appearance on *Good Morning America.* Neither George Sand nor Elizabeth Barrett Browning ever raced in a cab on a rainy morning to be interviewed on *Today.*

—MALCOLM BOYD (1923-)
AMERICAN MINISTER AND INSPIRATIONAL WRITER

The only thing that doesn't hurt me is to pick up a newspaper and read some libelous thing about me or some bad review of something. That doesn't bother me at all. But if I feel somebody has betrayed me in some way or been disloyal about something, I get terribly upset about it.

—TRUMAN CAPOTE (1924-1984)
AMERICAN WRITER

If success were based on what the audience actually wants, the films, radio, and TV would be a lot different. But it's not even about talent. It's about what promoters and producers think people are going to be comfortable with.

—SCOTT CAPURRO (1962-)
BRITISH COMEDIAN AND WRITER

The media is very flighty. AIDS is a little "last century," in terms of the media.

—ALAN CUMMING (1965-)
BRITISH ACTOR

If you look at network news, for instance, it's just a pack of lies, right? Well . . . it's not reflecting the truth and reality of society, anyway.

—DONNA DEITCH (1945-)
AMERICAN FILM DIRECTOR

If anybody's attacking you and in this case, it's the press that's attacked. . . . Incessantly you have two choices: You either take cover, or you can fight back. And the way you can fight back is by playing their game.

—SARA GILBERT (1975-)
AMERICAN ACTOR

What people accept as normal is formed largely by what the media serves up to them and what texts they come across.

—DREW GUMMERSON (1971–)
BRITISH WRITER

———————

That's the name of the name of the game in talk radio: Keep 'em guessing. . . . We've decided that it's a potentially great act of activism to show the world that gay men are interested in a wide range of issues. We're not a bunch of one-trick ponies.

—KAREL (ca. 1970–)
AMERICAN RADIO TALK SHOW HOST

———————

When I read things I've said in print, all it is, is black-and-white-words. I feel like the meaning is not as clear as I'd like it to be.

—STEVE KMETKO (1953–)
AMERICAN TV HOST

———————

CNN, is that Cashmere Cable Network or something?

—CARSON KRESSLEY (1969–)
AMERICAN FASHION EXPERT AND REALITY TV STAR

———————

I'm a real news junky. I can't get enough of that Boutrous Boutros-Ghali.

—CARSON KRESSLEY (1969–)
AMERICAN FASHION EXPERT AND REALITY TV STAR

———————

Listeners are dominated and intimated by the record stores and the radio into what they should listen to.

—K. D. LANG (1961–)
CANADIAN MUSICIAN

No matter how much everyone says they want hard news and nothing but the news, that all goes out the window when you find a story about the exploding python that tried to eat an alligator in Florida or convicted Ohio ex-Congressman James Traficant's hideous prison art sale on eBay. . . . "Believe it or not" stuff trumps newsy news any day.

—RACHEL MADDOW (1973-)
AMERICAN RADIO TALK SHOW HOST

———————

[The] mainstream American media . . . serves merely to consolidate the myths, power, and authority of the majority: "minorities" might be granted the right to speak and be heard, but only if we abide by the "master codes" of courteous speech, proper subject matter, conventional aesthetics, and "mainstream" appeal.

—MARLON RIGGS (1957-1994)
AFRICAN-AMERICAN FILMMAKER

———————

[A]s gay magazines have had to exclude sex ads that formerly funded the gay press in order to upscale and attract advertising from major corporations, they've lost the foundation of their funding. This has shifted the financial dependency of the gay press from sex, sex toys, pornography, masseurs, and escort service ads to viaticals.

—SARAH SCHULMAN (1958-)
FEMINIST WRITER AND AIDS ACTIVIST

———————

You have to be careful though, 'cause you don't want to try to be the spokesperson for the gay community, because we're so diverse. And you have to watch what you say 'cause—not to put down the press—but I have been misquoted.

—BOB SMITH (1960-)
AMERICAN COMEDIAN

I really admire people who regard any publicity attached to them as vulgar and odious. . . . To them, for a television crew to arrive one day and do a film of them in their gardens would be a terrible obscenity.

—STEPHEN SPENDER (1909-1995)
BRITISH POET AND WRITER

MEMORY

Either, or: it takes strength to remember, it takes another kind of strength to forget.

—JAMES BALDWIN (1924-1987)
AFRICAN-AMERICAN WRITER

I tend to think that the very act of working with language to refine and pinpoint meaning, is a kind of refining of memory itself.

—JUDITH BARRINGTON (1944-)
BRITISH POET AND WRITER

I have a very bad memory, so that comes in handy—not to dwell too much on what was. But you can make mistakes if you don't remember certain things.

—PETER BERLIN (1934-)
GERMAN MODEL AND GAY SEX ICON

I have learned by experience . . . that the one sure way to rid myself of haunting memories is to set them down in black and white—to write them out of my system.

—W. SOMERSET MAUGHAM (1874-1965)
BRITISH WRITER AND PLAYWRIGHT

And how will I be remembered, if at all, by those hundreds and hundreds of
nightpeople in that long goodbye that life turns into?

—JOHN RECHY (1934-)
AMERICAN WRITER

[I] wish to give shape to a fading impression at the back of my mind before that
impression should become irrecoverable. It is not only a personal impression, it is
an impression in a wider sense, of an age that I saw in the act of passing.

—VITA SACKVILLE-WEST (1892-1962)
BRITISH POET, NOVELIST, AND GARDENER

Instead of remembering here a scene and there a sound, I shall fit a plug
into the wall; and listen in to the past.

—VIRGINIA WOOLF (1882-1941)
BRITISH WRITER

THE MILITARY

SEE ALSO POLITICS, WAR

I wanted [the Marine Corps] to make me a tougher man. I wasn't thinking about
whether or not I was going to live my life as a gay man. I was thinking that the
Marines would make me the man I was supposed to be.

—ERIC ALVA (1974-)
FIRST U.S. SERVICEMAN INJURED IN THE IRAQ WAR

Boot camp was never about thinking, Oh, he looks cute across the room . . .
It was about being screamed at all day long by drill instructors and having maybe
90 seconds to eat. The showers were about getting in and out pretty quick,
because you still had things to do before you went to bed . . .

—ERIC ALVA (1974-)
FIRST U.S. SERVICEMAN INJURED IN THE IRAQ WAR

When my case started, the social climate was so bad that you couldn't
even say the word homosexual in public. Reporters who asked me
about it and the military officers who were trying the case would choke
on the word, which was always said with a cough.

—COPY BERG (1951–)
NAVAL OFFICER AND GAY RIGHTS ACTIVIST

"Don't ask, don't tell, don't pursue" suggests that even more dangerous
than the presence of gays in the military (everyone knows they're already there)
is the prospect of saying they're there.

—LEO BERSANI (1931–)
AMERICAN LITERARY THEORIST AND PROFESSOR OF FRENCH

Our attitude toward our servicemen is deeply shaming.

—NOËL COWARD (1899–1973)
BRITISH ACTOR AND PLAYWRIGHT

To me, the life of a guest in a warship is deeply satisfactory. I have passed some
of the happiest hours of my life [there]. . . Perhaps it is merely the complete
change of atmosphere that so englamours me; if so, I shall certainly take good
care never to outstay my welcome long enough to break it.

—NOËL COWARD (1899–1973)
BRITISH ACTOR AND PLAYWRIGHT

So let's be honest: the "don't ask, don't tell" policy is based on long-disproved
psychoanalytic theories of the "homosexual" as inherently sick and unreliable and
as such preserves prejudice, not military preparedness.

—ZSA ZSA GERSHICK (ca. 1970–)
AMERICAN PLAYWRIGHT

The real bar to good order and discipline [in the military], the real destroyer of unit cohesion—a fact well-documented but continually denied—is prejudice along with the bad behaviors, including harassment and violence, that it promotes.

—ZSA ZSA GERSHICK (ca. 1970-)
AMERICAN PLAYWRIGHT

I enlisted in the Army three days before my eighteenth birthday. They did ask, and I didn't tell. . . . I have resented for sixty-four years that I had to lie in order to serve my country.

—FRANK KAMENY (1925-)
AMERICAN GAY RIGHTS ACTIVIST

It's tough to say who "the military" really is. If it's the actual people fighting who don't care about serving next to gay people, then yes, they're supportive. If it's the group of human rights criminals who are making policies that punish people for homosexuality that you're talking about, then, no, they have not been supportive.

—REICHEN LEHMKUHL (1973-)
AMERICAN REALITY TV STAR AND CELEBRITY

When I think of the orgies that used to go on at air force bases, it's a wonder more people weren't caught. There was always this underground. People knew; there were certain codes.

—A. DAMIEN MARTIN (1934-1991)
AMERICAN GAY RIGHTS ACTIVIST

If then one could contrive that a state or an army should entirely consist of lovers and loved, it would be impossible for it to have a better organization that that which it would then enjoy through their avoidance of all dishonor and their mutual emulation; moreover, a handful of such men, fighting side by side, would defeat practically the whole world. A lover would rather be seen by all his comrades leaving his post or throwing always his arms than by his beloved; rather than that, he would prefer a thousand times to die.

— PLATO (427-347 BC)
GREEK PHILOSOPHER

The U.S. military has a stellar reputation for taking care of spouses in heterosexual marriages during deployment. . . . Gay service members are making the same amount of sacrifices as their heterosexual colleagues, and yet their loves are not cared for.

—STEVE RALLS (ca. 1975-)
AMERICAN GAY MILITARY LEGAL DEFENSE COUNSEL

I was on a submarine, and if you're on a submarine for twenty-two days, you want sex. We were either jacking each other off or sucking each other off. Everybody knew that everybody else was doing it.

—HAROLD ROBBINS (1916-1997)
AMERICAN WRITER

The Coast Guard tends to do things first. . . . It was the first branch of the military that allowed women to serve, and I think they are ready to do the same for gays. If given the green light, they would do it in a minute.

—BILL SHIPLEY (1960-)
AMERICAN COAST GUARD OFFICER

Gays in the military? The fact remains that lesbians get discharged more frequently than gay men.

—URVASHI VAID (1958–)
AMERICAN GAY RIGHTS ACTIVIST

On getting into uniform I could see from the attitude of friends and glances from strangers in the streets that my stock had increased in value, but instead of feeling encouraged, I was embarrassed, knowing that inside the uniform I was still myself.

—PATRICK WHITE (1912–1990)
AUSTRALIAN WRITER AND NOBEL LAUREATE

What better way to show how ridiculous [President Clinton and Sam Nunn] were than to come out on CNN? . . . [I] put another face on gays in the military than the one people like Sam Nunn wanted the public to see.

—JOSÉ ZUNIGA (1969–)
1992 U.S. ARMY SOLDIER OF THE YEAR

MISTAKES

We flung against their gods,
invincible, clear hate;
we fought;
frantic, we flung the last
imperious, desperate shaft
and lost.

—H. D., BORN HILDA DOOLITTLE (1886-1961)
AMERICAN ESSAYIST, NOVELIST, AND POET

I've made awful mistakes all along the line. And the awful thing is if I had my life to live a second time, I'd make the same errors all over again. All over again.

—W. SOMERSET MAUGHAM (1874–1965)
BRITISH WRITER AND PLAYWRIGHT

How terrible it is to be wrong, to go out on a limb and make an advance that isn't reciprocated. I thought of the topless stay-at-home wife, opening the door to the gay UPS driver. . . .

—DAVID SEDARIS (1956–)
AMERICAN WRITER

What lies before is my past. I have got to make myself look on that with different eyes, to make the world look on it with different eyes, to make God look on it with different eyes. This I cannot do by ignoring it, or slighting it, or praising it, or denying it. It is only to be done by fully accepting it as an inevitable part of the evolution of my life and character.

—OSCAR WILDE (1854–1900)
IRISH PLAYWRIGHT AND WRITER

You have a voice and you have to use it. . . . You might be spreading the wrong gospel, but at least you do something.

—FRANCO ZEFFIRELLI (1923–)
ITALIAN FILM DIRECTOR

MONEY

SEE ALSO BUSINESS, CLASS, WORK

In the world of cinema money is all that matters. In a museum or when you are writing you don't have to constantly think about money.

—CHANTAL AKERMAN (1950–)
BELGIAN FEMINIST AND DIRECTOR

That's mooch psychology: they most especially wouldn't help people who helped them. Well I've subsidized my last mooch.

—WILLIAM BURROUGHS (1914-1997)
AMERICAN WRITER

———————

To the problem of gold, as to any other, one should be totally devoted, and I admire those men who extract from it a strange kind of poetry.

—JEAN COCTEAU (1889-1963)
FRENCH WRITER AND FILMMAKER

———————

When out of work I am not able to rid myself of worries enough to accomplish anything. Some pecuniary assurances seem necessary to me to any opening of the creative channels.

—HART CRANE (1899-1932)
AMERICAN POET

———————

I do think money is dangerous, and I know more about its dangers than . . . [one might] suppose, for my great-grandfather was quite a famous banker, and some of his canniness runs in my blood, and tempts me to prefer money to the things it buys.

—E. M. FORSTER (1879-1970)
BRITISH WRITER

———————

You can't be poor, of course; the poor were disenfranchised last year. But if you have a credit card—and these days household pets have credit cards (thank God we're about to eliminate the deficit!)—you can charge enough to either make an independent film or run for state legislature.

—TONY KUSHNER (1956-)
AMERICAN PLAYWRIGHT

I will take money if a rich man will leave it to me. I like a rich man.

—VASLAV NIJINSKY (1890-1950)
RUSSIAN DANCER

———

The heir who carefully sets himself to exploit his heritage, to till every barren land, to afforest every waste place, has already expended not the least of his treasures.

—WALTER PATER (1839-1894)
BRITISH CRITIC AND WRITER

———

The income tax people have docked my pay. That's why I was overdrawn. Damn them.

—VITA SACKVILLE-WEST (1892-1962)
BRITISH POET, NOVELIST, AND GARDENER

———

I don't spend money. I own one pair of jeans, one pair of shoes. I wash my jeans a lot, so I'm not a stinky freak. But I just don't like shopping— I find the process of spending money to be a painful bore.

—DAN SAVAGE (1964-)
AMERICAN SEX COLUMNIST AND WRITER

———

Often with same-sex couples there's an income imbalance, and that can lead to weird game playing. I feel that two people have to pool their resources and treat money as "theirs," not "his money over here and my money over there." Keeping track of who owns and/or owes what is toxic.

—DAN SAVAGE (1964-)
AMERICAN SEX COLUMNIST AND WRITER

———

The best way I like to carry money, actually, is messily. Crumpled wads. A paper bag is good.

—ANDY WARHOL (1928-1987)
AMERICAN ARTIST

I do want to get rich, but I never want to do what there is to do to get rich.

—GERTRUDE STEIN (1874-1946)
AMERICAN EXPATRIATE WRITER

PINK DOLLARS

We went on an RV trip and we were very anonymous and a couple of times
we had problems with people not waiting on us because it was obvious
that we were girlfriends. We can't help ourselves. There's still that, and that's sad,
but people have their issues. That's sad. We usually leave the waitress who did
wait on us a huge tip. Like a crazy money tip.

—MELISSA ETHERIDGE (1961-)
AMERICAN GRAMMYAWARD-WINNING MUSICIAN AND BREAST CANCER ACTIVIST

Shout out from the gays—we're good people to wait on.

—TAMMY ETHERIDGE (1974-)
AMERICAN CELEBRITY WIFE

I suspect that the gay and lesbian community will achieve equal status
not through government and politics but through the private sector.
They're way ahead of the government.

—STEVE GUNDERSON (1951-)
AMERICAN CONGRESSMAN, AND FIRST OPENLY GAY REPUBLICAN REPRESENTATIVE

On the one hand, we are still hated, feared, and misunderstood.
On the other hand, we are seen as a "niche market" that can make
a lot of money. Caught in between, of course, is "us."

—MARIA MAGGENTI (1962-)
AMERICAN SCREENWRITER AND DIRECTOR, RAISED IN NIGERIA

POVERTY

Difference between pennilessness now and pennilessness then:
now we've got unquestioned credit.

—JOHN CAGE (1934-1992)
AMERICAN COMPOSER

In the hands of a poor man, coins are no longer the sign of wealth but of
its opposite.

—JEAN GENET (1910-1986)
FRENCH WRITER, CRIMINAL, AND POLITICAL ACTIVIST

There shouldn't be any millionaires and there shouldn't be
anyone asking for bread.

—MARSDEN HARTLEY (1877-1943)
AMERICAN ARTIST

Poverty lent my little dabblings a much-needed veneer of authenticity, and I imagined myself repaying the debt by gently lifting the lives of those around me, not
en masse, but one by one, the old fashioned way.

—DAVID SEDARIS (1956-)
AMERICAN WRITER

I was trying to think the other day about what you do now in America if you want
to be successful. Before, you were dependable and wore a good suit.
Looking around, I guess that today you have to do all the same things but not
wear a good suit. I guess that's all it is. Think rich. Look poor.

—ANDY WARHOL (1928-1987)
AMERICAN ARTIST

WEALTH

We see from experience that the majority of those born to riches
throw them away and die ruined.

—MICHELANGELO BUONARROTI (1475-1564)
ITALIAN PAINTER, SCULPTOR, POET, AND ENGINEER

The millionaires are all suffering from poverty and one can only pity them.

—MARSDEN HARTLEY (1877-1943)
AMERICAN ARTIST

High society here turns me off and I feel a bit of rage against all these rich guys
here, since I have seen thousands of people in the most terrible misery without
anything to eat and with no place to sleep.

—FRIDA KAHLO (1907-1954)
MEXICAN ARTIST AND INTELLECTUAL

In England or France or America people do not remember the industrial revolution
and the transition to prosperity. In Italy this transition has just taken place.

—PIER PAOLO PASOLINI (1922-1975)
ITALIAN FILM DIRECTOR

"I've been rich and I've been poor. It's better to be rich".

—GERTRUDE STEIN (1874-1946)
AMERICAN EXPATRIATE WRITER

MORALITY

SEE ALSO RELIGION

The ideology behind underground comics was to break through all the
bullshit representations of life. . . . I wanted to express my outrage
by raising these moral issues in a work of art.

—HOWARD CRUSE (1944-)
AMERICAN CARTOONIST

———————

"Kept women" and marital break-ups were big moral questions then.
Now, of course, everybody would be screwing everybody,
and everybody would know about it.

—GEORGE CUKOR (1899-1983)
AMERICAN FILM DIRECTOR

———————

I am afraid that this constant sacrifice to convention, assented to by more than one
poet or novelist . . . rather distorts psychology and greatly misleads public opinion.

— ANDRÉ GIDE (1869-1951)
FRENCH WRITER

———————

Morality should not be dependent on accidents of time and place
nor should it be based on supernatural considerations. It should be based on
what nature teaches; and the mouthpiece of nature is science.

—MAGNUS HIRSCHFELD (1868-1935)
GERMAN SEXOLOGIST AND PIONEER GAY RIGHTS ACTIVIST

What is the moral meaning of who we are? Let's suppose we know
who we are as Black and Gay or Lesbian or Bisexual human beings and then. . .
. What about that? How does any facet of your, or my, identity intersect,
for instance, with the fact that the average grade level of Black elementary or
high school children happens to be a D+? That's the situation in Oakland,
California. What about that?

—JUNE JORDAN (1936-2002)
AFRICAN-AMERICAN ACTIVIST

———————

I don't believe in dogmas and theologies. I just believe in being a good person.
I've always been honest with people. I've never lied. I think I've lived a moral life.

—ROBERT MAPPLETHORPE (1946-1989)
AMERICAN PHOTOGRAPHER

———————

Almost anybody of the writing, painting, musical, gigoloing, whoring, pimping or
drinking world was apt to turn up. . . . The so-called "bohemian" or art world has
. . . few intolerances about morals, or the way people make their living.

—ROBERT MCALMON (1896-1956)
AMERICAN WRITER AND PUBLISHER

———————

I was upset [by being expelled from the Boy Scouts] because they were
making some character determination of me that was false.
They implied in the letter that I'd done something wrong or illegal or immoral.
That offended me, because I hadn't.

—CHUCK MERINO (1955-)
FORMER POLICE OFFICER AND BOY SCOUT LEADER

[The police] interfere far too much with private morals—
whether people are having it off in the backs of cars, or smoking marihuana,
or doing the interesting little things that one does.

—JOE ORTON (1933-1967)
BRITISH PLAYWRIGHT

Morality is a weakness of the brain.

—ARTHUR RIMBAUD (1854-1891)
FRENCH POET

I can now declare with sincerity that my abnormal inclinations . . .
have brought me into close and profitable sympathy with human beings even
while I sinned against law and conventional morality.

—JOHN ADDINGTON SYMONDS (1840-1893)
ENGLISH POET AND CRITIC

There is no such thing as a moral or an immoral book. Books are well written,
or badly written. That is all.

—OSCAR WILDE (1854-1900)
IRISH PLAYWRIGHT AND WRITER

The tendency of all men who ever tried to write or talk Ethics or Religion
was to run against the boundaries of language. . . . This running against
the walls of our cage is perfectly, absolutely hopeless.

—LUDWIG WITTGENSTEIN (1889-1951)
AUSTRIAN PHILOSOPHER

MOTHERS AND MOTHERHOOD

SEE ALSO CHILDREN, FATHERS AND FATHERHOOD, GAY MARRIAGE, MARRIAGE,
ROLE MODELS

[Motherhood] . . . has enhanced my creativity, enhanced my ability to love, and
enhanced my tolerance for humanity. . . . It's made me a better director.

—JANE ANDERSON (1954–)
AMERICAN ACTOR AND DIRECTOR

My mother in Princeton got a cable from me, saying simply: "Opening bookshop
in Paris. Please send money," and she sent me all her savings.

—SYLVIA BEACH (1887–1962)
AMERICAN-BORN EXPATRIATE BOOKSELLER

[On becoming a mother] It's funny because Camille Paglia came to see my show
and said . . . "You're not going to get soft on me, are you?! You're not going to
lose your bitch?!" I said, "Did you see me on stage tonight, Camille? Was I any
less bitch and evil and strong than I ever have been?

—SANDRA BERNHARD (1955–)
AMERICAN ACTOR, COMEDIAN, AND MUSICIAN

He—or She—whom-I'm-carrying-in-my-flanks . . . bounds up and down,
until I wonder if I'm going to give birth to a Monegasque goat.

—SIDONIE-GABRIELLE COLETTE (1873–1954)
FRENCH WRITER

I am going to visit . . . my sainted mother [who] is insupportable. Not that she is
seriously ill, but she's having a crisis of "I wish to see my daughter."

—SIDONIE-GABRIELLE COLETTE (1873–1954)
FRENCH WRITER

The man who dies from a bullet on the field of battle with the cry of "Mother!" on his lips expresses with truculence that wish to be born again backwards, and to return to the place from which he emerged.

—SALVADOR DALÍ (1904-1989)
SPANISH ARTIST

———————

It was the dual proliferation of the pill and donor insemination that finally led me to understand there was no reason I couldn't be both a lesbian and a mother.

—LILLIAN FADERMAN (1940-)
LATVIAN-AMERICAN SCHOLAR AND WRITER

———————

You'd like my mom. She taught me tolerance. She's proud of me as a musician and as a gay man. She makes a really mean tabbouleh. And she's as American as you are.

—DAVE HALL (ca. 1970-)
ARAB-AMERICAN MUSICIAN

———————

I am my mother, OK? Just without the housedress and slippers.

—NATHAN LANE (1956-)
AMERICAN TONY AWARD–WINNING ACTOR AND COMEDIAN

———————

I went to visit my mother's grave for the first time. It is very odd reading a headstone with your own name on it. My name, her name too.

—ROSIE O'DONNELL (1962-)
AMERICAN ACTOR, COMEDIAN, AND TALK SHOW HOST

It was my mother who showed me how poetry could be written and
not just read in school. One fine day, mysteriously, she presented me with
a sonnet she'd composed in which she expressed her love for me
(I don't know through which contortions of rhyme the poem ended with the
words "of love for you I've lots.") A few days later, I wrote my first verses.

—PIER PAOLO PASOLINI (1922-1975)
ITALIAN FILM DIRECTOR

———————

What I can say is that I had a great love for my mother. . . . For a long time I
thought the whole of my erotic and emotional life was the result of this
excessive, almost monstrous love for my mother.

—PIER PAOLO PASOLINI (1922-1975)
ITALIAN FILM DIRECTOR

———————

When I told her [my mother] I was [gay], she thought about it for a
second and said, "Just look good at it."

—LINDA PERRY (1965-)
AMERICAN MUSICIAN

———————

I think that my emotional world or universe became something real very young
because I was an only child in a house of women. I played with other children—I
had friends on the street—but the world that touched me was a world based on
the people around me. It was my grandmother and my great-grandmother. My
environment was built around these two women.

—ANDRE LEON TALLEY (1949-)
AMERICAN FASHION EDITOR, *VOGUE*

———————

I could always escape into this demi-monde of homosexuality, which I feel really
indebted to. It stopped me being a mummy's boy.

—RUFUS WAINWRIGHT (1973-)
CANADIAN MUSICIAN

I absolutely wish I hadn't spent 15 years swimming in ambivalence about having a biological child. I tell everyone—gay, straight, bi, trans—who comes to my talks, workshops and readings the same thing: Your fertility is finite.

—REBECCA WALKER (1969-)
AMERICAN FEMINIST WRITER

———————

I was the people's artist. Miss Ethel Waters. Now I was also their big, fat, comforting Mama image.

—ETHEL WATERS (1896-1977)
AFRICAN-AMERICAN ACTOR AND MUSICIAN

MOVIES

SEE ALSO AUDIENCES, ENTERTAINMENT, HOLLYWOOD, TELEVISION

I don't believe you can overestimate the importance of music in movies, whether its Bernard Herrmann's scores for Hitchcock or John Williamson's scores for Spielberg—these are scores that transformed the films.

—CLIVE BARKER (1952-)
BRITISH WRITER AND DIRECTOR

———————

You know, when most people go to the movies, the ultimate compliment— for them—is to say, "We didn't notice the time pass!" With me, you see the time pass. And feel it pass. You also sense that this is the time that leads toward death.

—CHANTAL AKERMAN (1950-)
BELGIAN FEMINIST AND DIRECTOR

———————

Cinema can fill in the empty spaces of your life and your loneliness.

—PEDRO ALMODOVAR (1951-)
SPANISH FILM DIRECTOR

Before I was really out I was just so excited to see homosexuality in the movie that it really didn't matter to me that they were denigrated and brutalized, even; just the possibility of homoeroticism that was suggested in that movie was enough for me. I guess that's a reflection of how little there was and how desperate we were.

—ROB EPSTEIN (1955-)
AMERICAN FILM PRODUCER

My addiction to drugs is not much compared to my addiction to the cinema.

—ELOY DE LA IGLESIA (1944-2006)
SPANISH SCREENWRITER AND FILM DIRECTOR

A *Playgirl* centerfold movie without nudity is like a Paula Abdul concert without lip synching.

—CHRISTIAN MCLAUGHLIN (ca. 1973-)
AMERICAN TV WRITER AND PRODUCER

Screenwriting is thoroughly collaborative. A screenwriter is a field marshal for the ideas of others.

—RON NYSWANER (1956-)
AMERICAN SCREENWRITER

I do love movies. Especially if I'm in 'em.

—RUPAUL (1960-)
AMERICAN DRAG PERFORMER AND MUSICIAN

I saw that *Jurassic Park* remake. I don't understand why they didn't just rerelease the old one.

—DAVID SEDARIS (1956-)
AMERICAN WRITER

A giant, action, summer-event movie! I could think of no better place to spill out one's own personal problems and foist them onto the world.

—BRYAN SINGER (1965-)
AMERICAN FILM DIRECTOR

If cinephilia is dead, then movies are dead.

—SUSAN SONTAG (1933-2004)
AMERICAN WRITER AND CRITIC

Cinema's hundred years appear to have the shape of a life cycle: an inevitable birth, the steady accumulation of glories, and the onset in the last decade of an ignominious, irreversible decline.

—SUSAN SONTAG (1933-2004)
AMERICAN WRITER AND CRITIC

I guess that is the most subversive moment in my career—that I made a movie that tricked George Bush Sr. into thinking it was family values.

—JOHN WATERS (1946-)
AMERICAN DIRECTOR

DIRECTING

As a director, I am uncomfortable directing other people's words.

—JANE ANDERSON (1954-)
AMERICAN ACTOR AND FILM DIRECTOR

I don't set out to shock people. I make movies about how I truly see the world. If people like Bob Dole find that upsetting, then that's their problem.

—GREGG ARAKI (1959-)
JAPANESE-AMERICAN FILM DIRECTOR

If one is going to be in the business . . . one should be a director. He is the one who tells everyone what to do. In fact, he is the whole world.

—DOROTHY ARZNER (1897-1979)
AMERICAN FILM DIRECTOR

When people say, "Well what's it like being a woman director?" You know what, I don't know what it's like being a man director. I don't even know what it's like being a man! And in the same way, you know, is it different being a straight director, well, I don't know. I'm not straight. So it's hard for me to know.

—DONNA DEITCH (1945-)
AMERICAN FILM DIRECTOR

MOVIES AND HOMOSEXUALITY

Lesbian and gays, too, of all stripes, make up the fabric of life in America. But America wouldn't know it from the movies.

—LILLIAN FADERMAN (1940-)
AMERICAN SCHOLAR AND WRITER

[On *Philadelphia*, the movie] If you find any homosexuality in *Philadelphia*, you'd have to be Sherlock Holmes.

—LARRY KRAMER (1935-)
AMERICAN WRITER, PLAYWRIGHT, AND ACTIVIST

What does it say about our current political power that we need movies to save our lives? If we need them too much, then filmmakers are expected to somehow deliver liberation along with story, dialogue, subtext, good acting, philosophy, politics, a world view, and maybe a couple of laughs.

—MARIA MAGGENTI (1962-)
AMERICAN SCREENWRITER AND DIRECTOR

[On the making of *X-Men 3: The Last Stand*] It would be wonderful if the camera hovered over Magneto's bed, to discover him making love to Professor X.

—SIR IAN MCKELLEN, CBE (1939-)
BRITISH ACTOR

There shouldn't be such a label as "gay film." Just "film"—good and bad.

—TOMMY O'HAVER (1967-)
AMERICAN SCREENWRITER AND FILM DIRECTOR

I can see the guys' nervous titters. Then that kiss scene [in *Making Love*, 1982] happens and it's pandemonium. People start marching up the aisles. . . . I had to leave. I couldn't watch it.

—BARRY SANDLER (1947-)
AMERICAN WRITER AND FILM PRODUCER

[My 1984 film *Mala Noche*] came at a time in American cinema when there was no such thing as a gay film. There were foreign films that had gay characters and gay themes to them, but the American cinema never did.

—GUS VAN SANT (1952-)
AMERICAN FILM DIRECTOR

I think progress sometimes is when we can admit there's a bad gay movie.

—JOHN WATERS (1946-)
AMERICAN FILM DIRECTOR

MUSIC

SEE ALSO ART AND ARTISTS, AUDIENCES, DANCING, ENTERTAINMENT

What I like about music is its ability of being convincing, of carrying an argument through successfully to the finish, though the terms of this argument remain unknown quantities. What remains is the structure, the architecture of the argument.

—JOHN ASHBERY (1927-)
AMERICAN POET

Actually, believe it or not, I probably don't know any of our songs, fully. Seriously. I could not repeat the lyrics to any of our songs—that's how bad of a memory I have. I know my part. But I cannot sing any of the leads to anything.

—LANCE BASS (1979-)
AMERICAN MUSICIAN

And I just don't always buy that those [New Age gurus] are where they profess they want you to be. So, I'd rather take somebody like a Patti Smith or a Courtney Love and listen to their kind of raw screaming-out than a Marianne Williamson.

—SANDRA BERNHARD (1955-)
AMERICAN ACTOR, COMEDIAN, AND MUSICIAN

It's very important for me to be artistically successful first. . . . I'll do all the commercial things. I'll do interviews and make videos and everything else that's necessary. But when I'm making the album itself, my priority is that it really pleases me.

—DAVID BOWIE (1947-)
BRITISH MUSICIAN

It's easy to slip into glamorizing the rock 'n' roll lifestyle, but the hilarious paradox is: I never played rock 'n' roll 'til I got clean.

—LYNNE BREEDLOVE (1959-)
AMERICAN MUSICIAN AND WRITER

A tardy art, the art of Music. And why so slow? Is it because, once having learned a notation of pitches and durations, musicians will not give up their Greek?

—JOHN CAGE (1934-1992)
AMERICAN COMPOSER

———————

Let us invent an idiom for the proper transposition of jazz into words! Something clean, sparkling, elusive!

—HART CRANE (1899-1932)
AMERICAN POET

———————

The non-relationship of movement . . . is extended into a relationship with music. It is essentially a non-relationship.

—MERCE CUNNINGHAM (1919-)
AMERICAN CHOREOGRAPHER AND DANCER

———————

As prodigious as I was musically, I had been so retarded sexually up until that point. . . . Music was my only avenue of expression. It was a way to channel all of my locked up feelings.

—DAVID DEL TREDICI (1937-)
AMERICAN COMPOSER

———————

It's an incongruously quiet time for political song, given the political crisis we're all facing.

—ANI DIFRANCO (1970-)
AMERICAN SINGER-SONGWRITER

———————

It's really hard to take something so big that is infested with words that are very pedantic . . . you take a word like capitalism or patriarchy and try to make music out of it.

—ANI DIFRANCO (1970-)
AMERICAN SINGER-SONGWRITER

Yes. I remember that feeling of "Well, today people are opening their newspapers and reading about me—and my failure." That's how I felt. I remember playing the music, and it was so healing, this safe place I could go to when all this crap was going down. I don't care if anyone buys this record. It's served its purpose.

—MELISSA ETHERIDGE (1961–)
AMERICAN GRAMMY AWARD-WINNING MUSICIAN AND BREAST CANCER ACTIVIST

————

I loved those punky boys. I still go weak for a Mohican.

—BOY GEORGE (1961–)
BRITISH MUSICIAN

————

Light threatens, is active, is gone,
so it is with a song.

—H. D., BORN HILDA DOOLITTLE (1886-1961)
AMERICAN ESSAYIST, NOVELIST, AND POET

————

I never work with music. I hate background music, always did. I only like music in the foreground, meaning, deliberately listen to it.

—DAVID HOCKNEY (1937–)
BRITISH ARTIST

————

There's a new accessory in New York now: the large transistor radio cradled gracefully in one arm or hanging from a shoulder strap like a huge metallic communications purse. . . . If you love music, you may find yourself in the curious position of following a young man not because he is sexually interesting (or even sexually possible) but because he the radio he carries is playing "Do or Die."

—ANDREW HOLLERAN (1944–)
AMERICAN WRITER

My real compulsion is music. . . . It keeps everybody up and at 'em.

—TODD OLDHAM (1962–)
AMERICAN FASHION AND INTERIOR DESIGNER

———————

I like pop music. I collect old records and new ones on the basis that they may become part of pop history. That's all I'm interested in.

—JOE ORTON (1933-1967)
BRITISH PLAYWRIGHT

———————

I love this business [music business] because it's so sleazy.

—LINDA PERRY (1965–)
AMERICAN MUSICIAN

———————

I'm kind of a dick and very insensitive, because I'm afraid if I ever do fall in love with someone, it could jeopardize my music.

—LINDA PERRY (1965–)
AMERICAN MUSICIAN

———————

You can sing about anything . . . but does music enhance it? Is music necessary to it? Or is music merely a decorative way of our talking to each other?

—STEPHEN SONDHEIM (1930–)
AMERICAN MUSICAL THEATER COMPOSER AND PLAYWRIGHT

———————

I'm a firm believer that the ear hears things that the mind does not know, particularly in non-musicians, but even in musicians.

—STEPHEN SONDHEIM (1930–)
AMERICAN MUSICAL THEATER COMPOSER AND PLAYWRIGHT

CLASSICAL MUSIC

I don't listen [to classical music] when I'm writing. I can't do that because my own rhythms are more important to me than the rhythms of the composer. If I listen to music while I'm writing, the rhythms of the music will get in the way of the rhythms of my characters.

—EDWARD ALBEE (1928-)
AMERICAN TONY AWARD- AND PULITZER PRIZE-WINNING PLAYWRIGHT

I don't like classical music. There was a time when I tried to educate myself to liking it, but I just think it's a noise—a terrible racket, probably because I'm tone deaf.

—JOE ORTON (1933-1967)
BRITISH PLAYWRIGHT

I find the richness [of Bach] very, very exciting, thrilling, and disturbing in a way. . . . It doesn't seem like something by an old man. . . . He's taking strange journeys while searching out all the things he wants to find out.

—JEROME ROBBINS (1918-1998)
AMERICAN CHOREOGRAPHER

COMPOSING

When you get right down to it, a composer is simply someone who tells other people what to do. I find this an unattractive way of getting things done. I'd like our activities to be more social and anarchically so.

—JOHN CAGE (1934-1992)
AMERICAN COMPOSER

I would love to pretend that I'm the kind of artist who writes and writes
and doesn't give a damn about anybody else. But it's obvious
that I'm not a Dylan type, who's all involved with his art and the listeners feel
like they're just looking in on him when they hear his songs.

—MELISSA ETHERIDGE (1961-)
AMERICAN GRAMMY AWARD-WINNING MUSICIAN AND BREAST CANCER ACTIVIST

Usually what happens is that I've worked on it [melody] so much that the
unconscious takes over, and I arrive where I want to arrive.

—STEPHEN SONDHEIM (1930-)
AMERICAN MUSICAL THEATER COMPOSER AND PLAYWRIGHT

To a musician a score means something more than a collection of all kinds of
notes and pauses. It is a complete picture in which the central figures stand out
clearly form the accessories and the background.

—PETER ILYICH TCHAIKOVSKY (1840-1893)
RUSSIAN COMPOSER

DJS

DJs nowadays see themselves as a god.

—LADY BUNNY (1962-)
AMERICAN DRAG PERFORMER AND DJ

Yes, Boy George . . . just what England needs:
another queen who can't dress.

—GRAHAM NORTON (1963-)
IRISH COMEDIAN AND ACTOR

I know people who are just mixing with iPods and G4s, but I just don't get it. There's just no live feeling to that—you might just as well be a robot.

—JUNIOR VASQUEZ (1946–)
AMERICAN DJ AND RECORD PRODUCER

OPERA

I believe in the importance of the "experience" of going to the opera. The mere fact that one dresses specially to go there helps to create the special feeling of "occasion."

—PHILIP JOHNSON (1906–2005)
AMERICAN ARCHITECT

———————

I don't like opera, but I have a feeling that I wish I did.

—STEPHEN SONDHEIM (1930–)
AMERICAN MUSICAL THEATER COMPOSER AND PLAYWRIGHT

———————

The older I grow, the more convinced I am that symphony and opera are in every respect at the opposite poles of music.

—PETER ILYICH TCHAIKOVSKY (1840–1893)
RUSSIAN COMPOSER

PERFORMING

Singing torch songs is what inspires me. I long to simply stand on stage with a microphone and a spotlight.

—ANDY BELL (1964–)
BRITISH MUSICIAN

I'll never forget coming off the stage at a show in Ohio and these kids ran up to me and they wanted to touch me because I had met Britney Spears and done that thing on MTV with her. I was like "Honey, I've just done a forty-minute show and you might want to start off with 'I enjoyed your show' when you approach a sweaty drag queen."

—LADY BUNNY (1962-)
AMERICAN DRAG PERFORMER AND DJ

I should love to perform "There Are Fairies in the Bottom of My Garden" [Bea Lillie's signature song], but I don't dare. It might come out "There Are Fairies in the Garden of My Bottom."

—NOËL COWARD (1899-1973)
BRITISH ACTOR AND PLAYWRIGHT

As a folksinger and a storyteller it's really hard to stand on stage night after night for a month and have anything to say to anybody.

—ANI DIFRANCO (1970-)
AMERICAN SINGER-SONGWRITER

Performing is like being possessed sometimes, because when I sing and it's really on and it's Zen, I have nothing to do with what's coming out. Honestly, I don't. All I do is provide the channel. Because the voice is not really mine at all.

—K.D. LANG (1961-)
CANADIAN MUSICIAN

Onstage it's all about me, whether it should be or not.

—MICHAEL STIPE (1960-)
AMERICAN MUSICIAN

NATURE

Living in the country gives you faith. All you have to do is get up
and look at the mountains and look at the other animals to realize that your
problems are mostly made up or exacerbated by humans. But human life
isn't necessarily life. There's so much more out there.

—RITA MAE BROWN (1944-)
AMERICAN WRITER

There is no concept of waste in nature . . . but humans throw away things they
don't want, as though there is really any "away" to throw things.

—DARBY HOOVER (1964-)
AMERICAN ENVIRONMENTALIST

Nature tells you what to do, and nature is the overriding spirit of everything—
it's what is natural. It isn't just pretty flowers, it's order.

—STEPHEN SONDHEIM (1930-)
AMERICAN MUSICAL THEATER COMPOSER AND PLAYWRIGHT

Thank God, I have again become fully receptive to nature seeing and comprehend-
ing in each leaf and flower something unattainably beautiful, reposeful, peaceful.

—PETER ILYICH TCHAIKOVSKY (1840-1893)
RUSSIAN COMPOSER

I struggle with you against the laws of gravity.

—MONIQUE WITTIG (1935-2003)
FRENCH FEMINIST AND WRITER

OPPRESSION

SEE ALSO HATRED, THE HOLOCAUST, RACE AND RACISM, SUFFERING

The appearance in our time of dictatorships and one-party states has made it easier for us to understand what the doctrine of the Divine Right of Kings really meant.

—W. H. AUDEN (1907-1973)
ANGLO-AMERICAN POET AND CRITIC

———

The only real defiance of totalitarianism is by refusing the terms of the tyrant, by creating a reality beyond the reality of politics.

—SIMON CALLOW, CBE (1949-)
BRITISH ACTOR

———

What are the words you do not yet have? What do you need to say?
What are the tyrannies you swallow day by day and attempt to make your own,
until you will sicken and die of them, still in silence?

—AUDRE LORDE (1934-1992)
AFRICAN-AMERICAN WRITER, POET, AND ACTIVIST

———

I believe that the worst part of being in an oppressed culture is that
the oppressive culture—primarily because it controls the production
and dispersal of images in the media—can so easily make us feel ashamed
of ourselves, of our sayings, our doings, and our ways.

—ALICE WALKER (1944-)
AFRICAN-AMERICAN FEMINIST AND PULITZER PRIZE-WINNING WRITER

ORIGINALITY

SEE ALSO CREATION AND CREATIVITY, IDENTITY, IMAGINATION,
INDIVIDUALISM, STEREOTYPES

Because they designate unique beings, proper names are untranslatable.

—W. H. AUDEN (1907-1973)
ANGLO-AMERICAN POET AND CRITIC

My hair has always grown in every direction, and my teeth also, and the bristles
of my beard. My nerves and my soul must be planted in the same way.
That is what makes me insoluble to people who develop in one direction.

—JEAN COCTEAU (1889-1963)
FRENCH WRITER AND FILMMAKER

Unless one has some new, intensely personal viewpoint to record,
say on the eternal feelings of love. . . . I say, why write about it?
Nine chances out of ten, if you know where in the past to look, you will find
words already written in the more-or-less exact tongue of your soul.

—HART CRANE (1899-1932)
AMERICAN POET

The desire constantly, systematically, and at any cost to do just the
opposite of what everybody else did pushed me to extravagances
that soon became notorious in artistic circles.

—SALVADOR DALÍ (1904-1989)
SPANISH ARTIST

The *Pink Panther* imitates nothing, it reproduces nothing,
it paints the world its color, pink on pink . . .

—GILLES DELEUZE (1925-1995)
FRENCH PHILOSOPHER AND CRITIC

I think it is most important that one should trust one's own inclination, instincts, and tastes, and should not go to other writers to find out what a novel is or ought to be.

—E. M. FORSTER (1879-1970)
BRITISH WRITER

I do not strive for originality.

—PHILIP JOHNSON (1906-2005)
AMERICAN ARCHITECT

Most people are other people. Their thoughts are someone else's opinions, their life a mimicry, their passions a quotation.

—OSCAR WILDE (1854-1900)
IRISH PLAYWRIGHT AND WRITER

OUTSIDERS

SEE ALSO INDIVIDUALISM, ORIGINALITY, THE PUBLIC, SOCIETY

I've always been an iconoclast, even as a kid. I led a revolution at school when I was 11. I don't trust authority figures, and I don't like anyone telling me what I can and cannot say.

—SCOTT CAPURRO (1962-)
BRITISH COMEDIAN AND WRITER

The freakish character, incapable of originality, discovers it in the trouble he causes you by the lack of coherence in his actions. He tries to startle you and only upsets you. He believes he is exceptional. He does not move any of the pawns who decide the game.

—JEAN COCTEAU (1889-1963)
FRENCH WRITER AND FILMMAKER

We are outsiders, driven by desire, and desire makes us temporary and unreal.

—E. M. FORSTER (1879-1970)
BRITISH WRITER

I'm a new phenomenon, a new thing, a new creature, this rogue renegade character.
I'm not Carson Kressley. I'm not some *Queer Eye for the Straight Guy* safe homo:
I'm dangerous. I'm not afraid to offend; I'm not afraid to push the envelope.

—PEREZ HILTON (1978-)
CUBAN-AMERICAN CELEBRITY BLOGGER

I am not much about rules—like to break 'em and don't like to make 'em.

—CARSON KRESSLEY (1969-)
AMERICAN FASHION EXPERT AND REALITY TV STAR

People used to stop me on the street, the same way they do now—"Oh, I love you,
I think it's so funny that you can actually sound exactly like Dionne Warwick." This
was before my voice changed, right? And it was always, "Oh, you're fabulous,"
but then, "Ha-ha, what a freak." That's what it was. And it feels the same now.
Whenever anyone on the street says, "Oh, you're so great, I love your work," it
always feels like they're with a gang of kids down the block, calling me a freak.

—ISAAC MIZRAHI (1961-)
AMERICAN FASHION DESIGNER

I don't seek sanitization and normalization: I stand with the prostitutes,
boy lovers, drag queens, and transgendered.

—CAMILLE PAGLIA (1947-)
AMERICAN SCHOLAR AND CRITIC

Contestation has always been an essential act. Saints, hermits and intellectuals, those few who have made history, are the ones who have said "no," not the courtesans and Cardinals' assistants.

—PIER PAOLO PASOLINI (1922-1975)
ITALIAN FILM DIRECTOR

A gay kid doesn't discover he or she is gay until around puberty. And their parents aren't gay necessarily, and their classmates aren't, and they feel truly alone in the world and have to find, sometimes never find, a way to live.

—BRYAN SINGER (1965-)
AMERICAN FILM DIRECTOR

I am adopted, and I'm an American, and I'm an only child, and Superman was you know, these three things, except what interests me is that he is the ultimate immigrant and he carries his—what makes him different—his special heritage— he carries it with pride.

—BRYAN SINGER (1965-)
AMERICAN FILM DIRECTOR

When I was young, I wondered, why do men have to dress all the same? Why do they have this boring uniformity? I always liked people who were out of the crowd, who were individuals, who were free, who had a real sense of style, which means their own sense of style. I believe in style. I believe in people who have something to express, who make statements.

—GIANNI VERSACE (1946-1997)
ITALIAN FASHION DESIGNER

[During WWII] the C.O., a martinet whom most of those under him disliked, had taken a fancy to me; perhaps an outsider recognizing another.

—PATRICK WHITE (1912-1990)
AUSTRALIAN WRITER AND NOBEL LAUREATE

PARANOIA

In the twenty-first century, culture is becoming more and more global,
so we're all starting to have the same paranoias.

—ALEJANDRO AMENÁBAR (1972-)
SPANISH FILM DIRECTOR

———

Almost everybody has this theory that everybody else has a fascinating social life.

—ELIZABETH BISHOP (1911-1979)
AMERICAN POET

———

Let me repeat that I am not basically paranoid, that is I do not have the character
structure of true paranoia. I am fundamentally quite reasonable and have sense of
fact unusually well developed. Nonetheless my state of soul is very bad indeed.

—WILLIAM BURROUGHS (1914-1997)
AMERICAN WRITER

———

Paranoia is often just a heightened sensitivity toward what is possible.

—MICHELLE TEA (1971-)
AMERICAN WRITER

PASSION

SEE ALSO LOVE, ROMANCE, SEX

I daresay that in a person like myself who has no very passionate grip upon life,
the soul is liable to try to slip away when it finds a chance.

—J. R. ACKERLEY (1896-1967)
BRITISH WRITER AND EDITOR

It is a great help in life if one can feel passionately about things.
I am too far gone in my relativistic approach to the world really to care very
much about labels. I have no faith whatever in anything.

—PHILIP JOHNSON (1906-2005)
AMERICAN ARCHITECT

———

Life will teach you passion.

—JAMES MERRILL (1926-1995)
AMERICAN PULITZER PRIZE-WINNING POET

———

There's a way for the passion we have about someone to be both carnal and spiritual. It's a rare thing. The great challenge has been to channel this explosive
atom bath of hormones into the spiritual growth that love can be.

—PAUL MONETTE (1945-1995)
AMERICAN WRITER AND AIDS ACTIVIST

———

When you're excited by and idea or passionate about some kind of vision
then it never really becomes about egos.

—SARA GILBERT (1975-)
AMERICAN ACTOR

THE PAST

SEE ALSO HISTORY, THE PRESENT

The terrifying part of it is that it is done. Not what we did, but that it is over.

—DJUNA BARNES (1892-1982)
AMERICAN WRITER

I was dealing with a lot of personal stuff for years. I had a pile of poop to shovel. And once that's cleared away, you have time to think about things other than Ugh, what have I done.

—ANI DIFRANCO (1970-)
AMERICAN SINGER-SONGWRITER

We have no wish to revolt against the past; we can acknowledge the leadership of our great elders. But we can be freer.

—PHILIP JOHNSON (1906-2005)
AMERICAN ARCHITECT

The past can't be erased and can only be effaced if we agree to forget, and what has been shouldn't be forgotten.

—TONY KUSHNER (1956-)
AMERICAN PLAYWRIGHT

PERSPECTIVE

SEE ALSO ART AND ARTISTS, EXPERIENCE, SELF-AWARENESS

Everybody has his own interpretation of a painting he sees. I don't mind if people have different interpretations of what I have painted.

—FRANCIS BACON (1909-1992)
BRITISH ARTIST

I don't really have a strictly contrary nature, I just like looking at the other side of things.

—LEIGH BOWERY (1961-1994)
BRITISH PERFORMANCE ARTIST

Anyone who looks at something special, in a very original way,
makes you see it in that way forever.

—GEORGE CUKOR (1899-1983)
AMERICAN FILM DIRECTOR

———

Any point of view is interesting that is a direct impression of life.

—HENRY JAMES (1843-1916)
AMERICAN WRITER

———

I don't consciously try to turn anything into a farce. But I do think that that's my
natural way of seeing the world.

—NICKY SILVER (1960-)
AMERICAN PLAYWRIGHT

PESSIMISM

I've never responded well to entrenched negative thinking.
When I'm faced with "that won't work" or "don't let's try that," I freeze up.
I try to put judgment on hold for as long as possible.

—DAVID BOWIE (1947-)
BRITISH MUSICIAN

———

I acquired then a certain disengagement from things which are not essential, a
certain habit of doubting appearances and disdaining trifles. . . . But the price
paid in disillusionment and moral befoulment outweighed the gain of mental grit.

—JOHN ADDINGTON SYMONDS (1840-1893)
ENGLISH POET AND CRITIC

I'm of the opinion that things are going to get a lot worse with the world before they get better. I'm a bit of an Armageddon type.

—RUFUS WAINWRIGHT (1973-)
CANADIAN MUSICIAN

PHOTOGRAPHY

SEE ALSO ART AND ARTISTS, CREATION AND CREATIVITY, MEDIA, PORNOGRAPHY

When you're making a picture of something like that [an earthquake], you have to strike the right balance. You're capturing people on the worst days of their lives, and you are trying not to be too intrusive, but you want to show them in the moment and show them with some dignity and respect.

—GINNY DIXON (CA 1961-)
PULITZER PRIZE-WINNING PHOTOGRAPHER

———

Photography's changing. The digits are a profound change. The hand is actually being brought back into the camera. Er, meaning it's going towards painting.

—DAVID HOCKNEY (1937-)
BRITISH ARTIST

———

I went into photography because it seemed like the perfect vehicle for commenting on the madness of today's existence.

—ROBERT MAPPLETHORPE (1946-1989)
AMERICAN PHOTOGRAPHER

POETRY

SEE ALSO ART AND ARTISTS, LANGUAGE, LITERATURE, WRITING

You have to write a lot of bad poetry to get a good line of prose.

—DOROTHY ALLISON (1942–)
AMERICAN WRITER

———————

All genuine poetry is in a sense the formation of private spheres
out of a public chaos.

—W. H. AUDEN (1907–1973)
ANGLO-AMERICAN POET AND CRITIC

———————

I'm not a "thinky" poet. Any analysis I might have about where the poems come
from, or what influences bear upon them, is strictly retrospective.

—JUDITH BARRINGTON (1944–)
BRITISH POET AND WRITER

———————

Sometimes I think if I had been born a man I probably would have written
more. Dared more, or been able to spend more time at it. I've wasted a great
deal of time.

—ELIZABETH BISHOP (1911–1979)
AMERICAN POET

———————

Our poetry now is the realization that we possess nothing.

—JOHN CAGE (1934–1992)
AMERICAN COMPOSER

———————

If a poet has a dream, it is not of becoming famous, but of being believed.

—JEAN COCTEAU (1889–1963)
FRENCH WRITER AND FILMMAKER

I admit to a slight leaning toward the esoteric, and am perhaps not to be taken seriously. I am fond of things of great fragility.

—HART CRANE (1899-1932)
AMERICAN POET

Poetry, the human feelings . . . [are] so crowded out of the humdrum, rushing, mechanical scramble of today that the man who would preserve them must duck and camouflage for dear life to keep them or keep himself from annihilation.

—HART CRANE (1899-1932)
AMERICAN POET

A lot of poetry is coming true today, in the same way that a photograph reveals itself as it's being developed.

—ALLEN GINSBERG (1926-1997)
AMERICAN POET

I admit the expression "poetry world" causes a brief shudder of distaste.

—MARILYN HACKER (1942-)
FEMINIST POET, CRITIC, AND ACTIVIST

Intellect is oftentimes the foe of poetry because it imitates too much.

—FEDERICO GARCIA LORCA (1898-1936)
SPANISH POET AND PLAYWRIGHT

A poetic image is always a transference of meaning.

—FEDERICO GARCIA LORCA (1898-1936)
SPANISH POET AND PLAYWRIGHT

Poetry is the way we help give name to the nameless so it can be thought.

—AUDRE LORDE (1934-1992)
AFRICAN-AMERICAN WRITER, POET, AND ACTIVIST

[My poetry] is found at the crossroads where what I know and can't get meets what is left of what I know and can bear without hatred.

—FRANK O'HARA (1926-1966)
AMERICAN POET

The first poetry one reads is unforgettable.

—PIER PAOLO PASOLINI (1922-1975)
ITALIAN FILM DIRECTOR

I was tempted by holiness. Poetry was how.

—PIER PAOLO PASOLINI (1922-1975)
ITALIAN FILM DIRECTOR

I think the present age an unfavorable one to poets.

—WALTER PATER (1839-1894)
BRITISH CRITIC AND WRITER

I am degrading myself as much as possible. Why? I want to be a poet.

—ARTHUR RIMBAUD (1854-1891)
FRENCH POET

Poetry is some sort of "life-force," or enthusiasm, which uses us. We must live, above all, naturally; and wait to be made use of by the daemon of Poesy. I wish she (or he) would come a little nearer Tufton Street.

—SIEGFRIED SASSOON (1886-1967)
BRITISH POET AND WRITER

The republic of letters is, in reality, an aristocracy. And "poet" has always been a *titre de noblesse.*

—SUSAN SONTAG (1933-2004)
AMERICAN WRITER AND CRITIC

A poet's prose is the autobiography of ardor.

—SUSAN SONTAG (1933-2004)
AMERICAN WRITER AND CRITIC

English poets do not, like their American colleagues, reflect bitterly that all they are doing is writing poetry for other poets. It is exactly this which they want to do.

—STEPHEN SPENDER (1909-1995)
BRITISH POET AND WRITER

I am not a Pisces in vain. All poets are Piscean regardless of the month in which they are born.

—STEPHEN SPENDER (1909-1995)
BRITISH POET AND WRITER

In those days we laughed at poverty, because the poet is always poor, even when his name is Byron, Lamartine, or Tennyson.

—PAUL VERLAINE (1844-1896)
FRENCH POET

POLITICS

SEE ALSO ACTIVISM, GAY RIGHTS, MEDIA, THE MILITARY, WAR

I have absolutely no patience with Pacifism as a political movement,
as if one could do all the things in one's personal life that create wars and then
pretend that to refuse to fight is a sacrifice and not a luxury.

—W. H. AUDEN (1907-1973)
ANGLO-AMERICAN POET AND CRITIC

———————

I wouldn't vote for my father for anything. . . . I don't believe in his politics;
I think they're dangerous.

—CHASTITY BONO (1979-)
AMERICAN GAY RIGHTS ACTIVIST AND DAUGHTER OF CHER AND SONNY BONO

———————

At that time, with the [Berlin] Wall still up, there was a feeling of terrific tension
throughout the city. It was either very young or very old people. There were no
family units in Berlin. It was a city of extremes. It vacillated between the absurd—the
whole drag, transvestite night-club type of thing—and real radical, Marxist political
thought. And it seemed like this really was the focus of the new Europe. It was right
here. For the first time, the tension was outside of me rather than within me.

—DAVID BOWIE (1947-)
BRITISH MUSICIAN

———————

I can't help feeling that not until that "political consciousness" is more
general that the world will get out of this mess.

—BENJAMIN BRITTEN (1913-1976)
BRITISH COMPOSER

———————

[On Anita Hill] A little nutty, a little slutty.

—DAVID BROCK (1962-)
AMERICAN CONSERVATIVE JOURNALIST

Democracy is cancerous, and bureaus are its cancer. A bureau takes root anywhere in the state, turns malignant like the Narcotics Bureau, and grows and grows, always reproducing more of its own kind.

—WILLIAM BURROUGHS (1914-1997)
AMERICAN WRITER

For me being mayor is like taking a vow of celibacy; I don't date and I'm not in a relationship; I don't have a wife out in public and then a secret boyfriend whose on the city payroll; and I don't surf the Web on the city computer looking for pornography. Living a lie just wasn't an option.

—CHRISTOPHER CABALDON (1965-)
AMERICAN POLITICIAN, MAYOR OF WEST SACRAMENTO, CALIFORNIA

As much as we have issues with Middle America stereotyping gays, it's equally true that gays stereotype what goes on in Middle America.

—BRUCE COHEN (ca. 1965-)
AMERICAN FILM PRODUCER

Faced with such palpable incompetence and dishonesty, I should have thought that the great majority of the people would realize that the present Government, for which they voted with such enthusiasm, was not very good; but I am afraid that the people of this country are too stupid and complacent to grasp what is happening.

—NOËL COWARD (1899-1973)
BRITISH ACTOR AND PLAYWRIGHT

The only thing I won't touch is Laura Bush's pudendum.

—LEA DELARIA (1958-)
AMERICAN COMEDIAN AND ACTOR

Peace is not possible without balance. And patriarchy is inherently imbalanced.

—ANI DIFRANCO (1970-)
AMERICAN SINGER-SONGWRITER

I'm young enough (or old enough, depending on your point of view) to have
been shaped by the notion that the personal is political.

—MARK DOTY (1953-)
AMERICAN POET

Russia, perhaps through no fault of her own, seems to be going in the wrong
direction; too much uniformity and too much bloodshed. Perhaps—
and perhaps under another name—Communism will restart after the next
European catastrophe and do better.

—E. M. FORSTER (1879-1970)
BRITISH WRITER

The Bush administration has squelched freedom of speech.
If you disagree with them, you're excommunicated. We live in a country of
differences, and we should be able to voice those differences.

—TOM FORD (1962-)
AMERICAN FASHION DESIGNER

Thanks to all the increased communication that television, film, and the Internet
have created, even people in small towns in Middle America are exposed to the
same things as people in urban areas. That gives me great hope for the future.

—TOM FORD (1962-)
AMERICAN FASHION DESIGNER

People forget—and politicians forget sometimes too—that they're working for us. We're their bosses.

—CANDACE GINGRICH (1966-)
AMERICAN LGBT RIGHTS ACTIVIST, HALF-SISTER OF NEWT GINGRICH

Once you participate in the system, that in itself involves compromise. . . . The flip side is that if we don't participate, we cannot expect to have our interests reflected.

—DEBORAH GLICK (1989-)
NEW YORK STATE ASSEMBLYPERSON

There is nothing essentially Arab about terrorism, nor are Arabs the only perpetrators of terrorist acts.

—DAVE HALL(ca. 1970-)
ARAB-AMERICAN MUSICIAN

The state is a human tool designed for the benefit of humanity, not an absolute with metaphysical status nor an end in itself.

—KURT HILLER (1885-1972)
JEWISH WRITER AND PACIFIST

[On her committee's decision to impeach Nixon] My faith in the constitution is whole, it is complete, it is total. . . . I am not going to sit here and be an idle spectator to the diminution, the subversion, the destruction of the Constitution.

—BARBARA JORDAN (1936-1996)
AFRICAN-AMERICAN LEGISLATOR

There is nothing a government hates more than to be well-informed.

—JOHN MAYNARD KEYNES (1883-1946)
BRITISH ECONOMIST

It takes zillions of bucks and a severe personality disorder to become president.

—TONY KUSHNER (1956–)
AMERICAN PLAYWRIGHT

———————

People change, I believe deeply in the possibility of people changing,
but Bush? Sharon? Eight months have passed and look at the godforsaken
mess the feckless blood-spattered plutocrat and the unindicted
war criminal have wrought in the Mideast.

—TONY KUSHNER (1956–)
AMERICAN PLAYWRIGHT

———————

The problem with overtly political or social writing is that when the tide of feeling
goes out, the language begins to stink.

—JAMES MERRILL (1926–1995)
AMERICAN PULITZER PRIZE-WINNING POET

———————

I don't like the sort of liberal that is the reactionary underneath.

—JOE ORTON (1933–1967)
BRITISH PLAYWRIGHT

———————

The country is desperately seeking answers that combine some of the
best of conservative and liberal thinking.

—TORIE OSBORN (ca. 1950–)
AMERICAN GAY RIGHTS ACTIVIST

———————

Gays, who are vulnerable to abrupt changes in political climate, must have disci-
plined free minds to see the present and past without sentimentality or fear.

—CAMILLE PAGLIA (1947–)
AMERICAN SCHOLAR AND CRITIC

I'm not going to play only to a bunch of dykes and fags. I won't do that. I can do more for the gay community by . . . having my music reach somebody in Bumfuck, Ohio, who doesn't have any positive lesbian role models.

—LINDA PERRY (1965-)
AMERICAN MUSICIAN

When you live in San Francisco, with its liberal attitudes about sex and large gay community, you can forget that much of the rest of the country is very, very different. The moment you let your guard down, the cops will pounce.

—STEVEN SCARBOROUGH (ca. 1953-)
AMERICAN PORN PRODUCER AND DIRECTOR

As lesbians and gay men, we have spent our lives fearing eviction from our homes, the loss of our jobs, and beatings in the streets—simply because of who we are. . . . For us, the personal is the political.

—GERRY STUDDS (1937-2006)
AMERICAN CONGRESSMAN

There are already far too many in Washington who confuse themselves with the monuments.

—GERRY STUDDS (1937-2006)
AMERICAN CONGRESSMAN

My home state of Florida is as red as them come.

—JAMES ST. JAMES (1966-)
AMERICAN WRITER

You can only criticize capitalists and gay white men so much before they stop writing checks.

—RICH TAFEL (1962-)
AMERICAN FOUNDER OF THE LOG CABIN REPUBLICANS

I'm all for outing legislators and figures in government who are promoting antigay agendas and living their lives in a way that is hypocritical.

—ANDY TOWLE (1967–)
AMERICAN BLOGGER

———————

Politics is just my thing, you know—election night is like my Christmas Eve.

—RICK TROMBLY (1957–)
AMERICAN POLITICIAN AND STATE LEGISLATOR

Lesbians in leadership positions play a conventional kind of power politics invented by straight men.

—URVASHI VAID (1958–)
AMERICAN GAY RIGHTS ACTIVIST

———————

I was brought up in Washington. When you are brought up in a zoo, you know what's going on in the monkey house. You see a couple of monkeys loose and one is President and one is Vice President, you know it's trouble. Monkeys make trouble.

—GORE VIDAL (1925–)
AMERICAN WRITER AND POLITICAL ACTIVIST

———————

American laws don't work, but at least the laws of physics might work. And the Third Law is: There is no action without reaction. There should be a great deal of reaction to the total incompetence of this Administration. It's going to take two or three generations to recover what we had as of twenty years ago.

—GORE VIDAL (1925–)
AMERICAN WRITER AND POLITICAL ACTIVIST

I'm not a liberal, I mean, I voted for Ford. I liked his family better, and when Mrs. Carter said her idea of what she wanted to do was to bring square dancing back to the White House, well, that's when they lost my vote.

—JOHN WATERS (1946-)
AMERICAN DIRECTOR

You know, I can't give blood. I can't serve in the military. I mean, as a taxpayer, I'm funding my own discrimination! And then the government wants to give money to churches that discriminate against me.

—TOMMIE WATKINS
AMERICAN WRITER AND ACTIVIST

The fact that the rainbow flag—the worldwide symbol of gay rights—is waving today in front of Berlin's city hall is not a political act but one that goes without saying.

—KLAUS WOWEREIT (1953-)
GERMAN POLITICIAN AND MAYOR OF BERLIN

I have the feeling that people must be part of politics and must contribute to improve the situation of their own country. You can't just watch what happens and complain.

—FRANCO ZEFFIRELLI (1923-)
ITALIAN FILM DIRECTOR

GAY POLITICIANS

I am the first openly gay congressional committee chairman, which means I am the first openly gay or lesbian person in American history to have significant governmental powers. A lot of very important people in the country and in the world are going to have to deal with me on equal terms.

—BARNEY FRANK (1940-)
AMERICAN CONGRESSMAN

I'm sure we've had gay presidents before.

—STEVE HOWARD (1971-)
AMERICAN POLITICIAN AND STATE LEGISLATOR

I get some bad letters. But you can't separate if this is a reaction against a gay politician, or is it a reaction against a politician who is gay?

—KLAUS WOWEREIT (1953-)
GERMAN POLITICIAN AND MAYOR OF BERLIN

POLITICAL PARTIES

I never really felt that younger conservative crowd, the non-religious right crowd, was antigay. Younger, more hip members of the Right don't want the baggage of the religious right. I always found it hard to tell—and I was this way too—what conservative activists believed and what they were merely parroting. There was a lot of groupthink or party line and not a lot of independent thinking.

—DAVID BROCK (1962-)
CONSERVATIVE JOURNALIST

I am well aware of what a man risks who belongs to neither the right nor to the left. He is called an opportunist. For ists and isms are flourishing as usual.

—JEAN COCTEAU (1889-1963)
FRENCH WRITER AND FILMMAKER

I represent, I think, a large group of people who are fiscally conservative, who are pretty conservative on international affairs, and who happen to be gay. They would find the most comfort in the Republican Party, unless the Republican Party declares war on them.

—STEVE GUNDERSON (1951-)
OPENLY GAY AMERICAN CONGRESSMAN

It's not any more difficult, I think, for a candidate to deal with the gay issue than with the pro-choice issue in Republican Party and get nominated.

—STEVE GUNDERSON (1951-)
OPENLY GAY AMERICAN CONGRESSMAN

I had to come out as a Democrat before I came out gay.

—ERIC JOHNSON (1973-)
AMERICAN DOCUMENTARY STAR AND CONGRESSIONAL STAFFER

Bear culture emerged from the same phenomenon that gave us the Log Cabin Republicans.

—ERIC ROFES (1954-2006)
AMERICAN WRITER AND ACTIVIST

"Gay Republican" has always seemed like such a contradiction in terms.

—PAUL RUDNICK (1957-)
AMERICAN SCREENWRITER AND PLAYWRIGHT

It isn't an opposition party. I have been saying for the last thousand years that the United States has only one party—the property party. It's the party of big corporations, the party of money. It has two right wings; one is Democrat and the other is Republican.

—GORE VIDAL (1925-)
AMERICAN WRITER AND POLITICAL ACTIVIST

PORNOGRAPHY

SEE ALSO ENTERTAINMENT, MOVIES, PROSTITUTION, SEX, TELEVISION

I never watched pornography in my life, and I haven't even watched my films . . .
I just don't watch things, and especially not pornography—because it is sort of
the same thing I saw for real happening in the parks and things.

—PETER BERLIN (1934–)
GERMAN MODEL AND GAY SEX ICON

Did I ever tell you about the time I went to dirty movies in a Mexico City whore-
house and I had lost my glasses, and I said: "If that isn't the hairiest son of a
bitch I ever see fucking that cunt." Wind-up is it's a dog, a German police dog.

—WILLIAM BURROUGHS (1914-1997)
AMERICAN WRITER

Making trans porn came out of the same need that the book filled, with so little
out there I felt it necessary to try my hand at pornography. I really enjoyed making *Trannyfags* and I am anxious to direct my next video, which will have trans-
men having sex with women this time.

—MORTY DIAMOND (ca. 1976–)
AMERICAN FTM WRITER AND PORN PRODUCER

The lines between porn and the mainstream are getting thinner.

—COLTON FORD (1962–)
AMERICAN PORN STAR

Guys here [New York] are from all over the world. I like that, and I also like them to be uninhibited, nasty, and dirty. I want all of their nasty secrets and desires to be exposed for my cameras. I like them not only to fuck each other, I like them pissing on each other and eating each other's asses like there is no tomorrow. I am not interested in clean-cut vanilla sex.

—MICHAEL LUCAS (1972-)
RUSSIAN-BORN PORN PRODUCER

Here's my advice to all of you who are still broken up about *Brokeback Mountain*'s loss at the Oscars. Head to your local gay bookstore and shell out a few bucks for something besides porn.

—CHRISTOPHER RICE (1978-)
AMERICAN WRITER

What I do on camera is nothing like sex I have in private.
It's about making something look right for the camera.

—AIDEN SHAW (1966-)
BRITISH PORN STAR

Playgirl was a big influence on me as a kid. . . . I remember sneaking into my neighbor's house to peek at it when I was really young, nine and ten years old. And the amazing thing is all my friends have the same story!

—DIRK SHAFER (1962-)
AMERICAN MODEL, ACTOR, DIRECTOR, AND *PLAYGIRL*'S MAN OF THE YEAR IN 1992

So many people are flashing their own tools all over the Internet nowadays that we're all becoming increasingly desensitized—thank God!

—MICHAEL SOLDIER (1967-)
AMERICAN PORN STAR

I always knew I'd be some kind of artist. I thought I'd be an art teacher.
In fact, I am an art teacher. When I went into porn, I thought, oh I'll never be an
art teacher. But I'm hired now as an artist because I went into porn.

—ANNIE SPRINKLE (1954-)
AMERICAN PERFORMANCE ARTIST AND SEX EDUCATOR

But I don't make regular porn anymore. I make post-porn.

—ANNIE SPRINKLE (1954-)
AMERICAN PERFORMANCE ARTIST AND SEX EDUCATOR

Sex is the ultimate experience in someone's life—when I'm giving it to them!

—JEFF STRYKER (1962-)
AMERICAN PORN STAR

I'm resentful toward my parents for not giving birth to a porn star.

—RUFUS WAINWRIGHT (1973-)
CANADIAN MUSICIAN

[On what else people can do with their home video recorders]
Make the best pornography movies. It's going to be so great.

—ANDY WARHOL (1928-1987)
AMERICAN ARTIST

Maybe some people would still say it's kind of silly to say porn helps,
but now I know it does when I talk to people. And again I know a lot of movies
for guys in the Midwest who . . . don't live the life that maybe they wanted to.

—JOSH WESTON (ca. 1980-)
AMERICAN PORN STAR

A B role in a porn movie is anything that's not sex.

—JOSH WESTON (ca. 1980-)
AMERICAN PORN STAR

PREJUDICE

SEE ALSO HATRED, RACE AND RACISM

We still have a few prejudices hanging around and even if we don't
remove them ourselves, dear friends come in and do it for us.

—JOHN CAGE (1934-1992)
AMERICAN COMPOSER

————————

My own prejudice was the most difficult thing fro me to confront, and back then it
took me longer to admit congenital idiocy than it does now.

—JANIS IAN (1951-)
AMERICAN GRAMMY AWARD-WINNING MUSICIAN

————————

All of us make big mistakes in our thinking about people we don't know firsthand.

—ETHEL WATERS (1896-1977)
AFRICAN AMERICAN ACTOR AND MUSICIAN

THE PRESENT

SEE ALSO HISTORY, THE PAST

Since our centuries, in terms of God, last the space of a wink,
our picture is taken in slow motion. Slightly less speed would release all souls
and would remove from human intercourse its ferociousness.

—JEAN COCTEAU (1889-1963)
FRENCH WRITER AND FILMMAKER

We are going through a foggy chaos. Let us enjoy the multiplicity of it all.

—PHILIP JOHNSON (1906-2005)
AMERICAN ARCHITECT

What time in human history is comparable to this? It's nearly impossible to locate plausible occasions for hope. Foulness, corruption, meanness of spirit carry the day.

—TONY KUSHNER (1956-)
AMERICAN PLAYWRIGHT

Instead of a utopian moment, the time we live in is experienced as the end—more exactly, just past the end—of every ideal.

—SUSAN SONTAG (1933-2004)
AMERICAN WRITER AND CRITIC

The past only comes back when the present runs so smoothly that it is like the sliding surface of a deep river. Then one sees through the surface to the depths.

—VIRGINIA WOOLF (1882-1941)
BRITISH WRITER

PRISON

SEE ALSO CRIME

When I was at another facility I met a boy named Mike who I fell deeply in love with. I'd watch him in the mess hall and think to myself, "If only I could meet someone like that, then I wouldn't even mind being in jail!"

—MICHAEL ALIG (1966-)
AMERICAN FOUNDING MEMBER OF THE CLUB KIDS AND CONVICTED MURDERER

I can't say I'll never go to jail for a cause again, but I hope I never have any more jail bologna.

—MICHAEL CUNNINGHAM (1952–)
AMERICAN PULITZER PRIZE WINNING WRITER

Prison is that fortress, the ideal cave, the bandit's retreat against which the forces of the world beat in vain.

—JEAN GENET (1910–1986)
FRENCH WRITER, CRIMINAL, AND POLITICAL ACTIVIST

Well I was very popular in the L.A. County Jail . . . but I don't think for the right reasons! I'm a big talker, which is a great if you're in jail. Being able to tell stories helps a lot, especially if you're four foot eleven!

—LESLIE JORDAN (1955–)
AMERICAN EMMY AWARD-WINNING ACTOR

I don't have a chip on my shoulder about having been sent to prison. . . . No, I liked prison. I mean the only things I had against it were the small things.

—JOE ORTON (1933–1967)
BRITISH PLAYWRIGHT

PROMISCUITY

SEE ALSO PROSTITUTION, SEX

What's wrong with sluts? If sluttiness is what you like, what's wrong with that?

—TOM FORD (1962–)
AMERICAN FASHION DESIGNER

Give me the venom of the male sperm anytime over the placid life of the abstinent. Give me the drudgery of decaying health over the untouched skin that has never suffered the abrasions of heated love.

—FRANCISCO IBAÑEZ-CARRASCO (1963–)
CHILEAN-CANADIAN WRITER

Nature always extracts a price for sexual promiscuity.

—LARRY KRAMER (1935–)
AMERICAN WRITER, PLAYWRIGHT, ßAND ACTIVIST

The secret of sacred slutism . . . is being consciously aware of our slutty side, our animal side, nurturing that side of us, the wildwoman, the inner whore in all of us.

—ANNIE SPRINKLE (1954–)
AMERICAN PERFORMANCE ARTIST AND SEX EDUCATOR

I can also defend, on what appears to me sufficient grounds, a large amount of promiscuity. In the very nature of the sexual contact between two males there inheres an element of instability. No children come of the connection. There can be no marriage ceremonies. . . . Therefore the parties are left free, and the sexual flower of comradeship may spring afresh for each of them wherever favorable soil is found.

—JOHN ADDINGTON SYMONDS (1840-1893)
ENGLISH POET AND CRITIC

PROSTITUTION

SEE ALSO BUSINESS, MONEY, PROMISCUITY, SEX, WORK

I have been to a Japanese bath; it is a communal affair, everyone, men and boys, sit all together in a large sunken tiled bath of hot water . . .

—J. R. ACKERLEY (1896-1967)
BRITISH WRITER AND EDITOR

They have an arrangement here [in Tangier] I never saw elsewhere in all my experience as a traveler: Private Turkish bath cubicles "à deux" 60 cents. This solves the hotel problem. But the boys got like a union. They all expect $5.

—WILLIAM BURROUGHS (1914-1997)
AMERICAN WRITER

When a young person comes in to eat another man's relishes and to place a noncontributory hand upon the provender, you may assume that he'll be paying the bill overnight.

—EPHIPPUS (4TH CENTURY, BC)
GREEK POET

I really agonized over it [paid sex with evangelist Ted Haggard] for quite a while and finally decided I needed to say something . . . on principle, for the gay community. . . . I wish Haggard peace. . . . I do not wish him ill."

—MIKE JONES (1958-)
FORMER HUSTLER WHO OUTED TELEVANGELIST TED HAGGARD

The defiant rise of the stripper in the 1990s is the ultimate challenge to the old-guard feminist establishment with its genteel middle-class values.

—CAMILLE PAGLIA (1947-)
AMERICAN SCHOLAR AND CRITIC

When I was 10, men would come up to me and say, "Do you want an ice-cream
cone? If you do this, I'll give you the money to buy an ice-cream cone."
I thought that was normal; I didn't think there was anything wrong with it,
except that they didn't have Kleenexes in those days!

—HAROLD ROBBINS (1916-1997)
AMERICAN WRITER

Set my hair alight at a gas-jet in the Turkish Bath!

—SIEGFRIED SASSOON (1886-1967)
BRITISH POET AND WRITER

I didn't even know I was doing prostitution for three months. . . .
I really thought I was a masseuse.

—ANNIE SPRINKLE (1954-)
AMERICAN PERFORMANCE ARTIST AND SEX EDUCATOR

I'm interested in the new prostitution—for example, prostitutes for lesbians. . . .
There's a lot of new stuff happening. The image of the sacred
prostitute is coming back very strong.

—ANNIE SPRINKLE (1954-)
AMERICAN PERFORMANCE ARTIST AND SEX EDUCATOR

[During WWII] I learned a lot about the whore's mentality, and the
variations on her one client, in fact the whole tragicomedy of sex.

—PATRICK WHITE (1912-1990)
AUSTRALIAN WRITER AND NOBEL LAUREATE

The [go-go] boys wear G-strings only—so you can be pretty sure what you're getting. I would recommend, however, that penetration be avoided, as they are most probably all infected with clap in the ass. And I'd also recommend that you get them to the bath as their hours are long and sweaty. And that you have a pubic pesticide such as A-200.

—TENNESSEE WILLIAMS (1911-1983)
AMERICAN PLAYWRIGHT

HUSTLERS

Not to feel intact, not to [be] able to expose oneself to certain contacts because of self-consciousness—that really is an awful nuisance, and I spend a good deal of time now with people who are (vaguely speaking) my inferiors, and to whom I can very easily be kind.

—E. M. FORSTER (1879-1970)
BRITISH WRITER

I fell in love with a hustler who lied about every detail of his identity, even his name. In other words, I fell in love with the idea of someone, rather than a real person. And I lied to myself about myself.

—RON NYSWANER (1956-)
AMERICAN SCREENWRITER

He was one of the many to be found sunbathing on the pier on weekday afternoons, one of the many with no visible means of support, with time on their hands, a cultivated affability that is their best asset, a lifestyle somehow more pastoral than urban—in other words, a hustler.

—GEORGE WHITMORE (1946-1989)
AMERICAN WRITER AND PLAYWRIGHT

PSYCHOLOGY

SEE ALSO STATES OF MIND, THERAPY, THOUGHT

I think we all do what we have to do, that is to say what is dictated by
our psychologies.

—J. R. ACKERLEY (1896–1967)
BRITISH WRITER AND EDITOR

———————

After all, it is highly futile . . . to worry about neurotic homosexuals when the
world itself, led and ruled by the strong heterosexual "normal" men is in such
chaotic condition, and knows not where to turn. It is quite possible that if
called upon, the homosexuals in this country would put up the money to send
[a doctor] to Washington to examine these great big "normal" men, who guide
the destinies of millions, to find their "neurosis" and to cure it.

—HENRY GERBER (1892–1972)
GERMAN-BORN GAY RIGHTS ACTIVIST

———————

There are surely compensations for whatever type of mind a person may have,
but surely the mere memory mind is a great barrier to human relationships.

—ROBERT MCALMON (1896–1956)
AMERICAN WRITER AND PUBLISHER

———————

It's rather difficult to talk about my relations with my father and mother because
I know something about psychoanalysis, so I am not certain whether to talk
about them simply in terms of poetic, anecdotal memory or whether to
talk about them in psychoanalytic terms.

—PIER PAOLO PASOLINI (1922–1975)
ITALIAN FILM DIRECTOR

I don't mess around with my subconscious. . . . I try to keep wide awake.

—ROBERT RAUSCHENBERG (1925-)
AMERICAN ARTIST

———————

I am no longer in the mood to reveal the workings of my thought-processes
for the benefit of unbegotten generations of psychopathic subjects.

—SIEGFRIED SASSOON (1886-1967)
BRITISH POET AND WRITER

———————

A psychiatrist I once knew told me that the unconscious, that irritating retard, can't
distinguish between abandoning someone and being abandoned by him. I guess
he meant that even though I left you, it's come to seem as though you left me.

—EDMUND WHITE (1940-)
AMERICAN WRITER AND CRITIC

THE PUBLIC

SEE ALSO AUDIENCES, SOCIETY

The public is a billowy sea. It causes nausea.

—JEAN COCTEAU (1889-1963)
FRENCH WRITER AND FILMMAKER

———————

I am very free from Puritanical preoccupations—as much as from excessive
elegance. What I lament is that gross attitude of the crowd that is really
degrading and which is so easily forced upon us before we know it.

—HART CRANE (1899-1932)
AMERICAN POET

My patience with ordinary people has given out.

—E. M. FORSTER (1879–1970)
BRITISH WRITER

———

As for the stupid public, one must simply mind that at one time as little as at another. It is always there and is always a perfectly neglectable quantity, in regard to any question of letters or of art.

—HENRY JAMES (1843–1916)
AMERICAN WRITER

———

Ah, the public ain't so bad, they suffer too.

—JACK KEROUAC (1922–1969)
AMERICAN WRITER

———

The public, and mind you I do not say the people, can be taught. I know they can. I heard them boo Debussy and Ravel a few years ago, but I heard an ordinary audience shower their works with applause a couple of years later.

—FEDERICO GARCIA LORCA (1898–1936)
SPANISH POET AND PLAYWRIGHT

———

You may think I'm being old-fashioned, but I happen to know the public better than you do. I know their likes and dislikes. That's why I'm a bestseller throughout the world. Why proclaim from the rooftops that . . . you are predominantly homosexual?

—W. SOMERSET MAUGHAM (1874–1965)
BRITISH WRITER AND PLAYWRIGHT

———

I went through a period where I was really tired of seeing and reading about myself. If I'm tired of me, I'm sure the public is as well.

—MICHAEL STIPE (1960–)
AMERICAN MUSICIAN

I was called a "star," but being a star was to me just a nice way of saying I was a servant to my public.

—ETHEL WATERS (1896-1977)
AFRICAN-AMERICAN ACTOR AND MUSICIAN

Art should never try to be popular; the public should try to make itself artistic.

—OSCAR WILDE (1854-1900)
IRISH PLAYWRIGHT AND WRITER

QUEERNESS

SEE ALSO GAY COMMUNITY, GAY PRIDE, GAY RIGHTS, GAYS VS. LESBIANS, GAYS VS. STRAIGHTS, GENDER BENDING, LESBIANS

Some of the best people have been queers (all the old gang are trotted out once more, Shakespeare Tchaikovsky, etc).

—J. R. ACKERLEY (1896-1967)
BRITISH WRITER AND EDITOR

———

The only queer people are those who don't love anybody.

—RITA MAE BROWN (1944-)
AMERICAN WRITER

———

I'm the bad guy. . . . I'm not acting like a good little queer should.
I'm not being silent about issues that don't concern a modern gay man, like hair dos and don'ts.

—SCOTT CAPURRO (1962-)
BRITISH COMEDIAN AND WRITER

———

America I'm putting my queer shoulder to the wheel.

—ALLEN GINSBERG (1926-1997)
AMERICAN POET

———

You're neither unnatural, nor abominable, nor mad; you're as much a part of what people call nature as anyone else.

—RADCLYFFE HALL (1880-1943)
BRITISH NOVELIST AND POET

You see, I was a quarter normal and three-quarters queer, but I tried to persuade myself it was the other way round. That was my greatest mistake.

—W. SOMERSET MAUGHAM (1874–1965)
BRITISH WRITER AND PLAYWRIGHT

[Magnus] Hirschfeld was conducting his psychoanalytic school and a number of souls unsure of their sexes or of their inhibitions competed with each other in looking or acting freakishly, several Germans declared themselves authentic hermaphrodites, and one elderly variant loved to arrive at the smart cabarets each time as a different type of woman—elegant, or as a washerwoman, or a street vendor, or as a modest mother of a family.

—ROBERT MCALMON (1896–1956)
AMERICAN WRITER AND PUBLISHER

My work is always about community. . . . But do I have to do queer work to be part of the queer community?

—CATHERINE OPIE (1961–)
AMERICAN PHOTOGRAPHER

When I was living as a dyke, before transition, I dated women you could consider Bears. Well, they were certainly more butch than many of the boys at the Lone Star. But yeah, I'm a fag who likes Bears.

—MATT RICE (ca. 1970–)
AMERICAN FTM BEAR

I'm in a queer excited state . . .

—VITA SACKVILLE-WEST (1892–1962)
BRITISH POET, NOVELIST, AND GARDENER

The best gift we queer folks can give the rest of the world is a new angle on love.

—NICK STREET (1967-)
AMERICAN WRITER AND EDITOR

If homosexuality is a disease, let's all call in queer to work: "Hello. Can't work today, still queer."

—ROBIN TYLER (ca. 1955-)
AMERICAN GRASSROOTS ACTIVIST

There is no quintessential queer obsession—queers are obsessed with everything from their wardrobe to Section 28.

—JEANETTE WINTERSON (1959-)
BRITISH WRITER

RACE AND RACISM

SEE ALSO HATRED, IDENTITY, GAY RIGHTS, OUTSIDERS, POLITICS

Can I just reiterate: I don't hate white people. I hate stupid people.

—JOHN AMAECHI (1970-)
BRITISH NBA BASKETBALL PLAYER

———————

If Santa Claus did come from the North Pole, he would look more indigenous, more Eskimo, not like a big white bloke.

—JUSTIN CHIN (1967-)
ASIAN-AMERICAN WRITER AND PERFORMANCE ARTIST

———————

I believe that the consequences of racism are worse than the consequences of homophobia.

—TONY KUSHNER (1956-)
AMERICAN PLAYWRIGHT

———————

The history of white women who are unable to hear Black women's words, or to maintain dialogue with us, is long and discouraging.

—AUDRE LORDE (1934-1992)
AFRICAN-AMERICAN WRITER, POET, AND ACTIVIST

———————

Wherever an ethnologically related group of people is exploited by others, the exploiters often operate on the principle of granting certain concessions as sops. In Harlem the exploiting group is overwhelmingly white. And it gives no sops.

—CLAUDE MCKAY (1889-1948)
JAMAICAN WRITER

I think I've experienced racism—and every other -ism—from every angle: from gays, from lesbians, from blacks, from women. You would think that people who would have been oppressed would go, "Oh, I see what's going on here." But they don't.

—RUPAUL (1960-)
AMERICAN DRAG PERFORMER AND MUSICIAN

I was brought up on movies, so I thought the Japanese were a lot of people with buck teeth and glasses who tortured Americans.

—STEPHEN SONDHEIM (1930-)
AMERICAN MUSICAL THEATER COMPOSER AND PLAYWRIGHT

So, you know, to stereotype a group of people in these one-dimensional images is very damaging. I know that as a Japanese American who spent time in the years of World War II in prison for no good reason other than the fact that we happened to look like the people who bombed Pearl Harbor.

—GEORGE TAKEI (1937-)
AMERICAN ACTOR

Now, I hadn't always loved white people, I can tell you. I'll be candid, I did not love them. In fact, I just didn't like them—period.

—ETHEL WATERS (1896-1977)
AFRICAN-AMERICAN ACTOR AND MUSICIAN

Between puberty and an awareness of sexuality, the thing I knew the most was race, and I wrestled with those dynamics while everything else was put on hold because it was too much at once.

—GEORGE C. WOLFE (1954-)
AFRICAN-AMERICAN PLAYWRIGHT AND DIRECTOR

BLACKNESS

Yet do I marvel at this curious thing:
To make a poet black, and bid him sing!

—COUNTEE CULLEN (1903-1946)
AFRICAN-AMERICAN POET

_____

Once you go black, you can never go back.

—ROBERT MAPPLETHORPE (1946-1989)
AMERICAN PHOTOGRAPHER

_____

I was told that *Black Inches* wouldn't print a layout of me because I wasn't black enough. That is the only time that I've ever been discriminated against.

—MATTHEW RUSH (1972-)
AMERICAN PORN STAR

_____

After years of short hair, of cutting my hair back each time it raised its head, so to speak, I have begun to feel each time as if I am mutilating my antenna . . . and attenuating my power.

—ALICE WALKER (1944-)
AFRICAN-AMERICAN FEMINIST AND PULITZER PRIZE-WINNING WRITER

_____

Let us understand that to keep alive in us the speech and the voices of the ancestors is not only to "lively up" the old spirits through the great gift of memory, but to "lively up" our own selves, as well.

—ALICE WALKER (1944-)
AFRICAN-AMERICAN FEMINIST AND PULITZER PRIZE-WINNING WRITER

RELATIONSHIPS

SEE ALSO COMMUNICATION, FATHERS AND FATHERHOOD, FRIENDS AND FRIENDSHIP, GAY MARRIAGE, LOVE, MARRIAGE, MOTHERS AND MOTHERHOOD, ROMANCE, SEX, UNDERSTANDING

There is a lack of understanding in almost every love story.

—PEDRO ALMODOVAR (1951-)
SPANISH FILM DIRECTOR

———

I'm not sure if I'd be good at relationships anymore. You have to compromise to a certain extent—and I don't think I'm prepared to do that.

—MICHAEL ARDITTI (ca. 1960-)
BRITISH WRITER

———

After a day of battling [right-wing politicians] . . . you don't have to come home to the dinner table and yell "Give me the butter!" Just "Pass the butter" is fine, dear.

—KATE CLINTON (1947-)
AMERICAN WRITER AND COMEDIAN

———

Science, when applied to personal relationships, is always just wrong. . . . Art is a better guide than science.

—E. M. FORSTER (1879-1970)
BRITISH WRITER

———

Being gay is very different from being straight in the area of relationships. Of course, there are gay people who've had a long-term relationship for fifty years, but they're not the rule. And it's difficult to be in a relationship with someone as well known and wealthy as I am. There's a disparity that works in heterosexual relationships that doesn't work in homosexual relationships.

—DAVID GEFFEN (1943-)
AMERICAN RECORD MOGUL

It will always remain a mysterious thing to me, a relationship between
two incommensurables.

—ANDRÉ GIDE (1869-1951)
FRENCH WRITER

———————

Two male egos together are very tough. Men are just not raised to kowtow to
other men.

—ANDREW HOLLERAN (1944-)
AMERICAN WRITER

———————

When you meet that first person, you think this is who you're supposed to be with
for the rest of your life. And when it's 99 percent work, you still think this is who
you're supposed to be with for the rest of your life.

—CHERRY JONES (1956-)
AMERICAN TONY AWARD–WINNING ACTOR

———————

[On writer and editor Bryher and poet H. D.] [Bryher's] idea of a loving relationship was somewhat the same as her father's. The beloved was to be reduced to a
state of shrieking, trembling hysteria, and then she would be conciliatory and say,
"there, there, calm, calm. It's a nice kitten" . . . in tones calculated to bring
apoplexy up on the already infuriated lady.

—ROBERT MCALMON (1896-1956)
AMERICAN WRITER AND PUBLISHER

———————

The couple has become an obsession, an incubus; young people feel they must
couple off. This is also a misuse of sex.

—PIER PAOLO PASOLINI (1922-1975)
ITALIAN FILM DIRECTOR

Being single is not a pathology.

—CYNTHIA PORT (1969–)
AMERICAN FEMINIST SCHOLAR AND AGING EXPERT

———————

It's really ironic that he [my boyfriend] should end up in a long-term relationship with a writer who writes about him, because he's just a really private person.

—DAN SAVAGE (1964–)
AMERICAN SEX COLUMNIST AND WRITER

———————

My former boyfriend read it [my diary] once, and he was mainly mad because he wasn't in it. I said, "Yes, you are." Then I looked, and he wasn't mentioned. It was as if he didn't exist. If you read somebody's diary, you get what you deserve.

—DAVID SEDARIS (1956–)
AMERICAN WRITER

———————

I haven't really been successful in relationships with men or women. . . . The men think I'm a big dyke, and the women think I'm a fake lesbian, so no one comes up to me except little kids with braces. And I'm like, Do you have parents?

—JILL SOBULE (1961–)
AMERICAN SINGER-SONGWRITER

———————

A special thanks to all my exes for teaching me how to be a good partner . . .

—ANNIE SPRINKLE (1954–)
AMERICAN PERFORMANCE ARTIST AND SEX EDUCATOR

———————

Relationships require heroism on the part of both people . . . you're opening yourself up completely to another person, and you can't know who this human being is, other than what they choose to reveal to you.

—DANIEL TAMMET (1979–)
BRITISH AUTISTIC SAVANT

I've had many sorts of artistic relationships, and I would definitely say that I've spent most of my energy whittling away and crafting my musical chops, but in terms of human relationships and the art of love, I'm quite retarded.

—RUFUS WAINWRIGHT (1973-)
CANADIAN MUSICIAN

It's hard for women to have sex and not bond emotionally. It's near impossible. So what happens a lot of times is a one-night-stand that should never go past a one-night-stand can sometimes turn into a relationship.

—JACKIE WARNER (1968-)
AMERICAN REALITY TV STAR AND CELEBRITY TRAINER

There is nothing worse than a twinsy fag couple.

—LYNN WARREN (1977-)
AMERICAN REALITY TV STAR

I've got two dogs. They're my kids! . . . [I'm] a bit lost without them. They're such constant companions. I don't do very well when I'm not with them.

—JOSH WESTON (ca. 1980-)
AMERICAN PORN STAR

I cannot distinguish your silhouette from the place I occupy.

—MONIQUE WITTIG (1935-2003)
FRENCH FEMINIST AND WRITER

Perhaps modern relationships should be counted like cats' and dogs' lives.

—GEORGE WHITMORE (1946-1989)
AMERICAN WRITER AND PLAYWRIGHT

Human relations, at least between the sexes, were carried on as relations between countries are now—with ambassadors, and treaties.

—VIRGINIA WOOLF (1882-1941)
BRITISH WRITER

DATING

I was seeing someone for a short time. But then he said, "I feel like I'm dating someone who comes with a manual."

—GREG LOUGANIS (1960-)
AMERICAN OLYMPIC GOLD MEDALIST, DIVING

One of the annoying myths about celebrity is that it might get you laid.

—GRAHAM NORTON (1963-)
IRISH COMEDIAN AND ACTOR

I had never, from the age of 16, been out to dinner with anyone. . . . I thought you just went to bed with people.

—DUSTY SPRINGFIELD (1939-1999)
BRITISH MUSICIAN

We're gay people. We know how to break up.

—SUZANNE WESTENHOEFER (1961-)
AMERICAN ACTOR AND COMEDIAN

I like the idea that people in New York now have to wait in line for movies. . . . It costs so much money just to live now, and if you're on a date, you can spend your whole date time in line, and that way it saves you money.

—ANDY WARHOL (1928-1987)
AMERICAN ARTIST

MONOGAMY

There are some men who are completely comfortable with monogamy
and rarely lust for anything they don't already have.
Unfortunately they're generally very dreary men.

—BRAD FRASER (1959-)
CANADIAN PLAYWRIGHT AND SCREENWRITER

The very fact that it takes so many laws to enforce monogamy
at once labels it only an ideal but not a natural institution.
One never hears of laws compelling people to eat!

—HENRY GERBER (1892-1972)
GERMAN-BORN GAY RIGHTS ACTIVIST

To say to some twenty-year-old gay man, "You should become monogamous"
is crazy, since what they really want is a lot of sex.

—EDMUND WHITE (1940-)
AMERICAN WRITER AND CRITIC

RELIGION

SEE ALSO MORALITY, POLITICS, SUPERSTITION

I'm not saying that God created me with a love of Edith Piaf—which I think he
did—I'm saying that a loving God would not create me, or anybody else, with
the idea that something so fundamental as one's sexuality could be evil.

—MICHAEL ARDITTI (ca. 1960-)
BRITISH WRITER

Perhaps everybody has a garden of Eden, I don't know; but they have scarcely seen their garden before they see the flaming sword. Then, perhaps, life only offers the choice of remembering the garden or forgetting it.

—JAMES BALDWIN (1924-1987)
AFRICAN-AMERICAN WRITER

[Cousin Jerry Falwell] "He's had how many years to stand at his bully pulpit? . . . I'm certainly entitled to the same thing . . .

—BRETT BEASLEY (ca. 1962-)
COUSIN OF AMERICAN TELEVANGELIST JERRY FALWELL

I have no doubt that in heaven the angels will regard the blessed as a necessary evil.

—ALAN BENNETT (1934-)
BRITISH WRITER AND ACTOR

You can argue about Scripture until you're blue in the face . . . nobody's ever going to win that argument. But you can make a persuasive case that these "ex-gay" ministries are harmful.

—WAYNE BESEN (ca. 1971-)
AMERICAN WRITER AND GAY RIGHTS ADVOCATE

But I am afraid that we are threatened all over again with a rebirth of a mediaeval kind of religion and that we will be victims again of the same intolerance and bigotry, which in the name of morality once forbade my books to be sold in bookstores. . . . I hope never again to see a time when the same kind of of religious hysteria will trample on works of art.

—MARIE-CLAIRE BLAIS (1939-)
CANADIAN WRITER AND PLAYWRIGHT

Obviously you can't stop a bullet with a book; although indeed it happened on occasions, sometimes we put a book in our pocket here before getting into action . . . and very often the bullet would hit that and not go through. You'd be very bruised and you'd be very hurt, and maybe you'd crack a rib, but sometimes you were saved . . . and it was often the Bible!

—DIRK BOGARDE (1921-1999)
BRITISH ACTOR AND WRITER

Heathenism is a state of mind. You can take it that I'm referring to one who does not see his world. He has no mental light. He destroys almost unwittingly. He cannot feel any God's presence in his life. He is the twenty-first century man.

—DAVID BOWIE (1947-)
BRITISH MUSICIAN

I don't believe in demons. I don't think there is such a thing. Or evil. I don't believe in some force outside of ourselves that creates bad things. I just think of it as all dysfunctionalism of one kind of another. No Satan, no devil. The devil only really appears in the New Testament.

—DAVID BOWIE (1947-)
BRITISH MUSICIAN

I have an extreme sympathy with all fanatics, and yet am an ardent admirer of law and order!

—RUPERT BROOKE (1887-1915)
BRITISH POET

I have, much to my surprise, discovered that I am going to Heaven.

—RUPERT BROOKE (1887-1915)
BRITISH POET

Now I'm no longer cynical about it [the Church of England]. I hate it; and work against it; because I think it teaches untrue things; and that it is bad for people to believe untrue things. It leads to misery.

—RUPERT BROOKE (1887-1915)
BRITISH POET

———————

That there is a region of consciousness removed beyond what we usually call mortality, into which we humans can yet pass, I practically do not doubt; but granting that this is a fact, its explanation still remains for investigation.

—EDWARD CARPENTER (1844-1929)
BRITISH SOCIALIST POET AND GAY ACTIVIST

———————

Whenever any one denomination does something big— whether it's for better or for worse—it can't help impacting the other traditions. . . . We're all inexplicably related to one another.

—OTIS CHARLES (1926-)
EPISCOPALIAN BISHOP

———————

I'm in a place where it's just me and God. Black churches are still like, "Lord, how is she going to be gay all these years and then just stop on the dime?"

—CHARLENE COTHRAN (ca. 1955-)
AMERICAN EX-GAY PUBLISHER

———————

So many people refer to God in relation to the gay movement and the gay struggle. . . . People are thinking that in order to appease the religious right they need to bring God into gay issues. . . . Religion should be kept out of civil rights.

—ALAN CUMMING (1965-)
BRITISH ACTOR

The Judeo-Christian ethic established a patriarchal dictatorship-religion, a religious world of masters and slaves, a cause for which, over the centuries, more blood has been shed than in all the wars of history.

—ROBERT FERRO (1941–1988)
AMERICAN WRITER AND GAY RIGHTS ACTIVIST

Church dogma is at the true heart of the victim myth.

—ROBERT FERRO (1941–1988)
AMERICAN WRITER AND GAY RIGHTS ACTIVIST

I have to feel like and be a spiritual aristocrat because I'm made that way. . . . It is my native substance.

—MARSDEN HARTLEY (1877–1943)
AMERICAN ARTIST

Let me start with religion. . . . I am highly suspicious about anything religious— I think that most world religions are institutions of power. They use the same tool to control and oppress people; they take away what is so natural and essential for human beings; their sexuality! And then make them feel guilty about it.

—WIM HELDENS (1954–)
DUTCH PAINTER

I am conscious of making a great allowance to the questions agitated by religion, in feeling that conclusions and decisions about them are tolerably idle.

—HENRY JAMES (1843–1916)
AMERICAN WRITER

Well someone once said, "religion is for people who are afraid of going to Hell, and spirituality is for people who have already been there."

—LESLIE JORDAN (1955–)
AMERICAN EMMY AWARD-WINNING ACTOR

I have fallen in love with you, God. Take care of us all, one way or the other.

—JACK KEROUAC (1922-1969)
AMERICAN WRITER

Growing up, I was a devout Catholic—in fact, I wanted to be a priest. But I was suffering tremendous turmoil because I was gay. . . . The fact that I was a real horny kid and was very sexually active just intensified the conflict.

—A. DAMIEN MARTIN (1934-1991)
AMERICAN GAY RIGHTS ACTIVIST

I'm not Jesus Christ because He could do things that I can't. And the whole business of life was infinitely more simple for Him than it is for me.

—W. SOMERSET MAUGHAM (1874-1965)
BRITISH WRITER AND PLAYWRIGHT

Well, if you haven't developed your own relationship with God by the time you're twenty years old, then something is wrong anyway.

—ARMISTEAD MAUPIN (1944-)
AMERICAN WRITER

Instead of the usual religious crises in one's adolescent life, I had studied logic and metaphysics and remained agnostic.

—ROBERT MCALMON (1896-1956)
AMERICAN WRITER AND PUBLISHER

The fact is that more people have been slaughtered in the name of religion than for any other single reason. That, that my friends, is true perversion.

—HARVEY MILK (1930-1978)
AMERICAN POLITICIAN AND GAY RIGHTS ACTIVIST

It's very difficult to work out a spiritual life, especially for gays and lesbians, when so many religions are like political action committees. Judgmental is the first and last thing that they are.

—PAUL MONETTE (1945-1995)
AMERICAN WRITER AND AIDS ACTIVIST

I don't want people to drink and to have spiritualistic séances. It is bad for the health.

—VASLAV NIJINSKY (1890-1950)
RUSSIAN DANCER

People have said I'm anti-Catholic: I'm not really, I just think they're very funny.

—JOE ORTON (1933-1967)
BRITISH PLAYWRIGHT

[Mary and Joseph] are two earthly creatures to whom something monstrously divine is happening, which they are not equal to. There is an obvious disproportion between them and the celestial powers which are descending to them.

—PIER PAOLO PASOLINI (1922-1975)
ITALIAN FILM DIRECTOR

That monastic religion of the Middle Age was, in fact, in many of its bearings, like a beautiful disease or disorder of the senses: and a religion which is a disorder of the senses must always be subject to illusions.

—WALTER PATER (1839-1894)
BRITISH CRITIC AND WRITER

Religion, I sometimes think, is the only way in which poetry can really reach the hard-worked poor.

—WALTER PATER (1839-1894)
BRITISH CRITIC AND WRITER

A spiritual battle is as brutal as a battle of men.

—ARTHUR RIMBAUD (1854-1891)
FRENCH POET

I intend to unveil all mysterious: religious mysteries or those of nature, death, birth, the future, the past, cosmogony, the void. I am a master of hallucinations.

—ARTHUR RIMBAUD (1854-1891)
FRENCH POET

I believe that the acceptance of gay and lesbian people into the life of the church is something that is going to happen. . . . It may not happen in my lifetime, but that is all right. It will happen in God's own time.

—REVEREND GENE ROBINSON (1947-)
AMERICAN EPISCOPAL BISHOP

Spiritual sickness overshadows me. My mind is somehow diseased and distorted. I live in myself—seek freedom in myself—self-poisoned, self-imprisoned.

—SIEGFRIED SASSOON (1886-1967)
BRITISH POET AND WRITER

I have a spirituality that I keep very much to myself. I don't talk about it much, because I'm a filmmaker, I'm not a preacher.

—BRYAN SINGER (1965-)
AMERICAN FILM DIRECTOR

But when you grow up in a Judeo-Christian culture, these things find their way into your subconscious and your storytelling.

—BRYAN SINGER (1965-)
AMERICAN FILM DIRECTOR

So Christianity is the religion which recognizes everyone is "I." Marxism is the religion of "he."

—STEPHEN SPENDER (1909-1995)
BRITISH POET AND WRITER

We are invested with God. He is there in our flesh and in our blood. Skeptics say it is merely the imagination of the faithful, but it is not.

—PAUL VERLAINE (1844-1896)
FRENCH POET

Black homosexuals have a unique role in the spirituality discussion. We've always been at the forefront—musicians, preachers, all of those people— and to have the clergy say now that we can't exist is just asinine.

—TOMMIE WATKINS (ca. 1977-)
AMERICAN WRITER AND ACTIVIST

When man is truly humbled, when he has learned that he is not God, then he is nearest to becoming so.

—PATRICK WHITE (1912-1990)
AUSTRALIAN WRITER AND NOBEL LAUREATE

Sins of the flesh are nothing. They are maladies for physicians to cure, if they should be cured. Sins of the soul alone are shameful.

—OSCAR WILDE (1854-1900)
IRISH PLAYWRIGHT AND WRITER

ATHEISM

Don't you think that most atheists are people who are overzealous God-believers but are basically just mad at God? Because I think that even if you say, "Oh, I'm atheist," it's still acknowledging that there is a God.

—RUPAUL (1960-)
AMERICAN DRAG PERFORMER AND MUSICIAN

I'm borderline agnostic. Probably more toward the atheist side if anything. But that's just me. I kinda think that if there's a higher being, they're either really mean or they don't give a crap, or they'd be doing something by now.

—CANDACE GINGRICH (1966-)
AMERICAN ACTIVIST, HALF-SISTER OF NEWT GINGRICH

CHRISTIANTY

If all the gay vicars and gay Catholic priests resigned then both Churches would crumble!

—NICK BAMFORD (1952-)
BRITISH PLAYWRIGHT

I think the Bible and religious illustrations are often the place where we first find the possibility of sexuality. Then later on you see the movies of these things . . . very sexual movies. What's interesting is that they've patterned themselves as being very innocent and righteous—which I always love because it proves you can be morally self-righteous and show a lot of flesh . . . absolutely justified by the scriptures.

—CLIVE BARKER (1952-)
BRITISH WRITER AND DIRECTOR

If Jesus were walking our streets today, what would the TV preachers make of his "family" of 12 men?

—BRUCE BAWER (1956-)
AMERICAN CRITIC AND WRITER

———————

I've always thought the reason we suspect saints is the ambiguous nature of all good deeds, the impossibility of ever knowing why they are being performed.

—ELIZABETH BISHOP (1911-1979)
AMERICAN POET

———————

I feel very strongly that the Christian concept of Sin is a blight on the earth that has occasioned incalculable misery.

—WILLIAM BURROUGHS (1914-1997)
AMERICAN WRITER

———————

Who will believe that God will damn men for not knowing what they were never taught?

—LORD BYRON (1788-1824)
BRITISH POET

———————

Going to Christian concerts, and having girls in tube tops screaming at these Christian bands. . . . It's weird because you're not supposed to have idolatry.

—BRIAN DANNELLY (1963-)
GERMAN-BORN SCREENWRITER AND DIRECTOR

———————

I became this little Jesus freak, and my parents were appalled. I had fallen in the movement out of a lack of any other thing to believe in and out of wanting to be part of something.

—KEITH HARING (1958-1990)
AMERICAN ARTIST AND ACTIVIST

They're not coming in as they used to even three years ago announcing, "I'm just church shopping, I'm just looking around." The people I've seen recently have come to me and said, "Sign me up, I'm ready."

—ELIZABETH KAETON (ca. 1950-)
AMERICAN REVEREND AND RECTOR, ST. PAUL'S EPISCOPAL CHURCH IN CHATTERHAM,
NEW JERSEY

"Tell me more, my child." I think a few priests have asked for elaborate confessions too many times.

—ARMISTEAD MAUPIN (1944-)
AMERICAN WRITER

Christ going round Palestine is really a revolutionary whirlwind: someone who walks up to a couple of people and says "drop your nets and follow me" is a total revolutionary.

—PIER PAOLO PASOLINI (1922-1975)
ITALIAN FILM DIRECTOR

The Bible is like a mirror. You end up reading it not as a reflection of how it is but of how you are. If you're a bigoted, narrow person, you will find bigotry in the Bible.

—DANIEL TAMMET (1979-)
BRITISH AUTISTIC SAVANT

When I was a small child, until I was about eight or nine years old, I worried if I didn't go forward and get saved every Sunday—which I couldn't do, it was absolutely too humiliating to see these adults flailing and beating their breasts and sobbing, and I thought, Oh, my God, this is so ridiculous, so embarrassing—I could never bring myself to go forward. And I'd think, Oh, my God, if I don't go next Sunday, if the end of the world comes, I'll go to hell.

—LILY TOMLIN (1934-)
AMERICAN ACTOR AND COMEDIAN

Underneath Christ the divine I see,
The dear love of man for his comrade—the attraction of friend to friend.

—WALT WHITMAN (1819-1892)
AMERICAN POET

There will soon be no more priests. Their work is done.

—WALT WHITMAN (1819-1892)
AMERICAN POET

Christ's place indeed is with the poets. His whole conception of Humanity sprang right out of the imagination and can only be realized by it.

—OSCAR WILDE (1854-1900)
IRISH PLAYWRIGHT AND WRITER

JUDAISM

The Jewish religion says that you can not truly be a man until your father has died—maybe there is a certain amount of truth in that.

—CLIVE BARKER (1952-)
BRITISH WRITER AND DIRECTOR

I'm studying cabala, which is really the essence of Jewish spirituality. It's given me opportunities. I don't take things so personally in this business anymore.

—SANDRA BERNHARD (1955-)
AMERICAN ACTOR, COMEDIAN, AND MUSICIAN

Orthodox rabbis often don't know anything about the gay and lesbian experience. For them, it's very black and white.

—SANDI SIMCHA DUBOWSKI (1970-)
JEWISH-AMERICAN FILM DIRECTOR

Heaven knows if love for those I know and understanding of them racially, emotionally, and spiritually—would make me a Jew, I would be one surely by now.

—MARSDEN HARTLEY (1877-1943)
AMERICAN ARTIST

RELIGION AND POLITICS

If more self-styled Christians truly were Christian, then Christianity would be the chief bulwark of gay men and lesbians in the face of societal anathematization, rather than the bigots' principal tool.

—BRUCE BAWER (1956-)
AMERICAN CRITIC AND WRITER

———

Phil Gramm, Alan Keyes, and Pat Buchanan alternated between self-righteous Bible-thumping and vicious jabs at gay men and lesbians, among others. You'd have thought they were running for ayatollah.

—BRUCE BAWER (1956-)
AMERICAN CRITIC AND WRITER

———

The Christian Coalition has succeeded in creating a stereotype of the gay American because most of gay America has let it.

—STEVE GUNDERSON (1951-)
OPENLY GAY AMERICAN CONGRESSMAN

———

People in this country, including President Bush himself, have used the term "Islamo-fascism." We have to be equally careful about Christiano-fascism. The only reason they're not just as bad is, for the moment, they can't get away with what the Muslims can get away with in the Middle East. They would be perfectly happy to do so.

—FRANK KAMENY (1925-)
AMERICAN GAY RIGHTS ACTIVIST

Part of being free is to see the other side. So, okay, in this problem,
the other side doesn't see us. Even so, I feel smarter, more liberal,
and more intelligent. Unlike them, I am able to see the other side.
In the end, they will have no choice but to see me because I see them.

—IVRI LIDER (1974-)
ISRAELI MUSICIAN

The Right is desperate because we—queers and feminists—represent the
most serious obstacle to its efforts to achieve a theocratic state.

—URVASHI VAID (1958-)
AMERICAN GAY RIGHTS ACTIVIST

RELIGION AND SEXUALITY

Sex isn't a spiritually exclusive phenomenon.

—ROBERT GANT (1968-)
AMERICAN ACTOR

Someone long ago posited a connection between religious mania and sex. . . .
This was almost certainly why I fled to the arms of Jee-zuss.
Other boys at that church, I now realize, were also scrambling to escape their
homosexuality, though I didn't know it then.

—JOSEPH HANSEN (1923-2004)
AMERICAN WRITER

I've had to confront society and the Church, which says that homosexuals are
damned. That's absurd. How can someone who's born like this be judged? . . .
My gods made me the way I am.

—CHAVELA VARGAS (1919-)
COSTA RICAN MUSICIAN

REPRESSION

SEE ALSO SELF-HATE

I suppose what I'm trying to say is that if people's sexuality is repressed, either through self-denial or by an institution, they become monsters— and that is what the book is about.

—MICHAEL ARDITTI (ca. 1960–)
BRITISH WRITER

———————

People like that who deny themselves and their true natures, they're the ones who get out of control.

—ALAN BALL (1957–)
AMERICAN SCREENWRITER

———————

A passion of which the outlets are sealed, begets a tension of nerve, in which the sensible world comes to one with a reinforced brilliancy and relief— all redness is turned into blood, all water into tears.

—WALTER PATER (1839–1894)
BRITISH CRITIC AND WRITER

RESPONSIBILITY

Yes, I have been accused of irresponsibility, but how could one put up a Seagram Building if one thought only of social responsibility? What was needed was a lovely building.

—PHILIP JOHNSON (1906–2005)
AMERICAN ARCHITECT

I am an American and a Jew, and as such I believe I have a direct
responsibility for the behavior of Americans and Jews.

–TONY KUSHNER (1956-)
AMERICAN PLAYWRIGHT

With the police of their backs, many simply did what men have empowered themselves to do for centuries: They became as sexually adventurous and indulgent as
they wanted to be, denying any responsibility for themselves or others in the process.

–MICHELANGELO SIGNORILE (1960-)
AMERICAN JOURNALIST, WRITER, AND GAY ACTIVIST

REVENGE

SEE ALSO WRITING

Revenge is a kind of wild justice.

–SIR FRANCIS BACON (1561-1626)
BRITISH PHILOSOPHER AND STATESMAN

Think you I am not fiend and savage too?
Think you I could not arm me with a gun
And shoot down ten of you for every one
Of my black brothers murdered, burnt by you?

–CLAUDE MCKAY (1889-1948)
JAMAICAN WRITER

My drive for success at any cost comes as a form of revenge.
Nobody wanted to like me as a kid? Fine. Now you have to pay to sit
in a room and pay attention to what I have to say.

–RICK SKYE (ca. 1975-)
AMERICAN DRAG PERFORMER

Biography can be the most middle-class of all forms,
the judgment of little people avenging themselves on the great.

—EDMUND WHITE (1940-)
AMERICAN WRITER AND CRITIC

ROLE MODELS

I feel like I've led people down the wrong path. I mean people have
their own wills and everything, but the Club Kids really were role models
and we didn't always set the best example.

—MICHAEL ALIG (1966-)
AMERICAN FOUNDING MEMBER OF THE CLUB KIDS AND CONVICTED MURDERER

I'm a role model for kids. And it's weird, but what if they see their gay coach in a
Speedo or whatever and he's doing this gay magazine? What are they going to
think, you know? Am I going to let them down? What are their parents going to
think? And I know I shouldn't care what they think, but I do.

—J. P. CALDERON (1975-)
AMERICAN PROFESSIONAL VOLLEYBALL PLAYER, MODEL, AND REALITY TV STAR

How could I possibly be a role model when I don't even have it together yet?

—MICHAEL THOMAS FORD (1968-)
AMERICAN WRITER

A lot of people have said to me that I'm kind of a role model.
I never elected myself to be [one], but if I am going to be a role model,
I want to be one that I can be proud of.

—DAVID GEFFEN (1943-)
AMERICAN RECORD MOGUL

I do wish with all my heart that some very famous, very masculine actor or sports figure would come out, because the lesbians now have Rosie and they have Ellen. They have role models. And I still don't think there are really any role models on the big icon level for gay men. I wish we had a champion.

—LESLIE JORDAN (1955-)
AMERICAN EMMY AWARD-WINNING ACTOR

I'm doing this [coming out] because I know that there are kids out there, whether they're in my classroom or not, who need to be told and shown that it's OK to be who they are.

—GENE KUFFEL (1964-)
AMERICAN SCHOOLTEACHER AND MR. USA INTERNATIONAL IN 1997

We're all only human, and we make mistakes. People have to strive to be their own role models.

—GREG LOUGANIS (1960-)
AMERICAN OLYMPIC GOLD MEDALIST, DIVING

I don't have an agenda for how we must see positive role models. I've never had that agenda. I was pissed off, like a lot of other gay people, that for years we were just clowns or killers in films. But, that's also happened to every other minority in the country.

—ARMISTEAD MAUPIN (1944-)
AMERICAN WRITER

I'm not a role model for anyone—I deal in fiction.

—CHRISTOPHER RICE (1978-)
AMERICAN WRITER

I was the first openly gay news reporter to be hired at a mainstream newspaper anywhere in the country. The timing was ironic because this new gay disease had been detected just weeks before.

—RANDY SHILTS (1951-1994)
AMERICAN JOURNALIST, AIDS ACTIVIST, AND WRITER

———————

It is a very unimaginative nature that only cares for people on their pedestals. A pedestal may be a very unreal thing. A pillory is a terrible reality.

—OSCAR WILDE (1854-1900)
IRISH PLAYWRIGHT AND WRITER

HEROES

Heroes should have looks.

—ALLAN GURGANUS (1947-)
AMERICAN WRITER

———————

All heroes are forsaken in time.

—MARSDEN HARTLEY (1877-1943)
AMERICAN ARTIST

———————

Here's the truth: You can be a porn star and a hero. Homoerotic and wholesome. Gay and patriotic.

—ALEC MAPA (1965-)
FILIPINO ACTOR AND COMEDIAN

———————

I love that idea of a heroine—that she's ditzy, but she's capable of killing people.

—STEPHEN SONDHEIM (1930-)
AMERICAN MUSICAL THEATER COMPOSER AND PLAYWRIGHT

ROMANCE

SEE ALSO GAY MARRIAGE, LOVE, MARRIAGE, RELATIONSHIPS, SEX

Romance? Not in this weather.

—W. H. AUDEN (1907-1973)
ANGLO-AMERICAN POET AND CRITIC

I'm an over-the-top romantic. . . . And you know, in today's world
I don't think romance hurts anyone one bit.

—NICOLE CONN (1959-)
AMERICAN FILM DIRECTOR

I suppose I try to seduce everybody.

—TOM FORD (1962-)
AMERICAN FASHION DESIGNER

I was always with my girlfriend at the time backstage,
but I'm very private about my personal life. She was my makeup artist,
my manager, my hairdresser, my everything else.

—EVE SALVAIL (1973-)
CANADIAN SUPERMODEL

I'm crazy in love with my boyfriend. Isn't it sickening? I hate saying
this in public, because it feels like a huge jinx. All gay couples who yammer
on and on in public about their beautiful love wind up breaking up.

—DAN SAVAGE (1964-)
AMERICAN SEX COLUMNIST AND WRITER

Even if it's just eye contact with someone I pass on the street, I try to experience a little gay romance every day. It's all about making connections.

—NICK STREET (1967-)
AMERICAN WRITER AND EDITOR

Anyone, however monogamous he may have been, can learn all over again how to cruise, seduce, sparkle, and shine.

—GEORGE WHITMORE (1946-1989)
AMERICAN WRITER AND PLAYWRIGHT

ROUTINE

SEE ALSO CHANGE

I really like the routine, the constant sameness of things. When I was a kid I'd hate it when sitcoms sent the characters off on some adventure. Like when the Brady Bunch went to Hawaii. I found that really annoying. I just wanted them to be at home in their split-level house, doing what they always did.

—ALISON BECHDEL (1960-)
AMERICAN CARTOONIST AND GRAPHIC NOVELIST

I've been thinking about routine as art form and what distinguishes it from other forms. . . . In a sense the whole Nazi movement was a great, humorless, evil routine on Hitler's part.

—WILLIAM BURROUGHS (1914-1997)
AMERICAN WRITER

Now I just try to keep a sensible routine. I work four hours an afternoon, have dinner, and go to bed. Then in the morning, when I'm very clear, I go over what I wrote and straighten out anything that seems wrong. That way, I don't wake up to the sad emptiness of a blank page.

—TRUMAN CAPOTE (1924-1984)
AMERICAN WRITER

I fear the softness of habit. . . . I want to be a man of velleity, a traitor, an acrobat, an experimenter. A kind word would be: a magician.

—JEAN COCTEAU (1889-1963)
FRENCH WRITER AND FILMMAKER

My daily routine tends to benumb my faculties so much that at times I feel an infantile awe before any attempt whatever, critical or creative.

—HART CRANE (1899-1932)
AMERICAN POET

We have been abruptly plunged into horror: by 9/11 first and foremost. . . . We have been profoundly alienated from our "dailyness," from a certain familiarity and safety without which life becomes very difficult.

—TONY KUSHNER (1956-)
AMERICAN PLAYWRIGHT

I've got a grip on the details of everyday existence. But the details are so trivial and monotonous . . . life is woven of such details; an incessant washing of hands and face, and then discovering that they are dirty again.

—SIEGFRIED SASSOON (1886-1967)
BRITISH POET AND WRITER

Hospital, through a miracle of organized routines, never seems ordinary.

—STEPHEN SPENDER (1909-1995)
BRITISH POET AND WRITER

ROYALTY

SEE ALSO CELEBRITIES

The Queen is clearly the most enchanting woman.

—NOËL COWARD (1899-1973)
BRITISH ACTOR AND PLAYWRIGHT

[On Lunching with Queen Elizabeth II] It was all very merry and agreeable, but there is always, for me, a tiny pall of "best behavior" overlaying the proceedings. I am not complaining about this, I think it is right and proper, but I am constantly aware of it. It isn't that I have a basic urge to tell disgusting jokes and say "fuck" every five minutes, but I'm conscious of a faint resentment that I couldn't if I wanted to.

—NOËL COWARD (1899-1973)
BRITISH ACTOR AND PLAYWRIGHT

Princess Diana is the first person ever to enter Buckingham Palace who was good looking.

—QUENTIN CRISP (1908-1999)
BRITISH WRITER AND PERSONALITY

Who gives a fuck about royalty these days?

—W. SOMERSET MAUGHAM (1874-1965)
BRITISH WRITER AND PLAYWRIGHT

The Queen of England is a sensible person. . . . She's a strong-minded woman who knows her own mind. You won't find her sending me a telegram.

—W. SOMERSET MAUGHAM (1874–1965)
BRITISH WRITER AND PLAYWRIGHT

In the past, people were born royal. Nowadays, royalty comes from what you do.

—GIANNI VERSACE (1946–1997)
ITALIAN FASHION DESIGNER

S & M

SEE ALSO SEX, SEXUALITY

They say that the true sadist is the person who will not satisfy the masochist.

—EDWARD ALBEE (1928-)
AMERICAN TONY AWARD- AND PULITZER PRIZE-WINNING PLAYWRIGHT

S&M is nonetheless profoundly conservative in that its imagination
of pleasure is almost entirely defined by the dominant culture to which
it thinks of itself as giving "a stinging slap in the face."

—LEO BERSANI (1961-)
CRITIC AND THEORIST

S&M is a wonderful hobby for many, and those that have the time and the
finances to collect the pricey gear are lucky and know it.

—MARGARET CHO (1968-)
KOREAN-AMERICAN COMEDIAN

In sadism and masochism there is no mysterious link between pain and pleasure.
. . . There is no direct relation to pain; pain should be regarded as an effect only.

—GILLES DELEUZE (1925-1995)
FRENCH PHILOSOPHER AND CRITIC

There isn't a sadistic murderer *per se*; people always have to have the feeling that
the other person wants it.

—RAINER WERNER FASSBINDER (1945-1982)
GERMAN DIRECTOR

I remembered the corporal kicking with his nailed boot to get me up. . . .
I remembered smiling idly at him, for a delicious warmth,
probably sexual, was swelling through me.

—T. E. LAWRENCE, AKA LAWRENCE OF ARABIA (1888-1935)
BRITISH SOLDIER AND WRITER

If people want to believe I'm a dominatrix in my spare time, that's fine with me—I
mean, I'm definitely happy to smack people around if that's what they really want.

—JANE WIEDLIN (1958-)
AMERICAN MUSICIAN

SECRETS

SEE ALSO REPRESSION, COMING OUT

If there is anything about you that you have difficulty discussing or that you fear
your hearers will not like, don't tell them. Go on as though they already know.
The ideas they can accommodate. It is the words that are so irrevocable, so
embarrassing, so wounding.

—QUENTIN CRISP (1908-1999)
BRITISH WRITER AND PERSONALITY

The artist, painter, poet, or musician, by his decoration, sublime or beautiful, satisfies the aesthetic sense; but that is akin to the sexual instinct, and shares its bar-
barity: He lays before you also the greater gift of himself. To pursue his secret has
something of the fascination of a detective story.

—W. SOMERSET MAUGHAM (1874-1965)
BRITISH WRITER AND PLAYWRIGHT

I didn't share secrets with anybody. Some of them festered inside me
during the asthmatic summers and bronchial winters.

—PATRICK WHITE (1912-1990)
AUSTRALIAN WRITER AND NOBEL LAUREATE

SELF-AWARENESS

SEE ALSO IDENTITY, INDIVIDUALISM, SELF-DECEPTION, SELF-HATE

We learn about sex in a testosterone-charged playground where, even in today's
more enlightened society, to be gay is to be less than a man and therefore
beneath contempt. How can we not inherit low self-esteem?

—NICK BAMFORD (1952-)
BRITISH PLAYWRIGHT

I'm not Peter Berlin when I'm sitting with you. I'm this old guy who created Peter
Berlin. I mean, once in a while I slip into that character—last night, I had sex,
and whenever that happens, I slip into that character. And I still can see him. I
meet him. And I say hello to him, because when he's there, it's really fascinating.

—PETER BERLIN (1934-)
GERMAN MODEL AND GAY SEX ICON

My intentions are better than anything else about me.

—HART CRANE (1899-1932)
AMERICAN POET

To reach, not the point where one no longer says I, but the point where it
is no longer of any importance whether one says I. We are no longer ourselves.
Each will know his own. We have been aided, inspired, multiplied.

—GILLES DELEUZE (1925-1995)
FRENCH PHILOSOPHER AND CRITIC

I suspect that some kind of a sense of self-as-other—because of sexuality, or sensitivity, or any form of exile—is a prerequisite to the artistic life.

—MARK DOTY (1953-)
AMERICAN POET

—————

I'm a natural-born boss, I have to say. I just like to be good at things. Even as a child, I was boss of my family.

—TOM FORD (1962-)
AMERICAN FASHION DESIGNER

—————

What is important for each one is to know whether he has really put on all his own skins, one after the other, and not too much of the clothing of others . . .

—ANDRÉ GIDE (1869-1951)
FRENCH WRITER

—————

How do you participate in the world but not lose your integrity? It's a constant struggle.

—KEITH HARING (1958-1990)
AMERICAN ARTIST AND ACTIVIST

—————

One knows the most damning things about one's self.

—HENRY JAMES (1843-1916)
AMERICAN WRITER

—————

To each his own milieu. Enhance what was already in one's possession. In America Negroes sometimes talked loudly of this, but in their hearts they repudiated it. In their lives too. They didn't want to be like themselves.

—NELLA LARSEN (1891-1964)
AFRICAN-AMERICAN WRITER

I am not a dreamer, I have thought hard and coldly about what I believe. Like a true Andalusian, I know the secret of coldness, for I have ancient blood.

—FEDERICO GARCIA LORCA (1898-1936)
SPANISH POET AND PLAYWRIGHT

I am one of the most horrible old men alive today. I've been so wicked.

—W. SOMERSET MAUGHAM (1874-1965)
BRITISH WRITER AND PLAYWRIGHT

A generation ago "we" was the pronoun.

—JAMES MERRILL (1926-1995)
AMERICAN PULITZER PRIZE-WINNING POET

With no one around to answer the question, I made up my own.
I made a judgment, I deduced, I calculated, I became an authority
on nearly nothing and almost everything.

—ROSIE O'DONNELL (1962-)
AMERICAN ACTOR, COMEDIAN, AND TALK SHOW HOST

The last person to know oneself is oneself.

—PIER PAOLO PASOLINI (1922-1975)
ITALIAN FILM DIRECTOR

You had the feeling possibly of knowing where you were
but where you were was lost.

—ROBERT RAUSCHENBERG (1925-)
AMERICAN ARTIST

I've always been a person to know her own mind. I haven't understood myself—
still don't—I'm complex, but I know what I think and what I believe.

—ETHEL WATERS (1896-1977)
AFRICAN-AMERICAN ACTOR AND MUSICIAN

———

People put you down and people praise. It's hard to see yourself plain sometimes.

—ETHEL WATERS (1896-1977)
AFRICAN-AMERICAN ACTOR AND MUSICIAN

———

One, and no other figure, is the answer to all sums.

—PATRICK WHITE (1912-1990)
AUSTRALIAN WRITER AND NOBEL LAUREATE

SELF-DECEPTION

SEE ALSO DECEIT, SELF-AWARENESS, SELF-HATE

People who believe that they are strong-willed and the masters of their destiny can
only continue to believe this by becoming specialists in self-deception.

—JAMES BALDWIN (1924-1987)
AFRICAN-AMERICAN WRITER

———

The journey toward self-honesty includes the study of one's myths. Everybody has
them. So do you and I. Since we invariably create many of our personal myths, it
should not be extraordinarily difficult for us to perceive them honestly.

—MALCOLM BOYD (1923-)
AMERICAN MINISTER AND INSPIRATIONAL WRITER

One can't put all of oneself on paper; there are always contradictions,
divergences, complexities.

—MARK DOTY (1953–)
AMERICAN POET

―――――

But is there not real torture in the fact that, since the declaration of science,
and Christianity, man deludes himself, proving obvious truth,
puffing up with the pleasure of repeating his proofs . . . ?

—ARTHUR RIMBAUD (1854–1891)
FRENCH POET

―――――

Some sorts of self-deceit are crimes. They are the sign of a soul's
willingness to accept the second best and to give the second best, instead of
waiting through all suffering and all privation for the best in life.

—JOHN ADDINGTON SYMONDS (1840–1893)
ENGLISH POET AND CRITIC

SELF-EXPRESSION

SEE ALSO ART AND ARTISTS, COMMUNICATION, LANGUAGE

To say that a poem is a personal utterance does not mean that it is an act
of self-expression.

—W. H. AUDEN (1907–1973)
ANGLO-AMERICAN POET AND CRITIC

―――――

One must be drenched in words, literally soaked with them to have
the right ones form themselves into the proper pattern at the right moment.
When they come . . . it is a matter of felicitous juggling!

—HART CRANE (1899–1932)
AMERICAN POET

"Personal expression" is a much abused expression.

—GEORGE CUKOR (1899-1983)
AMERICAN FILM DIRECTOR

———————

True artists—and I do think there are some fashion-designer artists—
create because they can't do anything but create. There is no purpose to their
work other than expression.

—TOM FORD (1962-)
AMERICAN FASHION DESIGNER

———————

In short, my philosophy is functional eclecticism. . . . Functional eclecticism
amounts to being able to choose form history whatever forms, shapes,
or directions you want to, and using them as you please.

—PHILIP JOHNSON (1906-2005)
AMERICAN ARCHITECT

———————

I got that feeling in my stomach, it's not a directly sexual one,
it's something more potent than that. I thought that if I could somehow bring
that element into art, if I could somehow retain that feeling, I would be
doing something that was uniquely my own.

—ROBERT MAPPLETHORPE (1946-1989)
AMERICAN PHOTOGRAPHER

———————

It is always hazardous to express what one has to say indirectly and allusively.

—WALTER PATER (1839-1894)
BRITISH CRITIC AND WRITER

When I speak up and want to be more than just a blowup doll, people say,
"Oh, she thinks she's really something." But if I play the game and just say
what they want me to say, then they think I'm all right.

—RUPAUL (1960–)
AMERICAN DRAG PERFORMER AND MUSICIAN

———

I've never fancied the ideology of writing as therapy or self-expression.

—SUSAN SONTAG (1933–2004)
AMERICAN WRITER AND CRITIC

SELF-HATE

SEE ALSO HATRED, IDENTITY, INDIVIDUALISM, SELF-AWARENESS, SELF-DECEPTION

It must be ecstatic to live comfortably in one's own skin.
From birth, my cargo has been badly stowed.

—JEAN COCTEAU (1889–1963)
FRENCH WRITER AND FILMMAKER

———

Sitting on the pews of a Baptist church in Tennessee is where
I really learned to hate myself.

—LESLIE JORDAN (1955–)
AMERICAN EMMY AWARD-WINNING ACTOR

———

To me, evil is most closely related to self-hatred and the urge to kill oneself. . . .
since there's such a biological imperative not to kill yourself,
I think evil is that suicidal urge turned outwards.

—GREGORY MAGUIRE (1954–)
AMERICAN WRITER

I have too many followers whose adherence degrades me and
unconsciously confirms all my own self-deprecation.

—THOMAS MANN (1875-1955)
GERMAN WRITER

I was so busy running away from myself I didn't have the
time to take care of myself.

—ROY SIMMONS (1956-)
AMERICAN NFL FOOTBALL PLAYER

It has been my destiny to make continual renunciation of my truest self,
because I was born out of sympathy with the men around me.

—JOHN ADDINGTON SYMONDS (1840-1893)
ENGLISH POET AND CRITIC

SELFISHNESS

SEE ALSO LITERATURE, SPORTS

I am fast becoming a good enough Englishman to respect, inveterately,
my own habits, and do, wherever I may be, only exactly what I want.

—HENRY JAMES (1843-1916)
AMERICAN WRITER

The abandonment of self required to make literature . . . invariably incurs
the stigma of selfishness in "real" life.

—SUSAN SONTAG (1933-2004)
AMERICAN WRITER AND CRITIC

I didn't do this [come out] to spearhead a wave of gay women athletes
coming out—I just did it to enhance the quality of my life. . . .
It was a very selfish act in that way.

—MUFFIN SPENCER-DEVLIN (1953-)
AMERICAN PROFESSIONAL GOLFER

SELF-PITY

SEE ALSO SELF-HATE

What is wrong with bad self-pity is the hermetic, incestuous,
luxurious wallowing in it, and above all the pitier's refusal of insight.

—WILLIAM BURROUGHS (1914-1997)
AMERICAN WRITER

———————

Anger is a healthier emotion for me than self-pity.

—NOËL COWARD (1899-1973)
BRITISH ACTOR AND PLAYWRIGHT

———————

I am not going to pity myself—but on the other hand, why should I
stretch my face continually into a kind of "glad" expression.

—HART CRANE (1899-1932)
AMERICAN POET

S E X

SEE ALSO GAY MARRIAGE, LOVE, MARRIAGE, PROMISCUITY, PROSTITUTION,
RELATIONSHIPS, ROMANCE, S&M, SEXUALITY

I never managed to be considerate in matters of sex, and I daresay it is better
that I should not start again. I doubt if it is a subject in which one gains wisdom
if one has never had any.

—J. R. ACKERLEY (1896-1967)
BRITISH WRITER AND EDITOR

———————

Human beings have been mean to themselves and each other in
various uncountable ways ever since they were orangutans, yet all the time,
as far as I know, no one's ever died from fucking a corpse.

—KATHY ACKER (1947-1997)
AMERICAN WRITER

———————

First of all, I've been training for twenty-two years. And if there's anything that
goes hand in hand with trainers and working out, it's sex. Everything revolves
around sex. The clients talk about it. The trainers are talking about it. When you
get good looking people with nice bodies and loads of testosterone together,
there's going to be a lot of sexual tension.

—DOUG BLASDELL (1962-2007)
AMERICAN CELEBRITY TRAINER AND REALITY TV STAR

———————

When I was fifteen, I believed that sex was nearly the same thing as softball.

—LUCY JANE BLEDSOE (1957-)
AMERICAN WRITER

Our duty is but to propagate the species successfully and then to wait quietly for the disintegration of our bodies.

—RUPERT BROOKE (1887-1915)
BRITISH POET

I think people are finding that they can pick up an erotica book, or order one online, and there's no stigma attached. Erotica is a safe way for people to explore sexual fantasies, first by themselves, reading . . . and then, if they like, by sharing the stories with a lover.

—RACHEL KRAMER BUSSEL (1975-)
AMERICAN COLUMNIST AND WRITER OF EROTICA

Sex is like sneezing. . . . I meant that literally. I was making a metaphor for orgasm. What is the nearest thing in physical sensation to an orgasm? And I came up with the idea that it was sneezing.

—TRUMAN CAPOTE (1924-1984)
AMERICAN WRITER

Obviously sex is not love. It's a temporary situation, isn't it? Sex can lead to love, but friendship, real friendship, inevitably leads to love.

—TRUMAN CAPOTE (1924-1984)
AMERICAN WRITER

Once you start imposing an obligation on individuals to release their rights to sexual privacy, it's a slippery slope.

—DAVID CLARENBACH (ca. 1959-)
AMERICAN ACTIVIST AND STATE LEGISLATOR

Our sexuality is a way of getting to know ourselves and our place in the world.

—STEVE COMPTON
AMERICAN ARTIST AND CURATOR

There is a kind of mysticism in perversion: the greater the renunciation, the greater and the more secure the gains; we might compare it to a "black" theology where pleasure . . . is abjured, disavowed, "renounced," the better to be recovered as a reward or consequence, and as a law.

—GILLES DELEUZE (1925-1995)
FRENCH PHILOSOPHER AND CRITIC

I took to sex like a duck to water . . . and I became as prodigious sexually as I was musically.

—DAVID DEL TREDICI (1937-)
AMERICAN COMPOSER

There really is something raw about sexuality that's real and good and we must continue to learn to not be ashamed of it.

—KYAN DOUGLAS (1970-)
AMERICAN REALITY TV STAR

I think it's our job to bring sexiness into the consciousness of people— instead of having it be our terrible little secret.

—MELISSA ETHERIDGE (1961-)
AMERICAN GRAMMY AWARD-WINNING MUSICIAN AND BREAST CANCER ACTIVIST

I found actually in the course of time that everybody I really loved and wanted to go to bed with, I finally did. It may have taken twenty or thirty years, and we may have both fallen into ruins and baldness and all our teeth fallen out, but desire always found its way, even if it took decades.

—ALLEN GINSBERG (1926-1997)
AMERICAN POET

What if no one taught you anything about sex? How would you feel about it? . . .
Sex would be a very natural thing.   .

—RANDAL KLEISER (1946-)
AMERICAN DIRECTOR

———

Sex is magic. If you channel it right, there's more energy in sex than there is in art.

—ROBERT MAPPLETHORPE (1946-1989)
AMERICAN PHOTOGRAPHER

———

I think we, as a nation, have to grow up about sexuality.
We all have fantasies of one form or another.

—ARMISTEAD MAUPIN (1944-)
AMERICAN WRITER

———

The reality of sex is that it's going to happen, and it does, and there's nothing
you can do to stop that. Nobody can stop it, unless it's Jesus Christ himself.
And when he gets enough of it, I guess—and I don't really know the Lord
that well—I imagine he'll come down here and let us know.

—NORMA (AKA "JANE ROE") MCCORVEY (1947-)
AMERICAN ABORTION ACTIVIST

———

Yes, there is an element of sex in my plays. But sex is in the air. It's everywhere.
People do want to have sex, but they also want love.

—TERRENCE MCNALLY (1939-)
AMERICAN PLAYWRIGHT

———

Even with the wrong person, sex can be wonderful.

—CHRISTINA MINNA (1969-)
AMERICAN MUSICIAN

If men were forbidden by law, as they should be, to form connections with young boys, they would be saved from laying out immense pains for a quite uncertain return; nothing is more unpredictable than whether a young boy will turn out spiritually and physically perfect or the reverse.

—PLATO (427-347 BC)
GREEK PHILOSOPHER

———————

Sex is great because it's one factor in our makeup that we're not in control of. . . . It's like a Greta Garbo emotion: totally mysterious with no basis in reason or logic.

—GUS VAN SANT (1952-)
AMERICAN FILM DIRECTOR

———————

Is there anything in life that which can be disconnected from this curse of sex?

—SIEGFRIED SASSOON (1886-1967)
BRITISH POET AND WRITER

———————

As we get older: there's some talk among some of my friends that the drive isn't there; the libido is lessened—but the arousal is there. So if you're waiting around to get turned on, and then do it: no. You just find time, and start doing it—and then the arousal kicks in, which is kind of a nice differentiation.

—ANNIE SPRINKLE (1954-)
AMERICAN PERFORMANCE ARTIST AND SEX EDUCATOR

———————

I thought that I had transcended crude sensuality through the aesthetic idealization of erotic instincts. I did not know how fallacious that method of expelling nature is.

—JOHN ADDINGTON SYMONDS (1840-1893)
ENGLISH POET AND CRITIC

I wonder, sometimes, how much of the cruising was for the pleasure of my cruising partner's companionship and for the sport of pursuit and how much was actually for the pretty repetitive and superficial satisfactions of the act itself.

—TENNESSEE WILLIAMS (1911-1983)
AMERICAN PLAYWRIGHT

———————

Suddenly the door opened and the long and sinister figure of Mr. Lytton Strachey stood on the threshold. He pointed his finger at a stain on Vanessa's white dress. "Semen?" he asked. Can one really say it? I thought, and we burst out laughing. With that one word all barriers of reticence and reserve went down. A flood of the sacred fluid seemed to overwhelm us. Sex permeated our conversation. The word bugger was never far from our lips. We discussed copulation with the same excitement and openness that we had discussed the nature of good.

—VIRGINIA WOOLF (1882-1941)
BRITISH WRITER

ANONYMOUS SEX

I have been driven at last to the parks. The first night brought me a most strenuous wooing and the largest instrument I have [yet] handled.

—HART CRANE (1899-1932)
AMERICAN POET

———————

While experience tells me sex with someone I know is generally better than with someone I don't know, that doesn't mean sex with a stranger can't be a lot of fun.

—BRAD FRASER (1959-)
CANADIAN PLAYWRIGHT AND SCREENWRITER

CELIBACY

A chastity which is not founded upon a deep reverence for sex is nothing but tight-arsed old maidery.

—W. H. AUDEN (1907-1973)
ANGLO-AMERICAN POET AND CRITIC

————

Gertrude Himmelfarb is going to be made the ayatollah of sex in Indiana. She will peddle her appealing message, "Bring back shame!" to all Hoosier teens!

—TONY KUSHNER (1956-)
AMERICAN PLAYWRIGHT

————

How the hell would I know what the big deal about sex is?
I haven't gotten laid in months.

—TONY KUSHNER (1956-)
AMERICAN PLAYWRIGHT

————

A lot of women find themselves celibate for a while and I encourage that, to have periods of celibacy sometimes—if someone's sick—there are all kinds of reasons for not having sex. But the best RX, the best medicine for no sex, is have sex.

—ANNIE SPRINKLE (1954-)
AMERICAN PERFORMANCE ARTIST AND SEX EDUCATOR

FETISHES

Two months ago, in the paper, a man and a woman made the headlines, a couple in their late forties. The only way they could have sex was if he put on a raincoat and a hat to look like Humphrey Bogart, and she would wear a Lauren Bacall wig. This is all true. She would say, "play it again Sam," and then they'd have sex.

—DIRK BOGARDE (1921-1999)
BRITISH ACTOR AND WRITER

In San Francisco in the 1980s, the highest form of art became interior decoration. The glory hole was thus converted to an eighteenth-century foyer.

—RICHARD RODRIGUEZ (1944–)
MEXICAN-AMERICAN WRITER

As much as I'm for the freedom of people [fetish communities], they have no sense of humor about it, and that to me is shocking. How can you be a pickle top and not laugh about it? Or even say it with a straight face?

—JOHN WATERS (1946–)
AMERICAN DIRECTOR

KISSING

A woman phoned me a little bit ago and wanted to know how to prevent her lipstick from failing. . . . I said never eat anything, never drink anything, never kiss anything.

—QUENTIN CRISP (1908–1999)
BRITISH WRITER AND PERSONALITY

Kisses: Don't waste them. But don't count them.

—MARLENE DIETRICH (1901–1992)
GERMAN-BORN ACTOR

MASTURBATION

Masturbation is not chastity, it is just a way of sidestepping the issue without even approaching the solution.

—WILLIAM BURROUGHS (1914–1997)
AMERICAN WRITER

For some time I had felt within my caressing hand something small, moist, bizarre.
I looked in surprised: it was my penis.

—SALVADOR DALÍ (1904-1989)
SPANISH ARTIST

I didn't even masturbate until I was a senior in college. It took me a long time
to realize that the principle was friction.

—DAVID DEL TREDICI (1937-)
AMERICAN COMPOSER

For reading is still the principal thing we do by ourselves in culture. . . .
We have "forgiven" masturbation in our erotic jurisdiction,
but have we even learned to "indict" reading?

—RICHARD HOWARD (1929-)
AMERICAN POET, CRITIC, AND TRANSLATOR

I had so much semen that I had to throw it away. . . . I threw it on the bed
in order to protect myself from catching a venereal disease.

—VASLAV NIJINSKY (1890-1950)
RUSSIAN DANCER

Between twelve and thirteen sensuality took possession of me.
Thenceforward, unless my hands remained by my sides, I think it is true to
say that they usually moved to the place which I judged to be good.

—PAUL VERLAINE (1844-1896)
FRENCH POET

SAFE SEX

There's nothing I enjoy more than buying condoms.

—SANDRA BERNHARD (1955-)
AMERICAN ACTOR, COMEDIAN, AND MUSICIAN

In my young and repressed mind, a condom prohibited the "bonding"
I was seeking. I wanted to share everything with this guy, even if it was bad.

—RICH MERRITT (1967-)
AMERICAN, PORN STAR, WRITER AND U.S. MARINE

After more than fifteen years of telling people to "use a condom every time,"
you're certainly going to increase desire for people to fuck without condoms.

—ERIC ROFES (1954-2006)
AMERICAN WRITER AND ACTIVIST

SEXUALITY

SEE ALSO GENDER BENDING, HOMOSEXUALITY, LESBIANS, SEX

If heterosexuals were not projecting so much on us, if they were not so intent on
controlling or denying our sexuality, what might they discover about their own?

—DOROTHY ALLISON (1942-)
AMERICAN WRITER

Sexual abnormalities should not be ignored in a conspiracy of silence.
Even sexual minorities have certain rights.

—MAGNUS HIRSCHFELD (1868-1935)
GERMAN SEXOLOGIST AND PIONEER GAY RIGHTS ACTIVIST

Straight people were mad because I was gay. The dykes were mad because I wasn't gay enough.

—RITA MAE BROWN (1944–)
AMERICAN WRITER

———

[To Marcel Proust] No one—but no one in the world—has ever written comparable pages on inversion! Years ago I wanted to write a study of sexual inversion myself, and it was the substance of your pages that I wanted to express.

—SIDONIE-GABRIELLE COLETTE (1873–1954)
FRENCH WRITER

———

I think we all sort of know what our sexuality is; we just don't have a name for it.

—JONATHAN MURRAY (1955–)
AMERICAN TV PRODUCER

———

I'm kind of different in that I don't think about being gay that much. You just choose to be with someone of the same sex. Everything else is the same.

—DAVID PICHLER (1968–)
AMERICAN OLYMPIC DIVER

———

[In] American culture, sexuality as such remains taboo. Black heterosexuality is shrouded by even deeper layers of silence and aversion. And black homosexuality, the triple taboo, equates in their minds with an unspeakable obscenity.

—MARLON RIGGS (1957–1994)
AFRICAN-AMERICAN FILMMAKER

———

Too many people are hung up about whether it's heterosexuality, homosexuality, whatever sexuality. To me it's just sexuality.

—IAN ROBERTS (1965–)
OPENLY GAY AUSTRALIAN PROFESSIONAL RUGBY PLAYER

I never went through the agonies of choosing between this or that
sexual way of life. I was chosen.

—PATRICK WHITE (1912-1990)
AUSTRALIAN WRITER AND NOBEL LAUREATE

_____

Sexuality is an emanation, as much in the human being as the animal.
Animals have seasons for it. But for me it was a round-the-calendar thing.

—TENNESSEE WILLIAMS (1911-1983)
AMERICAN PLAYWRIGHT

_____

The category of sex is the political category that founds society as heterosexual.

—MONIQUE WITTIG (1935-2003)
FRENCH FEMINIST AND WRITER

BISEXUALITY

Do I like women? I like women. Do I like them sexually? Yeah, I do. Totally.
As for fooling around, I think when I was younger I was with a lot of women.

—DREW BARRYMORE (1975-)
AMERICAN ACTOR AND PRODUCER

_____

I wrote to maids, and wrote to lads no less,
Some things I wrote, 'tis true, which treat of love;
And songs of mine have pleased both he's and she's.

—BAUDRI OF MEUNG-SUR-LOIRE (1046-1130)
FRENCH ARCHBISHOP

_____

Human law calls a vice the great prudence with which nature
avoids overpopulation.

—JEAN COCTEAU (1889-1963)
FRENCH WRITER AND FILMMAKER

I must confess that I am both elated and terrified by the possibilities of "a bisexual moment." . . . What becomes of our political movement if we openly acknowledge that sexuality is flexible and fluid, that gay and lesbian does not signify "a people" but rather a "sometime behavior"?

—LILLIAN FADERMAN (1940-)
AMERICAN SCHOLAR AND WRITER

We play roles as who we are every day. And if that's true, we can change them—we can try this and we can try that. 'Cause in a way the bisexuality of the period is what's even more radical in some ways and disquieting to gay people and to straight people. It really pushes all those boundaries.

—TODD HAYNES (1961-)
AMERICAN FILM DIRECTOR

Bisexuality means I am free and I am as likely to want to love a woman as I am likely to want to love a man, and what about that? Isn't that what freedom implies?

—JUNE JORDAN (1936-2002)
AFRICAN-AMERICAN ACTIVIST

I used to think that when people said they were bisexual, they were just copping out because they didn't want to admit they were full-fledged queers. . . . Now I think that's so close-minded. I believe there's a whole spectrum of sexuality.

—JILL SOBULE (1961-)
AMERICAN SINGER-SONGWRITER

I'm as capable of being swayed by a girl as by a boy. More and more people feel that way. I don't see why I shouldn't.

—DUSTY SPRINGFIELD (1939-1999)
BRITISH MUSICIAN

SHAME

SEE ALSO SECRETS

Our shame, our fear, our incorrigible staginess, all wish and no resolve, are still,
and more intensely than ever, all we have.

—W. H. AUDEN (1907-1973)
ANGLO-AMERICAN POET AND CRITIC

———————

I've always felt that the only way around the enormous stigma and bigotry that's
been placed on homosexuality is to be matter-of-fact about it, to assume that
there's nothing to be ashamed of.

—ARMISTEAD MAUPIN (1944-)
AMERICAN WRITER

———————

What hours and days and weeks and months of weariness I have endured
by the alternate indulgence and repression of my craving imagination. . . .
What have I suffered in violent and brutal pleasures of the senses,
snatched furtively with shame on my part, with frigid toleration on the part
of my comrades and repented of with terror.

—JOHN ADDINGTON SYMONDS (1840-1893)
ENGLISH POET AND CRITIC

SHOCK

SEE ALSO ENTERTAINMENT, THEATER

If you meet a chap in shock, you must allow that you haven't met the chap at all,
you've met . . . the shock.

—TONY KUSHNER (1956-)
AMERICAN PLAYWRIGHT

Nobody was shocked by anything . . . A lot of the people I met came from these really decadent families where the married men were gay and nobody thought anything about it. I became the toast of London.

—ROBERT MAPPLETHORPE (1946–1989)
AMERICAN PHOTOGRAPHER

———

The good old days, the '60s. Experimentation! Shock! Outrage!

—TERRENCE MCNALLY (1939–)
AMERICAN PLAYWRIGHT

———

Those who undergo the shock of spiritual or intellectual change sometimes fail to recognize their debt to the deserted cause: how much of the heroism, or other high quality, of their rejection has really been the growth of what they reject?

—WALTER PATER (1839–1894)
BRITISH CRITIC AND WRITER

SILENCE

I distrust all silences; they are a cover for metamorphosis.

—ANDRÉ GIDE (1869–1951)
FRENCH WRITER

———

I was going to die, if not sooner then later, whether or not I had ever spoken myself. My silences had not protected me. Your silence will not protect you.

—AUDRE LORDE (1934–1992)
AFRICAN-AMERICAN WRITER, POET, AND ACTIVIST

Controlling through silence. Whoever speaks less is the stronger.

—SUSAN SONTAG (1933-2004)
AMERICAN WRITER AND CRITIC

How can anyone enjoy the absence of all sound, you will ask?
If you were a musician, perhaps you, too, would have the gift of hearing,
when all is still in the dead silence of night, the deep bass note which seems
to come from the earth in its flight through space.

—PETER ILYICH TCHAIKOVSKY (1840-1893)
RUSSIAN COMPOSER

SISSIES

SEE ALSO MASCULINITY

What, exactly, was a faggot? How did faggots run? Clearly, it wasn't a
good thing. It was probably the worst thing imaginable. It equaled weakness
and timidity, everything a budding, insecure jock wanted to avoid.
We were only kids. How were we supposed to know the truth?

—BILLY BEAN (1964-)
AMERICAN FORMER MAJOR LEAGUE BASEBALL PLAYER

When I was eight . . . the guys all told me I threw a ball like a girl so I asked the
girls if I threw a ball like a girl and they said, "No, you throw a ball like a sissy."
The point is, as far as the boys were concerned, sissy and girl are the same thing,
but as far as the girls are concerned the two are very different.

—HARRY HAY (1912-2002)
BRITISH-BORN GAY RIGHTS ACTIVIST

Please, dear God, don't let my wrists go limp today. Amen.

—STEVE KMETKO (1953-)
AMERICAN TV HOST

Real men don't sit in a saloon here [in New York] as they do at home.
I suppose it would be sissified. There's a bar for them to lean on and drink
and joke as long as they feel like.

—CLAUDE MCKAY (1889-1948)
JAMAICAN WRITER

I did want to play with the boys . . . but they made fun of me. They would call me
"Sissie" and other affectionate nicknames. Once when I tried to throw a ball, they
all laughed at me and told me I was a girl, not a boy. I went home crying and
asked my mother to put me in dresses.

—MR. B.
FROM DR. WILLIAM LEE HOWARD'S PSYCHOLOGICAL CASE STUDY, PUBLISHED 1904

Bike-riding and tree-climbing may be typically boyish, but they were merely
means to my sissified ends; I wanted, like an eight-year-old Garbo, to be alone.

—DAN SAVAGE (1964-)
AMERICAN SEX COLUMNIST AND WRITER

SMOKING

SEE ALSO VICE

The other day I brought 55 years of it [smoking] to an abrupt end. I've been rather
restless and I drink rather more than usual; my somber misanthropic outlook on life
has not been flooded with any new transforming light, but I no longer cough.

—J. R. ACKERLEY (1896-1967)
BRITISH WRITER AND EDITOR

The one unbreakable hang-up I have is with cigarettes. They have a bad effect on me. They make me extremely nervous. But I started smoking at twelve, and I've never written a word without a cigarette in my hand.

—TRUMAN CAPOTE (1924-1984)
AMERICAN WRITER

———————

All they that love not tobacco and boys are fools.

—CHRISTOPHER MARLOWE (1564-1593)
ENGLISH WRITER

———————

I smoke endless cigarettes, which help to addle my brain. I long for vigor and clear thought but only meet chaos.

—VITA SACKVILLE-WEST (1892-1962)
BRITISH POET, NOVELIST, AND GARDENER

———————

My aunt Lorraine's a chain-smoker. She's always lighting up. True story. She once saved a man's life by giving him mouth-to-mouth resuscitation. Six months later, he was dead from emphysema.

—BOB SMITH (1960-)
AMERICAN COMEDIAN

SOCIETY

SEE ALSO COMMUNICATION, THE PUBLIC

For me society seems preferable to the demi-monde, but . . . neither can ever suit me. I therefore have to find or found a milieu that fits my aspirations: a society composed of all those who seek to focus and improve their lives through an art that can give them pure presence. These are the only people with whom I can get along.

—NATALIE BARNEY (1876-1972)
AMERICAN WRITER

I think we are becoming more and more linked, and before long, we'll all be one culture. It's happening in every field, not just fashion. Actually, I think the only hope for peace is if culture is homogenized.

—TOM FORD (1962-)
AMERICAN FASHION DESIGNER

I prefer to see culture swept away by what's bad rather than by what's good.

—E. M. FORSTER (1879-1970)
BRITISH WRITER

In spite of all the restraints imposed upon it, sex has everywhere and at all times been the central fact around which the life of the individual and the community and all cultural life has been built.

—MAGNUS HIRSCHFELD (1868-1935)
GERMAN SEXOLOGIST AND PIONEER GAY RIGHTS ACTIVIST

We do not know how the Greeks lived—like pigs, some tell us—but their temples we remember, their art we remember, their poetry we remember.

—PHILIP JOHNSON (1906-2005)
AMERICAN ARCHITECT

The smallest divisible human unit is two people, not one; one is a fiction. From such nets of souls societies, the social world, human life springs.

—TONY KUSHNER (1956-)
AMERICAN PLAYWRIGHT

We've reached what I think is a critical point in our culture where we're all so fucking afraid of one another that we're losing any sense of a world—as the world gets smaller and smaller.

—PETER PAIGE (1969-)
AMERICAN ACTOR

There is no possibility of true culture without altruism.

—SUSAN SONTAG (1933-2004)
AMERICAN WRITER AND CRITIC

———————

I renounced all the follies of this world, actually hating civilization, and feeling entirely above the formalities of society. I resolved on the spot to be a barbarian.

—CHARLES WARREN STODDARD (1843-1909)
AMERICAN TRAVEL WRITER

———————

I tell these stories about the self-destruction and dissolution of families as if I were recounting a Requiem. . . . What has always interested me is the analysis of a sick society.

—LUCHINO VISCONTI (1906-1976)
ITALIAN ARISTOCRAT AND FILM DIRECTOR

———————

Consider what immense forces society brings to play upon each of us, how that society changes from decade to decade; and also from class to class; well, if we cannot analyze these invisible presences . . . how futile life-writing becomes.

—VIRGINIA WOOLF (1882-1941)
BRITISH WRITER

———————

The society of buggers has many advantages—if you are a woman. It is simple, it is honest, it makes one feel, as I noted, in some respects at one's ease. But it has this drawback—with buggers one cannot, as nurses say, show off.

—VIRGINIA WOOLF (1882-1941)
BRITISH WRITER

SOLITUDE

SEE ALSO RELATIONSHIPS

I live very much by myself. I don't meet people. I'm very quickly bored by people.

—PETER BERLIN (1934-)
GERMAN MODEL AND GAY SEX ICON

Writing . . . was a way of being less alone. To be printed, and to be "famous," would be an instant shortcut to identity, and an escape from solitude, because then other people would know one as admirers, friends, lovers, suitors, etc.

—ELIZABETH BISHOP (1911-1979)
AMERICAN POET

Communication is very important to me, though paradoxically, I am not a gregarious person . . . I am, in fact, a classic loner who needs to integrate one's own life with others, yet sets up barricades and spins spider webs.

—MALCOLM BOYD (1923-)
AMERICAN MINISTER AND INSPIRATIONAL WRITER

A disquieting loneliness came into my life, but it induced no hunger for friends of longer acquaintance: They seemed now like a salt-free, sugarless diet.

—TRUMAN CAPOTE (1924-1984)
AMERICAN WRITER

It is a social crime—or so it appears—to want solitude.

—JEAN COCTEAU (1889-1963)
FRENCH WRITER AND FILMMAKER

In school my state of mind became aggressive toward anything or anyone who deliberately or otherwise challenged my solitude. The children who ventured to come near me—growing progressively fewer to be sure—I received with a look and an attitude so hateful that I was safe from intrusion.

—SALVADOR DALÍ (1904-1989)
SPANISH ARTIST

Writing was a way of turning that sort of extreme loneliness on its head— it's a survival strategy.

—JOHN GRAYSON (1960-)
CANADIAN DIRECTOR

An hour of solitude—a way to consciously enjoy what one otherwise would have to let pass unnoticed.

—ANDREW HOLLERAN (1944-)
AMERICAN WRITER

I have come to the conclusion that solitude is the last refuge of civilized people. It is much more civilized than social intercourse, really, although at first sight the reverse might appear to be the case. Social relations are just the descendants of the primitive tribal need to get together for purposes of defense.

—VITA SACKVILLE-WEST (1892-1962)
BRITISH POET, NOVELIST, AND GARDENER

My own efforts have been an attempt to detach myself from the intimate trivial social happenings around me: resulting in apparent rudeness (which I enjoy). This is what I call "refusing to be messed about."

—SIEGFRIED SASSOON (1886-1967)
BRITISH POET AND WRITER

So I seem to sail between the devil and the deep blue sea, having—at the same time—an indescribable repugnance and horror toward making acquaintances and yet a feeling of depression in solitude.

—PETER ILYICH TCHAIKOVSKY (1840-1893)
RUSSIAN COMPOSER

SPORTS

[Written at age 9, in a note to his mother] I was meant to be a composer and will be I'm sure. . . . Don't ask me to try to forget this unpleasant thing and go play football—please.

—SAMUEL BARBER (1910-1981)
AMERICAN COMPOSER

———————

I had some mystic experiences and convictions when I was practicing Yoga. . . . My final decision was that Yoga is no solution for a Westerner. . . . Yoga should be practiced, yes, but not as final, a solution, but rather as we study history and comparative cultures.

—WILLIAM BURROUGHS (1914-1997)
AMERICAN WRITER

———————

I had my first ski lesson at one and since then I have been skating and tobogganing as well. I don't miss a chance to fall!

—SIDONIE-GABRIELLE COLETTE (1873-1954)
FRENCH WRITER

[On prize-fights] Many matches are boresome, but provide two sublime machines of human muscle-play in the vivid light of a "ring"—stark darkness all around with yells from all sides and countless eyes gleaming, centered on the circle,—and I get a real satisfaction and stimulant.

—HART CRANE (1899-1932)
AMERICAN POET

What's great about the Gay Games is that anyone can participate. . . . It's just fun to meet people from throughout the world who you don't have to explain yourself to.

—BILLIE JEAN KING (1943-)
AMERICAN TENNIS CHAMPION

I was marketable to the corporate world in every way but one.

—MARTINA NAVRATILOVA (1956-)
CZECH-BORN WORLD TENNIS CHAMPION

You could field a major-league all-star team with all the players that are gay.

—DAVE PALLONE (1951-)
AMERICAN MAJOR LEAGUE BASEBALL PLAYER

Where no true-identity romance was possible, a slow dance with nihilism appeared magnetic. And along came bodybuilding, pulling me in with a new way to fight against the downward spiral of life's gravity.

—BOB PARIS (1959-)
AMERICAN ACTIVIST AND MR. UNIVERSE INTERNATIONAL IN 1983

Eroticism did not draw me to bodybuilding nor keep me there.
The intersection between this particular sport and my young queer self
came about because I was desperate for something—anything—that would
lend focus and discipline to a fractured identity.

—BOB PARIS (1959-)
AMERICAN ACTIVIST AND MR. UNIVERSE INTERNATIONAL IN 1983

———

A lot of us who were gay were the best divers too. So people could say what
they wanted, but when they shut their mouths whenever you beat them.

—DAVID PICHLER (1968-)
AMERICAN OLYMPIC DIVER

———

I dream that I am a little boy in a private school. It is always the moment
when we are sent out to play football. . . . I never get beyond that.
I mean I have never got out into the football field as yet—but I always have the
impression that I am in disgrace for something—and being jeered at . . .

—VITA SACKVILLE-WEST (1892-1962)
BRITISH POET, NOVELIST, AND GARDENER

———

I don't understand sports. I don't understand basketball. Why is the hoop so high?
Why can't they lower it so we all can play?

—JASON STUART (1959-)
AMERICAN ACTOR AND COMEDIAN

———

I have confidence in the growing influence of young heterosexual tolerance
in sports—and in the irresistible power of young homosexual
athlete's courage, skill, and will.

—PATRICIA NELL WARREN (1936-)
AMERICAN WRITER

The runner's need to reach deep inside and "find more" spurred
my self-discovery as a woman and my consciousness-raising concerning women's
rights. Only then, through running could I finally catch up with those
long-festering questions about sexual orientation.

—PATRICIA NELL WARREN (1936–)
AMERICAN WRITER

Sports are a major arena in which American society hard-wires "traditional"
notions about gender roles and orientation into its citizens.

—PATRICIA NELL WARREN (1936–)
AMERICAN WRITER

SPORTS AND COMING OUT

People need to have some empathy for some of these young men in the NBA and
NFL and major-league baseball and any other professional sport, and understand
it's going to be different fore each different person. Not everybody is resilient.
Not everybody is outspoken. Not everybody is well-spoken.

—JOHN AMAECHI (1970–)
BRITISH NBA BASKETBALL PLAYER

But athletes need to know the truth. They need to be aware. If your livelihood was
specifically contingent upon your ability to work among people who might perse-
cute you, then it's a fair decision to keep your life private—in my world and from
my experience. And I think if we are judging, as a gay and lesbian community,
people who don't have [the ability to come out] yet, I don't think it's fair.

—BILLY BEAN (1964–)
AMERICAN MAJOR LEAGUE BASEBALL PLAYER

I realize that athletes look at Martina Navratilova and realize that she has lost millions in endorsements because she is openly lesbian. . . . I have been fortunate that discrimination has not held me back in my career. All I can say is that people will ultimately respect you most for being honest about who you are.

—MISSY GIOVE (1972-)
AMERICAN PROFESSIONAL DOWNHILL MOUNTAIN BIKE CHAMPION

I know it's not politically correct in the gay community to say that Troy [Aikman] is not gay, but I have a sense that he's not. Then again, you never know for sure.

—DAVE KOPAY (1942-)
AMERICAN NFL FOOTBALL PLAYER

I wish I could get across to gay athletes just how rewarding it is to come out . . . It is the greatest feeling imaginable when a kid comes up to you and tells you how much what you did meant to him. it's a reward that goes well beyond all the heartache.

—DAVE KOPAY (1942-)
AMERICAN NFL FOOTBALL PLAYER

I left Czechoslovakia for a lot of reasons, and it was a big risk. . . . It was frightening. I was only 18. If you spoke your mind there, you would go to jail. So for me to be in this country and be quiet [about being lesbian] because somebody else is uncomfortable with it—well, I'm not going to do that!

—MARTINA NAVRATILOVA (1956-)
CZECH-BORN WORLD TENNIS CHAMPION

FIGURE SKATING

People have the misconception that skating is all gay. . . . But that's not true. . . . Skating was the last place I came out.

—DONI DIGIOVANNI (1981-)
AMERICAN FIGURE SKATER AND MODEL

It's funny how people think there are gay people in skating because it's an artistic sport. . . . People think when you are artistic, you are obviously gay. It's not true.

—RUDY GALINDO (1964-)
AMERICAN FIGURE SKATING CHAMPION

When you get to nationals, these guys skate clean. They're really butch when they skate. They're just jump-jump-jump. They want just conservative— just really macho—men.

—RUDY GALINDO (1964-)
AMERICAN FIGURE SKATING CHAMPION

STATES OF MIND

SEE ALSO PSYCHOLOGY, THERAPY

Certainly there is a consent, between the body and the mind; and where nature erreth in the one, she ventureth in the other.

—SIR FRANCIS BACON (1561-1626)
BRITISH PHILOSOPHER AND STATESMAN

At the end I looked on the disorder of my mind as sacred.

—ARTHUR RIMBAUD (1854-1891)
FRENCH POET

Well, I feel some part of me can wake up and be very existential and the next day wake up and be sort of in love with the universe.

—LILY TOMLIN (1939-)
AMERICAN ACTOR AND COMEDIAN

ANXIETY

Great worrier that I am, tormented by too much happiness.

—ANDRÉ GIDE (1869-1951)
FRENCH WRITER

Notgeil, he called what I was enduring: A German word.
Notgeil was lust with insomnia. It was lust in a hurry. It was waiting room lust,
born of anxiety and boredom.

—DAVID LEAVITT (1961-)
AMERICAN WRITER

BOREDOM

Nothing can be more deadly than boredom and this applies if one
is either the cause of it or its victim.

—JAMES DEAN (1931-1955)
AMERICAN ACTOR

As for being bored, don't mind it. . . . You will never get hold of anything
in India unless you experience Indian boredom.

—E. M. FORSTER (1879-1970)
BRITISH WRITER

DEPRESSION

I either get super euphoric or darkly depressive, misery being my default
position. My soul flies erratically on the wings of what I would imagine
is a feeble bi-polarism.

—DAVID BOWIE (1947-)
BRITISH MUSICIAN

Despair is almost a necessary condition. . . . It is either the moment of defeat, or of breakthrough.

—STEPHEN SPENDER (1909-1995)
BRITISH POET AND WRITER

STEREOTYPES

SEE ALSO HOMOSEXUALITY, LESBIANS

I feel Hollywood now is fine with gay people and gay characters as long as we're making them laugh, doing their hair, giving the straight women therapy or decorating their homes. But it's sort of the same thing black people went through. As long as you're useful, you can sit at the table. We're sort of now in our Mammy role.

—CRAIG CHESTER (1965-)
AMERICAN ACTOR AND COMEDIAN

———

Gay characters in games are in the same place as gay characters in movies of the 1930s, '40s, '50s, even in the '70s. For the most part, gays are seen as a joke in the games. "Oh, look, I'm in a dress, I'm acting all fruity, ha ha ha!" Sadly that's where we're at.

—FLYNN DE MARCO (1967-)
AMERICAN GRAPHIC DESIGNER AND GAMER

———

I thought there was something really embarrassing and inauthentic about previous scenes of sexuality between women. . . . I wanted to make a believable love story between two women that did not end in a bisexual triangle or a suicide.

—DONNA DEITCH (1945-)
AMERICAN FILM DIRECTOR

We [GLAAD] want to be the people that scriptwriters and directors pick up the phone to call when their scripts are in development. . . . We want to make sure that we are talking about fair and accurate representations of gay people before those images make it to the screen.

—JOAN GARRY (1958-)
AMERICAN GAY RIGHTS ACTIVIST

People always like to put you in compartments. . . . I think compartments of any kind are bad. They do it in sex: "he's a leather fetishist" or "he likes little girls in pink knickers." Well, I think one should like everything, or try everything in all spheres of life.

—JOE ORTON (1933-1967)
BRITISH PLAYWRIGHT

I aspire to be the first openly gay actor to play openly straight roles on film. . . . I challenge Hollywood not to stereotype me.

—FELIX A. PIRE (1971-)
AMERICAN ACTOR

In this culture, anytime you deal in stereotypes, we lose.

—WILLIAM WAYBOURN (1947-)
AMERICAN PR EXECUTIVE AND GAY ACTIVIST, COFOUNDER OF THE GAY AND LESBIAN VICTORY FUND

STYLE

SEE ALSO APPEARANCES, BEAUTY, FASHION

I rehabilitate the commonplace.

—JEAN COCTEAU (1889-1963)
FRENCH WRITER AND FILMMAKER

Fortunately I am not one of those beings who when they smile are apt to expose remnants, however small, of horrible and degrading spinach clinging to their teeth.

—SALVADOR DALÍ (1904-1989)
SPANISH ARTIST

[On styling] It's the elevation of reality to a nicer place.

—PATRICIA FIELDS (1943-)
AMERICAN COSTUME DESIGNER

To have too much style is looked down upon in America, whereas for the French it is something to be celebrated.

—TOM FORD (1962-)
AMERICAN FASHION DESIGNER

Some people say that chairs are good-looking that are comfortable. Are they? I think that comfort is a function of whether you think the chair is good-looking or not.

—PHILIP JOHNSON (1906-2005)
AMERICAN ARCHITECT

Nothing can compete with the vulgarity of a snobbist or bought correct taste.

—ROBERT MCALMON (1896-1956)
AMERICAN WRITER AND PUBLISHER

Style isn't camp or chi-chi.

—JOE ORTON (1933-1967)
BRITISH PLAYWRIGHT

I hate naturalness. I reconstruct everything.

—PIER PAOLO PASOLINI (1922-1975)
ITALIAN FILM DIRECTOR

I don't know how I would describe myself because I'm so eclectic. People say they hear my style. I'm not sure I would recognize something I'd written.

—STEPHEN SONDHEIM (1930-)
AMERICAN MUSICAL THEATER COMPOSER AND PLAYWRIGHT

Elegance equals the largest amount of refusal.

—SUSAN SONTAG (1933-2004)
AMERICAN WRITER AND CRITIC

Style is knowing who you are, what you want to say, and not giving a damn.

—GORE VIDAL (1925-)
AMERICAN WRITER AND POLITICAL ACTIVIST

Any man under fifty that can pull off slicked-back hair so effortlessly without looking like a greaser from *The Outsiders* is a hottie in my book.

—DANIEL VOSOVIC (1981-)
AMERICAN FASHION DESIGNER AND REALITY TV STAR

I've always depended on charm both in life and in work.

—EDMUND WHITE (1940-)
AMERICAN WRITER AND CRITIC

SUCCESS

SEE ALSO BUSINESS, DETERMINATION, MONEY

Fortune is like the market; where many times if you can stay a little, the price will fall.

—SIR FRANCIS BACON (1561-1626)
BRITISH PHILOSOPHER AND STATESMAN

He that hath wife and children hath given hostages to fortune;
for they are impediments to great enterprises, either of virtue or mischief.
Certainly the best works, and of greatest merit for the public,
have proceeded from the unmarried or childless men.

—SIR FRANCIS BACON (1561-1626)
BRITISH PHILOSOPHER AND STATESMAN

———————

I sat on my ass for 30 years. That's an achievement in itself—think about it:
Peter Berlin hasn't done anything in 30 years.

—PETER BERLIN (1934-)
GERMAN MODEL AND GAY SEX ICON

———————

I was born prodigal . . . there is a race of Who loses wins,
and a race of Who wins loses.

—JEAN COCTEAU (1889-1963)
FRENCH WRITER AND FILMMAKER

———————

I am convinced that it would be foolish for me to be blinded by success.
The misunderstandings which success creates should not affect me
more than the misunderstandings which sarcasm directs at me.

—JEAN COCTEAU (1889-1963)
FRENCH WRITER AND FILMMAKER

———————

Move over Dorothy, there's a new girl in Oz.

—LOLA COLA (1963-)
AMERICAN TRANS DOCUMENTARY STAR

———————

If years of obscurity didn't deter me, it would be really silly
to be deterred by success.

—MICHAEL CUNNINGHAM (1952-)
AMERICAN PULITZER PRIZE-WINNING WRITER

It doesn't matter a bit whether a person really writes or only does it in his imagination . . . if he can summon up enough strength in his imagination to be successful in his imagination . . . then it's no different from someone who's really successful.

—RAINER WERNER FASSBINDER (1945-1982)
GERMAN DIRECTOR

It bothers me that so many people see being a successful gay artist as being someone who is embraced by the non-gay world.

—MICHAEL THOMAS FORD (1968-)
AMERICAN WRITER

I've earned all this money. I've worked for it. I didn't cheat anybody. I didn't issue junk bonds and put people out of work. I earned it.

—DAVID GEFFEN (1943-)
AMERICAN RECORD MOGUL

Having a driver is a great luxury—I aspire to have one again.

—BOY GEORGE (1961-)
BRITISH MUSICIAN

Other artists had been accusing me of selling out since my paintings started selling. I mean, I don't know what they intended me to do: Just stay in the subway the rest of my life? Somehow that would have made me stay pure?

—KEITH HARING (1958-1990)
AMERICAN ARTIST AND ACTIVIST

Until something lets me be expansive I can only limp along—an average life—and think of what I'd like to do if conditions would permit.

—MARSDEN HARTLEY (1877-1943)
AMERICAN ARTIST

I would always come in second. . . . I was the "best of the second best." In fact, I always said that if I wrote a book, that would be the title.

—GENE KUFFEL (1964-)
AMERICAN SCHOOLTEACHER AND MR. USA INTERNATIONAL IN 1997

It is a salutary discipline to consider the vast number of books that are written, the fair hopes with which their authors see them published, and the fate which awaits them. What chance is there that any book will make its way among that multitude? And the successful books are but the successes of a season.

—W. SOMERSET MAUGHAM (1874-1965)
BRITISH WRITER AND PLAYWRIGHT

My success means nothing to me. All I can think of now are my mistakes. I can think of nothing else but my foolishness.

—W. SOMERSET MAUGHAM (1874-1965)
BRITISH WRITER AND PLAYWRIGHT

How easy it is to be alive when we demand of life only the simple and crude reward of success in a steeplechase.

—SIEGFRIED SASSOON (1886-1967)
BRITISH POET AND WRITER

It's odd because you might work for years doing whatever it is that you do, and then when something happens it's made to appear as if you've sprung out overnight.

—DAVID SEDARIS (1956-)
AMERICAN WRITER

Show business is climbing the mountain and then coming back down. Nobody can stay at the top.

—ETHEL WATERS (1896-1977)
AFRICAN-AMERICAN ACTOR AND MUSICIAN

You cannot sit back and just look at the medals and the trophies of your career. You better throw them away.

—FRANCO ZEFFIRELLI (1923–)
ITALIAN DIRECTOR

SUFFERING

SEE ALSO DEATH, GRIEF, HATRED, OPPRESSION

Perhaps just this lesson I in the end must learn: that struggle itself is the peace of life.

—MERCEDES DE ACOSTA (1893–1968)
CUBAN-AMERICAN WRITER AND SOCIALITE

[On breakups] For several months I stayed in bed listening to Linda Rondstadt records. Linda Ronstadt, I felt sure, understood suffering.

—BLANCE MCCRARY BOYD (1945–)
WRITER

Art isn't the thing that makes one happy or miserable: it's Life. . . .
I don't extract misery from Art: if anything I occasionally am fortunate enough to find forgetfulness and watery reflection of content in it.

—RUPERT BROOKE (1887–1915)
BRITISH POET

I don't know which is better, the harm that helps or the good that hurts.

—MICHELANGELO BUONARROTI (1475–1564)
ITALIAN PAINTER, SCULPTOR, POET, AND ENGINEER

I assure you I have lately suffered very severely from kidneys within and creditors without.

—LORD BYRON (1788-1824)
BRITISH POET

Suffering is a habit. I am used to it.

—JEAN COCTEAU (1889-1963)
FRENCH WRITER AND FILMMAKER

I don't luxuriate in suffering. You can't. People are nattering at you, they bring their problems to you, and you have to very charmingly say, "Fuck that." . . . I think sour, disillusioned people are just bores.

—GEORGE CUKOR (1899-1983)
AMERICAN FILM DIRECTOR

Sorrow never scorned to speak
To any who
Were false or true.

—COUNTEE CULLEN (1903-1946)
AFRICAN-AMERICAN POET

My painting carries within it the message of pain. . . . Painting completed by life. I lost three children. . . . Paintings substituted for all of this.

—FRIDA KAHLO (1907-1954)
MEXICAN ARTIST AND INTELLECTUAL

Tragedy is the annihilation from whence new life springs, the Nothing out of which Something is born. Devastation can be a necessary prelude to a new kind of beauty. Necessary but always bloody.

—TONY KUSHNER (1956-)
AMERICAN PLAYWRIGHT

The gift of sympathy . . . is a charming faculty, but one often abused by those who are conscious of its possession: for there is something ghoulish in the avidity with which they will pounce upon the misfortune of their friends so that they may exercise their dexterity. It gushes forth like an oil-well, and the sympathetic pour out their sympathy with an abandon that is sometimes embarrassing to their victims.

—W. SOMERSET MAUGHAM (1874-1965)
BRITISH WRITER AND PLAYWRIGHT

If you don't have trouble paying the rent, you have trouble doing something else; one needs just a certain amount of trouble. Some people need more trouble to operate and some people need less.

—ROBERT RAUSCHENBERG (1925-)
AMERICAN ARTIST

I've had my share of laughs, but I'm also a connoisseur of suffering and bitter experience.

—ETHEL WATERS (1896-1977)
AFRICAN-AMERICAN ACTOR AND MUSICIAN

Suffering—curious as it may sound to you—is the means by which we exist, because it is the only means by which we become conscious of existing.

—OSCAR WILDE (1854-1900)
IRISH PLAYWRIGHT AND WRITER

Nothing is given us freely. You have to fight with your teeth and your nails in order to achieve something, in order to bring forth whatever gift you have received.

—FRANCO ZEFFIRELLI (1923-)
ITALIAN DIRECTOR

SUPERSTITION

SEE ALSO RELIGION

Superstition, without a veil, is a deformed thing; for, as it addeth deformity
to an ape, to be so like a man, so the similitude of superstition to religion,
makes it the more deformed.

—SIR FRANCIS BACON (1561-1626)
BRITISH PHILOSOPHER AND STATESMAN

———————

I am superstitious about going "back" to places . . . they have changed;
you have changed; even the weather may have changed.

—ELIZABETH BISHOP (1911-1979)
AMERICAN POET

———————

I only have one [superstition] with which I still drive people crazy. I won't have
three cigarettes in the same ashtray. I keep taking them out and putting them in
my pockets and all over my suit, just so I never have more than two cigarette butts
in other people's. I won't let other people have it either.

—TRUMAN CAPOTE (1924-1984)
AMERICAN WRITER

———————

I was very interested in horoscopes and things like that, and just one day
I took all of them and tore them up, and I'm not going to let myself be
victimized by this junk any longer.

—TRUMAN CAPOTE (1924-1984)
AMERICAN WRITER

TALENT

SEE ALSO ART AND ARTISTS, CREATION AND CREATIVITY, IMAGINATION, SUCCESS

Surely anything that is impossible for others to achieve by effort,
that is dangerous to imitate, and yet, like natural virtue, must be both admired
and imitated, always remains mysterious.

—ELIZABETH BISHOP (1911–1979)
AMERICAN POET

―――――――

Strange are the sweets of mediocrity.

—E. M. FORSTER (1879–1970)
BRITISH WRITER

―――――――

Talent is courtesy with respect to matter; it consists of giving song to what
was dumb.

—JEAN GENET (1910–1986)
FRENCH WRITER, CRIMINAL, AND POLITICAL ACTIVIST

―――――――

I think anyone who is talented can have a career today. Whether they can have
my career is a different story.

—TERRENCE MCNALLY (1939–)
AMERICAN PLAYWRIGHT

―――――――

Of my literary efforts I shall say nothing, except that they were appalling. . . .
I might call them masturbations, for they were certainly the fruit of my intellect
alone, deprived of all contact with good sense or discrimination.

—PAUL VERLAINE (1844–1896)
FRENCH POET

TECHNOLOGY

We have through electronic technology produced an extension of our brains to the world formerly outside of us.

—JOHN CAGE (1934-1992)
AMERICAN COMPOSER

My mobile phone had a breakdown and I was incommunicado for six days. No friends, lovers, agents, or relatives felt the need to investigate. . . . All that will be left of me will be a ribcage and a scrap of a Gucci scarf.

—JULIAN CLARY (1959-)
BRITISH COMEDIAN

A computer would deserve to be called intelligent if it could deceive a human into believing that it was human.

—ALAN TURING, OBE (1912-1954)
BRITISH MATHEMATICIAN AND CRYPTOGRAPHER

The only problem with the cell phone, I think, is that the substance that is in it that makes it work is from the Congo. You know this already. I'm convinced that the grief that the people are suffering in the Congo as they rip off this material will end up really hurting us. So, be very careful. Use that thing very, very little.

—ALICE WALKER (1944-)
AFRICAN-AMERICAN FEMINIST AND PULITZER PRIZE-WINNING WRITER

Well now there are a lot of clubs and DJs, and technology has made everything kind of boring. There's not a human side to DJs anymore, everything is electronic. It was different with vinyl—technology is taking away the warmth.

—JUNIOR VASQUEZ (1946-)
AMERICAN DJ AND RECORD PRODUCER

THE INTERNET

If you want titillation you'll go online.

—NICK BAMFORD (1952–)
BRITISH PLAYWRIGHT

———

I'm not this deranged Internet addict. I haven't got the concentration to be on there for ever. It's not my whole life. But there are lots of gay sites you can go on and meet people—I think in a way the Internet was the best thing that ever happened to gay culture. It's pretty hardcore.

—BOY GEORGE (1961–)
BRITISH MUSICIAN

———

I've never seen the Internet. I don't have e-mail. I just enjoy lying on the couch and reading a magazine. When people say, "You should visit my Web page," I'm always perplexed by it. Why? What do you do there?

—DAVID SEDARIS (1956–)
AMERICAN WRITER

———

The Net is the Godzilla of our modern age.

—BRUCE VILANCH (1948–)
AMERICAN COMEDY WRITER

———

Cyberspace is invented space. . . . It's at the intersection of those worlds that magic happens.

—JEANETTE WINTERSON (1959–)
BRITISH WRITER

TELEVISION

SEE ALSO AUDIENCES, ENTERTAINMENT, MEDIA, MOVIES

I get really bored with those kinds of shows telling me, "Hey, America, it's OK to be gay!" Because duh. It's the same feeling I have when TV shows tell me it's bad to be a racist. It's like, "Thanks for thinking I'm an idiot, and I can't figure that out on my own."

—ALAN BALL (1957-)
AMERICAN SCREENWRITER

————

The whole problem with television now is that it just goes for the lowest common denominator.

—SANDRA BERNHARD (1955-)
AMERICAN ACTOR, COMEDIAN, AND MUSICIAN

————

We're really very ungrateful to television.

—GEORGE CUKOR (1899-1983)
AMERICAN FILM DIRECTOR

————

[On seeing television for the first time as a child] I thought it was a miracle, an absolute miracle. I thought how can they do this. Isn't this incredible? Especially when it was, you know, the kinescopes I would watch but, but they were like, like ooh, it's gotta get better than this.

—BOB MACKIE (1940-)
AMERICAN FASHION DESIGNER

————

I love, love *Jackass*! Here's the thing: Cool gay men love it; square gay men hate it.

—JOHN WATERS (1946-)
AMERICAN DIRECTOR

I'm a big homo. I'm watching a lot of homo TV. . . . Now my TiVo knows I'm gay.

—SUZANNE WESTENHOEFER (1961–)
ACTOR AND COMEDIAN

THE L WORD

Yes, I do. I love to hate it [*The L Word*]. I admit that—love to hate it.

—AMANDA BEARSE (1958–)
AMERICAN ACTOR

————

They [*The L Word* creators] have an interesting challenge, trying to get a broad enough audience but not completely alienating their lesbian viewers. Sometimes that balance works, sometimes it seems like they're throwing some pretty meager bones to the lesbians.

—ALISON BECHDEL (1960–)
AMERICAN CARTOONIST AND GRAPHIC NOVELIST

REALITY TV

And a lot of reality television is the entertainment equivalent of traffic accidents on freeways. How can so many people not have a life?

—TOM BIANCHI (1945–)
AMERICAN PHOTOGRAPHER

————

You don't necessarily have to win a reality show to become successful from it. Just look at Jennifer Hudson.

—PAUL MCCULLOUGH (1971–)
AMERICAN CHEF AND REALITY TV STAR

I didn't want to go down in history for punching somebody on a reality show.

—JANE WIEDLIN (1958–)
AMERICAN MUSICIAN

TALK SHOWS

When somebody is antiwoman or anti-African-American, the [talk show] hosts will point it out quickly, saying, "Hey, you're being sexist or racist," or the audience will shout them down. . . . You don't hear hosts coming to the defense of gays and lesbians, and you don't hear the audience coming to their defense.

—STEVEN GOLDSTEIN (1962–)
AMERICAN TV PRODUCER AND GAY ACTIVIST

I was always afraid that at some talk show they'd take a question from the audience, and some guy would stand up and say, "I slept with you!"

—DIRK SHAFER (1962–)
AMERICAN MODEL, ACTOR, DIRECTOR, AND *PLAYGIRL'S* MAN OF THE YEAR IN 1992

The audiences have a mob mentality. . . . These things become frenzies.
I don't see how the hosts think they can control these situations.

—WILLIAM WAYBOURN (1947–)
AMERICAN PR EXECUTIVE AND GAY ACTIVIST, COFOUNDER OF THE GAY AND LESBIAN
VICTORY FUND

THEATER

SEE ALSO ART AND ARTISTS, AUDIENCES, ENTERTAINMENT, HOLLYWOOD,
MOVIES, WRITING

A play is more convincing than a film because a film is a story of phantoms.
Movie spectators do not exchange waves with flesh and blood actors.

—JEAN COCTEAU (1889-1963)
FRENCH WRITER AND FILMMAKER

The theatre is a furnace. The man who does not realize this is either
consumed in it sooner or later, or burned immediately.

—JEAN COCTEAU (1889-1963)
FRENCH WRITER AND FILMMAKER

Nothing bores me more than the usual solid, well-produced play.

—RAINER WERNER FASSBINDER (1945-1982)
GERMAN DIRECTOR

You learn to go out into the world after you see a play that you really loved,
and look at politics and love and all sorts of other human phenomena
in the same way. It's real and yet it isn't.

—TONY KUSHNER (1956-)
AMERICAN PLAYWRIGHT

The theater is an extremely useful instrument for the edification of a country,
and the barometer that measures its greatness or decline.

—FEDERICO GARCIA LORCA (1898-1936)
SPANISH POET AND PLAYWRIGHT

Plays are about what people do, not what they say, that dialogue is only the tip of the iceberg.

—TERRENCE MCNALLY (1939-)
AMERICAN PLAYWRIGHT

"Writing for the theater"—that royal road to megalomania.

—JAMES MERRILL (1926-1995)
AMERICAN PULITZER PRIZE-WINNING POET

In a scene, the character does not get affected by the words, the words get affected by the character.

—STEPHEN SONDHEIM (1930-)
AMERICAN MUSICAL THEATER COMPOSER AND PLAYWRIGHT

I was born with the smell of the stage in my nose.

—LUCHINO VISCONTI (1906-1976)
ITALIAN ARISTOCRAT AND DIRECTOR

When I say I had flipped through most of Shakespeare by the age of nine, I wasn't quite the prig it makes me sound. I understood less of the language than the average adult, but enjoyed the blood and thunder, the come and go, the stage directions (that magic word *exeunt*).

—PATRICK WHITE (1912-1990)
AUSTRALIAN WRITER AND NOBEL LAUREATE

THERAPY

SEE ALSO PSYCHOLOGY, STATES OF MIND

Single is new to me. That's why I'm seeing a therapist.

—DOUG BLASDELL (1962-2007)
AMERICAN CELEBRITY TRAINER AND REALITY TV STAR

But I realized something. About art. And psychiatry. They're both
self-perpetuating systems. Like religion. All three of them promise you a sense
of inner worth and meaning, and spend a lot of time telling you about
the suffering you have to go through to achieve it.

—SAMUEL R. DELANY (1942-)
AMERICAN WRITER

I've always used various addictions to anesthetize myself—drag, drugs, fame,
sex, religion, food—and there's been a lot of things in my life
that I've wanted to run away from. Therapy opens up a window.
You can try to close it, but the realization remains.

—BOY GEORGE (1961-)
BRITISH MUSICIAN

Offering counsel is repugnant to the discreet mind.

—HENRY JAMES (1843-1916)
AMERICAN WRITER

It took me 16 years of drug addiction and alcoholism to actually have the humility
to say, "I need help." Because, I figured that, because I was a successful man, I
was wealthy, I was, you know, seemingly intelligent—even that I am not intelligent
enough to ask for help. It took me 16 years to say those three words—I need help.

—SIR ELTON JOHN, CBE (1947-)
BRITISH GRAMMY AND ACADEMY AWARD-WINNING MUSICIAN

I used to pull out my pee pee in malls to get attention! My mother always said,
"Can't you just whisper your problems out to a therapist instead of acting them
out for the world to see?"

—LESLIE JORDAN (1955-)
AMERICAN EMMY AWARD–WINNING ACTOR

I think I have OCD or ADD or some other three-initial ditty.
Whatever it is, it is exhausting.

—ROSIE O'DONNELL (1962-)
AMERICAN ACTOR, COMEDIAN, AND TALK SHOW HOST

THOUGHT

SEE ALSO GENIUS, INTELLIGENCE AND INTELLECTUALS

But enough of "abstract speculation," marked as it is by a very concrete stupidity.

—HENRY JAMES (1843-1916)
AMERICAN WRITER

I don't know how to organize thoughts. I don't know how to have thoughts.

—JASPER JOHNS (1930-)
AMERICAN ARTIST

For there are no new ideas. There are only new ways of making them felt.

—AUDRE LORDE (1934-1992)
AFRICAN-AMERICAN WRITER, POET, AND ACTIVIST

When a man once gets bitten with the virus of the ideal not all the King's doctors
and not all the King's surgeons can rid him of it.

—W. SOMERSET MAUGHAM (1874-1965)
BRITISH WRITER AND PLAYWRIGHT

TRAVEL

SEE ALSO AMERICA, CITIES AND STATES, EUROPE

To lose your prejudices you must travel.

—MARLENE DIETRICH (1901-1992)
GERMAN-BORN ACTOR

[On Bangkok] They don't call it the Big Mango for nothing. . . . It's fruity!

—GRANT THATCHER
BRITISH–BORN, HONG KONG BASED TRAVEL EDITOR

Florence and Me. It seemed that at night the place was abandoned to sensation and a whole new set of inchoate longings I scarcely recognized.

—ROBERT FERRO (1941-1988)
AMERICAN WRITER AND GAY RIGHTS ACTIVIST

I feel American in Europe and exotic at home.

—JAMES MERRILL (1926-1995)
PULITZER PRIZE-WINNING POET

Once travel was itself an anomalous activity . . . [but now] to travel becomes the very condition of modern consciousness, of a modern view of the world—the acting out of longing or dismay.

—SUSAN SONTAG (1933-2004)
AMERICAN WRITER AND CRITIC

There is a fate in Tahiti that is known only to the initiated.

—CHARLES WARREN STODDARD (1843-1909)
AMERICAN TRAVEL WRITER

TRUTH

SEE ALSO DECEIT, HONESTY

I play with what is legend and what is true. Mostly because nobody knows.

—DOROTHY ALLISON (1942–)
AMERICAN WRITER

And I think as an artist my job isn't to preach, but to lay open the truth
about certain situations, gently.

—JANE ANDERSON (1954–)
AMERICAN ACTOR AND DIRECTOR

I don't know why people don't just embrace the truth. Strength comes out of that.

—ALEXIS ARQUETTE (1969–)
AMERICAN ACTOR AND DRAG PERFORMER

To lie, even with the best of intentions, is a deadly sin, for every time we tell
someone a lie. . . We not only forfeit for ever the right to his faith in us;
we undermine his faith in all men and all speech.

—W. H. AUDEN (1907–1973)
ANGLO-AMERICAN POET AND CRITIC

Expectation thus becomes the basic condition of truth: truth . . .
is what is at the end of expectation.

—ROLAND BARTHES (1915–1980)
FRENCH CRITIC AND THEORIST

[A Greek] found fault the other day with the English language,
because it had so few shades of a Negative, whereas a Greek can so modify
"No" to a "Yes," and vice versa, by the slippery qualities of his language,
that prevarication may be carried to any extent and still leave a loop-hole through
which perjury may slip without being perceived.

—LORD BYRON (1788-1824)
BRITISH POET

I don't care what anybody says about me as long as it isn't true.

—TRUMAN CAPOTE (1924-1984)
AMERICAN WRITER

It is worse to mistrust people than to be a sucker.

—STEPHEN FRY (1957-)
BRITISH COMEDIAN, WRITER, AND ACTOR

One can, of course, tell the truth, but I shouldn't think that would be
necessary to give the illusion of a True Confession.

—JAMES MERRILL (1926-1995)
AMERICAN PULITZER PRIZE-WINNING POET

Whatever satisfies the soul is truth.

—WALT WHITMAN (1819-1892)
AMERICAN POET

UNDERSTANDING

SEE ALSO COMMUNICATION

I offer an olive branch to you. . . . I say to you, Walk a mile in my pumps.

—TOM AMMIANO (1941-)
AMERICAN COMEDIAN, ACTIVIST, AND POLITICIAN

———

You have not been wronged as I have been. You cannot know my pain.

—COUNTEE CULLEN (1903-1946)
AFRICAN-AMERICAN POET

———

Together we organize the world for ourselves, or at least we organize our under-standing of it; we reflect it, refract it, criticize it, grieve over its savagery.

—TONY KUSHNER (1956-)
AMERICAN PLAYWRIGHT

———

I think I like either those people who completely understand whatever I say—at all levels—or those who understand hardly any of it. . . . Understanding has more than one face.

—JAMES MERRILL (1926-1995)
AMERICAN PULITZER PRIZE-WINNING POET

———

I see now that these nonsensical expressions were not nonsensical because I had not yet found the correct expressions, but that their nonsensicality was their very essence.

—LUDWIG WITTGENSTEIN (1889-1951)
AUSTRIAN PHILOSOPHER

VANITY

SEE ALSO APPEARANCES, BEAUTY, IDENTITY, INTELLIGENCE AND INTELLECTUALS,
FASHION, WORKING OUT

When people talk endlessly about themselves I associate the habit
with vanity or an absence of discretion. But there is also an element
of vanity in the decision not to talk.

—MARIE-CLAIRE BLAIS (1939-)
CANADIAN WRITER AND PLAYWRIGHT

———

A picture is a different matter—everybody sits for their picture;
but a bust looks like putting up pretensions to permanency, and smacks of something of a hankering for public fame rather than private remembrance.

—LORD BYRON (1788-1824)
BRITISH POET

———

I loved noting that fleeting look of pleased surprise in people's eyes when it was
suddenly brought to their attention that, in spite of theatrical success and excessive publicity, I was really quite pleasant and unaffected. This, of course, was all
nonsense, but I was at least no more affected than anyone else.

—NOËL COWARD (1899-1973)
BRITISH ACTOR AND PLAYWRIGHT

———

I feel an enormous power in me—that seems almost supernatural.
If this power is not too dissipated in aggravation and discouragement I may
amount to something sometime. I can say this now with perfect equanimity
because I am notoriously drunk.

—HART CRANE (1899-1932)
AMERICAN POET

But my mind (yours)
has its peculiar ego-centric
personal approach
to the eternal realities,
and differs from every other
in minute particulars.

—H. D., BORN HILDA DOOLITTLE (1886-1961)
AMERICAN ESSAYIST, NOVELIST, AND POET

The attempt to arouse and retain the interest of other people in oneself and one's
goings on . . . [is] a black art which most of us practice.

—E. M. FORSTER (1879-1970)
BRITISH WRITER

Though people may be flattered to appear in a book, they hate nothing more
than to appear foolish and will be down upon you like a ton of bricks.

—W. SOMERSET MAUGHAM (1874-1965)
BRITISH WRITER AND PLAYWRIGHT

There's the secret hope that people will love you for being so damned honest
about yourself. Even there, there's a certain amount of vanity involved.
You're aware of the effect that you're making.

—ARMISTEAD MAUPIN (1944-)
AMERICAN WRITER

You have no idea how silly the tiny refinements of introspection can become.

—VITA SACKVILLE-WEST (1892-1962)
BRITISH POET, NOVELIST, AND GARDENER

VICE

SEE ALSO ALCOHOL, DRUGS, SMOKING

You refer to—quite often think—people you are fond of as "clean and whole-some." Are such words allowed? I thought they belonged exclusively to the lan-guage of those persons—reformers, head-masters, scout-masters, etc.—who wish to stamp out vice (which includes you and me) and generally disinfect the country.

—J. R. ACKERLEY (1896-1967)
BRITISH WRITER AND EDITOR

If one is not scandalous it is difficult to write at all.

—J. R. ACKERLEY (1896-1967)
BRITISH WRITER AND EDITOR

All poets have sought one single thing: the angel. But their vice of congenital neg-ativism has confused and perverted their taste and turned them to evil angels.

—SALVADOR DALÍ (1904-1989)
SPANISH ARTIST

Over-indulgence of anything is a great way to live. I would never eat a whole gateaux in one sitting. But pleasure in life is a great thing.

—DAVID DANDRIDGE (ca. 1970-)
BRITISH PLAYWRIGHT AND WRITER

Casinos are desperate places—but you forget that quickly once you are in them. [They] irresistibly invite you to leave reality outside.

—RICHARD KWIETNIOWSKI (1957-)
BRITISH DIRECTOR

We drove past Sodom. . . . [It's] difficult to think of anyone ever getting anything as enjoyable as sin out of what is geographically, as well as its having been once morally, the lowest spot of the world.

—STEPHEN SPENDER (1909-1995)
BRITISH POET AND WRITER

———————

Vice and virtue are to the artist materials for an art.

—OSCAR WILDE (1854-1900)
IRISH PLAYWRIGHT AND WRITER

ADDICTION

Never say never to an addict. I've had my ups and downs over the years. Right now I'm in a good place. But I take it one day at a time.

—ROY SIMMONS (1956-)
AMERICAN NFL FOOTBALL PLAYER

———————

[Homosexuality is not] a matter of bad habit, of a vice, of a habitual behavior subject to correction through energetic self-cultivation, of something subject to remedy, something unnatural. But it is a matter of nature.

—KURT HILLER (1885-1972)
JEWISH WRITER AND PACIFIST

———————

I had to stop eating cookies, cakes, pies, and candies because I'm just way out of control—a junkie; I had to cut that out. I don't drink, I don't smoke, I don't do drugs; but I was out of control—that was my drug of choice.

—ANNIE SPRINKLE (1954-)
AMERICAN PERFORMANCE ARTIST AND SEX EDUCATOR

GREED

Avarice is a great sin, and nothing can come to a good end where there is sin.

—MICHELANGELO BUONARROTI (1475-1564)
ITALIAN PAINTER, SCULPTOR, POET, AND ENGINEER

———————

After dinner got sick with a terrible pain in the intestines. Castor oil. . . .
Punished for being a glutton.

—PETER ILYICH TCHAIKOVSKY (1840-1893)
RUSSIAN COMPOSER

VIOLENCE

SEE ALSO HATRED, SUFFERING

But this violence of my life, the violence which I've lived amongst,
I think it's different to the violence in painting. When talking about the violence
of paint, it's nothing to do with the violence of war. It's to do with an
attempt to remake the violence of reality itself.

—FRANCIS BACON (1909-1992)
BRITISH ARTIST

———————

I started having dreams that there was a home for me there. The desert motivates
me in a very different way than the city. There's a very harsh brutality that calls
upon your survival instincts. It's a harshness that is very beautiful to me. I feel very
much a part of this wilderness.

—ANA CASTILLO (1953-)
CHICANA POET, NOVELIST, AND ESSAYIST

In principle, violence is something that does not speak, or speaks but little, while sexuality is something that is little spoken about.

—GILLES DELEUZE (1925-1995)
FRENCH PHILOSOPHER AND CRITIC

———————

Time passes, but the violence done is not undone. It never is.

—ANDREA DWORKIN (1946-)
AMERICAN FEMINIST CRITIC AND ANTI-PORN ACTIVIST

———————

How sad is it that we're scared to go to an inner city school? There's so much publicity about violence that we're now afraid to go to places that should be shelters.

—SARA GILBERT (1975-)
AMERICAN ACTOR

———————

I feel the same about violence against gays in the Middle East as I do about anti-gay violence in Wyoming—terrible.

—DAVE HALL (ca. 1970-)
ARAB-AMERICAN MUSICIAN

———————

You know only 14 percent of Americans have passports.
And that's one of the reasons when they see bombs falling on other countries, they don't know what it's falling on.

—ALICE WALKER (1944-)
AFRICAN-AMERICAN FEMINIST AND PULITZER PRIZE-WINNING WRITER

VOYEURISM

Yes, I've always liked to think that I can stand off and observe
myself in any situation without participating in it.

—EDWARD ALBEE (1928-)
AMERICAN TONY AWARD- AND PULITZER PRIZE-WINNING PLAYWRIGHT

I have breezed through other lives . . . like an emotionally uninvolved tourist.

—JOHN RECHY (1934-)
AMERICAN WRITER

I don't write autobiographically, and I never have, but there's something in there,
as an observer, as a voyeur, taking in the world around me, breathing it in and
really, really observing, which is what I do best.

—MICHAEL STIPE (1960-)
AMERICAN MUSICIAN

Observed the Schillings having supper, through my binoculars.
A strange inquisitiveness! . . . Spied on the Schillings . . . .
why is it that I like to see and know so much how others live?

—PETER ILYICH TCHAIKOVSKY (1840-1893)
RUSSIAN COMPOSER

What I have tried to create is not an irreal atmosphere,
but a reality which is re-created, elaborated, mediated. I have detached
myself from a documented exact reality.

—LUCHINO VISCONTI (1906-1976)
ITALIAN ARISTOCRAT AND DIRECTOR

WAR

SEE ALSO THE MILITARY, POLITICS

War is an ugly thing . . . [soldiers] leave one way and come back another.

—ERIC ALVA (1974-)
FIRST U.S. SERVICEMAN INJURED IN THE IRAQ WAR

———

I woke up in recovery [after hitting a minefield in Iraq], and I was so drugged.
The first thing I did was look down, and my leg was gone. I remember just crying
and thinking, It's OK. They'll put it back on. They probably have it somewhere,
like a broken leg. They'll fix it.

—ERIC ALVA (1974-)
FIRST U.S. SERVICEMAN INJURED IN THE IRAQ WAR

———

In times of war even the crudest kind of positive affection between persons seems
extraordinarily beautiful, a noble symbol of the peace and forgiveness of which
the whole world stands so desperately in need.

—W. H. AUDEN (1907-1973)
ANGLO-AMERICAN POET AND CRITIC

———

I do not know what it would be like to be well and in a war,
possibly less terrifying than being ill, for ill one is doubly trapped,
or one thinks so, which amounts to the same thing.

—DJUNA BARNES (1892-1982)
AMERICAN WRITER

———

The people who didn't read [during the war], who just lay on their bed
scratching their genitals and farting and talking about banging women,
they found it difficult to survive. Those who read survive.

—DIRK BOGARDE (1921-1999)
BRITISH ACTOR AND WRITER

The world is sick with fear of war, and yet its bloody leaders
are dragging it steadily into it.

—BENJAMIN BRITTEN (1913-1976)
BRITISH COMPOSER

———

Two or three unimportant bombs this morning. One of them fell near here,
and I had a look at it. It looks like a machine made expressly to frighten people.

—SIDONIE-GABRIELLE COLETTE (1873-1954)
FRENCH WRITER

———

I don't intend to change my outlook because of war, until war forces me to
change it. . . . I don't, because the ship is sinking, want to join in.

—E. M. FORSTER (1879-1970)
BRITISH WRITER

———

Under Saddam, though we had a tyrannical government, homosexuals were
allowed some sexual freedom, a certain tolerance in Baghdad, as long as it was
not an in-your-face sexuality. We were constricted, but we did not have outright
fear for our lives. In contrast, today every gay person fears being killed.

—ALI HILI (1973-)
IRAQI EXILE AND GAY RIGHTS ACTIVIST

———

By 1968, you were supposed to have been excused from the draft because you
were already climbing the career ladder, or, as befitted a young man with a
future, married, or a father. Getting drafted meant you were none of those: still
drifting. Indecisive. Not grown up. Lacking purpose. Getting drafted, I felt certain
when it happened, meant you deserved to be.

—ANDREW HOLLERAN (1944-)
AMERICAN WRITER

We destroyed and annihilated them [Iraqis] . . . We destroyed the infrastructure.
We dismantled their abilities to defend against outside invaders.
We didn't even do that in Germany in World War II. You don't do that unless
your plan is to stay—to occupy.

—JEFF KEY (1966-)
AMERICAN WRITER, DOCUMENTARIST, AND U.S. MARINE

———————

Terrorism is not an enemy; it's a tactic. . . . Any kind of warfare is terrorism.
Terrorism is defending your ideology in any way you can.

— JEFF KEY (1966-)
AMERICAN WRITER, DOCUMENTARIST, AND U.S. MARINE

———————

Progress is a soiled creed . . . black with coal dust and gunpowder.

—JOHN MAYNARD KEYNES (1883-1946)
BRITISH ECONOMIST

———————

[On being kidnapped in Iraq in 2006] When I can get through an
ordinary day without shaking legs and a pounding heart. . . . I think that
will be a sign that I can start to tell my story.

—JAMES LONEY (1964-)
CANADIAN HUMANITARIAN KIDNAPPED IN IRAQ

———————

Within the war we are all waging with the forces of death, subtle and otherwise,
conscious or not—I am not only a casualty, I am also a warrior.

—AUDRE LORDE (1934-1992)
AFRICAN-AMERICAN WRITER, POET, AND ACTIVIST

———————

This is the war of wars, and the cause? Has this writhing worm of men a cause?

—AMY LOWELL (1874-1925)
PULITZER PRIZE-WINNING POET

We may never stop war, and it isn't likely that we will, actually. But what we're doing as we try to stop war externally, what we're trying to do is stop it in ourselves. That's where war has to end. And until we can control our own violence, our own anger, our own hostility, our own meanness, our own greed.

—ALICE WALKER (1944-)
AFRICAN-AMERICAN FEMINIST AND PULITZER PRIZE-WINNING WRITER

———————

We didn't know they hadn't found any weapons of mass destruction until we got back. . . . But we all kind of knew we were going there for oil. The minute we crossed the border from Kuwait, we saw the Iraqis had set the oil fields on fire.

—GAGE WESTON (ca. 1960-)
IRAQ WAR VETERAN AND PORN STAR

———————

The boredom and futility of war blanketed all those engaged in it.

—PATRICK WHITE (1912-1990)
AUSTRALIAN WRITER AND NOBEL LAUREATE

NUCLEAR WAR

The whole world is crazy with mutual suspicions, but I think it is time that someone took a risk, disarmed, and saw what happened.

—J. R. ACKERLEY (1896-1967)
BRITISH WRITER AND EDITOR

———————

Sometimes I think the indifference and skepticism of many people in the face of the nuclear threat, as though they are hiding their heads in the sand or passively accepting the inevitable, comes from their inability to imagine the horror of it.

—MARIE-CLAIRE BLAIS (1939-)
CANADIAN WRITER AND PLAYWRIGHT

The papers are full of the atomic bomb which is going to revolutionize everything and blow us all to buggery. Not a bad idea.

—NOËL COWARD (1899-1973)
BRITISH ACTOR AND PLAYWRIGHT

I think we are all taking it much too seriously. It is either going to be over in a couple of years or it is not.

—PHILIP JOHNSON (1906-2005)
AMERICAN ARCHITECT

Disarmament must also occur in the heart and in the spirit.

—ALICE WALKER (1944-)
AFRICAN-AMERICAN FEMINIST AND PULITZER PRIZE-WINNING WRITER

WEIGHT

SEE ALSO APPEARANCES, WORKING OUT

I'm getting bigger, very slowly but surely. I feel pregnant above all in the evening—about eight o'clock not a dress or a belt seems to fit.

—SIDONIE-GABRIELLE COLETTE (1873-1954)
FRENCH WRITER

I am also suffering both physically and psychically from the fact that all No. 4 underwear is now too small for me, No. 5 too big.

—THOMAS MANN (1875-1955)
GERMAN WRITER

I was both fat and blue and nobody knew it better than sixty-one-year-old
Ethel Waters.

—ETHEL WATERS (1896-1977)
AFRICAN-AMERICAN ACTOR AND MUSICIAN

WOMEN

SEE ALSO FEMINISM, LESBIANS, MASCULINITY

Women are stronger than us. They face more directly the problems that confront
them, and for that reason they are much more spectacular to talk about.

—PEDRO ALMODOVAR (1951-)
SPANISH FILM DIRECTOR

———————

Nowadays, if you go to a bullfighting school around seven out of
twenty of the students are women. I think the idea of a female bullfighter
is a very noble concept.

—PEDRO ALMODOVAR (1951-)
SPANISH FILM DIRECTOR

———————

The menopausal armies mass on the brink of every city and suburb; everything
that was is over and there is nothing left there to keep our sights lowered.
See the rifles raised? This army doesn't travel on its uterus any more.

—JUNE ARNOLD (1926-1982)
AMERICAN WRITER

———————

Every woman with a sense of humor is a lost woman.

—DJUNA BARNES (1892-1982)
AMERICAN WRITER

One is not born a woman, but rather becomes one.

—SIMONE DE BEAUVOIR (1908-1986)
FRENCH FEMINIST WRITER AND PHILOSOPHER

When a woman is earning money, has pretty dresses, a man in her bed, another man pleading to get into her bed, a third man—moreover, a good-looking and enamored gigolo—clamoring for the same privilege—and this same woman is sad and sallow—watch out for her liver!

—SIDONIE-GABRIELLE COLETTE (1873-1954)
FRENCH WRITER

Women are still second-class citizens . . . so this job of director and cinematographer is somehow still relegated to men. It's thought of as that power job, and that power job, like all of the power jobs in our society, are still the domain of men.

—DONNA DEITCH (1945-)
AMERICAN FILM DIRECTOR

To my mind, women don't exist to turn men on . . . women, more than men, are obliged to resort to underhanded methods to avoid being mere objects.

—RAINER WERNER FASSBINDER (1945-1982)
GERMAN DIRECTOR

Why is Xena such a hit? . . . I guess people were really ready to see a woman superhero kicking butt and being a full-on action hero.

—LIZ FRIEDMAN (ca. 1970-)
AMERICAN TV PRODUCER AND WRITER

Woman does not have a sex.

—LUCE IRIGARAY (1930-)
BELGIAN FEMINIST AND THEORIST

For women, then, poetry is not a luxury. It is a vital necessity of our existence. It forms the quality of the light within which we predicate our hopes and dreams toward survival and change.

—AUDRE LORDE (1934–1992)
AFRICAN-AMERICAN WRITER, POET, AND ACTIVIST

Those hard-boiled wisecracking girls. . . . I have learned to suspect to be the softest and greatest sentimentalists and liars-to-themselves of any.

—ROBERT MCALMON (1896–1956)
AMERICAN WRITER AND PUBLISHER

There is actually a new male fear of genuinely powerful women who are CEOs and judges and senators and women holding positions of great authority.

—PAUL RUDNICK (1957–)
AMERICAN SCREENWRITER AND PLAYWRIGHT

I write my women like I like my women.

—ROSE TROCHE (1964–)
AMERICAN DIRECTOR, PRODUCER, AND SCREENWRITER

There is no story more moving to me personally than one in which one woman saves the life of another, and saves herself, and slays whatever dragon has appeared.

—ALICE WALKER (1944–)
AFRICAN-AMERICAN FEMINIST AND PULITZER PRIZE-WINNING WRITER

MISOGYNY

I'm not a gay man. There's a difference between being a gay man and
any kind of woman—for one thing, misogyny.

—SANDRA BERNHARD (1955-)
AMERICAN ACTOR, COMEDIAN, AND MUSICIAN

The love for what I speak of reaches higher;
Woman's too much unlike, no heart by rights
Ought to grow hot for her, if wise and male.

—MICHELANGELO BUONARROTI (1475-1564)
ITALIAN PAINTER, SCULPTOR, POET, AND ENGINEER

I have one request to make, which is never mention a woman again
in any letter to me, or even allude to the existence of the sex.
I won't ever read a word of the feminine gender.

—LORD BYRON (1788-1824)
BRITISH POET

Truly, the gods should have made some other animal for men to couple
with and to get children by, instead of women. Then we might
have had more comfort and peace of mind.

—COUNTEE CULLEN (1903-1946)
AFRICAN-AMERICAN POET

We will marry. We will all have as many births as our individual situations allow.
And pass the word on to our daughters. . . . Men will continue to notice us only
for their sexual and nesting needs—which is what we want them to do. And by
the time they observe that there has been an astonishing number of births of baby
girls, it will be much too late.

—KATHERINE V. FORREST (1939-)
AMERICAN WRITER

Dismissal of lesbian writing is misogyny rendered acceptable to women-loathing liberals.

—JOHN WEIR (ca. 1966–)
AMERICAN SCHOLAR AND WRITER

WORK

SEE ALSO ACTORS AND ACTING, AMBITION, BUSINESS, CAREERS, HOLLYWOOD, JOURNALISM, MEDIA, MONEY, MOVIES, PROSTITUTION, SUCCESS, TELEVISION, THEATER

I had a gay résumé and a straight résumé when I first started looking for work. . . . I wasn't sure how gay you could be in the publishing world.

—CHARLOTTE ABBOTT (ca. 1973–)
AMERICAN BOOK EDITOR

I don't declare I'm gay when I go on meetings, but eventually all my producers know. And hell, it's so chic right now!

—JANE ANDERSON (1954–)
AMERICAN ACTOR AND DIRECTOR

That's another thing, you look weird for jobs sometimes, and you go around and people on the street are staring at you. It's like whatever, I'm working, I'm getting paid for this, who cares.

—ALEXIS ARQUETTE (1969–)
AMERICAN ACTOR AND DRAG PERFORMER

All day I had been finding pretexts to avoid work, reading magazines, making fudge, cleaning my shot-gun.

—WILLIAM BURROUGHS (1914–1997)
AMERICAN WRITER

I made the decision some decades ago to live a lightweight life.
I would see if it was possible to earn a living from talking about gay sex
and being rude about people's hair.

—JULIAN CLARY (1959-)
BRITISH COMEDIAN

———————

Work is poisoning my life.

—SIDONIE-GABRIELLE COLETTE (1873-1954)
FRENCH WRITER

———————

You were right about the real estate job. Ogling poor people for small investments
against their will didn't appeal to me very long.

—HART CRANE (1899-1932)
AMERICAN POET

———————

Even greater than my joy at the prospect of one day being able to draw unem-
ployment insurance was my ecstasy at moving into a room of my own.

—QUENTIN CRISP (1908-1999)
BRITISH WRITER AND PERSONALITY

———————

I find as I grow older, that the only serious work I can do is story-spinning.

—HENRY JAMES (1843-1916)
AMERICAN WRITER

———————

I've stopped wanting to do any work at all. All work is bullshit. Everyone knows
that. No matter how many telephones and extensions, no matter how many secre-
taries, no matter how many names in the rolodex. It's all bullshit.

—IRENA KLEPFISZ (1941-)
POLISH-AMERICAN JEWISH FEMINIST POET, PROFESSOR, AND ACTIVIST

A banquet is a gathering of professional people to eat with us. It is also an unwieldy assortment of the people who care least about us in life.

—FEDERICO GARCIA LORCA (1898-1936)
SPANISH POET AND PLAYWRIGHT

It is a horrible admission, but some of us are driven to work at times to forget about living life.

—ROBERT MCALMON (1896-1956)
AMERICAN WRITER AND PUBLISHER

You become a better playwright by writing plays and not doing other jobs. Life experience is important, but it's hard to write a play and it's best if you can come to it fresh and not after eight hours of doing something else.

—TERRENCE MCNALLY (1939-)
AMERICAN PLAYWRIGHT

All over the country, they're reading about me, and the story doesn't center on me being gay. It's just about a gay person who is doing his job.

—HARVEY MILK (1930-1978)
AMERICAN POLITICIAN AND GAY RIGHTS ACTIVIST

Being a garbage collector is one of the loneliest jobs there is.
They are the phantoms of the city in the way that we see them but we don't pay attention; they are a part of the urban landscape.

—JOÃO PEDRO RODRIGUES (1966-)
PORTUGUESE DIRECTOR

So here I was, writing for this publication [the *Advocate*] that had all these dirty classified ads in it. I couldn't even send it to my parents because it was filled with "Gay white man wants somebody to piss on."

—RANDY SHILTS (1951-1994)
AMERICAN JOURNALIST, AIDS ACTIVIST, AND WRITER

———

I've never dealt with an erotic housecleaning service, but something tells me the employees are hired for their looks rather than their vacuuming skills. Something tells me they only surface clean.

—DAVID SEDARIS (1956-)
AMERICAN WRITER

———

The word work is great—if it's a speech—but sing the word *work*, and you are in serious trouble . . .

—STEPHEN SONDHEIM (1930-)
AMERICAN MUSICAL THEATER COMPOSER AND PLAYWRIGHT

———

The last thing I wanted to do was fuck when I got home from work. . . I'd just shot my wad, so to speak, by playing for eighteen hours at a time.

—JUNIOR VASQUEZ (1946-)
AMERICAN DJ AND RECORD PRODUCER

———

My father wanted me to work every summer in high school so that I might learn the value of a dollar. I did work, I did learn, and what I learned was that my dollar could buy me hustlers. I bought my first when I was fourteen.

—EDMUND WHITE (1940-)
AMERICAN WRITER AND CRITIC

WORKING OUT

SEE ALSO APPEARANCES, BEAUTY, SPORTS

I venture the timid workouts of a lady who fears breaking something on the one hand and being beaten by her husband on the other.

—SIDONIE-GABRIELLE COLETTE (1873-1954)
FRENCH WRITER

————————

But who told you [a girlfriend] that I have been neglecting physical culture? I just have a new method, that's all. The Sidi Method. It's excellent. But no public courses. Only private lessons . . . extremely private . . .

—SIDONIE-GABRIELLE COLETTE (1873-1954)
FRENCH WRITER

————————

For them [body-obsessed gays] life is not about real bodies with wrinkles or zits: it's the bronzed, buffed, young love god. . . . It is the body as commodity. We've created an ideal and we sometimes sacrifice our reality to it.

—STEVE COMPTON
AMERICAN ARTIST AND CURATOR

————————

Today I was actually riding my—you're gonna love this—riding my exercise bike, watching *A Star Is Born*. That's what I do; I watch movies and ride my bike.

—LEA DELARIA (1958-)
AMERICAN COMEDIAN AND ACTOR

————————

I don't go into the shower at the gym. That would be dangerous. They might storm the locker room. I'm afraid to pee there.

—JEFF STRYKER (1962-)
AMERICAN PORN STAR

I believe in living. I didn't before. I spent Fourth of July in the country, and I had forgot about living. It was so beautiful. I started going to Sam Ronny's Health Club on Broadway and West 73rd Street, every day for four hours. I get massaged, box, swim under water. . . . I want to be pencil thin . . . I want to like myself.

—ANDY WARHOL (1928-1987)
AMERICAN ARTIST

———————

Trainers are more like therapists than any other profession.

—JACKIE WARNER (1968-)
AMERICAN REALITY TV STAR AND CELEBRITY TRAINER

WRITING

SEE ALSO ART AND ARTISTS, CREATION AND CREATIVITY, IMAGINATION, LITERATURE, MUSIC, PHOTOGRAPHY, STYLE, TALENT, THEATER, WRITING

A man tried twice to board an underground train stark naked. He was wrapped in a blanket and hustled away: he wasn't wanted. I am inclined to believe that that would be the answer also to my book.

—J. R. ACKERLEY (1896-1967)
BRITISH WRITER AND EDITOR

———————

I'll say again that writing isn't just writing, it's a meeting of writing and living the way existence is the meeting of mental and material or language of idea and sign. It is how we live.

—KATHY ACKER (1947-1997)
AMERICAN WRITER

There seemed to be one thing common to all their "primitive" writing,
as I suppose it might be called, in contrast to primitive painting: its slipshoddiness
and haste. Where primitive painters will spend months or years, if necessary,
putting in every blade of grass and building up brick walls in low relief,
the primitive writer seems in a hurry to get it over with.

—ELIZABETH BISHOP (1911-1979)
AMERICAN POET

A writer can be ruined by too much or too little success.

—WILLIAM BURROUGHS (1914-1997)
AMERICAN WRITER

Very few authors, especially the unpublished, can resist an invitation to read aloud.

—TRUMAN CAPOTE (1924-1984)
AMERICAN WRITER

I said I was jealous of the words of other writers. It is because they are not mine.
Each writer has a bag of them, as in a lotto set, with which he has to win.

—JEAN COCTEAU (1889-1963)
FRENCH WRITER AND FILMMAKER

Too much detailed accuracy makes dull reading.

—NOËL COWARD (1899-1973)
BRITISH ACTOR AND PLAYWRIGHT

My first novel got over 100 rejection letters, so anything that promises spiritual
peace is bound to catch my attention.

—WARREN DUNFORD (1963-)
CANADIAN WRITER

The most satisfactory dead are those who have published books.

—E. M. FORSTER (1879-1970)
BRITISH WRITER

One is always late in writing; the annoying thing is that it stops development; there is always something within or beside one's self that is not up to date and that nags.

—ANDRÉ GIDE (1869-1951)
FRENCH WRITER

Language is surely too small a vessel to contain these emotions of mind and body that have somehow awakened a response in the spirit.

—RADCLYFFE HALL (1880-1943)
BRITISH NOVELIST AND POET

Writing (here's a sapphic line) is a difficult form of reading.

—MARILYN HACKER (1942-)
FEMINIST POET, CRITIC, AND ACTIVIST

Readers assuredly have a right to their entertainment, but I don't believe it is in me to give them, in a satisfactory way, what they require.

—HENRY JAMES (1843-1916)
AMERICAN WRITER

To write good prose is an affair of good manners.

—W. SOMERSET MAUGHAM (1874-1965)
BRITISH WRITER AND PLAYWRIGHT

The ordinary is the writer's richest field.

—W. SOMERSET MAUGHAM (1874-1965)
BRITISH WRITER AND PLAYWRIGHT

I've always been envious of playwrights who give interviews in which they make profound statements about their plays. But I just don't think that way.

—TERRENCE MCNALLY (1939-)
AMERICAN PLAYWRIGHT

As a gay man, it seems you're going to write gay characters. . . . It's just something that I did. It was an organic thing. It's just how the first thing that I wrote turned out.

—TERRENCE MCNALLY (1939-)
PLAYWRIGHT

Nobody knows how to make love. . . . We're their artists, and we're supposed to be telling them, but we're being so discreet.

—ISABEL MILLER, PEN NAME OF ALMA ROUTSONG (1924-1996)
AMERICAN WRITER

Years ago, sex was very big for readers. . . . Today, it's violence and murder.

—HAROLD ROBBINS (1916-1997)
AMERICAN WRITER

If I ever write a masterpiece, it will be the result of a month in bed; alone.

—SIEGFRIED SASSOON (1886-1967)
BRITISH POET AND WRITER

When you're a writer, you want to try to avoid clichés. Unfortunately, when you're writing about marriage or family, all clichés seem to apply.

—DAN SAVAGE (1964-)
AMERICAN SEX COLUMNIST AND WRITER

My idea of a writer: someone interested in "everything."

—SUSAN SONTAG (1933-2004)
AMERICAN WRITER AND CRITIC

As regards the literary side of it [my work] . . . I cannot describe how it exhausts me. How many penholders I gnaw to pieces before a few lines grow perfect! How often I jump up in sheer despair because I cannot find a rhyme, or the meter goes wrong.

—PETER ILYICH TCHAIKOVSKY (1840-1893)
RUSSIAN COMPOSER

I always think of it [writing] as being like those monkeys and the typewriters: put me in a room with a computer for a couple of years, and I'm bound to come up with something.

—SARAH WATERS (1966-)
BRITISH NOVELIST

I thought to write of my own experiences required a translation out of the crude patois of actual slow suffering, mean, scattered thoughts, and transfusion-slow boredom into the tidy couplets of brisk, beautiful sentiment, a way of at once elevating and lending momentum to what I felt. . . . [But] what if I could write about my life exactly as it was? What if I could show it in all its density and tedium and its concealed passion?

—EDMUND WHITE (1940-)
AMERICAN WRITER AND CRITIC

My vocation [as a writer] came closest to revealing itself in those visits
to the theatre, usually musical comedy, in the early bubblings of sexuality,
and expeditions through the streets observing, always observing.

—PATRICK WHITE (1912-1990)
AUSTRALIAN WRITER AND NOBEL LAUREATE

Writing is continually a pursuit of a very evasive quarry,
and you never quite catch it.

—TENNESSEE WILLIAMS (1911-1983)
AMERICAN PLAYWRIGHT

I find words frustrating as I sit year in year out reeling out an endless grey.
I try to splurge a bit of perhaps—perhaps to get a sudden impact—as a painter
squeezes a tube. But there isn't the physical relief a painter experiences
in the act of painting. I wish I had been a painter or composer.

—PATRICK WHITE (1912-1990)
AUSTRALIAN WRITER AND NOBEL LAUREATE

AUTOBIOGRAPHY

Writing those books kept me alive. . . . Especially the autobiography.
I didn't want to die until I had the final touches. It's my revenge.

—REINALDO ARENAS (1943-1990)
CUBAN WRITER AND PLAYWRIGHT

Autobiography has long been misrepresented in American fiction.
It has often been considered the recourse of a limited imagination and, as such,
writers have long suppressed or disguised that their writing was based
not on imagination but on the facts of their own lives.

—ROBERT FERRO (1941-1988)
AMERICAN WRITER AND GAY RIGHTS ACTIVIST

I always felt that there was something slightly pompous or self-centered about getting strictly autobiographical. Then I got over that. I realized that the closer I got to the truth, the stronger the ring of truth would be about the novel itself.

—ARMISTEAD MAUPIN (1944-)
AMERICAN WRITER

Here I come to one of the memoir writer's difficulties—one of the reasons why, though I read so many, so many are failures. They leave out the person to whom things happened. . . . And the events mean very little unless we know first to whom they happened.

—VIRGINIA WOOLF (1882-1941)
BRITISH WRITER

BIOGRAPHY

Were I a writer, and dead, how pleased I would be if my life, through the efforts of some friendly and detached biographer, were to reduce itself to a few details . . . whose distinction and mobility might travel beyond the limits of its fate, and come to touch . . . some future body.

—ROLAND BARTHES (1915-1980)
FRENCH CRITIC AND THEORIST

If I should ever become famous, and anyone should collect materials for my biography, your letter to-day would give a very false impression of me.

—PETER ILYICH TCHAIKOVSKY (1840-1893)
RUSSIAN COMPOSER

FICTION

Try as man may, he will never get the woman's viewpoint in telling certain stories.

—DOROTHY ARZNER (1897-1979)
AMERICAN DIRECTOR

American fiction today, with exceptions seems the result of a philosophy of the limited in the face of the too great. It is the writer himself made small in reaction to the sudden revelation of the complexities of life, of nature, and the cosmos—the overwhelming revelations of the moderns.

—ROBERT FERRO (1941-1988)
AMERICAN WRITER AND GAY RIGHTS ACTIVIST

What is told is always the telling.

—RICHARD HOWARD (1929-)
AMERICAN POET, CRITIC, AND TRANSLATOR

It is a misfortune for me that the telling of a story just for the sake of the story is not an activity that is in favor with the intelligentsia.

—W. SOMERSET MAUGHAM (1874-1965)
BRITISH WRITER AND PLAYWRIGHT

I've never written a story in my life. The story has come to me and demanded to be written.

—W. SOMERSET MAUGHAM (1874-1965)
BRITISH WRITER AND PLAYWRIGHT

To edit your life is to save it—for fiction, for yourself.

—SUSAN SONTAG (1933-2004)
AMERICAN WRITER AND CRITIC

To be sure, fiction of all kinds has always fed on writers' lives. Every detail in a work of fiction was once an observation or a memory or a wish, or is a sincere homage to a reality independent of itself.

—SUSAN SONTAG (1933-2004)
AMERICAN WRITER AND CRITIC

I had to regain a lot of my belief in fairy tales, in happy endings.
A childish innocence where you are not afraid all the time any more.

—RUFUS WAINWRIGHT (1973-)
CANADIAN MUSICIAN

WRITER'S BLOCK

I know nothing so dreary as the feeling that you can't make the sounds or write
the words that your whole creative being is yearning for.

—NOËL COWARD (1899-1973)
BRITISH ACTOR AND PLAYWRIGHT

But O, why can't I create something? I am as dry as a biscuit.

—SIEGFRIED SASSOON (1886-1967)
BRITISH POET AND WRITER

YOUTH

SEE ALSO AGE AND AGING, CHILDHOOD, CHILDREN

This general unease of youth is only aggravated by what would appear
to alleviate it, a grace of person which grants them without effort on their part,
a succession of sexual triumphs.

—W. H. AUDEN (1907-1973)
ANGLO-AMERICAN POET AND CRITIC

If it be sinne to loue a louely Lad:
Oh then sinne I, for whom my soule is sad.

—RICHARD BARNFIELD (1574-1627)
BRITISH POET

I think the biggest frightener now is the disturbing lack of interest . . . among a
certain proportion of younger people. . . . The fashionable dumbing down of a
generation. . . . When I was a teenager I felt much the same. I mean, I used to
get really pissed off when people were just, like, purposefully dumb.

—DAVID BOWIE (1947-)
BRITISH MUSICIAN

Youth is stranger than fiction.

—RUPERT BROOKE (1887-1915)
BRITISH POET

I like to be with young people. They teach me much more than older people.
Their insolence and their seriousness are like a cold shower.
They administer our hygiene.

—JEAN COCTEAU (1889-1963)
FRENCH WRITER AND FILMMAKER

The young are unjust. They owe this to themselves. They fight against the invasion of personalities stronger than themselves.

—JEAN COCTEAU (1889-1963)
FRENCH WRITER AND FILMMAKER

———

There's a whole generation of kids—not kids, they're in their twenties—who've a very loose attitude to AIDS and to safe sex. It's galling. They weren't educated in the same way my generation was.

—ALAN CUMMING (1965-)
BRITISH ACTOR

———

For oh! my dear, when the youth's in the year,
Yours is the face that I long to have near,
Yours is the face, my dear.

—ANGELINA WELD GRIMKÉ (1880-1958)
AFRICAN-AMERICAN POET

———

Youth is a terrifying thing often for youth has no respect for anything but itself.

—MARSDEN HARTLEY (1877-1943)
AMERICAN ARTIST

———

I see a vision of a great rucksack revolution thousands or even millions of young Americans wandering around with rucksacks, going up to mountains to pray, making children laugh and old men glad, making young girls happy and old girls happier, all of 'em Zen lunatics . . .

—JACK KEROUAC (1922-1969)
AMERICAN WRITER

The federal government . . . has just authorized spending $250 million to encourage teenagers to stop having sex. Simultaneously the house has decided to eliminate the National Endowment for the Arts. This is extremely unwise. With the NEA gone and almost no arts programs available, into what exactly will these horny teenagers channel their pent-up, unspent orgone?

—TONY KUSHNER (1956-)
AMERICAN PLAYWRIGHT

My youth was a little bit like *American Graffiti*. Driving around Mac's Drive-In in our cars, going to the beach and drinking beer. But there was also listening to the Saturday afternoon broadcast of the opera and reading poetry, and not being made to feel like a freak for it.

—TERRENCE MCNALLY (1939-)
AMERICAN PLAYWRIGHT

Young adults are really good at saying here's what reality is, here's what it should be, and my, isn't there an uncomfortable difference between them.

—JAKE REITAN
GAY RIGHTS ACTIVIST

Teenagers will crash into lampposts on their way home from proms, and there is nothing to be done about it. You cannot forbid tragedy.

—RICHARD RODRIGUEZ (1944-)
MEXICAN-AMERICAN WRITER

You know you're young when someone asks you for money and you take it as a compliment.

—DAVID SEDARIS (1956-)
AMERICAN WRITER

Boys are singular beings in this that they easily accept a situation
however abnormal it may be.

—JOHN ADDINGTON SYMONDS (1840-1893)
ENGLISH POET AND CRITIC

I wish young people could suggest something new, express some new ideas,
some fresh force. . . . But at the moment I'm very disappointed.

—LUCHINO VISCONTI (1906-1976)
ITALIAN ARISTOCRAT AND FILM DIRECTOR

"Helping kids" has become the nation's cause du jour.
But some of the kids in our community won't make it without the
economic safety nets that only we can weave for them.

—PATRICIA NELL WARREN (1936-)
AMERICAN WRITER

This war to control all American youth includes the smaller war
to crush its 10 percent of gay youth.

—PATRICIA NELL WARREN (1936-)
AMERICAN WRITER

Life is full of transient loves when you are young, even though you
may long for the comfort of a lasting companion.

—TENNESSEE WILLIAMS (1911-1983)
AMERICAN PLAYWRIGHT

I love going out on tour and acting like a twenty-year-old guy.
If I can get away with that, why not?

—JANE WIEDLIN (1958-)
AMERICAN MUSICIAN

GAY YOUTH

Sometimes I'm next to a couple of twenty-something lesbians and I want to ask them, "Have you ever seen a movie called *Desert Hearts*?" But I don't, in case they say, "What's that?" It's just like other aspects of culture. There are people of another generation who don't remember *Easy Rider*. People typically don't study historical origins of another era; they think suddenly they found the water in the well.

—DONNA DEITCH (1945-)
AMERICAN FILM DIRECTOR

I had clues . . . but nowhere to go with the clues—being in Girl Scout camp at age 11 and finding one of the girls cute, going to field hockey camp and thinking the captain is attractive, but knowing I could never say anything.

—CANDACE GINGRICH (1966-)
AMERICAN ACTIVIST, HALF-SISTER OF NEWT GINGRICH

People started to hear about us [The Institute for the Protection of Lesbian and Gay Youth] and, unfortunately, called up and said, "I have this gay kid, and I don't know what to do with him. Can you help me?"

—A. DAMIEN MARTIN
AMERICAN GAY RIGHTS ACTIVIST

In some ways the gay movement has actually made life considerably harder for gay youth . . . raw exposure spiked with vicious backlash and a promise that 50 percent of them will be infected by middle age with the world's most gruesome disease. Thanks a lot, Stonewall generation.

—GABRIEL ROTELLO (1953-)
AMERICAN WRITER AND FILMMAKER

The question of ideal beauty, incarnated in breathing male beings, or eternalized in everduring works of art, was leading me to a precipice, from which no exit seemed possible except in suicide what I then considered sin.

—JOHN ADDINGTON SYMONDS (1840-1893)
ENGLISH POET AND CRITIC

I could buy the *Advocate* at the drugstore without everybody in the place turning around and looking at me. . . . Then I'd go home, lock myself in the bathroom, and look at the vacation ads for hours on end.

—RUFUS WAINWRIGHT (1973-)
CANADIAN MUSICIAN